Constantin-F. Volney

The Ruins

A survey of the revolutions of empires. Third Edition

Constantin-F. Volney

The Ruins
A survey of the revolutions of empires. Third Edition

ISBN/EAN: 9783337273767

Printed in Europe, USA, Canada, Australia, Japan

Cover: Foto ©Andreas Hilbeck / pixelio.de

More available books at **www.hansebooks.com**

VOLNEY's

RUINS.

H. E. BARKER
Lincolniana
1922 SOUTH HOBART BOULEVARD
LOS ANGELES, CALIFORNIA

VOLNEY'S RUINS.

See Herndon's Lincoln, page 439,
for an account of this book in connection with Lincoln's reading.
"In 1834, while still living in
New Salem and before he (Lincoln) became a lawyer, he was surrounded by a
class of people exceedingly liberal in
matters of religion. Volney's "Ruins"
and Paine's "Age of Reason" passed from
hand to hand, and furnished food for
the evening's discussion in the tavern
and village store."

See also Wm. E. Barton's "The Soul
of Abraham Lincoln," pages 19, 63, 146
and 152, for further mention of this
work.

H. E. Barker

*Here an opulent City once flourished: this
was the seat of a powerful Empire.__ Yes,
these places, now so desert, a living Multitude
formerly animated &c.*

Chap.II.

THE

R U I N S:

OR

A SURVEY

OF THE

REVOLUTIONS

OF

EMPIRES.

By M. VOLNEY,

ONE OF THE DEPUTIES TO THE NATIONAL ASSEMBLY OF 1789;
AND AUTHOR OF TRAVELS INTO SYRIA AND EGYPT.

TRANSLATED FROM THE FRENCH.

THE THIRD EDITION.

I will dwell in solitude amidst the ruins of cities: I will enquire of the
monuments of antiquity, what was the wisdom of former ages: I will
ask the ashes of legiflators, what caufes have erected and overthrown
empires; what are the principles of national profperity and misfortune:
what the maxims upon which the peace of fociety and the happinefs of
man ought to be founded? Ch. iv. p. 24.

LONDON:
PRINTED FOR J. JOHNSON, ST. PAUL'S CHURCH-YARD.

M.DCC.XCVI.

PREFACE.

THE plan of this publication was formed nearly ten years ago; ana allusions to it may be seen in the Preface to Travels in Syria and Egypt, as well as at the end of that work, published in 1787. The performance was in some forwardness when the events of 1788 in France interrupted it. Persuaded that a developement of the theory of political truth could not sufficiently acquit a citizen of his debt to society, the author wished to add practice; and that particularly at a time when a single arm was of consequence in the defence of the general cause. The same desire of public benefit which induced him to suspend his work, has since engaged him to resume it; and though it may not possess the same merit as if it had appeared

a 3   *under*

under the circumstances that gave rise to it, yet he imagines that at a time when new paſſions are burſting forth, paſſions that muſt communicate their activity to the religious opinions of men, it is of importance to diſſeminate ſuch moral truths as are calculated to operate as a ſort of curb and reſtraint. It is with this view he has endeavoured to give to theſe truths, hitherto treated as abſtract, a form likely to gain them a reception. It was found impoſſible not to ſhock the violent prejudices of ſome readers; but the work, ſo far from being the fruit of a diſorderly and perturbed ſpirit, has been dictated by a ſincere love of order and humanity.

After reading this performance it will be aſked, how it was poſſible, in 1784, to have had an idea of what did not take place till the year 1790? The ſolution is ſimple: in the original plan, the legiſlator was a fictitious and hypothetical being: in the preſent, the author has ſubſtituted an exiſting legiſlator; and the reality has only made the ſubject additionally intereſting.

INVOCATION.

Solitary Ruins, facred Tombs,
ye mouldering and filent Walls, all
hail ! To you I addrefs my Invoca-
tion. While the vulgar fhrink from
your afpect with fecret terror, my
heart finds in the contemplation a
thoufand delicious fentiments, a thoufand admirable recollections. Preg-
nant, I may truly call you, with ufeful
leffons, with pathetic and irrefiftible

advice

advice to the man who knows how
to confult you. A while ago the
whole world bowed the neck in
filence before the tyrants that oppreffed it; and yet in that hopelefs
moment you already proclaimed the
truths that tyrants hold in abhorrence: mixing the duft of the proud-
eft kings with that of the meaneft
flaves, you called upon us to contemplate this example of EQUALITY. From
your caverns, whither the mufing
and anxious love of LIBERTY led me,
I faw efcape its venerable fhade, and
with unexpected felicity direct its
flight, and marfhal my fteps the way
to renovated France.

Tombs,

Tombs, what virtues and potency
do you exhibit! Tyrants tremble at
your afpect; you poifon with fecret
alarm their impious pleafures; they
turn from you with impatience, and,
coward like, endeavour to forget you
amid the fumptuoufnefs of their palaces. It is you that bring home the
rod of juftice to the powerful oppreffor; it is you that wreft the ill-
gotten gold from the mercilefs ex-
tortioner, and avenge the caufe of him
that has none to help; you com-
penfate the narrow enjoyments of
the poor, by dafhing with care the
goblet of the rich; to the unfortunate you offer a laft and inviolable
afylum;

afylum ; in fine, you give to the foul that juft equilibrium of ftrength and tendernefs, which conftitutes the wifdom of the fage and the fcience of life. The wife man looks towards you, and fcorns to amafs vain grandeur and ufelefs riches with which he muft foon part : you check his lawlefs flights, without difarming his adventure and his courage ; he feels the neceflity of paffing through the period affigned him, and he gives employment to his hours, and makes ufe of the goods that fortune has affigned him. Thus do you rein in the wild fallies of cupidity, calm the fever of tumultuous enjoyment, free

the

the mind from the anarchy of the
paffions, and raife it above thofe little
interefts which torment the mafs of
mankind. We afcend the eminence
you afford us, and, viewing with one
glance the limits of nations and the
fucceffion of ages, are incapable of
any affections but fuch as are fublime,
and entertain no ideas but thofe of
virtue and glory. Alas! when this
uncertain dream of life fhall be over,
what then will avail all our bufy paffions, unlefs they have left behind
them the footfteps of utility!

Ye Ruins, I will return once more
to attend your leffons! I will refume
my place in the midft of your wide

fpreading

fpreading folitude. I will leave the tragic fcene of the paffions, will love my fpecies rather from recollection than actual furvey, will employ my activity in promoting their happinefs, and compofe my own happinefs of the pleafing remembrance that I have haftened theirs.

CHAP.

5   CHAP.

R U I N S:

O R,

A SURVEY OF THE REVOLUTIONS OF EMPIRES.

C H A P. I.

THE TOUR.

IN the eleventh year of the reign of Abd-ul Hamid, fon of Ahmed, emperor of the Turks; when the Nogaian Tartars were driven from the Crimea, and a Muffulman prince, of the blood of Gengis Khan, became the vaffal and *guard* of a woman, a Chriftian, and a queen*; I journeyed in the empire of the Ottomans, and traverfed the provinces which formerly were kingdoms of Egypt and of Syria.

---

* That is to fay, in the year 1784. The reader is re-quefted not to lofe fight of this epocha. See the notes at the end of the volume.

B   Directing

Directing all my attention to what concerns the happines of mankind in a ftate of fociety, I entered cities, and ftudied the manners of their inhabitants; I gained admiffion into palaces, and obferved the conduct of thofe who govern; I wandered over the country, and examined the condition of the peafants: and no where perceiving aught but robbery and devaftation, tyranny and wretchednefs, my heart was oppreffed with forrow and indignation.

Every day I found in my route fields abandoned by the plough, villages deferted, and cities in ruins. Frequently I met with antiquemonuments; wrecks of temples, palaces, and fortifications; pillars, aqueducts, fepulchres. By thefe objects my thoughts were directed to paft ages, and my mind abforbed in ferious and profound meditation.

Arrived at Hamfa on the borders of the Orontes, and being at no great diftance from the city of Palmyra, fituated in the defert, I refolved to examine for myfelf its boafted monuments. After three days travel in barren folitude, and having paffed through a valley filled with grottoes and tombs, my

eyes

eyes were fuddenly ftruck, on leaving this
valley and entering a plain, with a moft aftonifhing fcene of ruins. It confifted of a
countlefs multitude of fuperb columns ftanding erect, and which, like the avenues of our
parks, extended in regular files farther than
the eye could reach. Among thefe columns
magnificent edifices were obfervable, fome
entire, others in a ftate half demolifhed. The
ground was covered on all fides with fragments of fimilar buildings, cornices, capitals,
fhafts, entablatures, and pilafters, all conftructed of a marble of admirable whitenefs
and exquifite workmanfhip. After a walk of
three quarters of an hour along thefe ruins,
I entered the inclofure of a vaft edifice which
had formerly been a temple dedicated to the
fun; and I accepted the hofpitality of fome
poor Arabian peafants, who had eftablifhed
their huts in the very area of the temple.
Here I refolved for fome days to remain, that
I might contemplate, at leifure, the beauty
of fo many ftupendous works.

Every day I vifited fome of the monuments which covered the plain; and one
evening that, my mind loft in reflection, I had

advanced

advanced as far as the *Valley of Sepulchres*, I afcended the heights that bound it, and from which the eye commands at once the whole of the ruins and the immenfity of the defert. ... The fun had juft funk below the horizon; a ftreak of red ftill marked the place of his defcent, behind the diftant mountains of Syria : the full moon, appearing with brightnefs upon a ground of deep blue, rofe in the eaft from the fmooth bank of the Euphrates: the fky was unclouded; the air calm and ferene ; the expiring light of day ferved to foften the horror of approaching darknefs ; the refrefhing breeze of the night gratefully relieved the intolerable fultrinefs of the day that had preceded it ; the fhepherds had led the camels to their ftalls; the grey firmament bounded the filent landfcape; through the whole defert every thing was marked with ftillnefs, undifturbed but by the mournful cries of the bird of night, and of fome *chacals* * .... The dufk increafed, and alreadyI could diftinguifh nothing more than the

---

* An animal confiderably like the fox, but lefs cunning, and of a frightful afpect. It lives upon dead bodies, and reeks and ruins are the places of its habitation.

pale

pale phantoms of walls and columns. .... The folitarinefs of the fituation, the ferenity of evening, and the grandeur of the fcene, impreffed my mind with religious thoughtfulnefs. The view of an illuftrious city deferted, the remembrance of paft times, their comparifon with the prefent ftate of things, all combined to raife my heart to a ftrain of fublime meditations. I fat down on the bafe of a column ; and there, my elbow on my knee, and my head refting on my hand, fometimes turning my eyes towards the defert, and fometimes fixing them on the ruins, I fell into a profound reverie.

CHAP.

C H A P.   II.

MEDITATIONS.

Here, faid I to myfelf, an opulent city once flourifhed ; this was the feat of a power-ful empire. Yes, thefe places, now fo defert, a living multitude formerly animated, and an active crowd circulated in the ftreets which at prefent are fo folitary. Within thofe walls, where a mournful filence reigns, the noife of the arts and the fhouts of joy and feftivity continually refounded. Thefe heaps of marble formed regular palaces, thefe proftrate pillars were the majeftic orna-ments of temples, thefe ruinous galleries pre-fent the outlines of public places. There a numerous people affembled for the refpect-able duties of its worfhip, or the anxious cares of its fubfiftence : there induftry, the fruitful inventor of fources of enjoyment, collected together the riches of every climate, and the purple of Tyre was exchanged for the precious thread of Serica ; the foft tiffues

of

of Caffimere for the fumptuous carpets of
Lydia ; the amber of the Baltic for the
pearls and perfumes of Arabia ; the gold of
Ophir for the pewter of Thule (*a*). . . .

And now a mournful fkeleton is all that
fubfifts of this opulent city, and nothing remains of its powerful government but a vain
and obfcure remembrance ! To the tumultuous throng which crowded under thefe
porticos, the folitude of death has fucceeded.
The filence of the tomb is fubftituted for
the hum of public places. The opulence of
a commercial city is changed into hideous
poverty. The palaces of kings are become
the receptacle of deer, and unclean reptiles
inhabit the fanctuary of the Gods. . . .What
glory is here eclipfed, and how many labours
are annihilated ! . . . Thus perifh the works
of men, and thus do nations and empires
vanifh away !

The hiftory of paft times ftrongly prefented itfelf to my thoughts. I called to
mind thofe diftant ages when twenty celebrated nations inhabited the country around
me. I pictured to myfelf the Affyrian on
the banks of the Tygris, the Chaldean on

thofe

thofe of the Euphrates, the Perfian whofe power extended from the Indus to the Mediterranean. I enumerated the kingdoms of Damafcus and Idumea; of Jerufalem and Samaria; and the warlike ftates of the Philiftines; and the commercial republics of Phenicia. This Syria, faid I to myfelf, now almoft depopulated, then contained a hundred flourifhing cities, and abounded with towns, villages, and hamlets (b). Every where one might have feen cultivated fields, frequented roads, and crowded habitations. Ah! what are become of thofe ages of abundance and of life? What are become of fo many productions of the hand of man? Where are thofe ramparts of Nineveh, thofe walls of Babylon, thofe palaces of Perfepolis, thofe temples of Balbec and of Jerufalem? Where are thofe fleets of Tyre, thofe dockyards of Arad, thofe work-fhops of Sidon, and that multitude of mariners, pilots, merchants, and foldiers? Where thofe hufbandmen, thofe harvefts, that picture of animated nature of which the earth feemed proud? Alas! I have traverfed this defolate country, I have vifited the places that were the

theatre

theatre of fo much fplendour, and I have nothing beheld but folitude and defertion ! I looked for thofe ancient people and their works, and all I could find was a faint trace, like to what the foot of a paffenger leaves on the fand. The temples are thrown down, the palaces demolifhed, the ports filled up, the towns deftroyed, and the earth, ftript of inhabitants, feems a dreary burying-place. ....Great God ! from whence proceed fuch melancholy revolutions ? For what caufe is the fortune of thefe countries fo ftrikingly changed ? Why are fo many cities deftroy-ed ? Why is not that ancient population re-produced and perpetuated ?

Thus abforbed in contemplation, new ideas continually prefented themfelves to my thoughts. Every thing, continued I, mif-leads my judgment, and fills my heart with trouble and uncertainty. When thefe coun-tries enjoyed what conftitutes the glory and felicity of mankind, they were an *unbelieving* people who inhabited them: it was the Phe-nician, offering human facrifices to Moloch, who brought together within his walls the riches of every climate ; it was the Chaldean, proftrating

proftrating himfelf before a ferpent *, who
fubjugated opulent cities, and laid wafte the
palaces of kings and the temples of the Gods;
it was the Perfian, the worfhipper of fire,
who collected the tributes of a hundred nations; they were the inhabitants of this very
city, adorers of the fun and ftars, who erected
fo many monuments of affluence and luxury.
Numerous flocks, fertile fields, abundant
harvefts, every thing that fhould have been
the reward of *piety*, was in the hands of *idolaters:* and now that a *believing* and *holy* people occupy the countries, nothing is to be
feen but folitude and fterility. The earth
under thefe *bleffed* hands produces only briars
and wormwood. Man fows in anguifh, and
reaps vexation and cares ; war, famine, and
peftilence, affault him in turn. Yet, are not
thefe the children of the prophets ? This
Chriftian, this Muffulman, this Jew, are they
not the elect of Heaven, loaded with gifts
and miracles? Why then is this race, beloved of the Divinity, deprived of the favours
which were formerly fhowered upon the

* The dragon Bel.

Heathen ?

Heathen? Why do thefe lands, confecrated by the blood of the martyrs, no l nger boaft their former temperature and fertility? Why have thofe favours been banifhed as it were, and transf rred for fo many ages to other nations and different climes?

And here, purfuing the courfe of viciffitudes which have in turn tranfmitted the fceptre of the world to people fo various in manners and religion, from thofe of ancient Afia down to the more recent ones of Europe, my native country, defignated by this name, was awakened in my mind, and turning my eyes towards it, all my thoughts fixed upon the fituation in which I had left it *.

I recollected its fields fo richly cultivated, its roads fo admirably executed, its towns inhabited by an immenfe multitude, its fhips fcattered over every ocean, its ports filled with the produce of either India; and comparing the activity of its commerce, the extent of its navigation, the magnificence of its buildings, the arts and induftry of its inhabitants, with all that Egypt and Syria

---

* In the year 1782, at the clofe of the American war.

could

could formerly boaſt of a ſimilar nature, I
pleaſed myſelf with the idea that I had found
in modern Europe the paſt ſplendour of Aſia:
But the charm of my reverie was preſently
diſſolved by the laſt ſtep in the compariſon.
Reflecting that if the places before me had
once exhibited this animated picture : who,
ſaid I to myſelf, can aſſure me that their
preſent deſolation will not one day be the lot
of our own country ? who knows but that
hereafter ſome traveller like myſelf will ſit
down upon the banks of the Seine, the
Thames, or the Zuyder ſea, where now, in
the tumult of enjoyment, the heart and the
eyes are too ſlow to take in the multitude of
ſenſations ; who knows but he will ſit down
ſolitary amid ſilent ruins, and weep a people
inurned, and their greatneſs changed into an
empty name ?

The idea brought tears into my eyes ; and
covering my head with the flap of my garment, I gave myſelf up to the moſt gloomy
meditations on human affairs. Unhappy
man ! ſaid I in my grief, a blind fatality plays
with thy deſtiny (c) ! a fatal neceſſity rules
by chance the lot of mortals ! But, no : they
are

are the decrees of celeftial juftice that are
accomplifhing! A myfterious God exercifes
his incomprehenfible judgments! he has
doubtlefs pronounced a revealed malediction
againft the earth ; he has ftruck with a curfe
the prefent race of men, in revenge of paft
generations. Oh ! who fhall dare to fathom
the depths of the Divinity ?

And I remained immoveable, plunged in
profound melancholy.

C H A P.

C H A P. III.

THE APPARITION.

In the mean time a noife ftruck my ear, like to the agitation of a flowing robe, and the flow fteps of a foot, upon the dry and ruftling grafs. Alarmed, I drew my mantle from my head; and cafting round me a timid glance, fuddenly, by the obfcure light of the moon, through the pillars and ruins of a temple, I thought I faw, at my left, a pale apparition, enveloped in an immenfe drapery, fimilar to what fpectres are painted when iffuing out of the tombs. I fhuddered; and while in this troubled ftate, I was hefitating whether to fly, or afcertain the reality of the vifion, a hollow voice, in grave and folemn accents, thus addreffed me :

How long will man importune the heavens with unjuft complaint? How long, with vain clamours, will he accufe Fate as the author of his calamities ? Will he then never open his eyes

eyes to the light, and his heart to the infinu-
ations of truth and reafon! This truth every
where prefents itfelf in radiant brightnefs;
and he does not fee it! The voice of reafon
ftrikes his ear; and he does not hear it! Unjuft man! if you can for a moment fufpend
the delufion which fafcinates your fenfes; if
your heart be capable of comprehending the
language of argumentation, interrogate thefe
ruins! read the leffons which they prefent to
you!....And you, facred temples! venerable
tombs! walls once glorious! the witneffes of
twenty different ages, appear in the caufe of
nature herfelf! come to the tribunal of found
underftanding, to bear teftimony againft an
unjuft accufation, to confound the declama-
tions of falfe wifdom or hypocritical piety,
and avenge the heavens and the earth of
man who calumniates them!

What is this blind fatality, that, without
order or laws, fports with the lot of mortals?
What this unjuft neceffity, which confounds
the iffue of actions, be they thofe of prudence
or thofe of folly? In what confifts the male-
dictions of Heaven denounced againft thefe
countries? Where is the divine curfe that
perpetuates

perpetuates this scene of desolation ? Monuments of past ages ! say, have the heavens
changed their laws, and the earth its course?
Has the sun extinguished his fires in the
region of space ? Do the seas no longer send
forth clouds? Are the rain and the dew fixed
in the air ? Do the mountains retain their
springs ? Are the streams dried up ? and do
the plants no more bear fruit and seed? An-
swer, race of falsehood and iniquity, has God
troubled the primitive and invariable order
which he himself assigned to nature ? Has
heaven denied to the earth, and the earth to
its inhabitants, the blessings that were formerly dispensed ? If the creation has remained the same, if its sources and its instru-
ments are exactly what they once were,
wherefore should not the present race have
every thing within their reach that their
ancestors enjoyed ? Falsely do you accuse
Fate and the Divinity: injuriously do you refer to God the cause of your evils. Tell me,
perverse and hypocritical race, if these places
are desolate, if powerful cities are reduced to
solitude, is it he that has occasioned the
ruin? Is it his hand that has thrown down
these

thefe walls, fapped thefe temples, mutilated
thefe pillars ? or is it the hand of man ? Is it
the arm of God that has introduced the
fword into the city and fet fire to the country,
murdered the people, burned the harvefts,
rooted up the trees, and ravaged the paftures?
or is it the arm of man ? And when, after
this devaftation, famine has ftarted up, is it
the vengeance of God that has fent it, or the
mad fury of mortals ? When, during the
famine, the people are fed with unwholefome
provifion, and peftilence enfues, is it inflicted
by the anger of Heaven, or brought about by
human imprudence ! When war, famine, and
peftilence united have fwept away the inhabitants, and the land is become a defert, is it
God who has depopulated it ? Is it his rapacity that plunders the labourer, ravages the
productive fields, and lays wafte the country ; or the rapacity of thofe who govern ?
Is it his pride that creates murderous wars,
or the pride of kings and their minifters ? Is
it the venality of his decifions that overthrows
the fortune of families, or the venality of the
organs of the laws? Are they his paffions
that, under a thoufand forms, torment in-

C   dividuals

dividuals and nations; or the paffions of
human beings? And if in the anguifh of
their misfortunes they perceive not the remedies, is it the ignorance of God that is in
fault, or their own ignorance? Ceafe, then,
to accufe the decrees of Fate or the judgments of Heaven! If God is good, will he
be the author of your punifhment? If he
is juft, will he be the accomplice of your
crimes? No, no; the caprice of which man
complains, is not the caprice of deftiny: the
darknefs that mifleads his reafon, is not the
darknefs of God; the fource of his calamities,
is not in the diftant heavens, but near to
him upon the earth; it is not concealed in
the bofom of the divinity; it refides in himfelf, man bears it in his heart.

You murmur, and fay: Why have an unbelieving people enjoyed the bleffings of heaven and of the earth? Why is a holy and chofen
race lefs fortunate than impious generations?
Deluded man! where is the contradiction at
which you take offence? Where the incon-
fiftency in which you fuppofe the juftice of
God to be involved? Take the balance of
bleffings and calamities, of caufes and effects,
and

and tell me—When thofe infidels obferved the laws of the earth and the heavens, when they regulated their intelligent labours by the order of the feafons and the courfe of the ftars, ought God to have troubled the equili-brium of the world to defeat their prudence? When they cultivated with care and toil the face of the country around you, ought he to have turned afide the rain, to have withheld the fertilizing dews, and caufed thorns to fpring up? When, to render this parched and barren foil productive, their induftry conftructed aqueducts, dug canals, and brought the diftant waters acrofs the deferts, ought he to have blighted the harvefts which art had created; to have defolated a country that had been peopled in peace; to have de-molifhed the towns which labour had caufed to flourifh; in fine, to have deranged and confounded the order eftablifhed by the wifdom of man? And what is this *infidelity* which founded empires by prudence, de-fended them by courage, and ftrengthened them by juftice; which raifed magnificent cities, formed vaft ports, drained peftilential marfhes, covered the fea with fhips, the earth

C 2   with

with inhabitants, and, like the creative fpirit, diffufed life and motion through the world. If fuch is impiety, what is true belief? Does holinefs confift in deftruction? Is then the God that peoples the air with birds, the earth with animals, and the waters with rep-tiles; the God that animates univerfal na-ture, a God that delights in ruins and fepul-chres? Does he afk devaftation for homage, and conflagration for facrifice? Would he have groans for hymns, murderers to worfhip him, and a defert and ravaged world for his temple? Yet fuch, *holy* and *faithful* genera-tion, are your works! Thefe are the fruits of your *piety!* You have maffacred the peo-ple, reduced cities to afhes, deftroyed all traces of cultivation, made the earth a foli-tude; and you demand the reward of your la-bours! Miracles are not too much for your advantage! For you the peafants that you have murdered fhould be revived; the walls you have thrown down fhould rife again; the harvefts you have ravaged fhould flourifh; the conduits that you have broken down fhould be renewed; the laws of heaven and earth, thofe laws which God has eftablifhed for the

difplay

difplay of his greatnefs and his magnificence,
thofe laws anterior to all revelations and to
all prophets, thofe laws which paffion cannot
alter, and ignorance cannot pervert, fhould
be fuperfeded. Paffion knows them not;
ignorance, which obferves no caufe and pre-
dicts no effect, has faid in the foolifhnefs of
her heart: " Every thing comes from
" chance; a blind fatality diftributes good
" and evil upon the earth; fuccefs is not to
" the prudent, nor felicity to the wife." Or
elfe, affuming the language of hypocrify,
fhe has faid: " Every thing comes from
" God; and it is his fovereign pleafure to
" deceive the fage, and to confound the
" judicious." And fhe has contemplated
the imaginary fcene with complacency.
" Good !" fhe has exclaimed. " I then am
" as well endowed as the fcience that de-
" fpifes me! The cold prudence which
" evermore haunts and torments me, I will
" render ufelefs by a lucky intervention of
" Providence." Cupidity has joined the
chorus. " I too will opprefs the weak; I
" will wring from him the fruits of his
" labour: for fuch is the decree of Heaven,

C 3   " fuch

" fuch the omnipotent will of fate."—For
myfelf, I fwear by all laws human and divine,
by the laws of the human heart, that the
hypocrite and the deceiver fhall be themfelves deceived; the unjuft man fhall perifh
in his rapacity, and the tyrant in his ufurpa-
tion: the fun fhall change its courfe, before
folly fhall prevail over wifdom and fcience,
before ftupidity fhall furpafs prudence in the
delicate art of procuring to man his true
enjoyments, and of building his happinefs
upon a folid foundation.

C H A P. IV.

THE HEMISPHERE.

Thus fpoke the Apparition. Aftonifhed at his difcourfe, and my heart agitated by a diverfity of reflections, I was for fome time filent. At length, affuming the courage to fpeak, I thus addreffed him : O Genius of tombs and ruins ! your fudden appearance and your feverity have thrown my fenfes into diforder, but the juftnefs of your reafoning reftores confidence to my foul. Pardon my ignorance. Alas ! if man is blind, can that which conftitutes his torment be alfo his crime ? I was unable to diftinguifh the voice of reafon ; but the moment it was known to me, I gave it welcome. Oh ! if you can read my heart, you know how defirous it is of truth, and with what ardour it feeks it ; you know that it is in this purfuit I am now found in thefe remote places. Alas ! I have wandered over the earth, I have vifited cities and

C 4   countries ;

countries; and perceiving every where mifery and defolation, the fentiment of the evils
by which my fellow creatures are tormented
has deeply afflicted my mind! I have faid to
myfelf with a figh: <u>Is man, then, created to
be the victim of pain and anguifh?</u> And I
have meditated upon human evils, that I
might find out their remedy.   I have faid, I
will feparate myfelf from corrupt focieties ;
I will remove far from palaces where the foul
is depraved by fatiety, and from cottages
where it is humbled by mifery. I will dwell
in folitude amidft the ruins of cities : I will
enquire of the monuments of antiquity what
was the wifdom of former ages : in the very
bofom of fepulchres I will invoke the fpirit that formerly in Afia gave fplendour to
ftates and glory to their people: I will enquire of the afhes of legiflators what caufes
have erected and overthrown empires; what
are the principles of national profperity and
misfortune ; what the maxims upon which
the peace of fociety and the happinefs of
man ought to be founded.

I ftopped ; and cafting down my eyes, I
waited the reply of the Genius.   Peace and
happinefs,

happinefs, faid he, defcend upon him who practifes juftice! Young man, fince your heart fearches after truth with fincerity; fince you can diftinguifh her form through the mift of prejudices which blind the eyes, your en- quiry fhall not be vain: I will difplay to your view this truth of which you are in purfuit; I will fhow to your reafon the knowledge which you defire; I will reveal to you the wifdom of the tombs, and the fcience of ages —Then approaching me, and placing his hand upon my head, Rife, mortal, faid he, and difengage yourfelf from that corporeal frame with which you are incumbered—In- ftantly, penetrated as with a celeftial flame, the ties that fix us to the earth feemed to be loofened; and lifted by the wing of the Genius, I felt myfelf like a light vapour con- veyed in the uppermoft region. There, from above the atmofphere, looking down towards the earth I had quitted, I beheld a fcene entirely new. Under my feet, float- ing in empty fpace, a globe fimilar to that of the moon, but fmaller, and lefs luminous, prefented to me one of its faces * ; and this

* See Plate I. reprefenting half the terreftrial globe.

face

face had the appearance of a diſk variegat- .
ed with ſpots, ſome of them white and ne-
bulous, others brown, green and grey; and
while I exerted my powers in diſcerning
and diſcriminating theſe ſpots—Diſciple of
truth, ſaid the Genius to me, have you any
recollection of this ſpectacle? O Genius, I
replied, if I did not perceive the moon in a
different part of the heavens, I ſhould ſuppoſe the orb below me to be that planet; for
its appearance reſembles perfectly the moon
viewed through a teleſcope at the time of an
eclipſe: one might be apt to think the va-
riegated ſpots to be ſeas and continents.

Yes, ſaid he to me, they are the ſeas and
continents of the very hemiſphere you inhabit.

What, exclaimed I, is that the Earth that
is inhabited by human beings?

It is, replied he. That brown ſpace which
occupies irregularly a conſiderable portion of
the diſk, and nearly ſurrounds it on all ſides,
is what you call the main ocean, which,
from the ſouth pole advancing towards the
equator, firſt forms the great gulf of Africa
and India, then ſtretches to the eaſt acroſs
the Malay Iſlands, as far as the confines of

Tartary,

Tartary, while at the weft it inclofes the continents of Africa and of Europe, reaching to the north of Afia.

Under our feet, that peninfula of a fquare figure is the defert country of Arabia, and on the left you perceive that great continent, fcarcely lefs barren in its interior parts, and only verdant as it approaches the fea, the inhabitants of which are diftinguifhed by a fable complexion *. To the north, and on the other fide of an irregular and narrow fea †, are the tracts of Europe, rich in fertile meadows and in all the luxuriance of cultivation. To the right from the Cafpian, extend the rugged furface and fnow-topt hills of Tartary. In bringing back the eye again to the fpot over which we are elevated, you fee a large white fpace, the melancholy and uniform defert of Cobi, cutting off the empire of China from the reft of the world. China itfelf is that furrowed furface which feems by a fudden obliquity to efcape from the view. Farther on, thofe vaft tongues of land and fcattered points, are the peninfula,

---

* Africa.　　　† The Mediterranean.

and

and iflands of the Malayans, the unfortunate proprietors of aromatics and perfumes. Still nearer you obferve a triangle which projects ftrongly into the fea, and is the too famous peninfula of India (*d*). You fee the crooked windings of the Ganges, the ambitious mountains of Thibet, the fortunate valley of Caffimere (12), the difcouraging deferts of Perfia, the banks of the Euphrates, and the Tigris, the rough bed of the Jordan (4), and the mouths of the folitary Nile. (See the Plate.)

O Genius, faid I, interrupting him, the organ of a mortal would in vain attempt to diftinguifh objects at fo great a diftance. Immediately he touched my eyes, and they became more piercing than thofe of the eagle; notwithftanding which rivers appeared to me no more than meandering ribbons, ridges of mountains irregular furrows, and great cities a neft of boxes varied among themfelves like the fquares in a chefs-board.

The Genius proceeded to point out the different objects to me with his finger, and to develope them as he proceeded. Thefe heaps of ruins, faid he, that you obferve in

this

this narrow valley, laved by the Nile, are all that remain of the opulent cities that gave luftre to the ancient kingdom of Ethiopia (e). Here is the monument of its fplendid metropolis, Thebes with its hundred palaces (f), the progenitor of cities, the memento of human frailty. It was there that a people, fince forgotten, difcovered the elements of fcience and art, at a time when all other men were barbarous, and that a race, now regarded as the refufe of fociety, becaufe their hair is woolly, and their fkin is dark, explored among the phenomena of nature, thofe civil and religious fyftems which have fince held mankind in awe. A little lower the dark fpots that you obferve are the pyramids (1) whofe maffes have overwhelmed your imagination. Farther on, the coaft (3) that you behold limited by the fea on one fide, and by a ridge of mountains on the other, was the abode of the Phenician nations; there flood the powerful cities of Tyre, Sidon, Afcalon, Gaza, and Berytus. This ftream of water, which feems to difembogue itfelf into no fea (4), is the Jordan; and thefe barren rocks were formerly the fcene of events, whofe

whofe tale may not be forgotten. Here you
find the defert of Horeb, and the hill of Si-
nai (5), where, by artifice which the vulgar
were unable to penetrate, a fubtle and daring leader gave birth to inftitutions of memorable influence upon the hiftory of mankind. Upon the barren ftrip of land which
borders upon this defert, you fee no longer
any trace of fplendour; and yet here was
formerly the magazine of the world. Here
were the ports of the Idumeans (g), from
whence the fleets of the Phenicians and the
Jews, coafting the peninfula of Arabia, bent
their voyages to the Perfian gulf, and imported from thence the pearls of Havila, the
gold of Saba and Ophir. It was here, on
the fide of Oman and Bahrain, that exifted
that fite of magnificent and luxurious commerce, which, as it was tranfplanted from
country to country, decided upon the fate of
ancient nations. Hither were brought the
vegetable aromatics, and the precious ftones
of Ceylon, the fhawls of Caffimere, the diamonds of Golconda, the amber of the Mal-
dives, the mufk of Thibet, the aloes of Co-
chin, the apes and the peacocks of the continent

tinent of India, the incenfe of Hadramut, the myrrh, the filver, the gold duft, and the ivory of Africa. From hence were exported, fometimes by the Black Sea, in fhips of Egypt and Syria, thefe commodities, which conftituted the opulence of Thebes, Sidon, Memphis, and Jerufalem ; fometimes afcending the courfe of the Tygris and the Euphrates, they awakened the activity of the Affyrians, the Medes, the Chaldeans, and the Perfians, and according as they were ufed or abufed, cherifhed or overturned their wealth and profperity. Hence grew up the magnificence of Perfepolis, of which you may obferve the mouldering columns (8) ; of Ecbatana (9), whofe feven-fold walls are levelled with the earth; of Babylon (10), the ruins of which are trodden under foot of men (*b*) ; of Nineveh (11), whofe name feems to be threatened with the fame oblivion, that has overtaken its greatnefs ; of Thapfacus, of Anatho, of Gerra, and of the melancholy and memorable Palmyra. O names, for ever glorious ! celebrated fields ! famous countries ! how replete is your afpect with fublime inftruction ! How many

I   profound

profound truths are written on the furface
of this earth! Ye places that here witneffed
the life of man, in fo many different ages, aid
my recollection while I endeavour to trace
the revolutions of his fortune! Say, what
were the motives of his conduct, and what
his powers! Unveil the caufes of his mif-
fortunes, teach him true wifdom, and let the
experience of paft ages become a mirror of
inftruction, and a germ of happinefs to prefent and future generations!

C H A P.

C H A P. V.

CONDITION OF MAN IN THE UNIVERSE.

A F T E R a fhort filence, the Genius thus
refumed his inftructions :

I have already obferved to you, O friend
of truth, that man vainly attributes his mif-
fortunes to obfcure and imaginary agents,
and fceks out remote and myfterious caufes,
from which to deduce his evils. In the general order of the univerfe, his condition is
doubtlefs fubjected to inconveniencies, and
his exiftence over-ruled by fuperior powers;
but thefe powers are neither the decrees of a
blind deftiny, nor the caprices of fantaftic
beings. Man is governed, like the world of
which he forms a part, by natural laws, regular in their operation, confequent in their
effects, immutable in their effence; and thefe
laws, the common fource of good and evil,
are neither written in the diftant ftars, nor
concealed in myfterious codes : inherent in
the nature of all terreftrial beings, identified

D   with

with their exiftence, they are at all times and
in all places prefent to the human mind; they
act upon the fenfes, inform the intellect, and
annex to every action its punifhment and its
reward. Let man ftudy thefe laws, let him
underftand his own nature, and the nature of
the beings that furround him, and he will
know the fprings of his deftiny, the caufes of
his evils, and the remedies to be applied.

When the fecret power that animates the
univerfe, formed the globe of the earth, he
ftamped on the beings which compofe it effential properties, that became the rule of
their individual action, the tie of their reciprocal connections, and the caufe of the harmony of the whole. He hereby eftablifhed
a regular order of caufes and effects, of principles and confequences, which, under an
appearance of chance, governs the univerfe,
and maintains the equilibrium of the world.
Thus he gave to fire motion and activity, to
air elafticity, to matter weight and denfity;
he made air lighter than water, metals heavier than earth, wood lefs cohefive than
fteel; he ordered the flame to afcend, the
ftone to fall, the plant to vegetate; to man,

                                    whom

whom he decreed to expofe to the encoun-
ter of fo many fubftances, and yet wifhed to
preferve his frail exiftence, he gave the faculty of perception. By this faculty, every
action injurious to his life gives him a fenfation of pain and evil, and every favourable
action a fenfation of pleafure and good. By
thefe impreffions, fometimes led to avoid
what is offenfive to his fenfes, and fometimes
attracted towards the objects that foothe and
gratify them, man has been neceffitated to
love and preferve his exiftence.   Self-love,
the defire of happinefs, and an averfion to
pain, are the effential and primary laws that
nature herfelf impofed on man, that the
ruling power, whatever it be, has eftablifhed
to govern him : and thefe laws, like thofe of
motion in the phyfical world, are the fimple
and prolific principle of every thing that
takes place in the moral world.

Such then is the condition of man : on
one fide, fubjected to the action of the elements around him, he is expofed to a variety
of inevitable evils ; and if in this decree Nature appears too fevere, on the other hand,
juft and even indulgent, fhe has not only

tempered

tempered thofe evils with an equal portion
of benefits, fhe has moreover given him the
power of augmenting the one, and diminifh-
ing the other. She has feemingly faid to
him, " Feeble work of my hands, I owe you
" nothing, and I give you life. The world
" in which I place you was not made on
" your account, and yet I grant you the ufe
" of it. You will find in it a mixture of
" good and evil. It is for you to diftinguifh
" them ; you muft direct your own fteps in
" the paths of flowers and of thorns. Be the
" arbitrator of your lot ; I place your deftiny
" in your hands."———Yes, man is become
the artificer of his fate; it is himfelf who
has created in turn the viciffitudes of his
fortune, his fucceffes and his difappoint-
ments ; and if, when he reflects on the for-
rows which he has affociated to human life,
he has reafon to lament his weaknefs and
his folly, he has perhaps ftill more right to
prefume upon his force, and be confident in
his energies, when he recollects from what
point he has fet out, and to what heights he
has been capable of elevating himfelf.

C H A P.

C H A P. VI.

ORIGINAL STATE OF MAN.

IN the origin of things, man, formed equally naked both as to body and mind, found
himfelf thrown by chance upon a land confufed and favage. An orphan, deferted by
the unknown power that had produced him,
he faw no fupernatural beings at hand to ad-
vertife him of wants that he owed merely to
his fenfes, and inform him of duties fpringing
folely from thofe wants. Like other animals, without experience of the paft, without knowledge of the future, he wandered in
forefts, guided and governed purely by the
affections of his nature. By the pain of
hunger he was directed to feek food, and he
provided for his fubfiftence; by the incle-
mencies of the weather, the defire was excited of covering his body, and he made
himfelf cloathing : by the attraction of a
powerful pleafure, he approached a fellow-
being, and perpetuated his fpecies,

D 3   Thus

Thus the impreſſions he received from external objeĉts, awakening his faculties, developed by degrees his underſtanding, and began to inſtruĉt his profound ignorance : his wants called forth his induſtry; his dangers formed his mind to courage ; he learned to diſtinguiſh uſeful from pernicious plants, to reſiſt the elements, to ſeize upon his prey, to defend his life ; and his miſery was alleviated.

Thus *ſelf-love, averſion to pain, and deſire of happineſs,* were the ſimple and powerful motives which drew man from the ſavage and barbarous ſtate in which Nature had placed him: and now that his life is ſown with enjoyment, that he can every day <u>count upon ſome pleaſure,</u> he may applaud himſelf and ſay: " <u>It is I</u> who have produced the " bleſſings that encompaſs me ; <u>I am</u> the " fabricator of my own felicity ; a ſecure " habitation, commodious raiment, an abun- " dance of wholeſome proviſion in rich va- " riety, ſmiling valleys, fertile hills, popu- " lous empires, theſe are the works of my " hand ; <u>but for me,</u> the earth, given up to " diſorder, would have been nothing more " than

" than a poifonous fwamp, a favage foreft,
" and a hideous defert !" True, mortal
creator ! I pay thee homage ! Thou haft
meafured the extent of the heavens, and
counted the ftars, thou haft drawn the light-
ning from the clouds ; conquered the fury
of the fea and the tempeft, and fubjected
all the elements to thy will ! But, oh ! how
many errors are mixed with thefe fublime
energies !

D 4   C H A P.

C H A P. VII.

PRINCIPLES OF SOCIETY.

In the mean time, wandering in woods
and upon the borders of rivers, in purfuit of
deer and of fifh, the firft human beings,
hunters and fifhermen, befet with dangers,
aſſailed by enemies, tormented by hunger, by
reptiles, and by the animals they chafed, felt
their individual weaknefs; and, impelled by
a common want of fafety, and a common
fentiment of the fame evils, they united their
powers and their ftrength.   When one man
was expofed to danger, numbers fuccoured
and defended him; when one failed in provifion, another fhared with him his prey.
Men thus aſſociated for the fecurity of their
exiftence, for the augmentation of their faculties, for the protection of their enjoyment; and the principle of fociety was that
of *felf-love*.

Afterwards, inftructed by the repeated experience of diverfe accidents, by the fatigues

§   of

of a wandering life, by the anxiety refulting from frequent fcarcity, men reafoned with themfelves, and faid: " Why fhould we con-
" fume our days in fearch of the fcattered
" fruits which a parfimonious foil affords ?
" Why weary ourfelves in the purfuit of
" prey that efcape us in the woods or the
" waters ? Let us affemble under our hand
" the animals that nourifh us ; let us apply
" our cares to the increafe and defence of
" them. Their produce will afford us a fup-
" ply of food, with their fpoils we may
" clothe ourfelves, and we fhall live exempt
" from the fatigues of the day, and folicitude
" for the morrow." And aiding each other, they feized the nimble kid and the timid fheep; they tamed the patient camel, the ferocious bull, and the impetuous horfe; and applauding themfelves on the fuccefs of their induftry, they fat down in the joy of their hearts, and began to tafte repofe and tranquillity: and thus *felf-love*, the principle of all their reafoning, was the inftigator to every art and every enjoyment.

Now that men could pafs their days in leifure, and the communication of their ideas,

they

they turned upon the earth, upon the heavens, and upon themfelves an eye of curiofity
and reflection. They obferved the courfe of
the feafons, the action of the elements, the
properties of fruits and plants; and they applied their minds to the multiplication of
their enjoyments. Remarking in certain
countries the nature of feeds, which contain
within themfelves the faculty of re-producing
the parent plant, they employed to their own
advantage this property of Nature: they committed to the earth barley, wheat, and rice,
and reaped a produce equal to their moft fan-
guine hopes. Thus they found the means
of obtaining within a fmall compafs, and
without the neceffity of perpetual wander-
ings, a plentiful and durable ftock of provifion; and encouraged by this difcovery,
they prepared for themfelves fixed habitations, they conftructed houfes, villages, and
towns; they affumed the form of tribes and
of nations: and thus was *felf-love* rendered
the parent of every thing that genius has
effected, or human power performed.

By the fole aid then of his faculties, has
man been able to raife himfelf to the aftonifhing

ing height of his prefent fortune. Too happy would have been his lot, had he, fcru-pulouſly obferving the law imprinted on his nature, conftantly fulfilled the object of it! But, by a fatal imprudence, fometimes over-looking and fometimes tranfgreffing its li-mits, he plunged in an abyſs of errors and misfortunes; and *felf-love*, now difordered, and now blind, was converted into a prolific ſource of calamities.

CHAP.

C H A P. VIII.

SOURCE OF THE EVILS OF SOCIETY.

In reality, fcarcely were the faculties of men expanded, than, feized by the attraction of objects which flatter the fenfes, they gave themfelves up to unbridled defires. The fweet fenfations which nature had annexed to their true wants, to attach them to life, no longer fufficed. Not fatisfied with the fruits which the earth offered them, or their induftry produced, they were defirous of heaping up enjoyments, and they coveted thofe which their fellow-creatures poffeffed. A ftrong man rofe up againft a weak one to tear from him the profit of his labour: the weak man folicited the fuccour of a neighbour, weak like himfelf, to repel the violence. The ftrong man in his turn affociated himfelf with another ftrong man, and they faid: " Why fhould we fatigue our arms in pro-" ducing enjoyments which we find in the " hands of the feeble, who are unable to de-" fend

" fend themfelves? Let us unite, and plun-
" der them. They fhall toil for us, and we
" fhall enjoy in indolence the fruit of their
" exertions." The ftrong thus affociating
for the purpofe of oppreffion, and the weak
for refiftance, men reciprocally tormented
each other, and a fatal and general difcord
was eftablifhed upon the earth, in which the
paffions, affuming a thoufand new forms,
have never ceafed to generate a regular train
of calamities.

Thus that very principle of felf-love,
which, when reftrained within the limits of
prudence, was a fource of improvement and
felicity, became transformed, in its blind and
difordered ftate, into a contagious poifon.
Cupidity, the daughter and companion of
ignorance, has produced all the mifchiefs
that have defolated the globe.

Yes, ignorance and the love of accumulation, thefe are the two fources of all the
plagues that infeft the life of man! They
have infpired him with falfe ideas of his
happinefs, and prompted him to mifconftrue
and infringe the laws of nature, as they related to the connection between him and
exterior

exterior objects. Through them his conduct has been injurious to his own exiftence, and he has thus violated the duty he owes to himfelf; they have fortified his heart againft compaffion, and his mind againft the dictates of juftice, and he has thus violated the duty he owes to others. By ignorance and inordinate defire, man has armed himfelf againft man, family againft family, tribe againft tribe, and the earth is converted into a bloody theatre of difcord and robbery. They have fown the feeds of fecret war in the bofom of every ftate, divided the citizens from each other, and the fame fociety is conftituted of oppreffors and oppreffed, of mafters and flaves. They have taught the heads of nations, with audacious infolence, to turn the arms of the fociety againft itfelf, and to build upon mercenary avidity the fabric of political defpotifm: or they have taught a more hypocritical and deep-laid project, that impofed, as the dictate of heaven, lying fanctions and a facrilegious yoke: thus rendering avarice the fource of credulity. In fine, they have corrupted every idea of good and evil, juft and unjuft,

unjuft, virtue and vice : they have mifled
nations in a never-ending labyrinth of calamity and miftake.   Ignorance and the love
of accumulation !....Thefe are the malevolent beings that have laid wafte the earth ;
thefe are the decrees of fate that have overturned empires; thefe are the celeftial ma-
lediétions that have ftruck thofe walls once
fo glorious, and converted the fplendour of a
populous city into a fad fpeétacle of ruins!...
Since then it was from his own bofom all
the evils proceeded that have vexed the life
of man, it was there alfo he ought to have
fought the remedies, where only they are to
be found.

C H A P,

C H A. P.   IX.

THE ORIGIN OF GOVERNMENT AND LAWS.

In truth, the period foon arrived when
men, tired of the ills they occafioned each
other, fighed after peace; and reflecting on
the nature and caufes of thofe ills, they faid:
" We mutually injute one another by our
" paffions, and from a defire to grafp every
" thing we in reality poffefs nothing. What
" one ravifhes to-day, another tears from
" him to-morrow, and our cupidity rebounds
" upon our own heads. Let us eftablifh
" arbitrators, who fhall decide our claims
" and appeafe our variances. When the
" ftrong rifes up againft the weak, the arbi-
" trator fhall repel him; and the life and
" property of each being under a common
" guarantee and protection, we fhall enjoy
" all the bleffings of nature."

Conventions, tacit or expreffed, were thus
introduced into fociety, and became the rule
of the actions of individuals, the meafure of
their

their claims, and the law of their reciprocal relations. Chiefs were appointed to enforce the obfervance of the compact, and to thefe the people entrufted the balance of rights, and the fword to punifh violations.

Then a happy equilibrium of powers and of action was eftablifhed, which conftituted the public fafety. The names of equity and juftice were acknowledged and revered. Every man, able to enjoy in peace the fruits of his labour, gave himfelf up to all the energies of his foul; and activity, awakened and kept alive by the reality or the hope of enjoyment, forced art and nature to difplay all their treafures. The fields were covered with harvefts, the valleys with flocks, the hills with vines, the fea with fhips, and man was happy and powerful upon the earth.

The diforder his imprudence had caufed, his wifdom thus remedied. But this wifdom was ftill the effect of the laws of nature in the organization of his being. It was to fecure his own enjoyments, that he was led to refpect thofe of another, and the defire of

E   accumulation

accumulation found its corrective in enlightened felf-love.

Self-love, the eternal fpring of action in
every individual, was thus the neceffary bafis
of all affociations ; and upon the obfervance
of this natural law has the fate of every nation depended. Have the factitious and
conventional laws of any fociety accorded
with this law, and correfponded to its demands ? In that cafe every man, prompted
by an overpowering inftinct, has exerted all
the faculties of his nature, and the public
felicity has been the refult of the various
portions of individual felicity. Have thefe
laws, on the contrary, reftrained the effort of
man in his purfuit of happinefs? In that cafe
his heart, deprived of all its natural motives,
has languifhed in inaction, and the oppreffion of individuals has engendered general
weaknefs.

Self-love, impetuous and rafh, renders
man the enemy of man, and of confequence
perpetually tends to the diffolution of fociety.
It is for the art of legiflation, and for the
virtue of minifters, to temper the grafping

felfifhnefs

felfifhnefs of individuals, to keep each man's
defire to poffefs every thing in a nice equi-
poife, and thus to render the fubjects happy,
in order that, in the ftruggle of this with
any other fociety, all the members fhould
have an equal intereft in the prefervation and
defence of the commonwealth.

From hence it follows, that the internal
fplendour and profperity of empires, have
been in proportion to the equity of their governments; and their external power re-
fpectively, in proportion to the number of
perfons interefted in the maintenance of the
political conftitution, and their degree of intereft in that maintenance.

On the other hand, the multiplication of
men by complicating their ties, having rendered the demarcation of their rights a point
of difficult decifion ; the perpetual play of
the paffions having given rife to unexpected
incidents; the conventions that were formed
having proved vicious, inadequate, or null ;
the authors of the laws having either mifunderftood the object of them, or diffembled
it, and the perfons appointed to execute
them, inftead of reftraining the inordinate

defires

defires of others, having abandoned themfelves to the fway of their own avidity—fociety has, by thefe caufes united, been thrown
into trouble and diforder; and defective laws
and unjuft governments, the refult of cupidity and ignorance, have been the foundation of the misfortunes of the people, and
the fubverfion of ftates.

CHAP.

CHAP. X.

GENERAL CAUSES OF THE PROSPERITY OF ANCIENT STATES.

Such, O man, who enquireſt after wiſdom, have been the cauſes of the revolutions of thoſe ancient ſtates of which you contemplate the ruins! Upon whatever ſpot I fix my view, or to whatever period my thoughts recur, the ſame principles of elevation and decline, of proſperity and deſtruction, preſent themſelves to the mind. If a people were powerful, if an empire flouriſhed, it was becauſe the laws of convention were conformable to thoſe of nature; becauſe the government procured, to every man reſpectively the free uſe of his faculties, the equal ſecurity of his perſon and property. On the contrary, if an empire has fallen to ruin or diſappeared, it is becauſe the laws were vicious or imperfect, or a corrupt government has checked their operation. If laws and government, at firſt rational and juſt, have afterwards become

E 3   depraved,

depraved, it is becaufe the alternative of good and evil derives from the nature of the heart of man, from the fucceffion of his inclinations, the progrefs of his knowledge, the combination of events and circumftances; as the hiftory of the human fpecies proves.

In the infancy of nations, when men ftill lived in forefts, all fubject to the fame wants, and endowed with the fame faculties, they were nearly equal in ftrength; and this equality was a circumftance highly advantageous to the formation of fociety. Each individual finding himfelf independent of every other, no one was the flave, and no one had the idea of being mafter of another. Untaught man knew neither fervitude nor tyranny. Supplied with the means of providing fufficiency for his fubfiftence, he thought not of borrowing from ftrangers. Owing nothing, and exacting nothing, he judged of the rights of others by his own. Ignorant alfo of the art of multiplying enjoyments, he provided only what was neceffary; and fuperfluity being unknown to him, the defire to engrofs of confequence remained unexcited; or if excited, as it attacked others

in

in thofe poffeffions that were wholly indif-
penfible, it was refifted with energy, and the
very forefight of this refiftance maintained a
falutary and immoveable equilibrium.

Thus original equality, without the aid
of convention, maintained perfonal liberty,
fecured individual property, and produced
order and good manners. Each man labour-
ed feparately and for himfelf: and his heart
being occupied, he wandered not in purfuit
of unlawful defires. His enjoyments were
few, but his wants were fatisfied: and as
nature had made thefe wants lefs extenfive
than his ability, the labour of his hands
foon produced abundance; abundance population; the arts developed themfelves, cultivation extended, and the earth, covered with
numerous inhabitants, was divided into different domains.

The relations of men becoming complicated, the interior order of fociety was more
difficult to maintain. Time and induftry
having created affluence, cupidity awoke
from its flumber; and as equality, eafy between individuals, could not fubfift between
families, the national balance was deftroyed.

E 4   It

It was neceſſary to ſupply the loſs by means of an artificial balance; it was neceſſary to appoint chiefs, and eſtabliſh laws; but as theſe were occaſioned by cupidity, in the experience of primitive times they could not but partake of the origin from which they ſprung. Various circumſtances however concurred to temper the diſorder, and make it indiſpenſible for governments to be juſt.

States being at firſt weak, and having external enemies to fear, it was in reality of importance to the chiefs not to oppreſs the ſubject. By diminiſhing the intereſt of the citizens in their government, they would have diminiſhed their means of reſiſtance; they would have facilitated foreign invaſion, and thus endangered their own exiſtence for ſuperfluous enjoyments.

Internally, the character of the people was repellent to tyranny. Men had too long contracted habits of independence; their wants were too limited, and the conſciouſneſs of their own ſtrength too inſeparable from their minds.

States being cloſely knit together, it was difficult to divide the citizens, in order to oppreſs

oppreſs ſome by means of others. Their communication with each other was too eaſy, and their intereſts too ſimple and evident. Beſide, every man being at once proprietor and cultivator, he had no inducement to ſell himſelf, and the deſpot would have been unable to find mercenaries.

If diſſenſions aroſe, it was between family and family, one faction with another; and a conſiderable number had ſtill one common intereſt. Diſputes, it is true, were in this caſe more warm, but the fear of foreign invaſion appeaſed the diſcord. If the oppreſſion of a party was effected, the earth being open before it, and men, ſtill ſimple in their manners, finding every where the ſame advantages, the party migrated and carried their independence to another quarter.

Ancient ſtates then enjoyed in themſelves numerous means of proſperity and power.

As every man found his well-being in the conſtitution of his country, he felt a lively intereſt in its preſervation; and if a foreign power invaded it, having his habitation and his field to defend, he carried to the combat the ardour of a perſonal cauſe, and his patriotic

triotic exertions were prompted by felf-defence.

As every action ufeful to the public excited its efteem and gratitude, each was eager to be ufeful, and talents and civil virtues were multiplied by felf-love.

As every citizen was called upon indifcriminately to contribute his proportion of property and perfonal effort, the armies and the treafuries of the ftate were inexhauftible.

As the earth was free, and its poffeffion eafy and fecure, every man was a proprietor, and the divifion of property, by rendering luxury impoffible, preferved the purity of manners.

As everyman ploughed his own field, cultivation was more active, provifions more abundant, and individual opulence conftituted the public wealth.

As abundance of provifion rendered fubfiftence eafy, population rapidly increafed, and ftates quickly arrived at their plenitude.

As the produce was greater than the confumption, the defire of commerce ftarted up, and exchanges were made between different naticns, which were an additional ftimulus to

their

their activity, and increafed their reciprocal enjoyments.

In fine, as certain places in certain epochas combined the advantage of good government with that of being placed in the road of circulation and commerce, they became rich magazines of trade, and powerful feats of dominion. It was in this manner that the riches of India and Europe, accumulated upon the banks of the Nile, the Tigris, and the Euphrates, gave fucceffive exiftence to the fplendour of a thoufand metropoliffes.

The people, become rich, applied their fuperfluity of means to labours of public utility; and this was, in every ftate, the æra of thofe works, the magnificence of which aftonifhes the mind; thofe wells of Tyre (*i*), thofe artificial banks of the Euphrates, thofe conduits of Medea (*k*), thofe fortreffes of the Defert, thofe aqueducts of Palmyra, thofe temples, thofe porticos.... And thefe immenfe labours were little oppreffive to the nations that completed them, becaufe they were the fruit of the equal and united effort of individuals free to act and ardent to defire.

Thus

Thus ancient ſtates proſpered, becauſe ſocial inſtitutions were conformable to the true
laws of nature, and becauſe the ſubjects of
thoſe ſtates, enjoying liberty and the ſecurity
of their perſons and their property, could
diſplay all the extent of their faculties, and
all the energy of ſelf-love.

CHAP. XI.

GENERAL CAUSES OF THE REVOLUTIONS AND RUIN OF ANCIENT STATES.

In the mean time the inordinate defire of accumulation had excited a conftant and univerfal ftruggle among men, and this ftruggle, prompting individuals and focieties to reciprocal invafions, occafioned perpetual commotions and fucceffive revolutions.

At firft, in the favage and barbarous ftate of the firft human beings, this inordinate defire, daring and ferocious in its nature, taught rapine, violence, and murder; and the progrefs of civilization was for a long time at a ftand.

Afterwards, when focieties began to be formed, the effect of bad habits communicating itfelf to laws and government, civil inftitutions became corrupt, and arbitrary and factitious rights were eftablifhed, which gave the people depraved ideas of juftice and morality.

Becaufe

Becaufe one man, for example, was ftronger than another, this inequality, the refult of
accident, was taken for the law of nature (*l*);
and becaufe the life of the weak was in his
power, and he did not take it from him, he
arrogated over his perfon the abfurd right of
property, and individual flavery prepared the
way for the flavery of nations.

Becaufe the chief of a family could exercife an abfolute authority in his own houfe,
he made his inclinations and affections the
fole rule of his conduct; he conferred and
withheld the conveniences and enjoyments
of life without refpect to the law of equality
or juftice, and paternal tyranny laid the foundation of political defpotifm (*m*).

In focieties formed upon fuch bafes, time
and induftry having developed riches, inordinate defire, reftricted by the laws, became
*artificial without being lefs active. Under
the mafk of union and civil peace, it engendered in the bofom of every ftate an inteftine
war, in which the citizens divided into oppofite corps of orders, claffes, and families,
aimed to appropriate to themfelves, under
the name of *fupreme power*, the ability of
grafping

grafping and controlling every thing at the will of their paffions. It is this fpirit of rapacity, the difguifes of which are innumerable, but its operation and end uniformly the fame, that has been the perpetual fcourge of nations.

Sometimes oppofing focial compact, or deftroying that which already exifted, it has abandoned the inhabitants of a country to the tumultuous fhock of all their jarring principles; and the diffolved ftates, under the name of *anarchy*, have been tormented by the paffions of every individual member.

Sometimes a people jealous of its liberty, having appointed agents to adminifter, thefe agents have affumed to themfelves the powers of which they were only the guardians; have employed the public funds in corrupting elections, gaining partizans, and dividing the people againft itfelf. By thefe means, from temporary, they have become perpetual, from elective, hereditary magiftrates; and the ftate, agitated by the intrigues of the ambitious, by the bribes of the wealthy leaders of factions, by the venality of the indolent poor, by the empiricifm of declaim-

ers,

ers, has been troubled with all the inconveriences of *democracy*.

In one country, the chiefs, equal in strength, mutually afraid of each other, have formed vile compacts and coalitions, and portioning out power, rank, honours, have arrogated to themselves privileges and immunities; have erected themselves into separate bodies and distinct classes; have tyrannised in common over the people, and, under the name of *aristocracy*, the state has been tormented by the passions of the wealthy and the great.

In another country, tending to the same end by different means, *sacred impostors* have taken advantage of the credulity of the ignorant. In the secrecy of temples, and behind the veil of altars, they have made the Gods speak and act; have delivered oracles, worked pretended miracles, ordered sacrifices, imposed offerings, prescribed endowments; and, under the name of *theocracy* and *religion*, the state has been tormented by the passions of priests.

Sometimes, weary of its disorders or of its tyrants, a nation, to diminish the sources of its evils, gave itself a single master. In that case, if the powers of the prince were limited,

his

his only defire was to extend them ; if in-
definite, he abufed the truft that was con-
fided to him ; and, under the name of *monarchy*, the ftate was tormented by the paffions of kings and princes.

Then the factious, taking advantage of the
general difcontent, flattered the people with
the hope of a better mafter; they fcattered
gifts and promifes, dethroned the defpot to
fubftitute themfelves in his ftead ; and difputes for the fucceffion or the divifion of
power, have tormented the ftate with the diforders and devaftations of *civil war*.

In fine, among thefe rivals, one individual
more artful or more fortunate than the reft,
gaining the afcendancy, concentred the
whole power in himfelf. By a fingular phenomenon, one man obtained the maftery over
millions of his fellow-creatures, againft their
will, and without their confent; and thus
the art of *tyranny* appears alfo to have been
the offspring of inordinate defire. Obferving
the fpirit of egotifm that divided mankind,
the ambitious adroitly fomented this fpirit :
he flattered the vanity of one, excited the
jealoufy of another, favoured the avarice of a

F   third,

third, enflamed the refentment of a fourth,
irritated the paffions of all. By oppofing
interefts or prejudices, he fowed the feeds
of divifions and hatred. He promifed to the
poor the fpoil of the rich, to the rich the
fubjugation of the poor; threatened this
man by that, one clafs by another; and ifo-
lating the citizens by diftruft, he formed his
own ftrength out of their weaknefs, and impofed on them the yoke of *opinion*, the knots
of which they tied with their own hands.
By means of the army he extorted contributions; by the contributions he difpofed of
the army; by the correfponding play of
money and places, he bound all the people
with a chain that was not to be broken, and
the ftates which they compofed fell into the
flow decay of *defpotifm*.

Thus did one and the fame fpring, vary-
ing its action under all the forms that have
been enumerated, inceffantly attack the con-
tinuity of ftates, and an eternal circle of viciffitudes have fprung from an eternal circle
of paffions.

This conftant fpirit of egotifm operated
two principal effects equally deftructive: the
one,

one, that by dividing focieties into all their fractions, a ftate of debility was produced, which facilitated their diffolution; the other, that always tending to concentre the power in a fingle hand, it occafioned a fucceffive abforption of focieties and ftates, fatal to their peace and to their common exiftence (*n*).

Juft as in a fingle ftate, the nation had been abforbed in a party, that party in a family, and that family in an individual, there alfo exifted an abforption of a fimilar kind between ftate and ftate, attended with all the mifchiefs in the relative fituation of nations, that the other produced in the civil relation of individuals. One city fubjected its neighbour city, and the refult of the conqueft was a province; province fwallowed up province, and thus produced a kingdom; between two kingdoms a conqueft took place, and thus furnifhed an empire of unweildy bulk. Did the internal force of thefe ftates increafe in proportion to their mafs? On the contrary, it was diminifhed; and far from the condition of the people being happier, it became every day more oppreffive and

wretched,

wretched, by caufes inevitably flowing from the nature of things.

Becaufe, as the boundaries of ftates became extended, their adminiftration became more complicated and difficult; and to give motion to the mafs it was neceffary to increafe the prerogatives of the fovereign, and all proportion was thus annihilated between the duty of governors and their power.

Becaufe defpots, feeling their weaknefs, dreaded all thofe circumftances that developed the force of nations, and made it their ftudy to attenuate it.

Becaufe nations, eftranged from each other by the prejudices of ignorance and the ferocity of hatred, feconded the perverfity of governments, and employing a ftanding force for reciprocal offence, aggravated their flavery.

Becaufe, in proportion as the balance between ftates was broken, it became eafy for the ftrong to overwhelm the weak.

Becaufe, in proportion as ftate became blended with ftate, the people were ftripped of their laws, their cuftoms, every thing by which they were diftinguifhed from each other,

other, and thus loft the great mover *felfifh-nefs*, which gave them energy.

And defpots, confidering empires in the light of domains, and the people as their property, abandoned themfelves to depredations, and the licentioufnefs of the moft arbitrary authority.

And all the force and wealth of nations were converted into a fupply for individual expence and perfonal caprice; and kings, in the wearifomenefs of fatiety, followed the dictates of every factitious and depraved tafte (*o*). They muft have gardens conftructed upon arches, and rivers carried to the fummit of mountains; for them fertile fields muft be changed into parks for deer, lakes formed where there was no water, and rocks elevated in thofe lakes; they muft have palaces conftructed of marble and porphyry, and the furniture ornamented with gold and diamonds. Millions of hands were thus employed in fterile labours; and the luxury of princes being imitated by their parafites, and defcending ftep by ftep to the loweft ranks, became a general fource of corruption and empoverifhment.

F 3   And

And the ordinary tributes being no longer adequate to the infatiable thirft of enjoyment, they were augmented: the confequence of which was, that the cultivator, finding his toil increafe without any indemnity, loft his courage; the merchant, feeing himfelf robbed, took a difguft to induftry; the multitude, condemned to a ftate of poverty, exerted themfelves no farther than the procurement of neceffaries required, and every fpecies of productive activity was at a ftand.

And the furcharge of taxes rendering the poffeffion of lands burthenfome, the humble proprietor abandoned his field, or fold it to the man of opulence; and the mafs of wealth centered in a few individuals. As the laws and inftitutions favoured this accumulation, nations were divided into a fmall body of indolent rich, and a multiude of mercenary poor. The people, reduced to indigence, debafed themfelves; the great, cloyed with fuperfluity, became depraved; and the number of citizens interefted in the prefervation of the ftate decreafing, its ftrength and exiftence were by fo much the more precarious.

In

In another view, as there was nothing to excite emulation or encourage inftruction, the minds of men funk into profound ignorance.

The adminiftration of affairs being fecret and myfterious, there exifted no means of reform or hope of better times; and as the chiefs ruled only by violence and fraud, the people confidered them but as a faction of public enemies, and all harmony between the governed and the governors was at an end.

The ftates of opulent Afia become enervated by all thefe vices, it happened at length that the vagrant and poor inhabitants of the deferts and the mountains adjacent, coveted the enjoyments of the fertile plains, and inftigated by a common cupidity, they attacked polifhed empires, and overturned the thrones of defpots. Such revolutions were rapid and eafy, becaufe the policy of tyrants had enfeebled the citizens, razed the fortreffes, deftroyed the warlike fpirit of refiftance, and becaufe the oppreffed fubject was without perfonal intereft, and the mercenary foldier without courage.

Hordes of barbarians having reduced whole

nations

nations to a ftate of flavery, it followed that empires, formed of a conquering and a vanquifhed people, united in their bofom two claffes of men effentially oppofite and inimical to each other. All the principles of fociety were diffolved. There was no longer either a common intereft, or public fpirit: on the contrary, a diftinction of cafts and conditions was eftablifhed, that reduced the maintenance of diforder to a regular fyftem; and accordingly as a man was defcended from this or that blood, he was born vaffal or tyrant, live ftock or proprietor.

The oppreffors being in this cafe lefs numerous than the oppreffed, it became neceffary, in order to fupport this falfe equilibrium, to bring the fcience of tyranny to perfection. The art of governing was now nothing more than that of fubjecting the many to the few. To obtain an obedience fo contrary to inftinct, it was neceffary to eftablifh the moft fevere penalties; and the cruelty of the laws rendered the manners atrocious. The diftinction of perfons alfo eftablifhing in the ftate two codes of juftice, two fpecies of rights, the people, placed between

between the natural inclinations of their hearts, and the oath they were obliged to pronounce, had two contradictory confciences; and their ideas of juft and unjuft had no longer any foundation in the underftanding.

Under fuch a fyftem the people fell into a ftate of depreffion and defpair ; and the accidents of nature increafing the preponderance of evil, terrified at this groupe of calamities, they referred the caufes of them to fuperior and invifible powers : becaufe they had tyrants upon earth, they fuppofed there to be tyrants in heaven; and fuperftition came in aid to aggravate the difafters of nations.

Hence originated gloomy and mifanthropic fyftems of religion, which painted the Gods malignant and envious like human defpots. To appeafe them, man offered the facrifice of all his enjoyments, punifhed himfelf with privations, and overturned the laws of nature. Confidering his pleafures as crimes, his fufferings as expiations, he endeavoured to cherifh a paffion for pain, and to renounce felf-love ; he perfecuted his
fenfes;

senses, detested his life, and by a self-denying and unsocial system of morals, nations were plunged in the sluggishness of death.

But as provident nature had endowed the heart of man with inexhaustible hope, perceiving his desires disappointed of happiness here, he pursued it elsewhere; by a sweet illusion, he formed to himself another country, an asylum, where, out of the reach of tyrants, he should regain all his rights. Hence a new disorder arose. Smitten with his imaginary world, man despised the world of nature: for chimerical hopes he neglected the reality. He no longer considered his life but as a fatiguing journey, a painful dream; his body as a prison that withheld him from his felicity; the earth as a place of exile and pilgrimage, which he disdained to cultivate. A sacred sloth then established itself in the world; the fields were deserted, waste lands increased, empires were dispeopled, monuments neglected, and every where ignorance, superstition and fanaticism uniting their baleful effects, multiplied devastations and ruins.

Thus,

Thus, agitated by their own paffions, men, whether in their individual capacity, or as collective bodies, always rapacious and improvident, paffing from tyranny to flavery, from pride to abjectnefs, from prefumption to defpair, have been themfelves the eternal inftruments of their misfortunes.

Such was the fimplicity of the principles that regulated the fate of ancient ftates; fuch was the feries of caufes and effects, confecutive and connected with each other, according to which they rofe or fell in the fcale of human welfare, juft as the phyfical caufes of the human heart were therein obferved or infringed. A hundred divers nations, a hundred powerful empires, in their inceffant viciffitudes, have read again and again thefe inftructive leffons to mankind ... And thefe leffons are mute and forgotten ! The difcafes of paft times have appeared again in the prefent ! The heads of the different governments have practifed again, without reftraint, exploded projects of deception and defpotifm ! The people have wandered as before in the labyrinths of fuperftition and ignorance !

And

And what, added the Genius, calling up his energies afrefh, is the confequence of all this? Since experience is ufelefs, fince falutary examples are forgotten, the fcenes which were acted before are now about to be renewed; revolutions will again agitate people and empires; powerful thrones will, as before, be overturned; and terrible cataftrophes remind the human fpecies, that the laws of nature, and the precepts of wifdom and truth; cannot be trampled upon in vain.

C H A P. XII.

LESSONS TAUGHT BY ANCIENT, RE-
PEATED IN MODERN TIMES.

I N this manner did the Genius addrefs me. Struck with the reafonablenefs and coherence of his difcourfe, and a multiplicity of ideas crowding upon my mind, which, while they thwarted my habits, led my judgment at the fame time captive, I remained abforbed in profound filence. Meanwhile, as in this fombre and thoughtful difpofition I kept my eyes fixed upon Afia, clouds of fmoke and of flames at the north, on the fhores of the Black Sea, and in the fields of the Crimea, fuddenly attracted my attention. They appeared to afcend at once from every part of the peninfula, and paffing by the ifthmus to the continent, they purfued their courfe, as if driven by an eafterly wind, along the miry lake of Afoph, and were loft in the verdant plains of the Coban. Obferving more attentively the courfe of thefe clouds, I perceived

ceived that they were preceded or followed
by fwarms of living beings, which, like ants
difturbed by the foot of a paffenger, were in
lively action. Sometimes they feemed to
move towards and rufh againft each other,
and numbers after the concuffion remained
motionlefs. Difquieted at this fpectacle, I
was endeavouring to diftinguifh the objects,
when the Genius faid to me : Do you fee
thofe fires which fpread over the earth, and
are you acquainted with their caufes and
effects ?—O Genius, I replied, I fee columns
of flame and fmoke, and as it were infects
that accompany them ; but difcerning with
difficulty, as I do, the maffes of towns and
monuments, how can I diftinguifh fuch petty
creatures? I can fee nothing more than that
thefe infects feem to carry on a fort of mock
battles; they advance, they approach towards
each other, they attack, they purfue.—It is
no mockery, faid the Genius, it is the thing
itfelf.—And what name, replied I, fhall we
give to thefe foolifh animalculæ that deftroy
each other? Do they live only for a day, and
is this fhort life further abridged by violence
and murder ?—The Genius then once more
touched

touched my eyes and my ears. Liften, faid
he to me, and obferve.—Immediately, turning my eyes in the fame direction, alas ! faid
I, tranfpierced with anguifh, thefe columns
of flame, thefe infects, O Genius ! they are
men, and the ravages of war ! Thefe torrents of flame afcend from towns and villages fet on fire ! I fee the horfemen that
light them. I fee them fword in hand over-
run the country. Old men, women, and
children, in confufed multitudes, fly before
them. I fee other horfemen, who, with their
pikes upon their fhoulders, accompany and
direct them: I can even diftinguifh by their
led horfes, by their *kalpacks*, and by their
tufts of hair (*p*), that they are Tartars; and
without doubt thofe who purfue them in triangular hats and green uniforms are Mufcovites. I underftand the whole: I perceive
that the war has juft broken out afrefh between the empire of the Czars and the Sultans.—Not yet, replied the Genius; this is
only the prelude. Thefe Tartars have been,
and would ftill be troublefome neighbours;
the Mufcovites are ridding themfelves of
them. Their country is an object of conve-

nience

nience to their lefs uncivilized enemies; it rounds and makes complete their dominions; and as the firſt ſtep in the project that has been conceived, the throne of the Guerais is overturned.

In reality I ſaw the Ruſſian flag hoiſted over the Crimea, and their veſſels ſcattered upon the Euxine.

Meanwhile, at the cries of the fugitive Tartars, the Muſſulman empire was in commotion. " Our brethren," exclaimed the children of Mahomet, " are driven from their " habitations; the people of the prophet are " outraged; infidels are in poſſeſſion of a con- " ſecrated land (*q*), and profane the temples " of Iſlamiſm! Let us arm ourſelves to avenge " the glory of God and our own cauſe."

A general preparation for war then took place in the two empires. Armed men, proviſions, ammunition, and all the murderous accoutrements of battle, were every where aſſembled. My attention was particularly attracted by the immenſe crowds that in either nation thronged to the temples. On one ſide the Muſſulmans, aſſembled before their moſques, waſhed their hands and feet,

6 pared

pared their nails, and combed their beard: then fpreading carpets upon the ground, and turning themfelves towards the fouth, with their arms fometimes croffed and fometimes extended, they performed their genuflections and proftrations. Recollecting the difafters they had experienced during the laft war, they cried: " God of clemency and pity, haft " thou then abandoned thy faithful people ? " Why doft thou, who has promifed to thy " prophet the dominion of nations, and fig- " nalized religion by fo many triumphs, de- " liver up true believers to the fword of in- fidels?" And the Imans and the Santons faid to the people: " It is the chaftifement of " your fins. You eat pork, you drink wine, " you touch things that are unclean: God " has punifhed you. Do penance; purify " yourfelves; fay your creed *; faft from the " rifing of the fun to its fetting; give the " tenth of your goods to the mofques ; go " to Mecca; and God will make your arms " victorious." Then, affuming courage, the people gave a general fhout. " There is but

* There is but one God, and Mahomet is his prophet.

G   one

" one God," said they in a transport of rage,
" and Mahomet is his prophet! accursed be
" every one that believeth not! .... Indul-
" gent God! grant us the favour to exter-
" minate these Christians: it is for thy glory
" we fight, and by our death we are mar-
" tyrs to thy name."—And having offered sacrifices, they prepared themselves for
battle.

On the other hand, the Russians on their
knees exclaimed: " Let us give thanks to
" God, and celebrate his power: he has
" strengthened our arm to humble his ene-
" mies. Beneficent God! incline thine ear
" to our prayers. To please thee we will
" for three days eat neither meat nor eggs.
" Permit us to exterminate these impious
" Mahometans, and overthrow their empire,
" and we will give thee the tenth of the spoil,
" and erect new temples to thy honour."
The priests then filled the churches with
smoke, and said to the people: " We pray
" for you, and God accepts our incense, and
" blesses your arms. Continue to fast and
" to fight; tell us the faults you have secret-
" ly committed; bestow your goods on the
                                " church;

" church; we will abfolve you of your fins,
" and you fhall die in a ftate of grace." And
they fprinkled water on the people, diftributed among them little bones of departed
faints to ferve as amulets and talifmans; and
the people breathed nothing but war and
deftruction.

Struck with this contrafting picture of the
fame paffions, and lamenting to myfelf their
pernicious confequences, I was reflecting on
the difficulty the common Judge would find
in complying with fuch oppofite demands,
when the Genius, from an impulfe of anger,
vehemently exclaimed:

What madnefs is this which ftrikes my
ear? What blind and fatal infanity poffeffes
the human mind? Sacrilegious prayers, return to the earth from whence you came!
Ye concave heavens, repel thefe murderous
vows, thefe impious thankfgivings! Is it
thus, O man, you worfhip the Divinity? And
do you think that he, whom you call Father
of all, can receive with complacence the
homage of free-booters and murderers? Ye
conquerors, with what fentiments does he
behold your arms reeking with blood that he

G 2   has

has created? Ye conquered, what hope can
you place in ufelefs moans? Is he a man that
he fhould change, or the fon of man that he
fhould repent? Is he governed like you by
vengeance and compaflion, by rage and by
wearinefs! Bafe idea, how much unworthy
of the Being of Beings! Hear thefe men, and
you would imagine that God is a Being capricious and mutable; that now he loves, and
now he hates; that he chaflifes one, and in-
dulges another; that hatred is engendered
and nourifhed in his bofom; that he fpreads
fnares for men, and delights in the fatal effects of imprudence; that he permits ill, and
punifhes it; that he forefees guilt, and ac-
quiefces; that he is to be bought with gifts
like a partial judge; that he reverfes his edicts
like an undifcerning defpot; that he gives
and revokes his favours becaufe it is his will,
and is to be appeafed only by fervility like a
favage tyrant. I now completely underftand
what is the deceit of mankind, who have
pretended that God made man in his own
image, and who have really made God in
theirs; who have afcribed to him their weaknefs, their errors, and their vices; and in the
conclufion,

conclufion, furprifed at the contradictory
nature of their own affertions, have attempted to cloke it with hypocritical humility,
and the pretended impotence of human reafon, calling the delirium of their own underftandings the facred myfteries of heaven.

They have faid, God is without variable-
nefs, and they pray to him to change. They
have faid that he is incomprehenfible, and
they have undertaken to be interpreters of
his will.

A race of impoftors has made its appearance upon the earth, who, pretending to be
in the confidence of God, and taking upon
themfelves the office of inftructing the people, have opened the flood-gates of falfehood
and iniquity. They have affixed merit to
actions which either are indifferent or abfurd. They have dignified with the appellation of virtue the obfervance of certain pof-
tures, and the repetition of certain words
and names. They have taught the impiety
of eating certain meats on certain days rather than on others. It is thus the Jew
would fooner die than work on the fabbath.
It is thus the Perfian would endure fuffocation

before

before he would blow the fire with his breath. It is thus the Indian places fupreme perfection in fmearing himfelf with cow-dung, and myfteriously pronouncing the word *Aūm* (*r*). It is thus the Muffulman believes himfelf purified from all his fins by the ablution of his head and his arms; and difputes, fabre in hand, whether he ought to begin the ceremony at the elbow (*s*) or the points of his fingers. It is thus the Chriftian would believe himfelf damned, were he to eat the juice of animal food inftead of milk or butter. What fublime and truly celeftial doctrines! What purity of morals, and how worthy of apoftlefhip and martyrdom! I will cro's the feas to teach thefe admirable laws to favage people and diftant nations. I will fay to them: " Chil-
" dren of nature, how long will you wander
" in the paths of ignorance? How long will
" you be blind to the true principles of mo-
" rality and religion? Vifit civilized na-
" tions, and take leffons of pious and learn-
" ed people. They will teach you, that, to
" pleafe God, you muft in certain months
" of the year faint all day with hunger and
" thirft.

" thirft. They will teach you how you
" may fhed the blood of your neighbour,
" and purify yourfelves from the ftain, by
" repeating a profeffion of faith, and mak-
" ing a methodical ablution : how you may
" rob him of his goods, and be abfolved
" from the guilt, by fharing them with cer-
" tain perfons whofe profeffion it is to live
" in idlenefs upon the labour of others.''

Sovereign and myfterious Power of the
Univerfe ! fecret Mover of Nature ! univerfal Soul of every thing that lives ! infinite
and incomprehenfible Being, whom, under
fo many forms, mortals have ignorantly worfhipped ! God, who in the immenfity of the
heavens doft guide revolving worlds, and
people the abyfs of fpace with millions of
funs : fay, what appearance do thofe human
infects, which I can with difficulty diftinguifh upon the earth, make in thy eyes ?
When thou directeft the ftars in their orbits,
what to thee are the worms that crawl in
the duft ? Of what importance to thy infinite
greatnefs are their diftinctions of fects and
parties ? And how art thou concerned with
the fubtleties engendered by their folly ?

G 4   And

And you, credulous men, shew me the efficacy of your practices! During the many ages that you have obferved or altered them, what change have your *prefcriptions* wrought in the laws of nature? Has the fun shone with greater brilliance? Has the courfe of the feafons at all varied? Is the earth more fruitful, are the people more happy? If God be good, how can he be pleafed with your penances? If he be infinite, what can your homage add to his glory? Inconfiftent men, anfwer thefe queftions!

Ye conquerors, who pretend by your arms to ferve God, what need has he of your aid? If he wifhes to punifh, are not earthquakes, volcanoes, and the thunderbolt in his hand? And does a God of clemency know no other way of correcting but by extermination?

Ye Muffulmans, if your misfortunes were the chaftifements of heaven for the violation of the *five precepts*, would profperity be fhowered on the Franks who laugh at thefe things? If it is by the laws of the Koran that God judges the earth, what were the principles

principles by which he governed the nations
that exifted before the prophet, the numerous people who drank wine, ate pork, and
travelled not to Mecca, yet to whom it was
given to raife powerful empires? By what
laws did he judge the Sabeans of Nineveh
and of Babylon; the Perfian, who worfhipped fire; the Greek and Roman idolaters; the
ancient kingdoms of the Nile, and your own
progenitors the Arabs and Tartars? How
does he at prefent judge the various nations
that are ignorant of your worfhip, the numerous cafts of Indians, the vaft empire of the
Chinefe, the fwarthy tribes of Africa, the
iflanders of the Atlantic Ocean, the colonies
of America!

Prefumptuous and ignorant men, who arrogate to yourfelves the whole earth, were
God to fummon at once all paft and prefent
generations, what proportion would thofe
Chriftian and Muffulman fects, calling themfelves *univerfal*, bear in the vaft affemblage?
What would be the judgment of his fair and
impartial juftice refpecting the actual mafs
of mankind? It is in eftimating the general
fyftem of his government that you wander
                                        among

among multiplied abfurdities; and it is there that, in reality, truth prefents itfelf in all its evidence. It is there that we trace the fimple but powerful laws of nature and rea-fon; the laws of the common mover, the general caufe; of a God impartial and juft, who, that he might fend his rain upon a country, afks not who is its prophet; who caufes his fun equally to fhine on all tribes of men, whether diftinguifhed by a fair or a fable complexion, on the Jew as on the Muffulman, on the Chriftian as on the Hea-then; who multiplies the inhabitants of every country with whom order and induftry reign ; who gives profperity to every empire where juftice is obferved, where the powerful is reftrained, and the poor man protected by the laws; where the weak lives in fafety, and where all enjoy the rights which they derive from nature and an equitable compact.

Such are the principles by which nations are judged ! This is the true religion by which the fate of empires is regulated, and which, O Ottomans, has ever decided that of your own empire ! Interrogate your an-ceftors; afk them by what means they rofe

to

to greatnefs, when, idolators, few in number
and poor, they came from the deferts of
Tartary to encamp in thefe fertile countries?
Afk them if it was by iflamifm, at that period unknown to them, that they conquered
the Greeks and Arabs; or by their courage,
prudence, moderation, and unanimity, the
true powers of the focial flate? Then the
Sultan himfelf adminiftered juftice and maintained order: then the prevaricating judge
and the rapacious governor were punifhed,
and the multitude lived in eafe: the cultivator was fecure from the rapine of the jani-
zary, and the fields were productive: the
public roads were fafe, and commerce
flourifhed, It is true you were a league of
robbers, but among yourfelves you were
juft. You fubjugated nations, but you did
not opprefs them. Vexed by their own
princes they preferred being your tributaries.
" Of what importance is it to me, faid the
" Chriftian, whether my mafter be pleafed
" with images or breaks them in pieces,
" provided he is juft towards me? God will
" judge his doctrine in heaven." You were
temperate and hardy; your enemies foft and
effeminate:

effeminate: you were skilled in the art of battle; they had forgotten its principles: you had experienced chiefs, warlike and disciplined troops; the hope of booty excited ardour; bravery was recompenfed; difobedience and cowardice punished, and all the springs of the human heart were in action. You thus conquered a hundred nations, and out of the mafs founded an immenfe empire.

But other manners fucceeded. The laws of nature, however, did not lefs operate in your misfortunes than in your profperity. You deftroyed your enemies, and your grafping ambition, ftill in force, preyed upon yourfelves. Having become rich, you commenced an internal conteft refpecting the divifion and the enjoyment of your riches, and diforder was generated through every clafs of your fociety. The Sultan, intoxicated with his greatnefs, mifunderftood the object of his functions, and all the vices of arbitrary power prefently unfolded themfelves. Meeting with no obftacle to his defires, he became a depraved character. Weak, and arrogant at the fame time, he fpurned the people, and would no longer be influenced and directed by their voice.

voice. Ignorant, and yet flattered, he neglected all inftruction, all ftudy, and funk into total
incapacity. Become himfelf unqualified for
the conduct of affairs, he committed the
truft to hirelings, and thefe hirelings deceived him. To fatisfy their own paffions, they
ftimulated and increafed his; they multiplied his wants, and his enormous luxury
devoured every thing. He was no longer
content with the frugal table, the modeft
attire, and the fimple habitation of his anceftors: the earth and fea muft be exhaufted
to fatisfy his pride; fcarce furs muft be
fetched from the pole, and coftly tiffues from
the equator; he confumed at a meal the tribute of a city, and in a day the revenue of a
province. He became infefted with an army
of women, eunuchs, and courtiers. He
was told that the virtue of kings confifted
in liberality; and the munificence and treafures of the people were delivered into the
hands of parafites. In imitation of the mafter, the flaves were alfo defirous of having
magnificent houfes, furniture of exquifite
workmanfhip, carpets richly embroidered,
vafes of gold and filver for the vileft ufes; and all
the

the wealth of the empire was fwallowed up in the *Seraï*.

To fupply this inordinate luxury the flaves and the women fold their influence; and venality introduced a general depravation. They fold the favour of the prince to the Vifier, and the Vifier fold the empire. They fold the law to the Cadi, and the Cadi fold juftice. They fold the altar to the prieft, and the prieft fold heaven. And gold obtaining every thing, nothing was left unpractifed to obtain gold. For gold, friend betrayed friend; the child his father; the fervant his mafter; the wife her honour; the merchant his confcience; and there no longer exifted in the ftate either good faith, manners, concord, or ftability.

The Pacha, who purchafed his office, prefently had recourfe to the fyftem of farming it for a revenue, and exercifing upon it every fpecies of extortion. He fold the collection of the taxes, the command of the troops, the adminiftration of the diftricts; and in proportion as every employment was temporary, rapine, diffufing itfelf from rank to rank, was rapid and precipitate. The excifeman op-

6   preffed

preffed the merchant by his exactions, and trade was annihilated. The Aga ftript the hufbandman, and cultivation was degraded. The labourer, robbed of his little capital, had not wherewith to fow his field: taxes neverthelefs became due, and he was unable to pay them; he was threatened with corporal punifhment, and driven to the expedient of a loan : fpecie, for want of fecurity, was withdrawn from circulation; the intereft of money became enormous, and ufury aggravated the mifery of the poor.

Inclement feafons, periods of dearth, had rendered the harvefts abortive, but government would neither forgive nor poftpone its demands. Diftrefs began its career : a part of the inhabitants of the villages took refuge in the cities; the burthen upon thofe that remained became greater, their ruin was confummated, and the country depopulated.

Driven to the laft extremity by tyranny and infult, certain villages broke out into rebellion. The Pacha confidered the event as a fubject of rejoicing ; he made war upon them, took their houfes by ftorm, ranfacked their goods, and carried off their cattle. The foil

foil became a defert, and he exclaimed:
" What care I ; I fhall be removed from it
to-morrow."

Yet again, the want of cultivation led one
ftep farther. Periodical rains or fwelling
tides overflowed the banks and covered the
country with fwamps: thefe fwamps exhaled
a putrid air, which fpread chronical difeafes,
peftilence, and ficknefs of a thoufand forms,
and was followed by a ftill farther decreafe
of population, by penury and ruin.

Oh! who can enumerate all the evils of
this tyrannical fyftem of government!

Sometimes the Pachas make war of themfelves, and to avenge their perfonal quarrels,
provinces are laid wafte. Sometimes, dread-
ing their mafters, they aim at independence;
and draw upon their fubjects the chaftifement of their revolt. Sometimes, fear-
ing thefe very fubjects, they call to their
aid and keep in pay foreign troops, and to
be fure of them, they indulge them in every
kind of robbery. In one place, they commence an action againft a rich man, and
plunder him upon falfe pretences. In another, they fuborn witneffes, and impofe a

fine for an imaginary offence. On all occafions they excite the hatred of fects againft
each other, and encourage informations for
the fake of increafing their own corrupt advantages. They extort from men their property; they attack their perfons; and when
their imprudent avarice has heaped into one
mafs the riches of a province, the fupreme
government, with execrable perfidy, pretending to avenge the oppreffed inhabitants,
draws to itfelf their fpoil in the fpoil of the
culprit, and wantonly and vainly expiate in
blood the crime of which it was itfelf the
accomplice.

O iniquitous beings, fovereigns or minifters, who fport with the life and property
of the people! was it you who gave breath
to man, that you take it from him? Is it
you who fertilize the earth, that you diffipate
its fruits? Do you fatigue your arms with
ploughing the field? Do you expofe yourfelves to the heat of the fun, and endure
the torment of thirft in cutting down the
harveft and binding it into fheaves? Do you
watch like the fhepherd in the nocturnal

H   dew?

dew ? Do you traverfe deferts like the indefatigable merchant? Alas ! when I have reflected on the cruelty and infolence of the
powerful, my indignation has been roufed,
and I have faid in my anger : What ! will
there never appear upon the earth a race of
men who fhall avenge the people and punifh
tyrants! A fmall number of robbers devour
the multitude, and the multitude fuffer themfelves to be devoured ! O degraded people,
awake to the recognition of your rights !
authority proceeds from you, yours is all the
power.   Vainly do kings command you *in
the name of God* and *by their lance :* foldiers,
obey not the fummons. Since God fupports
the Sultan, your fuccour is ufelefs; fince the
fword of heaven fuffices him, he has no need
of yours; let us fee what he can do of himfelf. . . . The foldiers have laid down their
arms; and lo, the mafters of the world are as
feeble as the meaneft of their fubjects ! Ye
people, know then that thofe who govern
you are your chiefs and not your mafters ;
your guardians appointed by yourfelves, and
not your proprietors ; that your wealth is
                                                    your

your own, and to you they are accountable for the adminiſtration of it; that kings or ſubjects, God has made all men equal, and no human being has a right to opprefs his fellow-creature.

But this nation and its chiefs acknowledge not thefe facred truths. . . . Be it ſo; they will ſuffer the conſequences of their error. The decree is gone forth; the day approaches when this coloſſus of power ſhall be daſhed to pieces, and fall cruſhed by its own weight. Yes, I ſwear by the ruins of ſo many de-moliſhed empires, that the creſcent ſhall undergo the ſame fate as the ſtates whoſe mode of government it has imitated! A foreign people ſhall drive the Sultans from their metropolis; the throne of Orkhan ſhall be ſubverted; the laſt ſhoot of his race ſhall be cut off; and the horde of the Oguzians (t), deprived of their chief, ſhall be difperfed likc that of the Nogaians. In this diſſolution the ſubjects of the empire, freed from the yoke that held them together, will reſume their ancient diſtinctions, and a general anar-chy will take place, as happened in the em-

H 2   pire

pire of the Sophis (*u*), till there fhall arife
among the Arabs, the Armenians, or the
Greeks, legiflators who fhall form new ftates.
Oh! were a fagacious and hardy race of men
to be found, what materials of greatnefs and
glory are here! .... But the hour of deftiny
is arrived.   The cry of war ftrikes my ear,
and the cataftrophe is about to commence.
In vain the Sultan draws out his armies;
his ignorant foldiers are beaten and fcattered.
In vain he calls upon his fubjects: their
hearts are callous; his fubjects reply: " It
" is decreed; and what is it to us who is
" to be our mafter? we cannot lofe by the
" change." In vain thefe true believers invoke heaven and the prophet, the prophet
is dead, and heaven without pity anfwers:
" Ceafe to call upon me.   You are the au-
" thors of your calamities, find yourfelves
" their remedy.   Nature has eftablifhed
" laws, it becomes you to practife them.
" Examine and reflect upon the events that
" take place, and profit by experience.   It
" is the folly of man that works his deftruc-
" tion; it is his wifdom that muft fave him.
                                    " The

" The people are ignorant; let them get un-
" derftanding: their chiefs are depraved; let
" them correct their vices and amend their
" lives, for fuch is the decree of nature:
" *Since the evils of fociety flow from* IGNO-
" RANCE *and* INORDINATE DESIRE, *men*
" *will never ceafe to be tormented till they*
" *fhall become intelligent and wife; till they*
" *fhall practife the art of juftice, founded on*
" *a knowledge of the various relations in*
" *which they ftand, and the laws of their own*
" *organization* *."

CHAP.

* A fingular moral phenomenon made its appearance
in Europe in the year 1788. A great nation, jealous of
its liberty, contracted a fondnefs for a nation the enemy
of liberty; a nation friendly to the arts for a nation that
detefts them; a mild and tolerant nation for a perfecuting
and fanatic one; a focial and gay nation for a nation
whofe characteriftic are gloom and mifanthropy; in a
word, the French were fmitten with a paffion for the
Turks: they were defirous of engaging in a war for
them, and that at a time when a revolution in their own
country was juft at its commencement. A man who
perceived the true nature of the fituation, wrote a book
to diffuade them from the war : it was immediately pretended that he was paid by the government, which in
reality wifhed the war, and which was upon the point of
fhutting him up in a ftate prifon. Another man wrote

H 3   to

CHAP. XIII.

WILL THE HUMAN RACE BE EVER IN A BETTER CONDITION THAN AT PRESENT.

Oppressed with forrow at the predictions of the Genius, and the feverity of his reafoning : Unhappy nations, cried I, burfting

---

to recommend the war : he was applauded, and his word was taken in payment for the fcience, the politenefs and importance of the Turks. It is true that he believed in his own thefis, for he had found among them people who caft a nativity, and alchemifts who ruined his fortune; as he found Martinifts at Paris, who enabled him to fup with Sefoftris, and Magnetifers who concluded with deftroying his exiftence. Notwithftanding this, the Turks were beaten by the Ruffians, and the man who then predicted the fall of their empire, perfifts in the prediction. The refult of this fall will be a complete change of the political fyftem, as far as it relates to the coaft of the Mediterranean If, however, the French become important in proportion as they become free, and if they make ufe of the advantage they will obtain, their progrefs may eafily prove of the moft honourable fort, inafmuch as, by the wife decrees of fate, the true intereft of mankind evermore accords with their true morality.

ing into tears! Unhappy my own lot! I
now defpair of the felicity of man! fince
his evils flow from his own heart, fince he
muft himfelf apply the remedy, woe for
ever to his exiftence! For what can reftrain
the inordinate defire of the powerful? Who
fhall enlighten the ignorance of the weak?
Who inftruct the multitude in the knowledge of its rights, and force the chiefs to
difcharge the duties of their ftation? Individual will not ceafe to opprefs individual, one
nation to attack another nation, and never
will the day of profperity and glory again
dawn upon thefe countries. Alas! conquerors will come; they will drive away the
oppreffors, and will eftablifh themfelves in
their place; but, fucceeding to their power,
they will fucceed alfo to their rapacity, and
the earth will have changed its tyrants,
without leffening the tyranny.

Then turning towards the Genius: O
Genius! faid I, defpair has taken hold of
my heart. While you have inftructed me
in the nature of man, the depravity of governors, and the abjectnefs of thofe who

H 4   are

are governed, have given me a difguft to life ; and fince there is no alternative but to be the accomplice or the victim of oppreffion, what has the virtuous man to do but to join his afhes to thofe of the tombs!

The Genius, fixing upon me a look of feverity mixed with compaffion, was filent. After a few minutes he replied : Is it then in dying that virtue confifts ? The wicked man is indefatigable in the confummation of vice, and the juft difheartened at the firft obftacle which ftands in the way of doing good ! . . . . But fuch is the human heart: fuccefs-intoxicates it to prefumption, difappointment dejects and terrifies it. Always the victim of the fenfation of the moment, it judges not of things by their nature but by the impulfe of paffion. . . . Mortal, who defpaireft of the human race, upon what profound calculation of reafonings and events is your judgment formed ? Have you fcrutinized the organization of fenfible beings, to determine with precifion whether the fprings . that incline them to happinefs are weaker than thofe which repel ? or rather,

viewing

viewing at a glance the hiftory of the fpecies,
and judging of the future by the example
of the paft, have you hence difcovered with
certainty, that all proficiency is impoffible ?.
Let me afk : Have focieties, fince their
origin, made no ftep towards inftruction and
a better ftate of things ? Are men.ftill in
the woods, deftitute of every thing, ignorant, ftupid, and ferocious ? Are there no
nations advanced beyond the period, when
nothing was to be feen upon the face of the
globe but favage freebooters or favage flaves?
If individuals have at certain times, and in
certain places, become better, why fhould
not the mafs improve ? If particular focieties
have attained a confiderable degree of perfection, why fhould not the progrefs of the
general fociety advance ? If firft obftacles
have been overcome, why fhould fucceeding ones be infurmountable ?

But you are of opinion that the human
race is degenerating ? Guard yourfelf againft
the illufion and paradoxes of mifanthropy.
Diffatisfied with the prefent, man fuppofes
in the paft a perfection which does not exift,
                                                and

and which is merely the difcoloration of his
chagrin.   He praifes the dead from enmity
to the living, and employs the bones of the
fathers as an inftrument of chaftifement
againft the children.

To eftablifh this principle of a retrograde
perfection, it is neceffary that we fhould contradict the teftimony of facts and reafon.
Nor is this all; the facts of hiftory might
indeed be equivocal, but it is farther neceffary that we fhould contradict the living fact
of the nature of man; that we fhould affert
that he is born with a perfect fcience in the
ufe of his fenfes; that, previous to experience, he is able to diftinguifh poifon from
aliment; that the fagacity of the infant is
greater than that of his bearded progenitor;
that the blind man can walk with more
affurance than the man endued with fight;
that man, the creature of civilization, is lefs
favoured by circumftances than the canni-
bal; in a word, that there is no truth in
the exifting gradation of inftruction and experience.

Young man, believe the voice of tombs
                                    and

and the teftimony of monuments. There are countries which have doubtlefs fallen off from what they were at certain epochas: but if the underftanding were to analyfe thoroughly the wifdom and felicity of their inhabitants at thofe periods, their glory would be found to have lefs of reality than of fplendour; it would be feen, that even in the moft celebrated ftates of antiquity, there exifted enormous vices and cruel abufes, the precife caufe of their inftability; that in general the principles of government were atrocious; that, from people to people, audacious robbery, barbarous wars, and implacable animofities were prevalent (x); that natural right was unknown; that morality was perverted by fenfelefs fanaticifm and deplorable fuperftition; that a dream, a vifion, an oracle, were the frequent occafion of the moft terrible commotions. Nations are not perhaps yet free from the power of thefe evils; but their force is at leaft diminithed, and the experience of paft times has not been wholly loft. Within the three laft centuries efpecially, the light of knowledge has.

has been increafed and diffeminated; civilization, aided by various happy circumftances,
has perceptibly advanced, and even inconveniences and abufes have proved advantageous
to it : for if conquefts have extended kingdoms and ftates beyond due bounds, the
people of different countries, uniting under
the fame yoke, have loft that fpirit of ef-
trangement and divifion which made them
all enemies to one another. If the hands of
power have been ftrengthened, an additional
degree of fyftem and harmony has at leaft
been introduced in its exercife. If wars
have become more general in the mafs of
their influence and operation, they have been
lefs deftructive in their details. If the people carry to the combat lefs perfonality and
lefs exertion, their ftruggles are lefs fanguinary and ferocious. If they are lefs free,
they are lefs turbulent ; if they are more
effeminate, they are more pacific. Defpotifm itfelf feems not to have been unpro-
ductive of advantages : for if the government has been abfolute, it has been lefs perturbed and tempeftuous ; if thrones have
been

been regarded as hereditary property, they
have excited lefs diffention, and expofed the
people to fewer convulfions; in fine, if defpots, with timid and myfterious jealoufy have
interdicted all knowledge of their adminiftration, all rivalfhip for the direction of affairs, the paffions of mankind, excluded from
the political career, have fixed upon the arts
and the fcience of nature; the fphere of ideas
has been enlarged on every fide; man, devoted to abftract ftudies, has better underftood his place in the fyftem of nature, and
his focial relations; principles have been
more fully difcuffed, objects more accurately
difcerned, knowledge more widely diffufed,
individuals made more capable, manners
more fociable, life more benevolent and
pleafing; the fpecies at large, particularly
in certain countries, have been evidently
gainers : nor can this improvement fail to
proceed, fince its two principal obftacles,
thofe which have hitherto rendered it fo
flow, and frequently retrograde, the difficulty of tranfmitting ideas from age to age,
and communicating them rapidly from man
to man, have been removed.

With

With the people of antiquity, every canton and every city, having a language peculiar to itfelf, ftood aloof from the reft, and the refult was favourable to ignorance and anarchy : they had no communication of ideas, no participation of difcoveries, no harmony of interefts or of will, no unity of action or conduct. Befide, the only means of diffufing and tranfmitting ideas being that of fpeech, fugitive and limited, and that of writing, flow of execution, expenfive, and acquired by few, there refulted an extreme difficuity as to inftruction in the firft inftance, the lofs of advantages one generation might derive from the experience of another, inftability, retrogradation of fcience, and one unvaried fcene of chaos and childhood.

On the contrary, in the modern world, and particularly in Europe, great nations having allied themfelves by a fort of univerfal language, the firm of opinion has been placed upon a broader bafis ; the minds of men have fympathifed, their hearts have enlarged ; we have feen agreement in thinking, and concord in acting : in fine, that

2   facred

facred art, that memorable gift of celeftial genius, the prefs, furnifhed a means of communicating, of diffufing at one inftant any idea to millions of the fpecies, and of giving it a permanence which all the power of tyrants has been able neither to fufpend nor to fupprefs. Hence has the vaft mafs of inftruction perpetually increafed; hence has the atmofphere of truth continually grown brighter, and a ftrength of mind been produced that is in no fear of counteraction. And this improvement is the neceffary effect of the laws of nature; for by the law of fenfation, man as invincibly tends to make himfelf happy, as the flame to afcend, the ftone to gravitate, the water to gain its level. His ignorance is the obftacle which mifleads him as to the means, and deceives him refpecting caufes and effects. By force of experience he will become enlightened; by force of errors he will fet himfelf right; he will become wife and good, becaufe it is his intereft to be fo: and ideas communicating themfelves through a nation, whole claffes will be inftructed, fcience will be univerfally fully familiar, and all men will underſtand what are the principles of individual happineſs and of public felicity; they will underſtand what are their reſpective relations, their rights, and their duties, in the ſocial order; they will no longer be the dupes of inordinate deſire; they will perceive that morality is a branch of the ſcience of phyſics, compoſed it is true of elements complicated in their operation, but ſimple and invariable in their nature, as being no other than the elements of human organization itſelf. They will feel the neceſſity of being moderate and juſt, becauſe therein conſiſts the advantage and ſecurity of each; that to wiſh to enjoy at the expence of another is a falſe calculation of ignorance, becauſe the reſult of ſuch proceeding, are repriſals, enmity, and revenge; and that diſhoneſty is invariably the offspring of folly.

Individuals will feel that private happineſs is allied to the happineſs of ſociety:

The weak, that inſtead of dividing their intereſts, they ought to unite, becauſe equality conſtitutes their ſtrength:

The

The rich, that the meafure of enjoyment is limited by the conftitution of the organs, and that laffitude follows fatiety :

The poor, that the higheft degree of human felicity confifts in peace of mind and the due employment of time :

Public opinion, reaching kings on their thrones, will oblige them to keep themfelves within the bounds of a regular authority :

Chance itfelf, ferving the caufe of nations, will give them fometimes incapable chiefs, who, through weaknefs, will fuffer them to become free ; and fometimes enlightened chiefs, who will virtuoufly emancipate them:

Individuality will be a term of greater comprehenfion, and nations, free and enlightened will hereafter become one complex individual, as fingle men are now: the confequences will be proportioned to the ftate of things. The communication of knowledge will extend from fociety to fociety, till it comprehends the whole earth. By the law of imitation the example of one people will be followed by others, who will adopt its fpirit and its laws. Defpots themfelves, perceiving that they can no longer maintain

I   their

their power without juftice and beneficence, will be induced, both from neceffity and ri-valfhip, to foften the rigour of their government; and civilization will be univerfal.

Among nations there will be eftablifhed an equilibrium of force, which, confining them within the limits of juft refpect for their reciprocal rights, will put an end to the barbarous practice of war, and induce them to fubmit to civil arbitration the decifion of their difputes (*y*); and the whole fpecies will become one grand fociety, one individual family governed by the fame fpirit, by common laws, and enjoying all the felicity of which human nature is capable.

This great work will doubtlefs be long accomplifhing, becaufe it is neceffary that one and the fame motion fhould be communicated to the various parts of an immenfe body; that the fame leaven fhould affimilate an enormous mafs of heterogeneous elements: but this motion will effectually operate. Already fociety at large, having paffed through the fame ftages as particular focieties have done, promifes to lead to the fame refults. At firft, difconnected in its parts, each in-

dividual

dividual ſtood alone; and this intellectual
ſolitude conſtituted its age of anarchy and
childhood. Divided afterwards into ſections
of irregular ſize, as chance directed, which
have been called ſtates and kingdoms, it has
experienced the fatal effects which reſult
from the inequality of wealth and conditions; and the ariſtocracy by which great
empires have domineered over their depen-
dencies, have formed its ſecond age. In pro-
ceſs of time, theſe paramount chiefs of the
globe have diſputed with each other for ſupe-
riority, and then was ſeen the period of factions and civil broils. And now the parties,
tired of their diſcords and feeling the want of
laws, ſigh for the epocha of order and tranquillity. Let but a virtuous chief ariſe, a
powerful and juſt people appear, and the
earth will arrive at ſupreme power. It waits
a legiſlative people; this is the object of its
wiſhes and its prayers, and my heart hears its
voice..... Then turning to the quarter of
the Weſt: Yes, continued he, a hollow noiſe
already ſtrikes my ear; the cry of liberty,
uttered upon the farther ſhore of the Atlantic, has reached to the old continent. At

I 2   this

this cry a fecret murmur againft oppreffion is excited in a powerful nation ; a falutary alarm takes place refpecting its fituation ; it enquires what it is and what it ought to be ; it examines into its rights, its refources, and what has been the conduct of its chiefs . . . . One day, one reflection more . . . . and an immenfe agitation will arife, a new age will make its appearance, an age of aftonifhment to vulgar minds, of furprife and dread to tyrants, of emancipation to a great people, and of hope to the whole world.

CHAP.

C H A P. XIV.

GRAND OBSTACLE TO IMPROVEMENT.

THE Genius ſtopt. My mind however, preoccupied with gloomy forebodings, yielded not to perſuaſion ; but fearful of offending him by oppoſition, I made no reply. After a ſhort interval; fixing on me a look that tranſpierced my ſoul : You are ſilent, ſaid he, and your heart is agitated with thoughts which it dares not utter !—Confuſed and terrified : O Genius, I made anſwer, pardon my weakneſs : truth alone has doubtleſs proceeded from your lips; but your celeſtial intelligence can diſtinguiſh its traits, where to my groſs faculties there appear nothing but clouds. I acknowledge it, conviction has not penetrated my ſoul, and I feared that my doubts might give you offence.

And what is doubt, replied he, that it ſhould be regarded as a crime ? Has man the power of thinking contrary to the impreſſions that are made upon him ? If a truth

I 3

be

be palpable, and its obfervance important, let us pity the man who does not perceive it: his punifhment will infallibly fpring from his blindnefs. If it be uncertain and equivocal, how is he to find in it what does not exift? To believe without evidence and demonftration is an act of ignorance and folly. The credulous man involves himfelf in a labyrinth of contradictions; the man of fenfe examines and difcuffes every queftion, that he may be confiftent in his opinions; he can endure contradiction, becaufe from the collifion evidence arifes. Violence is the argument of falfehood; and to impofe a creed authoritatively, is the index and proceeding of a tyrant.

Emboldened by thefe fentiments, I replied: O Genius, fince my reafon is free, I ftrive in vain to welcome the flattering hope with which you would confole me. The fenfible and virtuous foul is prone enough to be hurried away by dreams of fancied happinefs; but a cruel reality inceffantly recals its attention to fuffering and wretchednefs. The more I meditate on the nature of man, the more I examine the prefent ftate of fociety, the lefs poffible does it appear to me

that

that a world of wifdom and felicity fhould
ever be realized. I furvey the face of our
whole hemifphere, and no where can I perceive the germ of a happy revolution. All
Afia is buried in the moft profound darknefs. The Chinefe, fubjected to an infolent defpotifm (z), dependent for their fortune upon the decifion of lots, and held in
awe by ftrokes of the bamboo, enflaved by
the immutability of their code, and by the
irremediable vice of their language, offer to
my view an abortive civilization and a race
of automata. The Indian, fettered by prejudice, and manacled by the inviolable inftitution of his cafts, vegetates in an incurable
apathy. The Tartar, wandering or fixed,
at all times ignorant and ferocious, lives in
the barbarity of his anceftors. The Arab,
endowed with a happy genius, lofes its force
and the fruit of his labour in the anarchy of
his tribes, and the jealoufy of his families.
The African, degraded from the ftate of
man, feems irremediably devoted to fervitude. In the North I fee nothing but ferfs,
reduced to the level of cattle, the live ftock
of the eftate upon which they live (1). Ig-

I 4   norance,

norance, tyranny, and wretchednefs have every where ftruck the nations with ftupor ; and vicious habits, depraving the natural fenfes, have deftroyed the very inftinct of happinefs and truth. In fome countries of Europe, indeed, reafon begins to expand its wings ; but even there, is the knowledge of individual minds common to the nation ? Has the fuperiority of the government been turned to the advantage of the people ? And thefe people, who call themfelves polifhed, are they not thofe who three centuries ago filled the earth with their injuftice? Are they not thofe who, under the pretext of com- merce, laid India wafte, difpeopled a new continent, and who at prefent fubject Africa to the moft inhuman flavery ? Can liberty fpring up out of the bofom of defpots, and juftice be adminiftered by the hands of ra- pacity and avarice? O Genius! I have be- held civilized countries, and the illufion of their wifdom has vanifhed from my fight. I faw riches accumulated in the hands of a few individuals, and the multitude poor and deftitute. I faw all right and power concentered in certain claffes, and the mafs

of

of the people paffive and dependent. I faw the palaces of princes, but no incorporation of individuals as fuch, no common-hall of nations. I perceived the deep attention that was given to the interefts of government; but no public intereft, no fympathetic fpirit. I faw that the whole fcience of thofe who command confifted in prudently oppreffing; and the refined fervitude of polifhed nations only appeared to me the more irremediable.

With one obftacle in particular my mind was fenfibly ftruck. In furveying the globe, I perceived that it was divided into twenty different fyftems of religious worfhip. Each nation has received, or formed for itfelf, oppofite opinions, and afcribing to itfelf exclufively the truth, has imagined every other to be in error. But if, as is the fact, in this difcordance the majority deceive themfelves, and deceive themfelves with fincerity, it follows that the human mind as readily imbibes falfehood as truth; and in that cafe how is it to be enlightened ? How are prejudices to be extirpated that firft take root in the mind ? How is the bandage to be removed from the eyes, when the firft article

in

in every creed, the firft dogma of all religions, is the profcription of doubt, of examination, and of the right of private judgment? How is truth to make itfelf known? If fhe refort to the demonftration of argument, pufilla- nimous man appeals againft evidence to his confcience. If fhe call in the aid of divine authority, already prepoffeffed, he oppofes an authority of a fimilar kind, and treats all in- novation as blafphemy. Thus, in his blind- nefs, riveting the chains upon himfelf, does he become the fport of his ignorance and paffions. To diffolve thefe fatal fhackles, a miraculous concurrence of happy circum- ftances would be neceffary. It would be neceffary that a whole nation, cured of the delirium of fuperftition, fhould no longer be liable to the impreffions of fanaticifm; that, freed from the yoke of a falfe doctrine, it fhould voluntarily embrace the genuine fyf- tem of morality and reafon; that it fhould be- come at once courageous and prudent, wife and docile; that every individual, acquainted with his rights, fhould fcrupuloufly obferve their limits; and the poor fhould know how to refift feduction, and the rich the allure-

ments

ments of avarice; that there fhould be found upright and difinterefted chiefs; that its tyrants fhould be feized with a fpirit of madnefs and folly; that the people, recovering their powers, fhould perceive their inability to exercife them, and confent to appoint delegates; that having firft created their magiftrates, they fhould know both how to refpeĉt and how to judge them; that in the rapid renovation of a whole nation pervaded with abufe, each individual, removed from his former habits, fhould fuffer patiently the pains and felf-denials annexed; in fine, that the nation fhould have the courage to conquer its liberty, the wifdom to fecure it, the power to defend it, and the generofity to communicate it. Can fober judgment expeĉt this combination of circumftances? Should fortune in the infinite variety of her caprices produce them, is it likely that I fhould live to fee that day? Will not this frame long before that have mouldered in the tomb?

Here, oppreffed with forrow, my heart deprived me of utterance. The Genius made no reply; but in a low tone of voice I heard him

him fay to himfelf: " Let us revive the hope
" of this man; for if he who loves his fellow-
" creatures be fuffered to defpair, what is to
" become of nations ? The paft is perhaps
" but too much calculated to dejeét him.
" Let us then anticipate futurity; let us un-
" veil the aftonifhing age that is about to
" arife, that virtue, feeing the end of its
" wifhes, animated with new vigour, may
" redouble its efforts to haften the accom-
" plifhment of it."

CHAP.

CHÁP. XV.

NEW AGE.

SCARCELY had the Genius uttered to himfelf thefe words than an immenfe noife proceeded from the Weft, and turning my eyes to that quarter, I perceived at the extre- mity of the Mediterranean, in the country of one of the European nations, a prodigious movement, fimilar to what exifts in the bo- fom of a large city when, pervaded with fedi- tion, an innumerable people, like waves, fluc- tuate in the ftreets and public places. My ear, ftruck with their cries, which afcend- ed to the very heavens, diftinguifhed at in- tervals thefe phrafes :

" What is this new prodigy ? What this " cruel and myfterious fcourge ? We are a " numerous people, and we want ftrength ! " We have an excellent foil, and we are " deftitute of provifion ! We are active and " laborious, and we live in indigence ! We " pay enormous tributes, and we are told

" that

" that they are not fufficient ! We are at
" peace without, and our perfons and pro-
" perty are not fafe within ! What then is
" the fecret enemy that devours us ?"

From the midft of the concourfe, fome
individual voices replied: " Erect a ftandard
" of diftinction, and let all thofe who, by
" ufeful labours, contribute to the fupport
" and maintenance of fociety, gather round
" it, and you will difcover the enemy that
" preys on your vitals."

The ftandard being erected, the nation
found itfelf fuddenly divided into two bodies
of unequal magnitude and diffimilar appearance: the one innumerable and nearly in-
tegral, exhibited, in the general poverty of
their drefs, and in their meagre and fun-
burnt faces, the marks of toil and wretchednefs; the other a pretty groupe, a valuelefs
faction, prefented, in their rich attire, embroidered with gold and filver, and in their
fleek and ruddy complexions, the fymptoms
of leifure and abundance. Confidering thefe
men more attentively, I perceived that the
large body was conftituted of labourers, arti-
fans, tradefmen, and every profeffion ufeful

to

to fociety ; and that in the leffer groupe there were none but priefts, courtiers, public accountants, commanders of troops, in fhort, the civil, military, or religious agents of government.

The two bodies being front to front affembled, and having looked with aftonifh-ment at each other, I faw the feelings of indignation and refentment fpring up in the one, and a fort of panic in the other ; and the large faid to the fmall body :

Why ftand you apart? Are you not of our number ?

No, replied the groupe ; you are the people; we are a privileged clafs; we have laws, cuftoms, and rights peculiar to ourfelves.

People.

And what labour do you perform in the fociety ?

Privileged Clafs.

None : we are not made to labour.

People.

How then have you acquired your wealth ?

Privileged Clafs.

By taking the pains to govern you.

2　　　　　　*People.*

People.

To govern us! and is this what you call governing? We toil, and you enjoy; we produce, and you diffipate; wealth flows ·from us, and you abforb it.... Privileged men, clafs diftinct from the people, form a nation apart, and govern yourfelves (2).

Then, deliberating on their new fituation, fome among the groupe faid: Let us join the people, and partake their burthens and cares; for they are men like ourfelves. Others replied: To mix with the herd would be degrading and vile; they are born to ferve us, who are men of a fuperior race. The civil govenors faid: the people are mild and naturally fervile; let us fpeak to them in the name of the king and the law, and they will return to their duty. ... People! the king decrees, the fovereign ordains.

People.

The king cannot decree any thing which the fafety of the people does not demand; the fovereign cannot ordain but according to law.

Civil Governors.

The law calls upon you for fubmiffion.

People.

People.

The law is the general will; and we will a new order.

Civil Governors.

You are in that cafe rebels.

People.

A nation cannot be a rebel; tyrants only are rebels.

Civil Governors.

The king is on our fide, and he enjoins you to fubmit.

People.

Kings cannot be feparated from the nation in which they reign. Our king cannot be on your fide; you have only the phantom of his countenance.

. Then the military governors advanced, and they faid : The people are timorous ; it is proper to threaten them ; they will yield to the influence of force....Soldiers, chaftife this infolent multitude !

People.

Soldiers, our blood flows in your veins ! will you ftrike your brothers? If the people be deftroyed, who will maintain the army ?

And the foldiers, grounding their arms,

K   faid

faid to their chiefs : We are a part of the people; we whom you call upon to fight againft them.

Then the ecclefiaftical governors faid: There is but one refource left. The people are fuperftitious; it is proper to overawe them with the names of God and religion.

Priefts.

Our dear brethren, our children, God has commiffioned us to govern you.

People.

Produce the patent of his commiffion.

Priefts.

You muft have faith; reafon leads men into guilt.

People.

And would you govern us without reafon?

Priefts.

God is the God of peace; religion enjoins you to obey.

People.

No; juftice goes before peace; obedience implies a law, and renders neceffary the cognizance of it.

Priefts.

This world was intended for trial and fuffering.

People.

People.

Do you then fhew us the example of fuffering.

Priefts.

Would you live without Gods or kings?

People.

We abjure tyranny of every kind.

Priefts.

You muft have mediators, perfons who
may act in your behalf.

People.

Mediators with God, and mediators with
the king! Courtiers and priefts, your fervices
are too expenfive; henceforth we take our
affairs into our own hands.

Then the fmaller groupe exclaimed: It is
over with us; the multitude are enlightened.
And the people replied: You fhall not be
hurt; we are enlightened, and we will commit no violence. We defire nothing but our
rights: refentment we cannot but feel, but
we confent to pafs it by: we were flaves,
we might now command; but we afk only
to be free, and free we are.

K 2   CHAP.

C H A P. XVI.

A FREE AND LEGISLATIVE PEOPLE.

I now reflected with myfelf that public power was at a ftand, that the habitual government of this people was annihilated, and I fhuddered at the idea of their falling into the diffolution of anarchy. But taking their affairs immediately into their confideration, they quickly difpelled my apprehenfions.

" It is not enough, faid they, that we
" have freed ourfelves from parafites and
" tyrants, we muft prevent for ever the re-
" vival of their power. We are human
" beings, and we know, by dear-bought ex-
" perience, that every human being incef-
" fantly graips at authority, and wifhes to
" enjoy it at the expence of others. It is
" therefore neceffary to guard ourfelves be-
" forehand againft this unfortunate propen-
" fity, the prolific parent of difcord; it is
" neceffary to eftablifh rules by which our
" rights

" rights are to be determined and our con-
" duct governed. But in this inveftigation
" abftrufe and difficult queftions are in-
" volved, which demand all the attention
" and faculties of the wifeft men. Occupied
" in our refpective callings, we have neither
" leifure for thefe ftudies, nor are we com-
" petent of ourfelves to the exercife of fuch
" functions. Let us felect from our body
" certain individuals, to whom the employ-
" ment will be proper. To them let our
" common powers be delegated, to frame for
" us a fyftem of government and laws: let us
" conftitute them the reprefentatives of our
" interefts and our wills; and that this re-
" prefentation may be as accurate as poffible,
" and have comprehended in it the whole
" diverfity of our wills and interefts, let the
" individuals that comprize it be numerous,
" and citizens like ourfelves."

The felection being made, the people thus
addreffed their delegates: " We have hither-
" to lived in a fociety formed by chance,
" without fixed claufes, without free con-
" ventions, without ftipulation of rights,
" without reciprocal engagements; and a

" multitude

" multitude of diforders and evils have been
" the refult of this confufed ftate of things.
" We would now, with mature deliberation,
" frame a regular compact; and we have
" made choice of you to draw up the articles
" of it. Examine then with care what
" ought to be its bafis and principles. In-
" veftigate the object and tendency of every
" affociation; obferve what are the rights
" which every individual brings into it, the
" powers he cedes for the public good, and
" the powers which he referves entire to
" himfelf. Communicate to us equitable
" laws and rules of conduct. Prepare for
" us a new fyftem of government, for we
" feel that the principles, which to this day
" have guided us, are corrupt. Our fathers
" have wandered in the paths of ignorance,
" and we from habit have trod in their fteps.
" Every thing. is conducted by violence,
" fraud, or delufion; and the laws of mo-
" rality and reafon are ftill buried in obfcu-
" rity. Do you unfold the chaos; difcover
" the time, order, and connexion of things;
" publifh your code of laws and rights; and
" we will conform to it."

6

And

And this people raifed an immenfe throne in the form of a pyramid, and feating upon it the men they had chofen, faid to them: " We raife you this day above us, that you " may take a more comprehenfive view of " our relations, and be exalted above the at- " mofphere of our paffions.

" But remember that you are citizens like " ourfelves; that the power which we con- " fer upon you belongs to us; that we give " it as a truft for which you are refponfible, " not as exclufive property, or hereditary " right; that the laws which you make, you " will be the firft to fubmit to; that to- " morrow you will defcend from your fta- " tions, and rank again with us; that you " will have acquired no diftinguifhing right, " but the right to our gratitude and efteem. " And oh! with what glory will the uni- " verfe, that reveres fo many apoftles of " error, honour the firft affembly of en- " lightened and reafonable men, who fhall " have declared the immutable principles of " juftice to mankind, and confecrated in the " very face of tyrants the rights of na- " tions!"

K 4   CHAP.

C H A P. XVII.

UNIVERSAL BASIS OF ALL RIGHT AND ALL LAW.

THESE men, chofen by the people to inveftigate the true principles of morality and
reafon, then proceeded to the objeςt of their
miffion: and after a long examination, having
difcovered a univerfal and fundamental principle, they faid to their conftituents: " We
" have employed our faculties in the invefti-
" gation you demand of us, and we conceive
" the following to be the primordial bafis
" and phyfical origin of all juftice and all
" right.

    " Whatever be the aςtive power, the mov-
" ing caufe that directs the univerfe, this
" power having given to all men the fame
" organs, the fame fenfations, and the fame
" wants, has thereby fufficiently declared
" that it has alfo given them the fame rights
" to the ufe of its benefits; and that in the
" order of nature all men are equal.

                              " Secondly,

" Secondly, inafmuch as this power has
" given to every man the ability of preferv-
" ing and maintaining his own exiftence, it
" clearly follows, that all men are conftitut-
" ed independent of each other, that they
" are created free, that no man can be fub-
" ject and no man fovereign, but that all
" men are the unlimited proprietors of their
" own perfons.

" Equality, therefore, and liberty, are two
" effential attributes of man, two laws of
" the Divinity, not lefs effential and immu-
" table, than the phyfical properties of ina-
" nimate nature.

" Again, from the principle, that every
" man is the unlimited mafter of his own
" perfon, it follows, that one infeparable
" condition in every contract and engage-
" ment is the free and voluntary confent of
" all the perfons therein bound.

" Farther, becaufe every individual is
" equal to every other individual, it fol-
" lows, that the balance of receipts and
" payments in political fociety, ought to be
" rigoroufly in equilibrium with each other;
" fo that from the idea of equality immedi-
" ately

" ately flows that other idea of equity and
" juſtice *.

" Finally, equality and liberty conſtitute
" the phyſical and unalterable baſis of every
" union of men in ſociety, and of conſe-
" quence the neceſſary and generating prin-
" ciple of every law and regular ſyſtem of
" government (3).

" It is becauſe this baſis has been invaded,
" that the diſorders have been introduced
" among you, as in every other nation, which
" have at length excited you to reſiſtance. It
" is by returning once more to a conformity
" with this rule, that you can reform abuſes
" and reconſtitute a happy order of ſociety.

" We are bound however to obſerve to
" you, that from this regeneration there will
" reſult an extreme ſhock to be endured in
" your habits, in your fortunes, and in your
" prejudices.   Vicious contracts muſt be
" diſſolved, unjuſt prejudices aboliſhed, ima-
" ginary diſtinctions ſurrendered, and iniqui-

---

* The etymology of the words themſelves trace out to
us this connexion: *equilibrium, equalitas, equitas,* are all of
one family, and the phyſical idea of *equality* in the ſcales
of a balance is the ſource and type of all the reſt.

" tous

" tous defcriptions of property abrogated :
" in fine, you muft fet out once more from
" the ftate of nature. Confider whether you
" are capable of thefe mighty facrifices."

They concluded : and while I reflected
upon the inherent cupidity of the human
heart, I was induced to believe that the people would reject a melioration prefented under fuch auftere colours. I was miftaken.
Inftantly a vaft crowd of men thronged to·
wards the throne, and folemnly abjured all
riches and all diftinctions. " Unfold to us,
" cried they, the laws of equality and liberty :
" we difclaim all future poffeffion that is not
" held in the facred name of juftice. _Equality_,
" _liberty, juftice_, thefe are our inviolable code,
" thefe names fhall infcribe our ftandard."

Immediately the people raifed a mighty
ftandard, varied with three colours, and upon
which thofe three words were written. They
unfurled it over the throne of the legiflators,
and now for the firft time the fymbol of
univerfal and equal juftice appeared upon
the earth. In front of the throne the people built an altar, on which they placed golden fcales, a fword, and a book, with this
legend :

legend: TO EQUAL LAW, THE PROTEC-
TOR, AND THE JUDGE.   They then drew
round the throne a vaſt amphitheatre, and
the nation ſeated itſelf to hear the publication of the law.   Millions of men, in act of
ſolemn appeal to heaven, lifted up their
hands together, and ſwore, "that they would
" live equal, free, and juſt; that they would
" reſpect the rights and property of each
" other ; that they would yield obedience to
" the law and its miniſters regularly ap-
" pointed."

A ſight like this, ſo full of ſublimity and
energy, ſo intereſting by the generous emo-
tions it implied, melted me into tears ; and
addreſſing myſelf to the Genius, I ſaid :
" Now may I live, for after this there is
" nothing which I am not daring enough to
" hope."

C H A P.

C H A P.   XVIII.

CONSTERNATION AND CONSPIRACY OF
TYRANTS.

MEANWHILE, fcarcely had the folemn cry of liberty and equality refounded through the earth, than aftonifhment and apprehenfion were excited in the different nations. In one place, the multitude, moved by defire, but wavering between hope and fear, between a fenfe of their rights and the habitual yoke of flavery, betrayed fymptoms of agitation: in another kings, fuddenly roufed from the fleep of indolence and defpotifm, were alarmed for the fafety of their thrones: every where thofe claffes of civil and religious tyrants, who deceive princes and opprefs the people, were feized with rage and confternation; and concerting plans of perfidy, they faid to one another: "Woe be to us, fhould "this fatal cry of liberty reach the ear of the "multitude, and this deftructive fpirit of "juftice

" juftice be diffeminated.".... And feeing the
ftandard waving in the air: " What a fwarm
" of evils, cried they, are included in thefe
" three words! If all men are equal, where
" is our exclufive right to honours and
" power? If all men are, or ought to be free,
" what becomes of our flaves, our vaffals,
" our property? If all are equal in a civil
" capacity, where are our privileges of birth
" and fucceffion, and what becomes of no-
" bility? If all are equal before God, where
" will be the need of mediators, and what
" is to become of the priefthood? Ah! let us
" accomplifh without a moment's delay the
" deftruction of a germ fo prolific and con-
" tagious! let us employ the whole force
" of our art againft this calamity. Let us
" found the alarm to kings, that they may
" join in our caufe. Let us divide the peo-
" ple; let us engage them in war, and turn
" afide their attention by conquefts and na-
" tional jealoufy. Let us excite their ap-
" prehenfions refpecting the power of this
" free nation. Let us form a grand league
" againft the common enemy. Let us pull
" down this facrilegious ftandard, demolifh
                                        " this

" this throne of rebellion, and quench this
" fire of revolution in its outfet."

And in reality, the civil and religious tyrants of the people entered into a general combination, and having gained, either by con-
ftraint or feduction, multitudes on their fide,
they advanced in an hoftile manner againft
the free nation. Surrounding the altar and
the throne of natural law, they demanded,
with loud cries: " What is this new and he-
" retical doctrine? What this impious altar,
" this facrilegious worfhip?....True believ-
" ers and loyal fubjects! Would you not fup-
" pofe that to day truth has been firft difco-
" vered, and that hitherto you have been in-
" volved in error? Would you not fuppofe
" that thefe men, more fortunate than your-
" felves, have alone the privilege of being
" wife? And you, rebel and guilty nation, do
" you not feel that your chiefs miflead you?
" That they adulterate the principles of your
" faith, and overturn the religion of your fa-
" thers? Tremble left the wrath of heaven
" be lighted againft you; and haften by fpeedy
" repentance to expiate your error."

But inacceffible to feduction as to terror,
the free nation kept filence : it maintained

an

an exact difcipline in arms, and continued to
exhibit an impofing attitude.

And the legiflators faid to the chiefs of
nations : " If when we went on with our
" eyes hood-winked, our fteps did not fail
" to be enlightened, why, now that the
" bandage is removed, fhould we conceive
" that we are involved in darknefs ? If we,
" who prefcribe to mankind to exert their
" faculties, deceive and miflead them, what
" can be expected from thofe who de-
" fire only to maintain them in blind-
" nefs ? Ye chiefs of nations, if you poffefs
" truth communicate it : we fhall receive it
" with gratitude; for with ardour we pur-
" fue it, and with intereft fhall engage in
" the difcovery.   We are men, and may be
" deceived ; but you alfo are men and as
" fallible as ourfelves.   Affift us in this la-
" byrinth, in which the human fpecies has
" wandered for fo many ages : affift us to
" diffipate the illufion of evil habits and
" prejudice.   Enter the lifts with us in
" the fhock of opinions which difpute for
" our acceptance, and engage with us in
" tracing the pure and proper character of
" truth.   Let us terminate to day the long
                              " combat

" combat of error : let us eftablifh between
" it and truth a folemn conteft : let us call
" in men of every nation to affift us in the
" judgment: let us convoke a general affem-
" bly of the world; let them be judges in
" their own caufe; and in the fucceffive trial
" of every fyftem, let no champion and no
" argument be wanting to the fide of preju-
" dice or of reafon. In fine, let a fair exami-
" nation of the refult of the whole, give birth
" to univerfal harmony of minds and opi-
" nions."

L   C H A P.

C H A P.   XIX.

GENERAL ASSEMBLY OF THE PEOPLE.

Thus fpoke the legiflators of this free people ; and the multitude, feized with the fpirit of admiration, which every reafonable propofition never fails to infpire, fhouted their applaufe, and the tyrants remained alone, overwhelmed with confufion.

A fcene of a new and aftonifhing nature then prefented itfelf to my view. All the people and nations of the globe, every race of men from every different climate, advancing on all fides, feemed to affemble in one inclofure, and form in diftinct groupes an immenfe congrefs. The motley appearance of this innumerable crowd, occafioned by their diverfity of drefs, of features and of complexion, exhibited a moft extraordinary and moft attractive fpectacle.

On one fide I could diftinguifh the European with his fhort and clofe habit, his triangular hat, fmooth chin, and powdered

I   hair ;

hair; and on the oppofite fide the Afiatic with a flowing robe, a long beard, a fhaved head and circular turban. Here I obferved the inhabitants of Africa, their fkin of the colour of ebony, their hair woolly, their body girt with white and blue fifh-fkin, and adorned with bracelets and collars of corals, fhells and glafs-beads; there the northern tribes inveloped in bags of fkin; the Laplander with his piked bonnet and his fnow fhoes; the Samoiede with glowing limbs and with a ftrong odour; the Tongoufe with his bonnet fhaped like a horn, and carrying his idols pendent from his neck; the Yakoute with his freckled fkin; the Calmuc with flattened nofe and with little eyes, forced as it were to have no correfpondence with each other. Farther in the diftance were the Chinefe, attired in filk, and with their hair hanging in treffes; the Japanefe of mingled race; the Malayans with fpreading ears, with a ring in their nofe, and with a vaft hat of the leaves of the palm-tree (4); and the *Tatoued* inhabitants of the iflands of the ocean and of the continent of the Antipodes *. The

* The country of the *Papons*, or New Guinea.

contemplation

contemplation of one fpecies thus infinitely
varied, of one underftanding thus modified
with extravagance, of one organization affuming fo contrary appearances, gave me a
a very complicated fenfation, and excited in
me a thoufand thoughts (5). I contemplated
with aftonifhment this gradation of colour,
from a bright carnation to a brown fcarcely
lefs bright, a dark brown, a muddy brown,
bronze, olive, leaden, copper, as far as to the
black of ebony and jet. I obferved the
Caffimerean, with his rofe-coloured cheek,
next in vicinity to the fun-burnt Hindoo;
the Georgian ftanding by the Tartar; and I
reflected upon the effect of climate hot or
cold, of foil mountainous or deep, marfhy
or dry, wooded or open. I compared the
dwarf of the pole with the giant of the temperate zone; the lank Arab with the pot-
bellied Hollander; the fquat figure of the
Samoiede with the tall and flender form of
the Sclavonian and the Greek; the greafy
and woolly head of the Negro with the
fhining locks of the Dane; the flat-faced
Calmuc, with his eyes angle- wife to each
other and his nofe crufhed, to the oval and
fwelling

fwelling vifage, the large blue eyes, and the aquiline nofe, of the Circaffian and the Abaffin. I contrafted the painted linens of India with the workmanlike cloths of Europe; the rich furs of Silefia; the various clothing of favage nations, fkins of fifhes, platting of reeds, interweaving of leaves and of feathers, together with the blue-ftained figures of ferpents, ftars, and flowers, with which their fkin is varied. Sometimes the general appearance of this multitude, reminded me of the enamelled meadows of the Nile and the Euphrates, when, after rains and inundations, millions of flowers unfold themfelves on all fides; and fometimes it refembled, in murmuring found and bufy motion, the innumerable fwarms of grafshoppers which alight in the fpring like a cloud upon the plains of Hauran.

At fight of fo many living and percipient animals, I recollefted, on one fide, the immenfe multitude of thoughts and fenfations which were crowded into this fpace; and on the other, reflefted on the conteft of fo many opinions and prejudices, and the ftruggle of fo many capricious paffions; and I was ftruck

L 3   with

with aſtoniſhment, admiration, and appre-
henſion. .... When the legiſlators, having
enjoined ſilence, preſently fixed my attention
on themſelves.

" Inhabitants of the earth, ſaid they, a
" free and powerful nation addreſſes you in
" the name of juſtice and of peace, and offers
" as the ſure pledge of its ſincerity, its convic-
" tion and experience. We were for a long
" time tormented with the ſame evils as you;
" we have enquired into their origin, and we
" have found them to be derived from vio-
" lence and injuſtice, which the inexperience
" of paſt ages eſtabliſhed into laws, and the
" prejudices of the preſent generation have
" ſupported and cheriſhed. Then, aboliſh-
" ing every factitious and arbitrary inſtitution,
" and aſcending to the ſource of reaſon and
" of right, we perceived that there exiſted in
" the order of the univerſe, and in the phyſi-
" cal conſtitution of man, eternal and immu-
" table laws, which waited only his obſer-
" vance to render him happy. O men of dif-
" ferent climes, look to the heavens that give
" you light, to the earth that nouriſhes you!
" Since they preſent to you all the ſame gifts;
" ſince

" since the Power that directs their motions
" has beſtowed on you the ſame life, the
" ſame organs, the ſame wants, has it not
" alſo given you the ſame right to the uſe of
" its benefits! Has it not hereby declared
" you to be all equal and free? What mortal
" then ſhall dare refuſe to his fellow-crea-
" ture that which is granted him by nature?
" O nations! let us baniſh all tyranny and
" diſcord; let us form one ſociety, one vaſt
" family; and ſince mankind are all conſti-
" tuted alike, let there henceforth exiſt but
" one law, that of nature; one code, that of
" reaſon; one throne, that of juſtice; one
" altar, that of union."

They ceaſed: and the multitude rended
the ſkies with applauſe and acclamation; and
in their tranſports made the earth refound
with the words *equality, juſtice, union*. But
different feelings preſently ſucceeded to this
firſt emotion. The doctors and chiefs of
the people exciting in them a ſpirit of diſpu-
tation, there aroſe a kind of murmur, which,
ſpreading from groupe to groupe, was converted into uproar, and from uproar into
diſorder of the firſt magnitude. Every na-

tion

tion affumed exclufive pretenfions, and claimed the preference for its own opinions and code.

"You are in error," faid the parties pointing at each other; "we alone are in poffeffion "of reafon and truth: ours is the true law, "the genuine rule of juftice and right, the "fole means of happinefs and perfection; all "other men are either blind or rebellious." And the agitation became extreme.

But the legiflators having proclaimed filence: "People," faid they, "by what im-"pulfe of paffion are you agitated? Where "will this quarrel conduct you? What ad-"vantage do you expect from this diffenfion? "For ages has the earth been a field of dif-"putation, and torrents of blood have been "fhed to decide the controverfy: what profit "have you reaped from fo many combats and "tears? When the ftrong has fubjected the "weak to his opinion, has he thereby fur-"thered the caufe of evidence and truth? O "nations, take council of your own wifdom! "If difputes arife between families, or in-"dividuals, by what mode do you reconcile "them! Do you not appoint arbitrators?

"*Yes,*"

" *Yes,*" exclaimed the multitude unanimoufly. " Treat then the authors of your pre-
" fent diffenfions in a fimilar manner. Com-
" mand thofe who call themfelves your in-
" ftructors, and who impofe on you their
" creed, to difcufs in your prefence the argu-
" ments on which it is founded. Since they
" appeal to your interefts, underftand in what
" manner your interefts are treated by them.
" ... And you, chiefs and doctors of the
" people, before you involve them in the
" difcordance of your opinions, let the rea-
" fons for and againft thefe opinions be
" fairly difcuffed. Let us eftablifh a folemn
" controverfy, a public inveftigation of truth,
" not before the tribunal of a frail indivi-
" dual, or a prejudiced party, but in prefence
" of the united information and interefts of
" mankind; and let the natural fenfe of the
" whole fpecies be our arbitrator and judge."

CHAP,

CHAP. XX.

INVESTIGATION OF TRUTH.

THE people having by shouts expressed their approbation, the legiflators said: "That " we may proceed in this grand work with " order and regularity, let a fpacious am- " phitheatre be formed in the fand before " the altar of union and peace: let each " fyftem of religion and each particular fect, " erect its proper and diftinguifhing ftandard " in points of the circumference; let its " chiefs and its doctors place themfelves " round it, and let their followers be ranged " in a right line terminated by the ftandard."

The amphitheatre being traced out, and order proclaimed, a prodigious number of ftandards were inftantly raifed, fimilar to what is feen in a commercial port, when, on days of feftivity, the flags of a hundred nations ftream from a foreft of mafts. At fight of this aftonifhing diverfity, I addreffed myfelf to the Genius: I fcarcely fuppofed the earth,

said

faid I, to be divided into more than eight or
ten different fyftems of religion, and I then
defpaired of conciliation : how can I now
hope for concord when I behold thoufands
of different parties !—Thefe, however, replied the Genius, are but a part of what exift;
and yet they would be intolerant !

As the groupes advanced to take their fta-
tions, the Genius, pointing out to me the
fymbols and attributes of each, thus explained to me their meaning.

That firft groupe, faid he, with a green
ftandard, on which you fee difplayed a crofs,
a bandage, and a fabre, is formed of the followers of the Arabian prophet.   To believe
in a God (without knowing what he is) ; to
have faith in the words of a man (without
underftanding the language in which he
fpeaks) ; to travel into a defert in order to
pray to the Deity (who is every where); to
wafh the hands with water (and not abftain
from blood) ; to faft all day (and practife
intemperance at night); to give alms of their
own property (and to plunder the property
of their neighbour) : fuch are the means of
perfection inftituted by Mahomet, fuch the
fignals

fignals and characteriftics of his true followers; and whoever profeffes not thefe
tenets, is confidered as a reprobate, has the
facred anathema denounced againft him, and
is devoted to the fword. A God of clemency,
the author of life, has, according to them,
inftituted thefe laws of oppreffion and murder; has inftituted them for the whole univerfe, though he has condefcended to reveal
them but to one man; has eftablifhed them
from all eternity, though they were made
known by him but yefterday. Thefe laws
are fufficient for all the purpofes of life, and
yet a volume is added to them; this volume
was to diffufe light, to exhibit evidence, to
lead to perfection and happinefs, and yet, in
the very life-time of its prophet, its pages,
every where abounding with obfcure, ambiguous, and contradictory paffages, needed
explanation and commentaries; and the perfons who undertook to interpret them, vary-
ing in opinion, became divided into fects and
parties oppofite and inimical to each other.
One maintains that Ali is the true fucceffor,
and another takes the part of Omar and
Aboubekre. This denies the eternity of the
Koran,

Koran, that the neceffity of ablutions and prayers. The Carmite profcribes pilgrimage, and allows the ufe of wine; the Hakemite preaches the doctrine of tranfmigration, and thus are there fects to the number of feventy-two, of which you may enumerate the different ftandards (6). In this difcordance, each afcribing the evidence exclufively to itfelf, and ftigmatizing the reft with herefy and rebellion, has turned againft them its fanguinary zeal. And this religion, which celebrates a beneficent and merciful God, the common parent of the whole human race, converted into a torch of difcord and an incentive to war, has never ceafed for twelve hundred years to whelm the earth in blood, and fpread ravage and defolation from one extremity of the ancient hemifphere to the other (7).

The men you fee diftinguifhed by their vaft white turbans, their hanging fleeves and long rofaries, are the Imans, the Mollas, and the Muftis; and not far from them are the Dervifes with a pointed bonnet, and the Santons with their facred tonfure. They utter with vehemence their feveral confeffions

fions of faith; they difpute with eagernefs
refpecting the more or lefs important fources
of impurity; the mode of performing ablutions; the attributes and perfections of God;
the Chaîtan and the good and evil Genii;
death; the refurrection; the interrogatory
which fucceeds the tomb; the paffage of the
perilous bridge, and its hair-breadth efcapes;
the balance of good and bad works; the
pains of hell, and the joys of paradife.

By the fide of thefe, that ftill more numerous groupe, with ftandards of a white
ground ftrewed with croffes, confifts of the
worfhippers of Jefus. Acknowledging the
fame God as the Muffulmans, founding their
belief on the fame books, admitting like
them a firft man, who loft the whole human
race by eating an apple, they yet feel towards them a holy horror; and from motives
of *piety*, thefe two fects reciprocally treat
each other as *impious* men and blafphemers.
Their chief point of diffenfion is, that the
Chriftian, after admitting the unity and indivifibility of God, proceeds to divide him
into three perfons, making of each an entire
and complete God, and yet preferving an
                                    identical

identical whole : he adds, that this Being, who fills the univerſe, reduced himſelf to the ſtature and form of a man, and aſſumed material, periſhable, and limited organs, without ceaſing to be immaterial, eternal, and infinite. The Muſſulman, on the contrary, not able to comprehend theſe myſteries, though he readily conceives of the eternity of the Koran, and the miſſion of the prophet, treats them as abſurdities, and rejects them as the viſions of a diſordered brain. Hence reſult the moſt implacable animoſities.

Divided among themſelves, the Chriſtian ſects are not leſs numerous than thoſe of the Muſſulman religion ; and the quarrels that agitate them are by ſo much the more violent, ſince the objects for which they contend being inacceſſible to the ſenſes, and of conſequence incapable of demonſtration, the opinions of each ſectary can have no other foundation than that of his will or caprice. Thus agreeing that God is an incomprehenſible and unknown being, they nevertheleſs diſpute reſpecting his eſſence, his mode of acting, and his attributes. Agreeing that his ſuppoſed transformation into man, is an

enigma

enigma above the human underftanding, they ftill difpute refpecting the confufion or the diftinction of two wills and two natures, the change of fubftance, the real or fictitious prefence, the mode of incarnation, &c. &c. Hence innumerable fects, of which two or three hundred have already perifhed, and three or four hundred others ftill exift, and are reprefented by that multitude of colours in which your fight is bewildered. The firft in order, furrounded by a groupe abfurd and difcordant in their attire, red, purple, black, white, and fpeckled, with heads wholly or partially fhaved, or with their hair fhort, with red caps, fquare caps, here with mitres, there with beards, is the ftandard of the Roman pontiff, who, applying to the prieft-hood the pre-eminence of his city in the civil order, has erected his fupremacy into a point of religion, and made of his pride an article of faith.

At the right, you fee the Greek Pontiff, who, proud of the rivalfhip fet up by his metropolis, oppofes equal pretenfions, and fupports them againft the Weftern church, by the fuperior antiquity of that of the Eaft.

At

At the left, are the ftandards of two recent chiefs *, who, throwing off a yoke that was become tyrannical, have, in their reform, erected altars againft altars, and gained half Europe from the Pope. Behind them are the inferior fects into which thefe grand parties are again fubdivided, the Neftorians, the Eutycheans, the Jacobites, the Icono-clafts, the Anabaptifts, the Prefbyterians, the Wiclifites, the Ofiandrins, the Manicheans, the Pietifts, the Adamites, the Enthufiafts, the Quakers, the Weepers, together with a hundred others (8); all of diftinct parties, of a perfecuting fpirit when ftrong, tolerant when weak, hating each other in the name of a God of peace, forming to themfelves an exclufive paradife in a religion of univerfal charity, each dooming the reft, in another world, to endlefs torments, and realizing here the imaginary hell of futurity.

Next to this groupe, obferving a fingle ftandard of a hyacinth colour, round which were gathered men in all the various dreffes of Europe and Afia: Here, faid I to the Genius, we fhall at leaft find unanimity.—

---

* Luther and Calvin.

M   At

At firſt fight, replied he, and from an incidental and temporary circumſtance this would feem to be the cafe: but do you not know what fyſtem of worſhip it is ?—Then perceiving in Hebrew letters the monogram of God, and branches of the palmtree in the hands of the Rabbins : Are not thefe, faid I, the children of Mofes, difperfed over the earth, and who, holding every nation in abhorrence, have been themfelves univerfally defpifed and perfecuted ?—Yes, replied the Genius, and it is for this very reafon that, having neither time nor liberty to difpute, they have preferved the appearance of unanimity.   But in their re-union, no fooner ſhall they compare their principles, and reafon upon their opinions, than they will be divided, as formerly, at leaſt into two principal feɛts *, one of which, taking advantage of the filence of their legiſlator, and confining itfelf to the literal fenfe of his books, will deny every dogma not therein clearly underſtood, and of confequence will reject as inventions, the immortality of the foul, its tranfmigration into an abode of hap-

* The Sadducees and the Pharifees.

pinefs

pinefs or feat of pain, its refurrection, the laft judgment, the exiftence of angels, the revolt of a fallen fpirit, and the poetical fyf-tem of a world to come: and this favoured people, whofe perfection confifts in the cut-ting off a morfel of their flefh, this atom of people that in the ocean of mankind is but as a fmall wave, and that pretends that the whole was made for them alone, will far-ther reduce by one half, in confequence of their fchifm, their already trivial weight in the balance of the univerfe.

The Genius then directed my attention to another groupe, the individuals of which were clothed in white robes, had a veil co-vering the mouth, and were ranged round a ftandard of the colour of the clouds gilded by the rifing fun. On this ftandard was painted a globe, one hemifphere of which was black and the other white. The fate of thefe difciples of Zoroafter (9), conti-nued he, this obfcure remnant of a people once fo powerful, will be fimilar to that of the Jews. Difperfed as they are at prefent among other nations, and perfecuted by all, they receive without difcuffion the precepts

M 2   that

that are taught them : but fo foon as their Mobed and their Deftours (10) fhall be reftored to their full prerogatives, the con-troverfy will be revived refpecting the good and the bad principle, the combats of Or-muz, God of light, and Ahrimanes, God of darknefs; the literal or allegorical fenfes of thefe combats; the good and evil Genii; the worfhip of fire and the elements; pol-lution and purificaticn; the refurrection of the body, or the foul, or both (11); the renovation of the prefent world, or the pro-duction of a new which is to fucceed it. The Parfes will ever divide themfelves into fects, by fo much the more numerous as their families fhall have contracted different manners or opinions during their difperfion.

Next to thefe are ftandards which exhibit upon a blue ground monftrous figures of human bodies, double, triple, or quadruple, with the heads of lions, boars, and elephants, and tails of fifhes, tortoifes, &c. Thefe are the ftandards of the Indian fects, who find their Gods amidft the animal creation, and the fouls of their kindred in reptiles and infects. Thefe men anxioufly fupport hof-
pitals

pitals for the reception of hawks, ferpents, and rats, and look with horror upon their brethren of mankind! They purify themfelves with the dung and urine of a cow, and confider themfelves as polluted by the touch of a heretic! They wear a net over their mouths, left by accident a fly fhould get down their throat, and they fhould thus interrupt the progrefs of a purified fpirit in its purgatory; but with all this humanity in unintelligible cafes, they think themfelves obliged to let a Paria (12) perifh with hunger rather than relieve him! They worfhip the fame Gods, but inlift themfelves under hoftile ftandards.

This firft ftandard, feparated from the reft, and on which you fee reprefented a figure with four heads, is the ftandard of Brama, who, though the Creator of the univerfe, has neither followers nor temples, and who, reduced to ferve as a pedeftal to the Lingam (13), receives no other mark of attention than a little water fprinkled every morning over his fhoulder by the Bramin, and a barren fong in his praife.

The fecond ftandard on which you fee

M 3   painted

painted a kite, his body fcarlet and his head white, is that of the Vichenou, who, though preferver of the univerfe, has paffed a part of his life in malevolent actions. Some-times you fee him under the hideous forms of a boar and a lion tearing the entrails of mankind; fometimes under that of a horfe (14), foon to appear upon the face of the earth, with a fabre in his hand, to deftroy the prefent inhabitants of the world, to darken the ftars, to drive the planets from their fpheres, to fhake the whole earth, and to oblige the mighty ferpent to vomit a flame which fhall confume the globes.

The third ftandard is that of Chiven, the deftroyer of all things, the God of defola-tion, and who neverthelefs has for his em-blem the inftrument of production; he is the moft deteftable of the three, and he has the greateft number of followers. Proud of his attribute and character, his partizans in their devotions (15) exprefs every fort of contempt for the other Gods, his equals and his brothers, and imitating the incon-fiftency that characterifes him, they profefs modefty and chaftity, and at the fame time publicly

publicly crown with flowers, and bathe with
milk and honey, the obfcene image of the
Lingam.

Behind them came the lefs magnificent
ftandards of a multitude of Gods, male, female, and hermaphrodite, related to and
connected with the three principal, who pafs
their lives in inteftine war, and are in this
refpect imitated by their worfhippers. Thefe
Gods have need of nothing, and receive offerings without ceafing. Their attributes
are omnipotence and ubiquity, and a Bramin
with fome petty charm imprifons them in
an image, or in a pitcher, and retails their
favours according to his will and pleafure.

At a ftill greater diftance you will obferve
a multitude of other ftandards, which, upon
a yellow ground, common to them all, have
different emblems figured, and are the ftandards of one God, who, under various names,
is acknowledged by the nations of the Eaft.
The Chinefe worfhip him under the name
of *Fôt* (16); the Japanefe denominate him
Budſo; the inhabitants of Ceylon, *Beddhou*;
the people of Laos, *Chekia*; the Peguan,
Phta; the Siamefe, *Sommona-Kodom*; the

M 4   people

people of Thibet, *Budd* and *La*; all of them agree as to moft points of his hiftory; they celebrate his penitence, his fufferings, his fafts, his functions of mediator and expiator, the enmity of another God his adverfary, the combats of that adverfary and his defeat: but they difagree refpecting the means of recommending themfelves to his favour, refpecting rites and ceremonies, refpecting the dogmas of their interior and their public doctrine. Thus the Japanefe Bonze, in a yellow robe, and with his head uncovered, preaches the eternity of fouls and their fucceffive tranfmigration into different bodies; while his rival, the Sintoift, denies that the foul can exift independently of the fenfes (17), and maintains that it is the mere refult of the organization with which it is connected, and with which it perifhes, as the found of a flute is annihilated when you break it in pieces. Near him the Siamefe, with fhaved eye-brows, and with the Talipat fcreen in his hand (18), recommends alms-giving, purifications and offerings, at the very time that he believes in blind neceffity and immutable fate. The Chinefe Ho-Chang

Ho-Chang facrifices to the fouls of his anceftors, while his neighbour, the follower
of Confucius, pretends to difcover his future
deftiny by the tofling of counters and the
conjunction of the ftars (19). Obferve this
infant attended by a numerous crowd of
priefts with yellow garments and bonnets :
he is the grand Lama, and the God of Thibet has juft become incarnate in his perfon
(20). He however has a rival on the banks
of the Baikal ; nor is the Calmuc Tartar in
this refpect any way behind the Tartar of
La-fa. They are agreed in this important
doctrine, that God can become incarnate
only in a human body, and fcorn the ftupidity of the Indian, who looks down with
reverence upon cow-dung, though they
themfelves preferve with no lefs awe the
excrements of their pontiff (21).

As thefe ftandards paffed, an innumerable
crowd of others prefented themfelves to our
eyes, and the Genius exclaimed : I fhould
never come to a conclufion, were I to detail
to you all the different fyftems of belief
which divide thefe nations. Here the Tartar
Hordes adore, under the figure of animals,
infects,

infects, and birds, the good and the evil
Genii, who, under a principal but indolent
divinity, govern the univerſe, by their idolatry giving us an image of the ancient pa-
ganiſm of the weſtern world. You ſee the
ſtrange dreſs of their Chamans, a robe of
leather fringed with little bells and rattles,
embroidered with idols of iron, claws of
birds, ſkins of ſerpents, and heads of owls :
they are agitated with artificial convulſions,
and with magical cries evoke the dead to
deceive the living. In this place you behold the ſooty inhabitants of Africa, who,
while they worſhip their *Fetiches*, entertain
the ſame opinions. The inhabitant of
Juida adores God under the figure of an
enormous ſerpent, which for their misfortune
the ſwine regard as a delicious morſel (22).
The Teleutean dreſſes the figure of his
God in a variety of gaudy colours, like a
Ruſſian ſoldier ; and the Kamchadale, finding that every thing goes on ill in this world
and under his climate, repreſents God to
himſelf under the figure of an ill-natured
and arbitrary old man (23), ſmoking his
pipe and ſitting in his *traineau* employed in
the

the hunting of foxes and martins. In fine, there are a hundred other favage nations, who, entertaining none of thefe ideas of civilized countries refpecting God, the foul, and a future ftate, exercife no fpecies of worfhip, and yet are not lefs favoured with the gifts of nature, in the irreligion to which nature has deftined them.

C H A P.

C H A P. XXI.

PROBLEM OF RELIGIOUS CONTRADIC-
TIONS.

THE different groupes having taken their
flations, and profound filence fucceeding to
the confufed uproar of the multitude, the
legiflators faid: " Chiefs and doctors of the
" people ! you perceive how the various
" nations of mankind, living apart, have hi-
" therto purfued different paths, each be-
" lieving its own to be that of truth.   If
" truth, however, is one, and your opinions
" are oppofite, it is manifeft that fome of
" you muft be in error : and fince fo many
" men deceive themfelves, what individual
" fhall dare fay, I am not miftaken ? Begin,
" then, by being indulgent refpecting your
" difputes and diffentions.   Let us all feek
" truth, as if none of us had poffeffion of it.
" The opinions which to this day have go-
" verned the earth, produced by chance,
" diffeminated in obfcurity, admitted with-
" out difcuffion, credited from a love of
                                     " novelty

" novelty and imitation, have in a manner
" clandeftinely ufurped their empire. It is
" time, if they are founded in reality, to
" give them the folemn ftamp of certainty,
" and to legitimate their exiftence. Let us
" this day cite them to a common and ge-
" neral examination; let each make known
" his creed; let the united affembly be the
" judge, and let us acknowledge that to be
" the only true one, which is proper for the
" whole human race."

Then, in order of pofition, the firft ftandard at the left being defired to fpeak :
" There can be no doubt," faid they, " that
" ours is the only true and infallible doc-
" trine. In the firft place, it is revealed
" by God himfelf."

" So alfo is ours," exclaimed all the other
ftandards, " and there can be no room for
" doubt."

" But it is at leaft neceffary to explain it,"
faid the legiflators, " for it is impoffible for
" us to believe any thing of which we are
" ignorant."

" Our doctrine," refumed the firft ftandard, " is proved by numerous facts, by a
" crowd of miracles, by refurrections from
" the

" the dead, by torrents fuddenly dried up,
" mountains removed from their fituations,
" &c. &c."

" We alfo," cried the reft, " are in poffef-
" fion of miracles without number;" and each
began to recite the moft incredible things.

" Their miracles," replied the firft ftandard, " are imaginary, or the preftiges of the
" evil fpirit who has deluded them."

To this it was anfwered by the others :
" They are yours, on the contrary, that are
" imaginary;" and each fpeaking of himfelf
added : " Ours are the only true ones, all
" other miracles are falfe."

" Have you living witneffes of their
" truth ?" the legiflators afked.

" No," they univerfally anfwered : " they
" are ancient facts, of which the witneffes
" are dead, but thefe facts are recorded."

" Be it fo," replied the legiflators : " but
" as they contradict each other, who fhall
" reconcile them ?"

" Juft arbiters !" cried one of the ftandards, " as a proof that our witneffes have
" feen the truth, they died in confirmation
" of it; and our creed is fealed with the
" blood of martyrs."

" So

"So alfo is ours," exclaimed the reft:
" we have thoufands of martyrs, who have
" died in the moft agonizing tortures, with-
" out in a fingle inftance abjuring the truth."
And the Chriftians of every fect, the Muffulmans, the Indians, the Japanefe, recounted endlefs legends of confeffors, martyrs,
penitents, &c.

One of thefe parties having denied the
martyrology of the others: "We are ready,"
cried they, " to die ourfelves to prove the
" infallibility of our creed."

Inftantly a crowd of men of every fect
and of every religion, prefented themfelves
to endure whatever torments might be inflicted on them; and numbers of them began to tear their arms, and to beat their
head and their breaft, without difcovering
any fymptom of pain.

But the legiflators putting a ftop to this
violence: " O men !" faid they to them,
" hear with compofure the words we ad-
" drefs to you. If you die to prove that two
" and two make four, will this truth gain
" additional confirmation by your death ?"

" No," was the general anfwer.

ı   " If

" If you die to prove they are five, will
" this make them five ?"

" No," they again replied.

" What, then, does your perfuafion prove,
" fince it makes no alteration in the exift-
" ence of things. Truth is one; your opi-
" nions are various; many of you muft
" therefore be miftaken. And fince man, as
" is evident, can perfuade himfelf of error,
" how can his perfuafion be regarded as the
" demonftration of evidence ? Since error
" has its martyrs, what is the fignet of
" truth ? Since the evil fpirit works mira-
" cles, what is the diftinguifhing character-
" iftic of the Divinity ? Befide, why this
" uniform refort to incomplete and infuffi-
" cient miracles ? Why not rather, inftead
" of thefe violations of nature, change the
" opinions of rational beings ? Why mur-
" der and terrify men, inftead of enlighten-
" ing and inftructing them ?

" O credulous mortals, and obftinate in
" your credulity ! as we are none of us cer-
" tain of what paffed yefterday, of what is
" paffing this very day before our eyes, how
" can we fwear to the truth of what hap-
                                    " pened

" pened two thoufand years ago ? Weak, and
" at the fame time proud beings ! the laws
" of nature are immutable and profound, our
" underftandings full of illufion and frivolity,
" and yet we would decide upon and com-
" prehend every thing. But in reality it is
" eafier for the whole human race to fall into
" error, than an atom of the univerfe to
" change its nature."

" Well then," faid one of the doctors,
" let us leave the evidence of facts, fince fuch
" evidence is equivocal, and let us attend to
" the proofs of reafon, and the intrinfic me-
" rit of the doctrine itfelf."

An Iman of the law of Mahomet, with
a look of confidence, then advanced in the
fand, and having turned himfelf towards
Mecca, and uttered with emphafis his confeffion of faith : " Let God be praifed !" faid
he, in a grave and authoritative voice ; " the
" light fhines in all its fplendour, and the
" truth has no need of examination." Then
exhibiting the Koran : " Behold the light
" and the truth in their genuine colours ! In
" this book every doubt is removed ; it will
" conduct the blind man fafely, who fhall

N   " receive

" receive without difcuffion the divine word,
" given to the prophet to fave the fimple
" and confound the wife. God hath ap-
" pointed Mahomet to be his minifter upon
" earth; he has delivered up the world to
" him, that he might fubdue by his fword
" fuch as refufe to believe in his law. Infi-
" dels difpute his authority, and refift the
" truth : their obduracy proceeds from God,
" who has hardened their hearts that he
" might inflict upon them the moft dreadful
" chaftifements *."

Here a violent murmur from all fides interrupted the Iman. " What man is this,"
cried every groupe, " who thus gratuitoufly
" commits outrage? By what right does he
" pretend, as conqueror and tyrant, to im-
" pofe his creed on mankind? Has not God
" created us as well as him with eyes, under-
" ftanding, and reafon? Have we not an equal
" right to make ufe of them in determining

---

* This paffage contains the fenfe and nearly the very
words of the firft chapter of the Koran; and the reader
will obferve in general, that, in the pictures that follow,
the writer has endeavoured to give as accurately as poffible
the letter and fpirit of the opinions of each party.

" what

" what we ought to reject, and what to be-
" lieve ? If he have the right to attack, have
" not we the right to defend ourfelves? If he
" be content to believe without examination,
" are we therefore not to employ our reafon
" in the choice of our creed ?

" And what is this *fplendid* doctrine which
" fears the *light?* What this apoftle of a God
" of clemency who preaches only carnage
" and murder? What this God of juftice who
" punifhes a blindnefs which himfelf has
" caufed? If violence and perfecution are the
" arguments of truth, mildnefs and charity
" muft they be the indices of falfehood?" ·

A man advancing from the next groupe
then faid to the Iman : " Admitting that
" Mahomet is the apoftle of the better doc-
" trine, the prophet of the true religion,
" condefcend to tell us, in practifing this
" doctrine whom we are to follow, his fon-
" in-law Ali, or his vicars Omar and Abou-
" bekre (24) ?"

At the mention of thefe names a terrible
fchifm arofe among the Muffulmans. The
partifans of Omar and of Ali, treating each
other as heretics and blafphemers, were

equally

equally lavifh of execrations. The difpute even became fo violent, that it was neceffary for the neighbouring groupes to interpofe to prevent their coming to blows.

Some degree of tranquillity being at length reftored, the legiflators faid to the Imans : " You fee what are the confequences which " refult from your principles! were they " carried into practice, you would by your " enmity deftroy each other till not an in- " dividual would remain : and is it not the " firft law of God, that man fhould live ?" Then addreffing themfelves to the other groupes : " This fpirit of intolerance and " exclufion," faid they, " is doubtlefs fhock- " ing to every idea of juftice, and deftroys " the whole bafis of morals and fociety: fhall " we not, however, before we entirely reject " this code, agree to hear fome of its dogmas " recited, that we may not decide from " forms only, without having inveftigated " the religion itfelf ?"

The groupes having confented to the pro- pofal, the Iman began to explain to them how God, who before time had fpoken to the nations funk in idolatry by twenty-four thoufand

thoufand prophets, had at length fent the laft, the extract and perfection of all the reft, Mahomet, in whom was vefted the falvation of peace : he informed them that to prevent the word of truth from being any more per- verted by infidels, the divine clemency had written with its own fingers the chapters of the Koran ; and that the Koran, by virtue of its character of the word of God, was, like its author, uncreated and eternal. He proceeded to explain to them the dogmas of Iflamifm; that this book had been tranfmitted from heaven leaf by leaf in twenty-four thoufand miraculous vifions of the angel Gabriel; that the angel announced his approach by a fmall ftill knocking, which threw the prophet into a cold fweat; that Mahomet had in one night traverfed ninety heavens, mounted upon the animal called Borak, one half woman and one half horfe; that being endowed with the gift of miracles, he walked in the funfhine unattended by a fhadow, caufed with a fingle word trees already withered to refume their verdure, filled the wells and the cifterns with water, and cut in two equal parts the body of the moon; that, authorized by a commiffion

N 3   from

from heaven, he had propagated, fword in
hand, a religion the moft worthy of God for
its fublimity, the moft fuitable to man for the
fimplicity of its injunctions, confifting indeed
only of eight or ten principal doctrines, fuch
as the unity of God; the authority of Mahomet, the only prophet of God ; our duty to
pray five times in a day ; to faft one month
in the year; to repair to Mecca once at leaft
in our lives ; to pay the tenth of all that we
poffefs ; to drink no wine, to eat no pork,
and to make war upon the infidels (25) ;
upon which conditions every Muffulman, being himfelf an apoftle and a martyr, fhould
enjoy in this life a thoufand bleffings, and in
the world to come, after a folemn trial, his
foul being weighed in the balance of good
works, his abfolution pronounced by the two
black angels, and his progrefs performed over
the bridge that croffes the infernal pit, as narrow as a hair and as keen as a razor, fhould
be received in the feat of delights, bathed in
rivers of milk and honey, embalmed in the
perfumes of India and Arabia, and live in
uninterrupted commerce with thofe chafte
females, the celeftial Houris, who prefent a
perpetually

perpetually renewed virginity to the elect, who preferve a perpetual vigour.

An involuntary fmile was vifible in the countenance of every one at this relation; and the various groupes, reafoning upon thefe articles of belief, unanimoufly faid: " Is it " poffible for reafonable beings to have faith " in fuch reveries? Might one not fuppofe " that a chapter had been juft read to us " from the *Thoufand and One Nights?*"

A Samoiede advancing in the fand then faid: " The paradife of Mahomet is in my " opinion excellent : but one of the means " of obtaining it puzzles me extremely. If, " as this prophet ordains, it is neceffary to " abftain from meat and drink between the " rifing and fetting of the fun, how in our " country is fuch a faft practicable, where " the fun continues above the horizon for fix " months together ?"

To vindicate the honour of their prophet, the Muffulman doctors denied the poffibility of this; but a hundred people bearing tefti-mony to the fact, the infallibility of Maho-met fuftained a violent fhock.

" It is fingular," faid a European, " that God " fhould

" fhould continually have revealed what was
" going on in heaven, without ever having
" informed us of what paffes upon earth."

" Their pilgrimage," faid an American,
" is to me an infuperable difficulty. For let
" us fuppofe a generation to be twenty-five
" years, and the number of males exifting on
" the globe to be a hundred millions : in
" this cafe, each being obliged to travel to
" Mecca once during his life, there would be
" annually engaged in the pilgrimage four
" millions of men ; and as it would be im-
" practicable for them to return in the fame
" year, the number would be doubled, or in
" other words would amount to eight mil-
" lions. Where are provifions, accommoda-
" tion, water, and veffels to be found for this
" univerfal proceffion ? What numerous mi-
" racles would it not be neceffary to work !"

" The proof," faid a Catholic Divine, " that
" the religion of Mahomet is not a revealed
" religion, is, that the majority of ideas upon
" which it is founded exifted for a long time
" before it, and that it is nothing more than a
" confufed mixture formed out of the truths
" of our holy religion and that of the Jews,
" which

" which an ambitious man has made ſerve.
" his proje
cts of dominion, and his worldly
" views. Turn over the pages of his book :
" you will ſee little elſe than the hiſtories of
" the Old and New Teſtament traveſtied
" into the moſt abſurd tales, and the reſt a
" tiſſue of vague and contradictory declama-
" tion, and ridiculous or dangerous precepts.
" Analyze the ſpirit of theſe precepts, and.
" the conduct of their apoſtle : you will find
" a ſubtle and daring character, which, to ar-
" rive at its end, works, it is true, with ad-
" mirable ſkill upon the paſſions of thoſe
" whom it wiſhes to govern. It addreſſes
" itſelf to ſimple and credulous men, and it.
" tells them of prodigies : they are ignorant
" and jealous, and it flatters their vanity by
" deſpiſing ſcience ; they are poor and rapa-
" cious, and it excites their avidity by the hope
" of plunder ; having nothing at firſt to give
" them on earth, it creates treaſures in hea-
" ven ; it makes them long for death, as the
" ſupreme bleſſing ; the daſtardly it threa-
" tens with hell ; to the brave it promiſes
" paradiſe ; the weak it ſtrengthens by the
" principle of fatality : in ſhort, it produces
" the

" the attachment it requires, by every al-
" lurement of the fenfes, and the fafcination
" of all the paffions.

" How different is the character of the
" Chriftian doctrine! and how much does its
" empire, eftablifhed on the wreck of every
" natural inclination and the extinction of
" all the paffions, prove its celeftial origin!
" How forcibly does its mild and compaf-
" fionate morality atteft its emanation from
" the Divinity! Many of its dogmas, it is
" true, are beyond the reach of human un-
" derftanding, and impofe on reafon a re-
" fpectful filence; but this very circum-
" ftance the more fully confirms its revela-
" tion, fince the faculties of men could never
" have invented fuch fublime myfteries."—
Then, with the Bible in one hand, and the
Four Evangelifts in the other, the doctor
began to relate that in the beginning, God
(after having paffed an eternity without doing any thing) conceived at length the defign (without apparent motive) of forming
the world out of nothing: that having in fix
days created the whole univerfe, he found
himfelf tired on the feventh: that having

5   placed

placed the firſt pair of human beings in a delightful garden to make them completely happy, he neverthelefs forbad them to taſte of the fruit of one tree which he planted within their reach : that thefe firſt parents having yielded to temptation, all their race (as yet unborn) were condemned to ſuffer the penalty of a fault which they had no ſhare in committing: that after permitting the human ſpecies to damn themſelves for four or five thouſand years, this God of compaſſion ordered his well-beloved ſon, engendered without a mother and of the ſame age as himſelf, to defcend upon the earth in order to be put to death, and this for the ſalvation of mankind, the majority of whom have neverthelefs continued in the road to ſin and damnation : that to remedy this inconvenience, this God, the ſon of a woman, who was at once a mother and a virgin, after having died and rifen again, commences a new exiſtence every day, and under the form of a morfel of dough is multiplied a thouſand fold at the pleafure of the bafeſt of mankind. Having explained thefe dogmas, he was going on to treat of the doctrine of
the

the Sacraments, of abfolution and anathema, of the means of purifying men from crimes of every fort with a drop of water and the muttering half a dozen words; but he had no fooner pronounced the names of indulgence, papal prerogative, fufficient grace, and effectual grace, than he was interrupted by a thoufand voices at once. It is a horrid corruption, cried the Lutherans, to pretend to fell for money the pardon of fin; it is contrary to the fenfe of the gofpel, faid the Calvinifts, to talk of the real prefence in the Sacrament. The Pope, exclaimed the Janfenifts, has no power to decide upon any thing without a council. Thirty fects at once mutually accufed each other of herefy and blafphemy, and their voices were fo confufed that it was no longer poffible to diftinguifh a word they uttered.

After fome time, filence being at length reftored, the Muffulmans faid to the legiflators: " Since you have rejected our doctrine " as containing things incredible, can you " poffibly admit that of the Chriftians, which " is ftill more contrary to juftice and com- " mon fenfe ? An immaterial and infinite " God

"God to transform himfelf into a man!
"To have a fon as old as himfelf! This
"God-man to become bread, which is eaten
"and undergoes digeftion! What abfurdi-
"ties have we equal to thefe? Is it to thefe
"men belong the exclufive right of exact-
"ing a blind obedience? And will you ac-
"cord to them privileges of faith, to our
"detriment?"

Some favage tribes then advanced: "What,"
faid they, "becaufe a man and a woman eat
"an apple fix thoufand years ago, is the
"whole human race to be involved in dam-
"nation? And do you call God juft? What
"tyrant ever made the children refponfible
"for the fins of their fathers? How can one
"man anfwer for the actions of another?
"Would not this be overthrowing every
"principle of equity and reafon?"

"Where," exclaimed others, "are the
"witneffes and proofs of all thefe pretended
"facts? It is impoffible to receive them
"without evidence. The moft trivial ac-
"tion in a court of judicature requires two
"witneffes, and are we to believe all this
"upon mere tradition and hearfay?"

A Jewifh

A Jewish Rabbin then, addressing the affembly, faid: " For the general facts we are
" indeed fureties; but as to the form and ap-
" plication of thofe facts, the cafe is different,
" and the Chriftians are here condemned out
" of their own mouth. They cannot deny
" that we are the ftock from which they are
" defcended, the trunk upon which they
" have been grafted : from whence it fol-
" lows by an inevitable dilemma, that either
" our law is from God, and then theirs is a
" herefy, fince it differs from ours; or our law
" is not from God, and then whatever proves
" its falfehood is deftructive of theirs."

" But there is a proper line of diftinction,"
faid the Chriftian, " to which it is neceffary
" to attend. Your law is of God as typical
" and preparative, not as final and abfolute;
" you are but the image, of which we are
" the reality."

" We are not ignorant," replied the Rabbin, " that fuch are your pretenfions; but
" they are perfectly fuppofitious and falfe.
" Your fyftem refts entirely on myftical (26),
" vifionary, and allegorical interpretations.
" You pervert the letter of our books, fub-
                                    " ftitute

" ftitute continually for the true fenfe of a
" paffage the moft chimerical ideas, and find
" in them whatever is agreeable to your
" fancy, juft as a roving imagination difco-
" vers figures in the clouds. You have thus
" imagined a fpiritual Meffiah, where our
" prophets fpeak only of a political king.
" You have interpreted into a redemption of
" the human race, what refers folely to the
" re-eftablifhment of our nation. Your pre-
" tended conception of the virgin is derived
" from a phrafe which you have wrefted
" from its true meaning. You conftrue
" every thing as you pleafe. You even find
" in our books your doctrine of the Trinity,
" though they contain not the moft indirect
" allufion to it, and though the idea was an
" invention of profane nations, and admitted
" into your code, together with a multitude
" of other opinions of every worfhip and fect
" of which it is compofed, during the chaos
" and anarchy of the three firft ages."

At thefe words, tranfported with indignation, and crying out facrilege, blafphemy !
the Chriftian doctors were difpofed to lay
violent hands upon the Jew : and a motley
                                        groupe

groupe of monks, fome in black, fome in white, advancing with a ftandard on which *pincers, a gridiron,* and *a funeral pile,* and the words *juftice, charity,* and *mercy,* were painted *, exclaimed : " It is proper to make an " example of this impious heretic, and to " burn him alive for the glory of God." And already they had pictured to their imaginations the fcene of torture, when the Muffulmans in a tone of irony faid to them : " Such is the religion of peace, whofe hum- " ble and humane fpirit you have fo loudly " vaunted ! Such that evangelical charity " which combats incredulity with no other " weapon than mildnefs, and oppofes only " patience to injuries ! Hypocrites, it is thus " you deceive nations ! It is in this manner " you have propagated your deftructive er- " rors ! When weak, you have preached li- " berty, toleration, and peace ; when power " has been in your hands, you have prac- " tifed violence and perfecution !" .... And they were beginning to recite the wars and murders of Chriftianity, when the legif-

---

* This defcription anfwers exactly to the colours of the Inquifition of Spanifh Jacobins.

lators, demanding filence, affuaged for a while the difcord.

" It is not," replied the monks in a tone of affected mildnefs and humility, "ourfelves " that we would avenge, we are defirous " only of defending the caufe and glory of " God."

" And what right have you," faid the Imans, " to conftitute yourfelves his repre- " fentatives more than we? Have you pri- " vileges that we are not favoured with? " Are you beings of a different nature from " us?"

" To take upon ourfelves to defend God, " is to infult his wifdom and power," faid another groupe. " Does he not know bet- " ter than mortals what is becoming his " dignity!"

" Certainly," rejoined the monks; " but " his ways are fecret."

" You, however," faid the Rabbins, "will " always find the difficulty infuperable of " proving that you enjoy the exclufive pri- " vilege of comprehending them." And the Jews, proud of finding their caufe fupported, fondly pleafed themfelves with the idea that

O   their

their books would be triumphant; when the Mobed * of the Parſes begged leave to ſpeak.

"We have heard," ſaid he to the legiſla-
"tors, the account of the Jews and Chriſtians
"reſpecting the origin of the world, and
"though they have introduced various cur-
"ruptions, they have related a number of
"facts which our religion admits; but we
"deny that they are to be attributed to the
"Hebrew legiſlator. It was not he who
"made known to mankind theſe ſublime
"dogmas, theſe celeſtial events: it was not
"to him that God revealed them, but to our
"holy prophet Zoroaſter; and proofs of
"this are to be found in the very books in
"queſtion. If you examine with attention
"the detail of laws, of rights, and of pre-
"cepts eſtabliſhed by Moſes, you will no
"where find the moſt tacit indication of
"what conſtitutes at preſent the baſis of the
"Jewiſh and Chriſtian theology. You will
"perceive no trace either of the immortality
"of the foul, or a life to come, or hell, or

* Highprieſt.

"paradiſe,

" paradife, or the revolt of the principal an-
" gel, author of all the evils which have af-
" flicted the human race, &c. Thefe ideas
" were unknown to Mofes, and this appears
" from indifputable evidence, fince it was not
" till four hundred years after him that they
" were firft promulgated by Zoroafter in
" Afia (27)."

The Mobed added, addreffing himfelf to
the Rabbins : " It was not till this epocha,
" till after the age of your firft kings, that
" thefe ideas appeared in your writings; and
" then their appearance was furtive and
" gradual, according as there grew up a po-
" litical relation between your anceftors and
" ours. It was particularly at the period
" when, conquered and difperfed by the
" kings of Nineveh and Babylon, your pro-
" genitors reforted to the banks of the Ti-
" gris and the Euphrates, and refided in our
" country for three fucceffive generations,
" that they imbibed our manners and opi-
" nions, which before they had regarded
" with averfion, as contrary to their law.
" When our king, Cyrus, had delivered them

O 2   " from

" from flavery they felt attached to us from
" fentiments of gratitude; they became our
" difciples and imitators, and introduced
" our peculiar doctrines into the corrected
" publication of their facred books (28);
" for your Genefis in particular was never
" the work of Mofes, but a compilation di-
" gefted after the return from the Babylo-
" nifh captivity, and containing in it the
" Chaldean opinions refpecting the origin
" of the world.

 " At firft the pure followers of the law,
" oppofing to the emigrants the letter of the
" text and the abfolute filence of the pro-
" phet, endeavoured to overpower thefe in-
" novations; but they ultimately prevailed,
" and our doctrines, modified according to
" your ideas, gave rife to a new fect. You
" expected a king, the reftorer of your poli-
" tical independence; we announced a God,
" the regenerator of the world, and the fa-
" viour of mankind. Thefe ideas blended
" together, conftituted the tenets of the Ef-
" fenians, and through them became the
" bafis of Chriftianity. Jews, Chriftians,
" Mahometans, however lofty may be your
                                    " pretenfions,

" pretenfions, you are, in your fpiritual and
" immaterial fyftem, only the blundering
" followers of Zoroafter !"

Having thus commenced his difcourfe, the
Mobed went on to the detail of his religion ;
and fupporting his fentiments by quotations
from the Zadder and the Zendavefta, he recounted in the fame order as they are found
in the book of Genefis, the creation of the
world in fix *gabans* (29) ; the formation of a
firft man and a firft woman in a peculiar and
celeftial habitation, under the reign of perfect
good ; the introduction of evil into the world
by the great lizard, the emblem of Ahrimanes;
the revolt and combat of this magnificent
genius of darknefs, againft Ormuz the benevolent God of light ; the diftribution of
angels into white and black, good and ill ;
their hierarchy confifting of cherubim, feraphim, thrones, dominions, &c. ; the end of
the world at the clofe of fix thoufand years ;
the coming of the Lamb, the regenerator of
nature ; the new world ; the life to come in
an abode of felicity or anguifh ; the paffage
of fouls over the bridge of the abyfs ; the
celebration of the myfteries of Mithra ; the

O 3   unleavened

unleavened bread that is set apart for the initiated : the baptifm of new-born children ;
extreme unction and auricular confeffion
(30'; in a word, he repeated fo many articles analogous to thofe of the three preceding religions, that his difcourfe feemed to
be a commentary or a continuation of the
Koran or the Apocalypfe.

But the Jewifh, Chriftian, and Mahometan doctors excepted to this detail, and treating the Parfes as idolatrous worfhippers of
fire, charged them with falfehood, invention,
and alteration of facts. A violent difpute
then arofe refpecting the dates of events, their
order and fucceffion, refpecting the origin of
opinions, their tranfmiffion from one people
to another, the authenticity of the books
which eftablifh them, the epocha when thefe
books were compofed, the character of their
compilers, the value of their teftimony ; and
the various parties proving, each againft the
reft, contradictions, improbabilities, and the
counterfeit nature of their books, accufed one
another of having founded their creed upon
popular rumours, upon vague traditions, upon abfurd fables, invented by folly, and admitted

mitted without examination by unknown, ignorant, or partial writers, at doubtful periods, and different from thofe to which their partifans referred them.

A loud rumour was now excited under the ftandards of the various Indian fects, and the Bramins, entering their proteft againft the claims of the Jews and the Parfes, faid: "What are thefe upftart and almoft un-" known people, who thus arrogantly con-" fider themfelves as the founders of nations, " and the depofitories of the facred archives? " To hear their calculations of five or fix " thoufand years, one would fuppofe that " the world was but of yefterday, whereas " our monuments prove a duration of many " thoufands of centuries. And in what re-" fpect are their books preferable to ours? " Are then the Vedes, the Chaftres, the " Pourans, inferior to the Bible, the Zenda-" vefta, the Sadder (31)? Is not the tefti-" mony of our progenitors and our Gods, of " equal value with that of the Gods and " progenitors of the weftern world? Oh! " were we permitted to reveal to profane " men the myfteries of our religion! Did

.O 4 ` " not

" not a facred veil juftly hide our doctrine
" from every eye !". ...

The Bramins fuddenly obferving a profound filence: " How," faid the legiflators,
" can we admit your doctrine, if you refufe
" to make it known? How could its firft
" authors propagate it, when, having fole
" poffeffion of it, they regarded even their
" own people as profane ? Has heaven re-
" vealed it that it might be kept a fecret?"

The Bramins however perfifted in their
filence; and a European at this moment offering to fpeak, remarked, that their fecrecy
was at prefent an empty form, that their facred books were divulged and their doctrine
explained: he accordingly undertook to re-
capitulate its feveral articles.

Beginning with an abftract of the four
Vedes, the twenty-eight Pourans, and the five
or fix Chaftres, he recounted how an immaterial, infinite, eternal, and *round* Being, after
having paffed an unlimited portion of time
in felf-contemplation, defirous at length of
manifefting himfelf, feparated the faculties
of male and female which were in him, and
operated an act of generation of which the

Lingam

Lingam remains the emblem: how from this firſt act were born three divine powers, of the names of Brama, Bichen, or Vichenou, and Chib or Chiven (32), the firſt deputed to create, the ſecond to preſerve, the third to deſtroy or change the form of the univerſe. He then detailed the hiſtory of their exploits and adventures, and related how Brama, proud of having created the world and the eight Bobouns (or ſpheres) of probation, and of being preferred to his equal Chib, this pride occaſioned between them a combat, in which the globes or celeſtial orbits were broken to pieces, as if they had been a baſket of eggs: how Brama overcome in this conteſt, was reduced to ſerve as a pedeſtal to Chib, metamorphoſed into the Lingam: how Vichenou, the preſerver of the univerſe, had, in the diſcharge of his function, aſſumed nine animal and mortal forms; how under the firſt, that of a fiſh, he ſaved from the univerſal deluge a family by whom the earth was re-peopled; afterwards, in the ſhape of a tortoiſe (33), drew from the ſea of milk the mountain *Mandreguiri* (the Pole); then, under that of a boar, tore the entrails of the
giant

giant *Erenniacheſſen*, by whom the earth had been ſunk in the abyſs of *Djole*, from which he delivered it; how he became incarnate under the form of the Black Shepherd, and bearing the name of *Chriſ-en* refcued the world from the venomous ferpent Calengam, whoſe head he cruſhed, after having himſelf received a wound in his heel.

Paſſing to the hiſtory of the ſecondary Genii, unfolded to the aſſembly how the Eternal, for the diſplay of his glory, had created divers orders of angels, whoſe office it was to ſing his praiſes and direct the uni-verſe: that a part of theſe angels had revolted under the conduct of an ambitious chief, who wiſhed to uſurp the power of God, and take the reigns of government into his own hands: that God precipitated them into a world of darkneſs as a puniſhment for their miſdeeds: that at laſt, touched with compaſſion, he conſented to withdraw them from thence, and to receive them again into favour, after previouſly ſubjecting them to a long ſtate of probation: that for this purpoſe, having created fifteen orbits or regions of planets, and bodies to inhabit them, he obliged theſe

rebellious

rebellious angels to undergo eighty-feven tranfmigrations: that the fouls, thus purified, returned to their primitive fource, to the ocean of life from which they had emanated: that as all living beings contained a portion of this univerfal foul, it was an act of great criminality to deprive them of it. He was proceeding to develope the rites and cere- monies of this religion, when, fpeaking of offerings and libations of milk and butter to Gods of wood and of brafs, he was interrupt- ed by a univerfal murmur mixed with loud burfts of laughter.

Each of the different groupes reafoned in its own particular manner refpecting this fyftem. "They are idolaters," faid the Muffulmans, " it is our duty to exterminate them "... " They are mad," faid the followers of Con- fucius, " it is our duty to cure them "... " What abfurd Gods," cried the reft, " a fet " of fat monkeys begrimmed with fmoke, " whom they wafh like children in clouts, " and from whom they drive away the flies, " lured by the tafte of honey, who would " otherwife defile them with their excre- " ments !"

At thefe words a Bramin, burfting with

§   indignation,

indignation, exclaimed : " Thefe are in-
" fcrutable myfteries, the profound em-
" blems of truth, which you are not wor-
" thy to know."

" And how comes it," replied a Lama of
Thibet, " that you are more worthy than we ?
" Is it becaufe you pretend to be fprung
" from the head of Brama, while the reft of
" mankind derive their origin from the lefs
" noble parts of his body ? If you would
" fupport the fable of your origin, and the
" vain diftinctions of your cafts, prove that
" you are of a nature different from us; prove
" at leaft by hiftorical teftimony the allego-
" ries you maintain; nay, prove that you are
" really the authors of this fyftem; for on our
" part we are able to prove, if that were
" neceffary, that you have only ftolen and
" disfigured it; that you have borrowed the
" ancient paganifm of the weftern world,
" and blended it by an abfurd conceit with
" the purely fpiritual nature of our Gods
" (34), a nature which ftoops not to addrefs
" itfelf to the fenfes, and was wholly unknown
" to the world till the miffion of Beddou."

Inftantly innumerable voices demanded to
be informed of this nature, and to hear of
that

that God with whofe very name the majority
of them were unacquainted. In purfuance
of this demand, the Lama refumed.

" In the beginning," faid he, " there was
" one God, felf-exiftent, who paffed through
" a whole eternity, abforbed in the contem-
" plation of his own reflections, ere he de-
" termined to manifeft thofe perfections to
" created beings, when he produced the
" matter of the world. The four elements,
" at their production, lay in a ftate of mingled
" confufion, till he breathed upon the face of
" the waters, and they immediately became
" an immenfe bubble, fhaped like an egg,
" which when complete became the vault or
" globe of the heavens in which the world is
" inclofed (35). No fooner was the earth
" and the bodies of animals produced, than
" God, the fource of motion, beftowed upon
" them as a living foul a portion of his fub-
" ftance. Thus the foul of every living
" thing, being only a fraction or feparate
" part of the univerfal foul, no percipient
" being is liable to perifh, but merely changes
" its form and mould as it paffes fucceffively
" into different bodies. But of all the fub-
                                    " ftantial

" ftantial forms that of man is moft pleafing
" to the Divine Being, as moft refembling
" his uncreated perfectiors; and man, when,
" by withdrawing himfelf from the com-
" merce of the fenfes, he becomes abforbed
" in the contemplation of his own nature,
" difcovers the Divinity that refides in it, and
" himfelf becomes worthy of Divinity. Thus
" is God inceffantly rendering himfelf incar-
" nate; but his greateft and moft folemn in-
" carnation was three thoufand years ago,
" in the province of Caffimere, under the
" name of Fôt or Beddou, for the purpofe of
" teaching the doctrine of felf-denial and felf-
" annihilation." The Lama proceeded to detail the hiftory of Fôt, obferving, that he had
fprung from the right intercoftal of a virgin of
the royal blood, who, when fhe became a mother, did not the lefs continue to be a virgin:
that the king of the country, uneafy at his
birth, was defirous to put him to death, and
caufed all the males who were born at the
fame period to be maffacred: that being faved
by fhepherds, Beddou lived in the defert to
the age of thirty years, at which time he
opened his commiffion, preaching the doctrine

trine of truth and cafting out devils : that he performed a multitude of the moft aftonifh-ing miracles, fpent his life in fafting and the fevereft mortifications, and at his death bequeathed to his difciples the volume in which the principles of his religion are contained. The Lama then began to read—

" He that forfaketh his father and his " mother," fays Fôt, " to follow me, fhall " become a perfect Samanean (a heavenly " being).

" He that keepeth my precepts to the " fourth degree of perfection, fhall acquire " the power of flying in the air, of moving " earth and heaven, of protracting or fhort-" ening his life, and of rifing again.

" The Samanean looks with contempt on " riches, and makes ufe only of fuch things " as are ftrictly neceffary. He mortifies the " flefh, fubdues his paffions, fixes his defires " and affections on nothing terreftrial, medi-" tates without ceafing upon my doctrine, " endures injuries with patience, and bears " no enmity againft his neighbour.

" Heaven and earth," fays Fôt, " fhall pafs " away; defpife therefore your bodies which

" are

" are compofed of the four perifhable ele-
" ments, and think only of your immortal foul.

" Hearken not to the fuggeſtions of the
" flefh : fear and forrow are the produce of
" the paffions : ſtifle the paſſions, and fear
" and forrow will thus be deſtroyed.

" Whoſoever dies," fays Fôt, " without
" having received my doctrine, becomes
" again and again an inhabitant of the earth,
" till he fhall have embraced it."

The Lama was going on with his ex-
tracts when the Chriſtians interrupted him,
obſerving, that this religion was an alteration of theirs; that Fôt was Jeſus himſelf
disfigured, and that the Lamas were nothing
more than a degenerate ſect of the Neſto-
rians and Manicheans.

But the Lama (36), fupported by all
the Chamans, Bonzes, Gonnis, Talapoins of Siam, of Ceylon, of Japan, and
of China, demonſtrated to the Chriſtians from their own Theologians, that
the doctrine of the Samaneans was known
through the Eaſt upwards of a thoufand years before Chriſtianity exiſted; that
their name was cited previous to the reign
of

of Alexander, and that that of Boutta or
Beddou could be traced to a more remote
antiquity than that of Jefus—" And now,
faid they, retorting upon the Chriftians,
" do you prove to us that you are not your-
" felves degenerated Samaneans; that the
" man whom you confider as the author of
" your fect is not Fôt himfelf in a different
" form. - Demonftrate his exiftence by hif-
" torical monuments of fo remote a period
" as thofe which we have adduced (37);
" for as it appears to be founded on no au-
" thentic teftimony, we abfolutely deny its
" truth; and we maintain that your gofpels
" are taken from the books of the Mythriacs
" of Perfia, and the Effenians of Syria, who
" were themfelves only reformed Sama-
" neans (38)."

Thefe words excited a general outcry on
the part of the Chriftians, and a new difpute more violent than any preceding one
was on the point of taking place, when a
groupe of Chinefe Chamans, and Talapoins
of Siam came forward, pretending that they
could eafily adjuft every difference, and produce in the affembly a uniformity of opi-

P   nion,

nion, and one of them fpeaking for the reft,
faid : " It is time that we fhould put an
" end to all thefe frivolous difputes, by
" drawing afide the veil and expofing to
" your view the *interior* and *fecret* doctrine
" which Fôt himfelf, on his death-bed, re-
" vealed to his difciples (39). Thefe va-
" rious theological opinions are mere chi-
" meras ; thefe accounts of the attributes,
" actions and life of the Gods are nothing.
" more than allegories and myfterious fym-
" bols, under which moral ideas, and the
" knowledge of the operations of nature in
" the action of the elements and the revo-
" lutions of the planets, are ingenioufly de-
" picted.

" The truth is, that there is no reality in
" any thing ; that all is illufion, appearance,
" a dream ; that the moral metemfychofis is
" nothing more than a figurative fenfe of
" the phyfical metemfychofis, of that fuc-
" ceffive motion by which the elements of
" which a body is compofed, and which
" never perifh, pafs, when the body itfelf
" is diffolved, into a thoufand others, and
" form new combinations. The foul is
                                        " merely

" merely the vital principle refulting from
" the properties of matter, and the action of
" the elements in bodies, in which they
" create a fpontaneous movement. To fup-
" pofe that this refult of organization, which
" is born with it, developed with it, fleeps
" with it, continues to exift when organiza-
" tion is no more, is a romance that may be
" pleafing enough, but that is certainly chi-
" merical. God himfelf is nothing more
" than the principal mover, the occult power
" diffufed through every thing that has be-
" ing, the fum of its laws and its properties,
" the animating principle, in a word, the
" foul of the univerfe; which, by reafon of
" the infinite diverfity of its connections and
" operations, confidered fometimes as fimple
" and fometimes as multiple, fometimes as
" active and fometimes as paffive, has ever
" prefented to the human mind an infolv-
" able enigma. What we can comprehend
" with greateft perfpicuity is, that matter
" does not perifh; that it poffeffes effential
" properties, by which the world is go-
" verned in a mode fimilar to that of a liv-
" ing and organifed being; that, with re-

" fpect

" fpect to man, the knowledge of its laws is
" what conftitutes his wifdom; that in their
" obfervance confift virtue and merit; and
" evil, fin, vice, in the ignorance and viola-
" tion of them; that happinefs and misfor-
" tune are the refpective refult of this ob-
" fervance or neglect, by the fame neceffity
" that occafions light fubftances to afcend,
" heavy ones to fall, and by a fatality of
" caufes and effects, the chain of which ex-
" tends from the fmalleft atom to the ftars of
" greateft magnitude and elevation (40)."

A crowd of Theologians of every fect inftantly exclaimed, that this doctrine was rank
materialifm, and thofe who profeffed it impious Atheifts, enemies both of God and
man, who ought to be extirpated from the
earth.—" Strange reafoning," replied the
Chamans. " Suppofing us to be miftaken,
" which is by no means impoffible, fince it
" is one of the attributes of the human mind
" to be fubject to illufion, what right have
" you to deprive beings like yourfelves of
" the life which God has given them ? If
" heaven confiders us as culpable, and looks
" upon us with horror, why does it difpenfe

" to

" to us the fame bleſſings as to you! If it
" treats us with endurance, what right have
" you to be leſs indulgent? Pious men,
" who ſpeak of God with ſo much certainty
" and confidence, condeſcend to tell us what
" he is; explain, ſo that we may compre-
" hend them, thoſe abſtract and metaphy-
" ſical beings which you call God and the
" ſoul; ſubſtances without matter, exiſt-
" ence without body, life without organs or
" ſenſations. If you diſcover theſe beings
" by means of your ſenſes, render them in
" like manner perceptible to us. If you
" ſpeak of them only upon teſtimony and
" tradition, ſhow us a uniform recital, and
" give an identical and determinate baſis to
" your creed."

There now aroſe a warm controverſy between the Theologians reſpecting the nature
of God and his mode of acting and mani-
feſting himſelf; reſpecting the ſoul and its
union with the body, whether it' has exiſtence previous to the organs, or from the
time of their formation only; reſpecting the
life to come and another world; and every
ſect, every ſchool, every individual, differing

P 3   from

from the reſt as to all theſe points, and aſ-
ſigning for its diſſent plauſible reaſons and
reſpectable but oppoſite authorities, they
were all involved in an inextricable labyrinth of contradictions.

At length, the legiſlators having reſtored
ſilence, recalled the diſpute to its true object,
and ſaid : " Leaders and inſtructors of the
" people, you came hither for the purpoſe
" of inveſtigating truth ; and at firſt every
" one of you, confident in his own infalli-
" bility, demanded an implicit faith : pre-
" ſently, however, you felt the contrariety
" of your opinions, and conſented to ſubmit
" them to a fair compariſon and a common
" rule of evidence. You proceeded to ex-
" poſe your proofs : you began with the
" allegation of facts ; but it preſently ap-
" peared that every religion and every ſect
" had its miracles and its martyrs, and had
" an equal cloud of witneſſes to boaſt, who
" were ready to prove the rectitude of their
" ſentiments by the ſacrifice of their lives,
" Upon this firſt point therefore the balance
" remained equal.

" You next paſſed to proofs of reaſoning :
                                                        " the

" the fame arguments were alternately ap-
" plied to the fupport of oppofite propofi -
" tions ; the fame affertions, equally gratui-
" tous were fucceffively advanced and re-
" pelled ; every one was found to have an
" equal reafon for denying his affent to the
" fyftem of the others. A farther confe-
" quence that arofe from thus confronting
" your fyftems was, that, notwithftanding
" their diffimilitude in fome points, their
" refemblance in others was not lefs ftrik-
" ing. Each of you claimed the firft de-
" pofit and the original difcovery ; each of
" you taxed his neighbour with adulteration
" and plagiarifm ; and a previous queftion
" to the embracing of any of your doctrines
" appeared to refult from the hiftory of opi-
" nions.

" A ftill greater embarraffment arofe
" when you entered into the explication of
" your doctrines : the more affiduous were
" your endeavours, the more confufed did
" they appear ; they refted upon a bafis in-
" acceffible to human underftanding, of
" confequence you had no means to judge
" of their validity, and you readily admitted

" that,

" that, in afferting them, you were the echos
" of your fathers. Hence it became impor-
" tant to know how they had come into the
" hands of that former generation, who had
" no means of learning them different from
" yourſelves. Thus the tranſmiſſion of theo-
" logical ideas from country to country, and
" their firſt riſe in the human underſtanding,
" were equally myſterious, and the queſtion
" became every moment more complicated
" with metaphyſical ſubtlety and antiquarian
" reſearch.

" But as theſe opinions, however extra-
" ordinary, have ſome origin; as all ideas,
" even the moſt abſtracted and fantaſtical,
" have in nature ſome phyſical model, we
" muſt aſcend to that origin in order to diſ-
" cover what this model is, and how the
" underſtanding came by thoſe ideas of
" Deity, the ſoul and immaterial beings,
" that are ſo obſcure, and which form the
" foundation of ſo many religious ſyſtems;
" we muſt trace their lineal deſcent and the
" alterations they have undergone in their
" various ſucceſſions and ramifications. If
" therefore there are in this aſſembly men
" who

" who have made thefe objects their pecu-
" liar ftudy, let them come forward and en-
" deavour to difpel, in the prefence of the
" nations of the earth, the obfcurity of opi-
" nions in which for fo long a period they
" have all wandered."

C H A P.

C H A P. XXII.

ORIGIN AND GENEALOGY OF RELIGIOUS IDEAS.

A T thefe words a new groupe, formed in an inftant of individuals from every ftandard, but undiftinguifhed by any, advanced in the fand, and one of the members, fpeaking in the name of the general body, faid :

" Legiflators, friends of evidence and of truth !

" That the fubject of which we treat fhould be involved in fo many clouds, is by no means aftonifhing, fince, befide the difficulties that are peculiar to it, thought itfelf has, till this moment, ever had fhackles impofed upon it, and free enquiry, by the intolerance of every religious fyftem, been interdicted. But now that thought is unreftrained, and may develope all its powers, we will expofe in the face of day, and fubmit to the common judgment of affembled nations, fuch rational truths as unprejudiced minds

minds have by long and laborious ftudy difcovered : and this, not with the defign of
impofing them as a creed, but from a defire
of provoking new lights, and obtaining better information.

" Chiefs and inftructors of the people,
you are not ignorant of the profound obfcurity in which the nature, origin, and hiftory
of the dogmas you teach are inveloped.
Impofed by force and authority, inculcated
by education, maintained by the influence
of example, they were perpetuated from age
to age, and habit and inattention ftrengthened their empire. But if man, enlightened by experience and reflection, fummon
to the bar of mature examination the prejudices of his infancy, he prefently difcovers a
multitude of incongruities and contradictions
which awaken his fagacity, and call forth
the exertion of his reafoning powers.

" At firft, remarking the various and oppofite creeds into which nations are divided,
we are led boldly to reject the infallibility
claimed by each ; and arming ourfelves alternately with their reciprocal pretenfions, to
conceive that the fenfes and the underftanding

ing emanating directly from God, are a law
not lefs facred, and a guide not lefs fure than
the indirect and contradictory codes of the
prophets.

"If we proceed to examine the texture
of the codes themfelves, we fhall obferve
that their pretended divine laws, that is to
fay, laws immutable and eternal, have rifen
from the complexion of times, of places,
and of perfons; that thefe codes iffue one
from another in a kind of a genealogical
order, mutually borrowing a common and
fimilar fund of ideas, which every inftitutor
modifies agreeably to his fancy.

"If we afcend to the fource of thofe ideas,
we fhall find that it is loft in the night of
time, in the infancy of nations, in the very
origin of the world, to which they claim alliance; and there, immerfed in the obfcurity
of chaos, and the fabulous empire of tradition, they are attended with fo many prodigies as to be feemingly inacceffible to the
human underftanding. But this prodigious
ftate of things gives birth itfelf to a ray of
reafoning, that refolves the difficulty; for if
the miracles held out in fyftems of religion
have

have actually exifted; if, for inftance, metamorphofes, apparitions, and the converfations
of one or more Gods, recorded in the facred
books of the Hindoos, the Hebrews, and the
Parfes, are indeed events in real hiftory, it
follows that nature in thofe times was perfectly unlike the nature that we are acquainted with now; that men of the prefent age
are totally different from the men that formerly exifted; and, confequently, that we
ought not to trouble our heads about them.

" On the contrary, if thofe miraculous
facts-have had no real exiftence in the phyfical order of things, they muft be regarded
folely as productions of the human intellect:
and the nature of man, at this day, capable
of making the moft fantaftic combinations,
explains the phenomenon of thofe monfters
in hiftory. The only difficulty is to afcertain how and for what purpofe the imagination invented them. If we examine with
attention the fubjects that are exhibited by
them, if we analize the ideas which they
combine and affociate, and weigh with accu-
racy all their concomitant circumftances,
we fhall find a folution perfectly conformable

able to the laws of nature. Thofe fabulous ftories have a figurative fenfe different from their apparent one, they are founded on fimple and phyfical facts : but thefe facts, being ill conceived and erroneoufly reprefented, have been disfigured and changed from their original nature by accidental caufes dependent on the human mind, by the confufion of figns made ufe of in the reprefentation of objects, by the equivocation of words, the defeat of language, and the imperfection of writing. Thefe Gods, for example, who act fuch fingular parts in every fyftem, are no other than the phyfical powers of nature, the elements, the winds, the meteors, the ftars, all which have been perfonified by the neceffary mechanifm of language, and the manner in which objects are conceived by the underftanding. Their life, their manners, their actions, are only the operation of the fame powers, and the whole of their pretended hiftory no more than a defcription of their various phenomena, traced by the firft naturalift that obferved them, but taken in a contrary fenfe by the vulgar who did not underftand it, or by fucceeding genera-

tions

tions who forgot it. In a word, all the
theological dogmas refpecting the origin of
the world, the nature of God, the revelation of his laws, the manifeftation of his
perfon, are but recitals of aftronomical facts,
figurative and emblematical narratives of
the motion and influence of the heavenly
bodies. The very idea itfelf of the Divinity, which is at prefent fo obfcure, ab-
ftracted, and metaphyfical, was in its origin
merely a compofit of the powers of the material univerfe, confidered fometimes analy-
tically, as they appear in their agents and
their phenomena, and fometimes fyntheti-
cally, as forming one whole, and exhibiting
an harmonious relation in all its parts. Thus
the name God has been beftowed fometimes
upon the wind, upon fire, water, and the
elements; fometimes upon the fun, the
ftars, the planets, and their influences;
fometimes upon the univerfe at large, and
the matter of which the world is compofed;
fometimes upon abftract and metaphyfical
properties, fuch as fpace, duration, motion,
and intelligence; but in every inftance, the
idea of a deity has not flowed from the miraculous revelation of an invifible world,
but

but has been the natural refult of human reflection, has followed the progrefs and undergone the changes of the fucceffive improvement of intellect, and has had for its fubject the vifible univerfe and its different agents.

" It is then in vain that nations refer the origin of their religion to heavenly infpiration; it is in vain that they pretend to defcribe a fupernatural ftate of things as firft in the order of events : the original barbarous ftate of mankind, attefted by their own monuments (41), belies all their affertions. Thefe affertions are ftill more victorioufly refuted by confidering this great principle, *that man receives no ideas but through the medium of his fenfes* (42): for from hence it appears, that every fyftem which afcribes human wifdom to any other fource than experience and fenfation, includes in it a υσερον προ]ερον, and reprefents the laft refults of underftanding as earlieft in the order of time. If we examine the different religious fyftems which have been formed refpecting the action of the Gods, and the origin of the world, we fhall difcover at every turn an anticipation in the order of narrating things,

which

which could only be fuggefted by fubfequent reflection. Reafon, then, emboldened by thefe contradictions, hefitates not to
reject whatever does not accord with the nature of things, and accepts nothing for hiftorical truth that is not capable of being eftablifhed by argument and ratiocination. Its
ideas and fuggeftions are as follow :

"Before any nation received from a neighbour nation dogmas already invented; before
one generation inherited the ideas of another,
none of thefe complicated fyftems had exiftence. The firft men, the children of nature,
whofe confcioufnefs was anterior to experience, and who brought no preconceived
knowledge into the world with them, were
born without any idea of thofe articles of
faith which are the refult of learned con-
tention ; of thofe religious rites which had
relation to arts and practices not yet in exiftence ; of thofe precepts which fuppofe the
paffions already developed ; of thofe laws
which have reference to a language and a
focial order hereafter to be produced ; of
that God, whofe attributes are abftractions
of the knowledge of nature, and the idea of

Q   whofe

whofe conduct is fuggefted by the experience
of a defpotic government; in fine, of that
foul and thofe fpiritual exiftences which are
faid not to be the object of the fenfes, but
which, however, we muft for ever have remained unacquainted with, if our fenfes
had not introduced them to us. Previoufly
to arriving at thefe notions, an immenfe ca-
talogue of exifting facts muft have been obferved. Man, originally favage, muft have
learned from repeated trials the ufe of his
organs. Succeffive generations muft have
invented and refined upon the means of fubfiftence; and the underftanding, at liberty to
difengage itfelf from the wants of nature,
muft have rifen to the complicated art of
comparing ideas, digefting reafonings, and
feizing upon abftract fimilitudes.

SECT. I. *Origin of the idea of God: Worfhip
of the elements, and the phyfical powers of
nature.*

"IT was not till after having furmounted
thofe obftacles, and run a long career in the
night of hiftory, that man, reflecting on his
ftate, began to perceive his fubjection to
forces

forces fuperior to his own and independent of his will. The fun gave him light and warmth ; fire burned, thunder terrified, the winds buffetted, water overwhelmed him ; all the various natural exiftences acted upon him in a manner not to be refifted. For a long time, an automaton, he remained paffive, without enquiring into the caufe of this action ; but the very moment he was defirous of accounting to himfelf for it, aftonifhment feized his mind; and paffing from the furprife of a firft thought to the reverie of curiofity, he formed a chain of reafoning.

" At firft, confidering only the action of the elements upon him, he inferred, relatively to himfelf, an idea of weaknefs, of fubjection, and relatively to them, an idea of power, of domination ; and this idea was the primitive and fundamental type of all his conceptions of the Divinity.

" The action of the natural exiftences, in the fecond place, excited in him fenfations of pleafure or pain, of good or evil ; by virtue of his organization, he conceived love or averfion for them, he defired or dreaded their

Q 2   prefence ;

prefence; and fear or hope was the principle of every idea of religion.

"Afterwards, judging every thing by comparifon, and remarking in thofe beings a motion fpontaneous like his own, he fuppofed there to be a will, an intelligence inherent in that motion, of a nature fimilar to what exifted in himfelf; and hence, by way of inference, he ftarted a frefh argument.— Having experienced that certain modes of behaviour towards his fellow-creatures wrought a change in their affections and governed their conduct, he applied thofe practices to the powerful beings of the univerfe. "When " my fellow-creature of fuperior ftrength," faid he to himfelf, " is difpofed to injure me, " I humble myfelf before him, and my prayer " has the art of appeafing him. I will pray " to the powerful beings that ftrike me. I " will fupplicate the faculties of the winds, " the planets, the waters, and they will hear " me. I will conjure them to avert the ca- " lamities, and to grant me the bleffings " which are at their difpofal. My tears will " move, my offerings propitiate them, and I " fhall enjoy complete felicity."

§ " And,

" And, fimple in the infancy of his reafon, man fpoke to the fun and the moon, he animated with his underftanding and his paffions the great agents of nature; he thought by vain founds and ufelefs practices to change their inflexible laws. Fatal error! He defired that the water fhould afcend, the mountains be removed, the ftone mount in the air; and fubftituting a fantaftic to a real world, he conftituted for himfelf beings of opinion, to the terror of his mind and the torment of his race.

" Thus the ideas of God and religion fprung, like all others, from phyfical objects, and were in the underftanding of man the produce of his fenfations, his wants, the circumftances of his life, and the progreffive ftate of his knowledge.

" As thefe ideas had natural beings for their firft models, it refulted from hence that the Divinity was originally as various and manifold as the forms under which he feemed to act : each being was a Power, a Genius, and the firft men found the univerfe crowded with innumerable Gods.

" In like manner the ideas of the Divinity having had for motors the affections of

Q 3   the

the human heart, they underwent an order of divifion calculated from the fenfations of pain and pleafure, of love and hatred: the powers of nature, the Gods, the Genii, were claffed into benign and maleficent, into good and evil ones: and this conftitutes the univerfality of thefe two ideas in every fyftem of religion.

"Thefe ideas, analogous to the condition of their inventors, were for a long time confufed and grofs. Wandering in woods, befet with wants, deftitute of refources, men in their favage ftate had no leifure to make comparifons and draw conclufions. Suffering more ills than they tafted enjoyments, their moft habitual fentiment was fear, their theology terror, their worfhip confined to certain modes of falutation, of offerings which they prefented to beings whom they fuppofed to be ferocious and greedy like themfelves. In their ftate of equality and independence, no one took upon him the office of mediator with Gods as infubordinate and poor as himfelf. No one having any fuperfluity to difpofe of, there exifted no parafite under the name of prieft, nor tribute under

under the name of victim, nor empire under the name of altar; their dogma and morality, jumbled together, were only felf-pre-
fervation; and their religion, an arbitrary
idea without influence on the mutual relations exifting between men, was but a
vain homage paid to the vifible powers of
nature.

"Such was the firft and neceffary origin
of every idea of the Divinity."

The orator then addreffing the favage nations, faid: "We appeal to you, who have
received no foreign fictitious ideas, whether
your conceptions have not been formed precifely in this manner? We afk you alfo,
learned theologians, if fuch be not the
unanimous record of all the monuments of
antiquity (43)?

SECT. II.   *Second fyftem: Worfhip of the
Stars, or Sabeifm.*

"BUT thofe fame monuments offer us a
more methodical and more complicated fyftem, that of the worfhip of all the ftars,
adored at one time under their proper form,
at another under emblems and figurative

Q 4   fymbols,

fymbols. This worfhip was alfo the effect of the knowledge of man in phyfics, and derived immediately from the firft caufes of the focial ftate; that is to fay, from wants and arts of the firft degree, the elements as it were in the formation of fociety.

" When men began to unite in fociety, they found it neceffary to enlarge the means of their fubfiftence, and confequently to apply themfelves to agriculture; and the practice of agriculture required the obfervation and knowledge of the heavens (44). It was neceffary to know the periodical return of the fame operations of nature, the fame phenomena of the fkies; it was neceffary to regulate the duration and fucceffion of the feafons, months and year. In order to this it was requifite to become acquainted with the march of the fun, which in its zodiacal revolution fhowed itfelf the firft and fupreme agent of all creation; then of the moon, which by its changes and returns regulated and diftributed time; finally of the ftars, and even of the planets, which, by their appearance and difappearance on the horizon and the nocturnal hemifphere, formed the minuteft

eft divifions. In a word it was neceffary to eftablifh an entire fyftem of aftronomy, to form an almanac; and from this labour there quickly and fpontaneoufly refulted a new manner of confidering the dominant and governing powers. Having obferved that the productions of the earth bore a regular and conftant connection with the phenomena of the heavens; that the birth, growth, and decay of each plant, were allied to the appearance, exaltation and decline of the fame planet, the fame groupe of ftars; in fhort, that the langour or activity of vegetation feemed to depend on celeftial influences, men began to infer from this an idea of action, of power, in thofe bodies, fuperior to terreftrial beings; and the ftars difpenfing fcarcity or abundance, became powers, Genii (45), Gods, authors of good and evil.

" As the ftate of fociety had already introduced a methodical hierarchy of ranks, employments and conditions, men, continuing to reafon from comparifon, transferred their new acquired notions to their theology, and the refult was a complicated fyftem of gradual Divinities, in which the fun, as the firft God,

God, was a military chief, a political king;
the moon, a queen, his confort; the planets,
fervants, bearers of commands, meffengers:
and the multitude of ftars, a nation, an army
of heroes, of Genii, appointed to govern the
world under the command of their officers;
every individual had a name, functions, attributes, drawn from its connections and influences, and even a fex derived from the gender of its appellation (46).

" As the ftate of fociety had introduced
certain ufages and complex practices, worfhip, leading the van, adopted fimilar ones.
Ceremonies, fimple and private at firft, became public and folemn; offerings were more
rich and more numerous; rites more methodical; places of affembly, chapels and temples
were erected; officers, pontiffs, created to
adminifter; forms and epochas were fettled ;
and religion became a civil act, a political tie.
But in this developement it altered not its
firft principles, and the idea of God was ftill
that of phyfical beings, operating good or
ill, that is to fay, impreffing fenfations of
pain or pleafure : the dogma was the knowledge of their laws or modes of acting; virtue
and

and fin the obfervance or infringement of thofe laws; and morality, in its native fimplicity, a judicious practice of all that is conducive to the prefervation of exiftence, to the well-being of the individual and of his fellow-creatures (47).

" Should it be afked at what epoch this fyftem took birth, we fhall anfwer, fupported by the authority of the monuments of aftronomy itfelf, that its principles can be traced back with certainty to a period of nearly feventeen thoufand years (48). Should we farther be afked to what people or nation it ought to be attributed, we fhall reply, that thofe felf-fame monuments, feconded by unanimous tradition, attribute it to the firft tribes of Egypt. And when reafon finds in that region a concurrence of all the phyfical circumftances calculated to give rife to it; when it finds at once a zone of heaven, in vicinity of the tropic, equally free from the rains of the equator, and the fogs of the north (49); when it finds there the central point of the antique fphere; a falubrious climate; an immenfe yet manageable river; a land fertile without art, without fatigue ; inundated,

inundated, without peftilential exhalations ; fituate between two feas which lave the fhores of the richeft countries—it becomes manifeft that the inhabitant of the diftricts of the Nile, inclined to agriculture from the nature of his foil ; to commerce, from the facility of communication; to geometry, from the annual neceffity of meafuring his poffef-fions ; to aftronomy, from the ftate of his heaven, ever open to obfervation, muft firft have paffed from the favage to the focial ftate, and confequently attained that phyfical and moral knowledge proper to civilized man.

"It was thus, upon the diftant fhores of the Nile, and among a nation of fable complexion, that the complex fyftem of the wor-fhip of the ftars, as connected with the pro-duce of the foil and the labours of agriculture, was conftructed. The worfhip of the ftars under their proper forms, or their natural attributes, was a fimple procefs of the human underftanding ; but in a fhort time the multiplicity of objects, their relations, their action and re-action, having confounded the ideas and the figns that reprefented them, a confequence

confequence refulted as abfurd in its nature as pernicious in its tendency.

Sect. III. *Third Syftem: Worfhip of fymbols, or idolatry.*

"From the inftant this agricolar race had turned an eye of obfervation on the ftars, they found it neceffary to diftinguifh in-dividuals or groupes, and to affign to each a proper name. A confiderable difficulty here prefented itfelf; for on the one hand, the celeftial bodies, fimilar in form, offered no peculiar character by which to denominate them; and on the other hand, language, poor and in a ftate of infancy, had no expref-fions for fo many new and metaphyfical ideas. The ufual ftimulus of genius, neceffity, con-quered all obftacles. Having remarked that in the annual revolution, the renewal and periodical appearance of the productions of the earth were conftantly connected with the rifing and fetting of certain ftars, and with their pofition relatively to the fun, the mind, by a natural mechanifm, affociated in its thought terreftrial and celeftial objects, which had in fact a certain alliance; and applying

to

to them the fame fign, it gave to the ftars
and the groupes it formed of them, the very
names of the terreſtrial objects to which they
bore affinity (50).

"Thus the Ethiopian of Thebes called
ftars of inundation, or of *Aquarius*, thofe under
which the river began to overflow * ; ftars
of the ox or bull, thofe under which it was
convenient to plough the earth ; ftars of the
lion, thofe under which that animal, driven
by thirft from the deferts, made his appearance on the banks of the Nile ; ftars of the
fheaf, or of the harveſt maid, thofe under
which the harvefts were got in ; ftars of the
lambs, ftars of the goat, thofe under which
thofe valuable animals brought forth their
young; and thus was a firft part of the difficulty refolved.

"On the other hand, man, having remarked in the beings that furrounded him certain
qualities peculiar to each fpecies, and having
invented a name by which to defign them,
fpeedily difcovered an ingenious mode of ge-
neralizing his ideas, and transferring the name

* This muft have been June.   See Note (46).

already

already invented to every thing bearing a fimilar or analogous property or agency, enriched his language with a multiplicity of metaphors and tropes.

" Thus the fame Ethiopian, having obferved that the return of the inundation anfwered conftantly to the appearance of a very beautiful ftar towards the fource of the Nile, which feemed to warn the hufbandman againft being furprifed by the waters, he compared this action with that of the animal who by barking gives notice of danger, and called this ftar the dog, the barker (Syrius). In the fame manner he called ftars of the crab, thofe which fhowed themfelves when the fun, having reached the bounds of the tropic, returned backwards and fideways like the crab or Cancer; ftars of the wild goat, thofe which, the fun being arrived at its greateft altitude, at the top of the horary gnomon, imitated the action of that animal who delights in climbing the higheft rocks; ftars of the balance, thofe which, the days and nights being of the fame length, feemed to obferve an equilibrium like that inftrument; ftars of the fcorpion, thofe which were perceptible when certain regular winds brought a burning vapour like

like the poifon of the fcorpion. In the fame
manner he called by the name of rings and
ferpents the figured traces of the orbits of the
ftars and planets (51); and this was the general means of appellation of all the heavenly bodies, taken in groupes or indivi-
dually, according to their connection with
rural and terreftrial operations, and the analogies which every nation found them to
bear to the labours of the field and the objects of their climate and foil.

"From this proceeding it refulted, that
abject and terreftrial beings entered into affociation with the fuperior and powerful beings
of the heavens ; and this affociation became
more rivetted every day by the very conftitution of language and the mechanifm of the
mind. Men would fay, by a natural metaphor: " The bull fpreads upon the earth the
" germins of fecundity (in fpring); and
" brings back abundance by the revival of
" vegetation. The lamb (or ram) delivers
" the heavens from the malevolent Genii of
" winter; and faves the world from the fer-
" pent (emblem of the wet feafon). The
" fcorpion pours out his venom upon the
" earth, and fpreads difeafes and death, &c."

This

" This language, underſtood by every body, was at firſt attended with no incon-- venience; but, in procefs of time, when the almanac had been regulated, the people, who could do without further obfervation of the ſkies, loſt fight of the motive which led to the adoption of thefe expreffions; and the allegory ſtill remaining in the practices of life, became a fatal ſtumbling-block to the underſtanding and reaſon. Habituated to join to ſymbols the ideas of their models, the mind finally confounded them; then thofe fame animals which the imagination had raifed to heaven, defcended again on the earth; but in this return, decked in the livery and inveſted with the attributes of the ſtars, they impofed upon their own authors. The people, imagining that they faw their Gods before them, found it a more eafy taſk to offer up their prayers. They demanded of the ram of their flock, the influence which they expected from the celeſtial ram; they prayed the fcorpion not to pour out his venom upon Nature; they revered the fiſh of the river, the crab of the fea, and the fcarabeus of the ſlime; and by a feries of

R   corrupt,

corrupt, but inseparable analogies, they loft themselves in a labyrinth of consequent absurdities.

" Such was the origin of this ancient and singular worship of animals ; such the train of ideas by which the character of the Divinity became common to the meaneft of the brute creation; and thus was formed the vaft, complicated, and learned theological fyftem which, from the banks of the Nile, conveyed from country to country by commerce, war, and conqueft, invaded all the old world ; and which, modified by times, by circumftances, and by prejudices, is ftill to be found among a hundred nations, and fubfifts to this day as the fecret and infeparable bafis of the theology of thofe even who defpife and reject it."

At thefe words, murmurs being heard in various groupes : " I repeat it," continued the orator. " People of Africa ! hence, for example, has arifen among you the adoration of your *Feteches*, plants, animals, pebbles, bits of wood, before which your anceftors would never have been fo abfurd as to proftrate themfelves, if they had not

feen

feen in them talifmans, partaking of the
nature of the ftars (52). Nations of Tartary! this is equally the origin of your
Marmouzets, and of the whole train of animals with which your Chamans ornament
their magic robes. This is the origin of
thofe figures of birds and ferpents, which
all the favage nations, with myftic and facred ceremonies, imprint on their fkin. Indians! it is in vain you cover yourfelves
with the veil of myftery: the hawk of your
God Vichenou is but one of the thoufand
emblems of the fun in Egypt, and his incarnations in a fifh, boar, lion, turtle, together
with all his monftrous adventures, are nothing more than the metamorphofes of the
fame ftar, which, paffing fucceffively through
the figns of the twelve animals *, was fuppofed to affume their forms, and to act their
aftronomical parts (53). Japanefe! your
bull which breaks the egg of the world, is
merely that of the heavens, which, in times
of yore, opened the age of the creation, the
equinox of Spring. Rabbins, Jews! that
fame bull is the *Apis* worfhipped in Egypt,

* The Zodiac.

R 2   and

and which your anceftors adored in the idol of the golden calf. It is alfo your bull, children of Zoroafter! that, facrificed in the fymbolic myfteries of Mithra, fhed a blood fertilizing to the world. Laftly, your bull of the Apocalypfe, Chriftians! with his wings, the fymbol of the air, has no other origin: your lamb of God, immolated, like the bull of Mithra, for the falvation of the world, is the felf-fame fun in the fign of the celeftial ram, which, in a fubfequent age, opening the equinox in his turn, was deemed to have rid the world of the reign of evil, that is to fay, of the ferpent, of the large fnake, the mother of winter and emblem of the Ahrimanes or Satan of the Perfians, your inftitutors. Yes, vainly does your imprudent zeal confign idolaters to the torments of the Tartarus which they have invented: the whole bafis of your fyftem is nothing more than the worfhip of the ftar of day, whofe attributes you have heaped upon your chief perfonage. It is the fun which, under the name of Orus, was born, like your God, in the arms of the celeftial virgin, and paffed through an obfcure, indigent,

digent, and deftitute childhood, anfwering
to the feafon of cold and froft. It is the
fun, which, under the name of Ofiris, perfecuted by Typhon and the tyrants of the
air, was put to death, laid in a dark tomb,
the emblem of the hemifphere of winter,
and which, rifing afterwards from the inferior zone to the higheft point of the heavens, awoke triumphant over giants and the
deftroying angels. Ye priefts! from whom
the murmurs proceed, you wear yourfelves
its figns all over your bodies. Your tonfure
is the difk of the fun; your ftole its Zodiac
(54); your rofaries the fymbols of the ftars
and planets. Pontiffs and prelates! your
mitre, your crofier, your mantle, are the
emblems of Ofiris; and that crucifix of
which you boaft the myftery, without comprehending it, is the crofs of Serapis, traced
by the hands of Egyptian priefts on the
plan of the figurative world, which, paffing
through the equinoxes and the tropics, became the emblem of future life and refurrection, becaufe it touched the gates of ivory
and horn through which the foul was to
pafs in its way to heaven."

R 3   Here

Here the doctors of the different groupes looked with aftonifhment at one another, but none of them breaking filence, the orator continued.

" Three principal caufes concurred to produce this confufion of ideas. Firft, the neceffity, on account of the infant ftate of language, of making ufe of figurative expreffions to depict the relations of things; expreffions that, paffing afterwards from a proper to a general, from a phyfical to a moral fenfe, occafioned, by their equivocal and fynonymous terms, a multiplicity of miftakes.

" Thus having at firft faid, that the fun furmounted and paffed in its courfe through the twelve animals, they afterwards fuppofed that it combated, conquered, and killed them, and from this was compofed the hiftorical life of Hercules.

" Having faid that it regulated the period of rural operations, of feed time and of harveft; that it diftributed the feafons, ran through the climates, fwayed the earth, &c. it was taken for a legiflative king, a conquering warrior, and hence they formed the

5   ftories

ftories of Ofiris, of Bacchus, and other fimilar Gods.

" Having faid that a planet entered into
a fign, the conjunction was denominated a
marriage, adultery, inceft (55): having farther faid, that it was buried, becaufe it funk
below the horizon, returned to light and
gained its ftate of eminence, they gave it the
epithet of dead, rifen again, carried into
heaven, &c.

" The fecond caufe of confufion was
the material figures themfelves, by which
thoughts were originally painted, and which,
under the name of hieroglyphics, or facred
characters, were the firft invention of the
mind. Thus to denote an inundation, and
the neceffity of preferving one's-felf from
it, they painted a boat, the veffel Argo; to
exprefs the wind, they painted a bird's wing;
to fpecify the feafon, the month, they deli-
neated the bird of paffage, infect, or animal,
which made its appearance at that epoch;
to exprefs winter they drew a hog, or a
ferpent, which are fond of moift and miry
places. The combination of thefe figures
had alfo a meaning, and was fubftituted for

R 4   words

words and phrafes * (56). But as there was
nothing fixed or precife in this fort of language, as the number of thofe figures and
their combinations became exceffive and
burdenfome to the memory, confufions and
falfe interpretations were the firft and obvious refult.   Genius having afterwards invented the more fimple art of applying figns
to founds, of which the number is limited,
and of painting the word inftead of the
thought, hieroglyphic pictures were, by
means of alphabetical writing, brought into
difufe ; and from day to day their forgotten
fignifications made way for a variety of illufions, equivoques, and errors.

" Laftly, the civil organization of the firft
ftates was a third caufe of confufion.   Indeed, when the people began to apply themfelves to agriculture, the formation of the
rural calendar requiring continual aftronomical obfervations, it was neceffary to chufe
individuals whofe province it fhould be to
watch the appearance and fetting of certain
ftars, to give notice of the return of the inundation, of particular winds and rains, and

* See the examples cited in note (45).

the

the proper time for fowing every fpecies of
grain. Thefe men, on account of their office, were exempted from the common occupations, and the fociety provided for their
fubfiftence. In this fituation, folely occupied in making obfervations, they foon penetrated the great phenomena of nature, and
dived into the fecret of various of her operations. They became acquainted with the
courfe of the ftars and planets; the connection which their abfence and return had with
the productions of the earth and the activity
of vegetation: the medicinal or nutritive
properties of fruits and plants; the action
of the elements, and their reciprocal affinities.
But, as there were no means of communicating this knowledge otherwife than by the
painful and laborious one of oral inftruction,
they imparted it only to their friends and
kindred; and hence refulted a concentration
of fcience in certain families, who, on this
account affumed to themfelves exclufive privileges, and a fpirit of corporation and feparate diftinction fatal to the public weal. By
this continued fucceffion of the fame labours
and enquiries, the progrefs of knowledge it
is true was haftened, but, by the myftery
that

that accompanied it, the people, plunged daily in the thickeſt darkneſs, became more ſuperſtitious and more ſlaviſh. Seeing human beings produce certain phenomena,announce, as it were at will, eclipſes and comets, cure diſeaſes, handle noxious ſerpents, they ſuppoſed them to have intercourſe with celeſtial powers; and, to obtain the good or have the ills averted which they expected from thoſe powers, they adopted theſe extraordinary human beings as mediators and interpreters. And thus were eſtabliſhed in the very boſom of ſtates ſacrilegious corporations of hypocritical and deceitful men, who arrogated to themſelves every kind of power; and prieſts, being at once aſtronomers, divines, naturaliſts, phyſicians, necromancers, interpreters of the Gods, oracles of the people, rivals of kings or their accomplices, inſtituted under the name of religion an empire of myſtery, which to this very hour has proved ruinous to the nations of mankind."

At theſe words the prieſts of all the groupes interrupted the orator; with loud cries, they accuſed him of impiety, irreligion, blaſphemy, and were unwilling he ſhould proceed: but the legiſlators having obſerved,

that

that what he related was merely a narrative
of hiftorical facts ; that if thofe facts were
falfe or forged, it would be an eafy matter
to refute them ; and that if every one were
not allowed the perfect liberty to declare his
opinion, it would be impoffible to arrive at
truth—he thus went on with his difcourfe.

" From all thefe caufes, and the perpetual
affociation of diffimilar ideas, there followed
a ftrange mafs of diforders in theology, morality, and tradition. And firft, becaufe the
ftars were reprefented by animals, the qualities of the animals, their likings, their fym-
pathies, their averfions, were transferred to
the Gods and fuppofed to be their actions.
Thus the God *Ichneumon* made war againft
the God crocodile; the God wolf wanted
to eat the God fheep; the God ftork devoured the God ferpent; and the Deity became a ftrange, whimfical, ferocious being,
whofe idea mifled the judgment of man, and
corrupted both his morals and his reafon.

" Again, as every family, every nation, in
the fpirit of its worfhip adopted a particular
ftar or conftellation for its patron, the affections and antipathies of the emblematical
brute

brute were transferred to the fectaries of this
worfhip; and the partifans of the God dog
were enemies to thofe of the God wolf; the
worfhippers of the God bull, abhorred thofe
who fed upon beef, and religion became the
author of combats and animofities, the fenfelefs caufe of frenzy and fuperftition (57).

" Farther, the names of the animal ftars
having, on account of this fame patronage,
been conferred on nations, countries, mountains, and rivers, thofe objects were alfo
taken for Gods; and hence there arofe a
medley of geographical, hiftorical, and mythological beings, by which all tradition was
involved in confufion.

" In fine, from the analogy of their fuppofed actions the planetary gods having been
taken for men, heroes, and kings; kings and
heroes took in their turn the actions of the
Gods for models, and became, from imitation, warlike, conquering, fanguinary, proud,
lafcivious, indolent; and religion confecrated the crimes of defpots, and perverted the
principles of governments.

SECT. IV. *Fourth fyflem: Worſhip of two principles, or Dualiſm.*

" MEANWHILE the aftronomical priefts, enjoying in their temples peace and abun- dance, made every day freſh progreſs in the fciences; and the fyftem of the world gra- dually difplaying itfelf before their eyes, they ftarted fucceſively various hypothefes as to its agents and effects, which became fo many fyftems of theology.

" The navigators of the maritime nations, and the caravans of the Afiatic and African Nomades, having given them a knowledge of the earth from the Fortunate Iflands to Serica, and from the Baltic to the fources of the Nile, they difcovered, by a comparifon of the different Zones, the rotundity of the globe, which gave rife to a new theory. Obferving that all the operations of Nature, during the annual period, were fummed up in two principal ones, that of producing and that of deftroying; that upon the major part of the globe, each of thefe operations was equally accomplifhed from one to the other equinox; that is to fay, that during the fix months

months of fummer all was in a ftate of pro-
creation and increafe, and during the fix
months of winter all in a ftate of languor
and nearly dead, they fuppofed nature to contain two contrary powers always ftruggling
with and refifting each other; and confidering in the fame light the celeftial fphere,
they divided the pictures, by which they reprefented it into two halves or hemifpheres,
fo that thofe conftellations which appeared
in the fummer heaven formed a direct and
fuperior empire, and thofe in the winter
heaven an oppofite and inferior one. Now
as the fummer conftellations were accompanied with the feafon of long, warm, and unclouded days, together with that of fruits
and harvefts, they were deemed to be the
powers of light, fecundity, and creation;
and by tranfition from a phyfical to a moral
fenfe, to be Genii, angels of fcience, beneficence, purity, virtue : in like manner the
winter conftellations, being attended with
long nights and the polar fogs, were regarded as genii of darknefs, deftruction, death,
and, by fimilar tranfition, as angels of wickednefs, ignorance, fin, vice. By this difpofal,

fal, heaven was divided into two domains, two factions; and the analogy of human ideas opened already a vaft career to the flights of imagination; but a particular circumftance determined, if it did not occafion the miftake and illufion. (Confult Plate II. at the end of the volume.)

" In the projection of the celeftial fphere drawn by aftronomical priefts (58), the Zodiac and the conftellations difpofed in a circular order, prefented their halves in diametrical oppofition: the winter hemifphere was adverfe, contrary, oppofite to, being the Antipodes of, that of fummer. By the continued metaphor thefe words were converted into a moral fenfe, and the adverfe angels and Genii became rebels and enemies (59). From that period the whole aftronomical hiftory of the conftellations was turned into a political hiftory; the heavens became a human ftate, where every thing happened as it does on earth. Now as the exifting ftates, for the moft part defpotic, had their monarchs, and as the fun was the apparent fovereign of the fkies, the fummer hemifphere (empire of light), and its conftellations (a nation of white angels), had for

king

king an enlightened, intelligent, creative, benign God; and as every rebellious faction muft have its chief, the hemifphere of winter (the fubterraneous empire of darknefs and woe), together with its ftars (a nation of black angels, giants, or demons), had for leader a malignant Genius, whofe part was affigned, by the different people of the earth, to that ftar which appeared to them the moft remarkable. In Egypt it was originally the Scorpion, the firft fign of the Zodiac after the Balance, and the hoary chief of the wintry figns: then it was the bear or the polar afs, called Typhon, that is to fay, deluge (60), on account of the rains which poured down upon the earth during the dominion of that ftar. In Perfia, at a fubfequent period (61), it was the ferpent, which, under the name of Ahrimanes, formed the bafis of the fyftem of Zoroafter; and it is the fame, Chriftians and Jews, that is become your ferpent of Eve (the celeftial origin), and that of the crofs; in both cafes the emblem of Satan, the great adverfary of the Ancient of Days, fung by Daniel. In Syria it was the hog or wild boar, enemy of Adonis, becaufe in that country the office of the

Northern

Northern bear was made to devolve upon the
animal whofe fondnefs for mire and dirt is
emblematical of winter. And it is for this
reafon that you, children of Mofes and of
Mahomet, hold this animal in abhorrence, in
imitation of the priefts of Memphis and Balbec, who detefted him as the murderer of
their God the fun. This is likewife, O Indians! the type of your Chib-en, which was
once the Pluto of your brethren the Greeks
and Romans; your Brama alfo (God the creator), is only the Perfian Ormuzd, and the
Ofiris of Egypt, whofe very name expreffes
a creative power, producer of forms. And
thefe Gods were worfhipped in a manner
analogous to their real or fictitious attributes;
and this worfhip, on account of the difference
of its objects, was divided into two diftinct
branches. In one, the benign God received
a worfhip of joy and love; whence are derived all religious acts of a gay nature (62),
feftivals, dances, banquets, offerings of
flowers, milk, honey, perfumes; in a word,
of every thing that delights the fenfes and
the foul. In the other, the malign God, on
the contrary, received a worfhip of fear and

S   pain;

pain; whence originated all religious acts of the fombre kind (63), tears, grief, mourning, felf-denial, blood-offerings, and cruel facrifices.

"From the fame fource flowed the divifion of terreftrial beings into pure and impure, facred or abominable, according as their fpecies was found among the refpective conftellations of the two Gods, and made a part of their domains. This produced, on one hand, the fuperftitions of pollution and purification; and on the other, the pretended efficacious virtues of amulets and talifmans.

"You now underftand," continued the orator, addrefling himfelf to the Indians, Perfians, Jews, Chriftians and Muffulmans, "you now underftand the origin of thofe ideas of combats and rebellion, which equally pervade your refpective mythology. You perceive what is meant by white and black angels; by the cherubs and feraphs with heads of an eagle, a lion or a bull; the Deus, devils or demons with horns of goats and tails of fnakes; the thrones and dominions, ranged in feven orders or gradations, like the feven fpheres of the planets; all of them beings

acting

acting the fame parts, partaking of the fame attributes in the Vedas, the Bibles, or the Zendavefta; whether their chief be Ormuzd or Brama, Typhon or Chib-en, Michael or Satan; whether their form be that of giants with a hundred arms and feet of ferpents, or that of Gods metamorphofed into lions, ftorks, bulls and cats, as they appear in the facred tales of the Greeks and Egyptians: you perceive the fucceffive genealogy of thefe ideas, and how in proportion to their remotenefs from their fources, and as the mind of man became refined, their grofs forms were purified, and reduced to a ftate lefs fhocking and repulfive.

" But, juft as the fyftem of two oppofite principles or deities originated in that of fymbols ; in the fame manner you will find a new fyftem fpring out of this, to which it ferved in its turn as a foundation and fupport."

SECT. V. *Myftical or moral worfhip, or the fyftem of a future ftate.*

" IN reality, when the vulgar heard talk of a new heaven and another world, they foon

gave

gave a body to thefe fictions; they erected on
it a folid ftage and real fcenes; and their
notions of geography and aftronomy ferved
to ftrengthen, if they did not give rife to
the allufion.

" On the one hand, the Phenician navigators, thofe who paffed the pillars of Hercules
to fetch the pewter of Thule and the amber
of the Baltic, related that at the extremity
of the world, the boundaries of the ocean
(the Mediterranean), where the fun fets to
the countries of Afia, there were fortunate
Iflands, the abode of an everlafting fpring;
and at a farther diftance, hyperborean regions, placed under the earth (relatively to the
tropics), where reigned an eternal night *.
From thefe ftories, badly underftood, and no
doubt confufedly related, the imagination of
the people compofed the Elyfian Fields (64),
delightful fports in a world below, having
their heaven, their fun and their ftars; and
Tartarus, a place of darknefs, humidity, mire,
and chilling froft. Now, inafmuch as mankind, inquifitive about all that of which they

* Nights of fix months duration.

are

are ignorant, and defirous of a protracted exiftence, had already exerted their faculties
refpecting what was to become of them after
death; inafmuch as they had early reafoned
upon that principle of life which animates the
body, and which quits it without changing
the form of the body, and had conceived to
themfelves airy fubftances, phantoms and
fhades, they loved to believe that they fhould
refume in the fubterranean world that life
which it was fo painful to lofe; and this
abode appeared commodious for the reception of thofe beloved objects which they
could not prevail on themfelves to renounce.

" On the other hand, the aftrological and
philofophical priefts told fuch ftories of their
heavens as perfectly quadrated with thefe
fictions. Having, in their metaphorical language, denominated the equinoxes and fol-
ftices the gates of heaven, or the entrance of
the feafons, they explained the terreftrial
phenomena by faying, that through the gate
of horn (firft the bull, afterwards the ram),
vivifying fires defcended, which, in fpring,
gave life to vegetation , and aquatic Spirits,
which caufed, at the folftice, the overflowing

S 3   of

of the Nile : that through the gate of ivory
(originally the Bowman, or Sagittarius, then
the Balance) and through that of Capricorn,
or the urn, the emanations or influences of
the heavens returned to their fource and re-
afcended to their origin; and the milky Way
which paffed through the doors of the fol-
ftices, feemed to them to have been placed
there on purpofe to be their road and ve-
hicle (65). The celeftial fcene farther prefented, according to their Atlas, a river (the
Nile, defignated by the windings of the
Hydra) ; together with a barge (the veffel
Argo), and the dog Sirius, both bearing relation to that river of which they forboded
the overflowing. Thefe circumftances added to the preceding ones, increafed the probability of the fiction ; and thus, to arrive
at Tartarus or Elyfium, fouls were obliged
to crofs the rivers Styx and Acheron, in the
boat of Charon the ferryman, and to pafs
through the doors of horn and ivory,
which were guarded by the maftiff Cerbe-
rus. At length a civil ufage was joined
to all thefe inventions, and gave them con-
fiftency.

" The

" The inhabitants of Egypt having remarked that the putrefaction of dead bodies
became in their burning climate the fource
of peftilence and difeafes, the cuftom was
introduced in a great number of ftates, of
burying the dead at a diftance from the
inhabited diftricts, in the defert which lies
at the Weft. To arrive there it was neceffary to crofs the canals of the river in a boat,
and to pay a toll to the ferryman, otherwife
the body, remaining unburied, would have
been left a prey to wild beafts. This cuftom
fuggefted to her civil and religious legiflators, a powerful means of affecting the manners of her inhabitants ; and addreffing favage and uncultivated men with the motives
of filial piety and reverence for the dead,
they introduced, as a neceffary condition,
the undergoing that previous trial which
fhould decide whether the deceafed deferv-
ed to be admitted upon the footing of his family honours into the *black city*. Such an
idea too well accorded with the reft of the
bufinefs not to be incorporated with it : it
accordingly entered for an article into religious creeds, and hell had its Minos and its

S 4   Radaman-

Radamanthus, with the wand, the chair, the guards and the urn, after the exact model of this civil tranfaction. The Divinity then, for the firft time, became a fubject of moral and political confideration, a legiflator, by fo much the more formidable as, while his judgment was final and his decrees without appeal, he was unapproachable to his fub-jects. This mythological and fabulous creation, compofed as it was of fcattered and difcordant parts, then became a fource of future punifhments and rewards, in which divine juftice was fuppofed to correct the vices and errors of this tranfitory ftate. A fpiritual and myftical fyftem, fuch as I have mentioned, acquired fo much the more credit as it applied itfelf to the mind by every argument fuited to it. The oppreffed looked thither for an indemnification; and entertained the confoling hope of vengeance; the oppreffor expected by the coftlinefs of his offerings to fecure to himfelf impunity, and at the fame time employed this principle to infpire the vulgar with timidity : kings and priefts, the heads of the people, faw in it a new fource of power, as they referved to

themfelves

themfelves the privilege of awarding the favours or the cenfure of the great judge of all, according to the opinion they fhould inculcate of the odioufnefs of crimes and the meritorioufnefs of virtue.

" Thus, then, an invifible and imaginary world entered into competition with that which was real. Such, O Perfians, was the origin of your renovated earth, your city of refurrection, placed under the equator, and diftinguifhed from all other cities by this fingular attribute, that the bodies of its inhabitants caft no fhade (66). Such, O Jews and Chriftians, difciples of the Perfians, was the fource of your new Jerufalem, your paradife and your heaven, modelled upon the aftrological heaven of Hermes. Meanwhile, your hell, O ye Muffulmans, a fubterraneous pit furmounted by a bridge, your balance of fouls and good works, your judgment pronounced by the angels Monkir and Nekir, derives its attributes from the myfterious ceremonies of the cave of Mithra (67) ; and your heaven is exactly coincident with that of Ofiris, Ormudz and Brama."

SECT. VI. *Sixth System: The animated world, or worship of the universe under different emblems.*

" WHILE the nations were losing themselves in the dark labyrinth of mythology and fables, the physiological priests, pursuing their studies and enquiries about the order and disposition of the universe, came to fresh results, and set up fresh systems of powers and moving causes.

" Long confined to simple appearances, they had only seen in the motion of the stars an unknown play of luminous bodies, which they supposed to roll round the earth, the central point of all the spheres; but from the moment they had discovered the rotundity of our planet, the consequences of this first fact led them to other considerations, and from inference to inference they rose to the highest conceptions of astronomy and physics.

" In truth, having conceived the enlightened and simple idea, that the celestial globe is a small circle inscribed in the greater circle of the heavens, the theory of the concentral circles

circles naturally prefented itfelf to their hypothefis, to refolve the unknown circle of the
terreftrial globe by known points of the celeftial circle ; and the meafure of one or feveral degrees of the meridian, gave precifely
the total circumference. Then taking for
compafs the diameter of the earth, a fortunate genius defcribed with aufpicious boldnefs the immenfe orbits of the heavens; and,
by an unheard of abftraction, man, who
fcarcely peoples the grain of fand of which
he is the inhabitant, embraced the infinite
diftances of the ftars, and launched himfelf
into the abyfs of fpace and duration. There a
new order of the univerfe prefented itfelf, of
which the petty globe that he inhabited no
longer appeared to him to be the center: this
important part was transferred to the enormous mafs of the fun, which became the in-
flamed pivot of eight circumjacent fpheres,
the movements of which were henceforward
fubmitted to exact calculation.

" The human mind had already done a great
deal, by undertaking to refolve the difpofition
and order of the great beings of nature ; but
not contented with this firft effort, it wifhed
alfo

alfo to refolve its mechanifm, and difcover its origin and motive principle. And here it is that, involved in the abftract and metaphy-fical depths of motion and its firft caufe, of the inherent or communicated properties of matter, together with its fucceffive forms and extent, or, in other words, of boundlefs fpace and time, thefe phyfiological divines loft themfelves in a chaos of fubtle argument and fcholaftic controverfy.

" The action of the fun upon terreftrial bodies, having firft led them to confider its fubftance as pure and elementary fire, they made it the focus and refervoir of an ocean of igneous and luminous fluid, which, under the name of ether, filled the univerfe, and nourifhed the beings contained therein. They afterwards difcovered, by the analyfis of a more accurate philofophy, this fire, or a fire fimilar to it, entering into the compofition of all bodies, and perceived that it was the grand agent in that fpontaneous motion, which in animals is denominated life, and in plants vegetation. From hence they were led to conceive of the mechanifm and action of the univerfe, as of a homogeneous WHOLE,

a fingle

a fingle body, whofe parts, however diftant
in place, had a reciprocal connection with
each other (69) ; and of the world as a living
fubftance, animated by the organical circulation of an ingneous or rather electrical
fluid (70), which, by an analogy borrowed
from men and animals, was fuppofed to have
the fun for its heart (71).

   " Meanwhile, among the theological philofophers, one fect beginning from thefe principles, the refult of experiment, faid: That
nothing was annihilated in the world; that
the elements were unperifhable ; that they
changed their combinations, but not their
nature ; that the life and death of beings
were nothing more than the varied modifi-
cations of the fame atoms; that matter contained in itfelf properties, which were the
caufe of all its modes of exifting ; that the
world was eternal (72), having no bounds
either of fpace or duration. Others faid:
That the whole univerfe was God; and, according to them, God was at once effect and
caufe, agent and patient, moving principle
and thing moved, having for laws the invariable properties which conftitute fatality;

and

and they defignated their idea fometimes by
the emblem of PAN (the GREAT ALL); or
of Jupiter, with a ftarry front, a planetary
body, and feet of animals; or by the fymbol
of the Orphic egg *, whofe yolk fufpended
in the middle of a liquid encompaffed by a
vault, reprefented the globe of the fun
fwimming in ether in the middle of the vault
of heaven (73); or by the emblem of a large
round ferpent, figurative of the heavens,
where they placed the firft princicle of motion, and for that reafon of an azure colour,
ftudded with gold fpots (the ftars), and de-
vouring his tail, that is, re-entering into himfelf, by winding continually like the revolutions of the fpheres; or by the emblem of a
man, with his feet preffed and tied together to
denote immutable exiftence, covered with a
mantle of all colours, like the appearance of
nature, and wearing on his head a fphere of
gold (74), figurative of the fphere of the planets; or by that of another man fometimes
feated upon the flower of *Lotos*, borne upon the
abyfs of the waters, at others reclined upon

* Vide Œdip. Ægypt. tom. II. p. 205.

a pile

a pile of twelve cushions, signifying the twelve celeftial figns. And this, O nations of India, Japan, Siam, Thibet, and China, is the theology, which, invented by the Egyptians, has, been tranfmitted down and preferved among yourfelves, in the pictures you give of Brama, Beddou, Sommanacodom, and Omito. This, O ye Jews and Chriftians, is the counterpart of an opinion, of which you have retained a certain portion, when you defcribe God as *the breath of life moving upon the face of the waters*, alluding to the wind (75), which at the origin of the world, that is, at the departure of the fpheres from the fign of the Crab, announced the overflowing of the Nile, and feemed to be the preliminary of creation."

Sect. VII. *Seventh Syftem: Worfhip of the* Soul *of the* World, *that is, the element of fire, the vital principle of the univerfe.*

" BUT a third fet of the theological philofophers, difgufted with the idea of a being at once effect and caufe, agent and patient, and uniting in one and the fame nature all contrary attributes, diftinguifhed the moving principle from the thing moved; and laying

7   it

it down as a datum that matter was in itfelf,
inert, they pretended that it received its properties from a diftinct agent of which it was
only the envelope or cafe. Some made this
agent the igneous principle, the acknowledged author of all motion; others made it
the fluid called ether, becaufe it was thought
to be more active and fubtile: now, as they
denominated the vital and motive principle
in animals, a foul, a fpirit; and as they always reafoned by comparifon, and particularly by comparifon with human exiftence,
they gave to the motive principle of the
whole univerfe the name of foul, intelligence,
fpirit; and God was the vital fpirit, which,
diffufed through all beings, animated the vaft
body of the world. This idea was reprefented fometimes by You-piter, effence of
motion and animation, principle of exiftence,
or rather exiftence itfelf (76); at other times
by Vulcan, or *Phtha*, elementary principle of
fire, or by the altar of Vefta, placed cen-
trally in her temple, like the fun in the
fpheres; and again by *Kneph*, a human being
dreffed in deep blue, holding in his hands a
fceptre and a girdle (the Zodiac), wearing on
his

his head a cap with feathers, to exprefs the fugacity of thought, and producing from his mouth the great egg (77).

"As a confequence from this fyftem, every being containing in itfelf a portion of the igneous or etherial fluid, the univerfal and common mover, and that fluid, foul of the world, being the Deity, it followed that the fouls of all beings were a part of God himfelf, partaking of all his attributes, that is, being an indivifible, fimple, and immortal fubftance; and hence is derived the whole fyftem of the immortality of the foul, which at firft was eternity (78). Hence alfo its tranfmigrations known by the name of metempfychofis, that is to fay, paffage of the vital principle from one body to another; an idea which fprung from the real tranfmigration of the material elements. Such, O Indians, Budfoifts, Chriftians, Muffulmans, was the origin of all your ideas of the fpirituality of the foul! Such was the fource of the reveries of Pythagoras and Plato, your inftitutors, and who were themfelves but the echoes of another, the laft fect of vifionary philofophers that it is neceffary to examine.

T   SECT.

SECT. VIII. *Eighth fyftem: The world a machine : worſhip of the. Demi-ourgos, or
ſupreme artificer.*

" HITHERTO the theologians,. in exercifing their faculties on the detached and
fubtile fubſtances of ether and the igneous
principle, had not however ceafed to treat
of exiftences palpable and perceptible to
the fenfes, and their theology had continued to be the theory of phyfical powers,
placed fometimes exclufively in the ſtars, and
fometimes diſſeminated through the univerfe.
But at the period at which we are arrived,
fome fuperficial minds, lofing the chain of
ideas which had directed thefe profound enquiries, or ignorant of the facts which ferved
as their bafis, rendered abortive all the refults
that had been obtained from them, by the
introduction of a ſtrange and novel chimera.
They pretended that the univerfe, the heavens, the ſtars, the fun, differed in no refpect from an ordinary machine ; and applying
to this hypothefis a comparifon drawn from
the works of art, they erected an edifice of
the moft whimfical fophifms. " A machine,"
faid

faid they, "cannot form itfelf, there muft be
" a workman to conftruct it ; its very exift-
" ence implies this. The world is a machine ;
" it has therefore an artificer (79)."

" Hence the *Demi-ourgos*, or fupreme artificer, the autocrator and fovereign of the
univerfe. It was in vain that the ancient philofophy objected to the hypothefis, that this
artificer did not ftand in lefs need of parents
and an author, and that a fcheme, which added only one link to the chain by taking the
attribute of eternity from the world and giving
it to the creator, was of little value. Thefe
innovators, not contented with a firft para-
dox, added a fecond, and applying to their artificer the theory of human underftanding,
pretended that the *Demi-ourgos* fafhioned his
machine upon an archetype or idea extant in
his mind. In a word, juft as their mafters, the
natural philofophers, had placed the *primum
mobile* in the fphere of the fixed ftars, under
the appellation of intelligence and reafon,
fo their apes, the fpiritualifts, adopting the
fame principle, made it an attribute of the
Demi-ourgos, reprefenting this being as a diftinct fubftance, neceffarily exifting, to which
they

they applied the terms of *Mens* or *Logos*, in other words, underftanding and fpeech. Separately from this being, they held the exiftence of a folar principle, or foul of the world, which, taken with the preceding, made three gradations of divine perfonages; firft, the *Demi-curgos*, or fupreme artificer; fecondly, the *Logos*, underftanding or fpeech : and thirdly, the fpirit or foul of the world (80). And this, O Chriftians, is the fiction on which you have founded your doctrine of the Trinity; this is the fyftem, which, born a Heretic in the Egyptian temples, tranfmitted a Heathen to the fchools of Greece and Italy, is now Catholic or Orthodox by the converfion of its partifans, the difciples of Pythagoras and Plato, to Chriftianity.

" Thus the Deity, after having been originally confidered as the fenfible and various action of meteors and the elements ; then as the combined power of the ftars, confidered in their relation to terreftrial objects ; then as thofe terreftrial objects themfelves, in confequence of confounding fymbols with the things they reprefented ; then as the complex power of Nature, in her two principal operations

operations of production and deftruction; then as the animated world without diftinction of agent and patient, caufe and effect; then as the folar principle or element of fire acknowledged as the fole caufe of motion— the Deity, I fay, confidered under all thefe different views, became at laft a chimerical and abftract being; a fcholaftic fubtlety of fubftance without form, of body without figure; a true delirium of the mind beyond the power of reafon at all to comprehend. But in this its laft transformation, it feeks in vain to conceal itfelf from the fenfes: the feal of its origin is indelibly ftamped upon it. All its attributes, borrowed from the phyfical attributes of the univerfe, as immenfity, eternity, indivifibility, incomprehenfiblenefs; or from the moral qualities of man, as goodnefs, juftice, majefty; and its very names (81), derived from the phyfical beings which were its types, particularly the fun, the planets, and the world, prefent to us continually, in fpite of thofe who would corrupt and difguife it, infallible marks of its genuine nature.

" Such is the chain of ideas through which

T 3   the

the human mind had already run at a period anterior to the pofitive recitals of hiftory; and fince their fyftematic form proves them to have been the refult of one fcene of ftudy and inveftigation, every thing inclines us to place the theatre of inveftigation, where its primitive elements were generated, in Egypt. There their progrefs was rapid, becaufe the idle curiofity of the theological philofophers had, in the retirement of the temples, no other food than the enigma of the univerfe, which was ever prefent to their minds; and becaufe, in the political diffentions which long difunited that country, each ftate had its college of priefts, who, being in turns auxiliaries or rivals, haftened by their dif-putes the progrefs of fcience and difcovery (82).

" On the borders of the Nile there hap-pened at that diftant period, what has fince been repeated all over the globe. In pro-portion as each fyftem was formed, it excited by its novelty quarrels and fchifms: then, gaining credit even by perfecution, it either deftroyed anterior ideas, or incorporated it-felf with and modified them. But political

inftitutions

inftitutions taking place, all opinions, by the aggregation of ftates and mixture of different people, were at length confounded; and the chain of ideas being loft, theology, plunged in a chaos, became a mere logogryph of old traditions no longer underftood. Religion, lofing its object, was now nothing more than a political expedient by which to rule the credulous vulgar; and was embraced either by men credulous themfelves and the dupes of their own vifions, or by bold and energetic fpirits, who formed vaft projects of ambition.''

SECT. IX. *Religion of Mofes, or worfhip of the foul of the world (You-piter).*

" Of this latter defcription was the Hebrew legiflator, who, defirous of feparating his nation from every other, and of forming a diftinct and exclufive empire, conceived the defign of taking for its bafis religious prejudices, and of erecting round it a facred rampart of rites and opinions. But in vain did he profcribe the worfhip of fymbols, the reigning religion, at that time, in Lower Egypt and Phenicia (83) : his God was not

T 4   on

on that account the lefs an Egyptian God, of
the invention of thofe priefts whofe difciple
Mofes had been; and *Yahouh* (84), detected
by his very name, which means eſſence of
beings, and by his ſymbol, the fiery buſh, is
nothing more than the foul of the world, the
principle of motion, which Greece ſhortly
after adopted under the fame denomination
in her *Yu-piter*, generative principle, and
under that of *El*, exiſtence (85); which the
Thebans confecrated by the name of *Kneph*;
which Sais worſhipped under the emblem of
Iſis veiled, with this infcription, *I am all that
has been, all that is, and all that will be, and
no mortal has drawn aſide my veil*; which Pythagoras honoured under the appellation of
Veſta, and which the Stoic philofophy defined
with precifion, by calling it the principle of
fire. In vain did Mofes wiſh to blot from
his religion whatever could bring to remembrance the worſhip of the ſtars; a multiplicity of traits in ſpite of his exertions ſtill
remained to point it out: the feven lamps
of the great candleſtick, the twelve ſtones
or figns of the Urim of the high-prieſt, the
feaſt of the two equinoxes, each of which at

that

that epocha formed a year, the ceremony of the lamb cr celeftial ram, then at its fifteenth degree ; laftly, the name of Ofiris even preferved in his fong (86), and the ark or coffer, an imitation of the tomb in which that God was inclofed ; all thefe remain to bear record to the genealogy of his ideas, and their derivation from the common fource."

SECT. X.   *Religion of Zoroafter.*

" ZOROASTER was alfo a man of the fame bold and energetic ftamp, who, five centuries after Mofes, and in the time of David, revived and moralized among the Medes and Bactrians the whole Egyptian fyftem of Ofiris, under the names cf Ormuzd and Ahrimanes. He called the reign of fummer, virtue and good ; the reign of winter, fin and evil ; the renovation of nature in fpring, creation ; the revival of the fpheres in the fecular periods of the conjunction, refurrection ; and his future life, hell, paradife, were the Tartarus and Elyfium of the ancient aftrologers and geographers; in a word, he only confecrated the already exifting reveries of the myftic fyftem."

SECT.

SECT. XI. *Budoifm, or religion of the Samaneans.*

In the fame rank muft be included the promulgators of the fepulchral doctrine of the Samaneans, who, on the bafis of the me-tempfychofis, raifed the mifanthropic fyftem of felf-renunciation and denial, who, laying it down as a principle, that the body is only a prifon where the foul lives in impure confinement; that life is but a dream, an illufion, and the world a place of paffage to another country, to a life without end; placed virtue and perfection in abfolute infenfibility, in the abnegation of phyfical organs, in the annihilation of all being: whence refulted the fafts, penances, macerations, folitude, contemplations, and all the deplorable practices of the mad-headed Anchorets."

SECT. XII. *Braminifm, or the Indian fyftem.*

" FINALLY, of the fame caft were the founders of the Indian fyftem, who, refining after Zoroafter upon the two principles of creation and deftruction, introduced an intermediate one, that of confervation, and upon their trinity in unity, of Brama, Chiven, and Bichenou,

Bichenou, accumulated a multitude of traditional allegories, and the alembicated subtleties of their metaphyfics."

" Thefe are the materials which, fcattered through Afia, there exifted for many ages, when, by a fortuitous courfe of events and circumftances, new combinations of them were introduced on the banks of the Euphrates, and on the fhores of the Mediterranean."

SECT. XIII. *Chriftianity, or the allegorical worfhip of the Sun, under the cabaliftical names of* CHRIS-EN *or* CHRIST, *and* Yês-US *or* JESUS.

" IN conftituting a feparate people, Mofes had vainly imagined that he fhould guard them from the influence of every foreign idea: but an invincible inclination, founded on affinity of origin, continually called back the Hebrews to the worfhip of the neighbouring nations; and the relations of commerce that neceffarily fubfifted between them, tended every day to ftrengthen the propenfity. While the Mofaic inftitution maintained its ground, the coercion of government and the laws, was a confiderable obftacle to the inlet

of

of innovations ; yet even then the principal
places were full of idols, and God the fun
had his chariot and horfes painted in the
palaces of kings, and in the very temple of
Yahouh : but when the conquefts of the
kings of Nineveh and Babylon had diffolved
the bands of public power, the people left
to themfelves, and folicited by their conquerors, no longer kept a reftraint on their inclinations, and profane opinions were openly
profeffed in Judea, At firft the Affyrian
colonies, placed in the fituation of the old
tribes, filled the kingdom of Samaria with
the dogmas of the Magi, which foon penetrated into Judea. Afterwards Jerufalem
having been fubjugated, the Egyptians, Syrians and Arabs, entering this open country,
introduced their tenets, and the religion of
Mofes thus underwent a fecond alteration.
In like manner the priefts and great men,
removing to Babylon, and educated in the
fcience of the Chaldeans, imbibed, during a
refidence of feventy years, every principle of
their theology, and from that moment the
dogmas of the evil Genius (Satan), of the
archangel Michael (87), of the Ancient of
Days

Days (Ormuzd), of the rebellious angels, the celeſtial combats, the immortality of the ſoul, and the reſurrection, dogmas unknown to Moſes, or rejected by him, ſince he obſerves a perfect ſilence reſpecting them, became naturalized among the Jews.

" On their return to their country, the emigrants brought back with them theſe ideas; and at firſt the innovations occaſioned diſputes between their partiſans, the Phari- ſees, and the adherents to the ancient na- tional worſhip, the Sadducees: but the for- mer, ſeconded by the inclination of the peo- ple, and the habits they had already con- tracted, and ſupported by the authority of the Perſians, their deliverers, finally gained the aſcendancy, and the theology of Zoro- aſter was conſecrated by the children of Moſes (88).

" A fortuitous analogy between two lead- ing ideas, proved particularly favourable to this coalition, and formed the baſis of a laſt ſyſtem, not leſs ſurpriſing in its fortune than in the cauſes of its formation.

" From the time that the Aſſyrians had deſtroyed the kingdom of Samaria, ſome ſa- gacious

gacious fpirits forefaw, announced, and predicted the fame fate to Jerufalem : and all
their predictions were ftamped by this parti-
cularity, that they always concluded with
prayers for a happy re-eftablifhment and regeneration, which were in like manner fpoken
of in the way of prophefies. The enthufiafm
of the Hierophants had figured a royal deliverer, who was to re-eftablifh the nation in
its ancient glory : the Hebrews were again to
become a powerful and conquering people,
and Jerufalem the capital of an empire that
was to extend over the whole world.

  " Events having realized the firft part of
thofe predictions, the ruin of Jerufalem, the
people clung to the fecond with a firmnefs
of belief proportioned to their misfortunes;
and the afflicted Jews waited with the impatience of want and of defire for that victorious king and deliverer that was to come,
in order to fave the nation of Mofes, and reftore the throne of David.

  " The facred and mythological traditions
of precedent times had fpread over all Afia a
tenet perfectiy analogous. A great mediator,
a final judge, a future faviour, was fpoken of,

  ß   who,

who, as king, God, and victorious legiſlator,
was to reſtore the golden age upon earth (89),
to deliver the world from evil, and regain for
mankind the reign of good, the kingdom of
peace and happineſs. Theſe ideas and expreſſions were in every mouth, and they con-
ſoled the people under that deplorable ſtate
of real ſuffering into which they had been
plunged by ſucceſſive conqueſts and conquerors, and the barbarous deſpotiſm of their
governments. This reſemblance between
the oracles of different nations and the predictions of the prophets, excited the attention
of the Jews ; and the prophets had doubtleſs been careful to infuſe into their pictures,
the ſpirit and ſtyle of the ſacred books employed in the Pagan myſteries. The arri-
val of a great ambaſſador, of a final ſaviour,
was therefore the general expectation in Judea, when at length a ſingular circumſtance
was made to determine the preciſe period
of his coming.

" It was recorded in the ſacred books of
the Perſians and the Chaldeans, that the
world, compoſed of a total revolution of
twelve thouſand periods, was divided into
two

two partial revolutions, of which one, the age and reign of good, was to terminate at the expiration of fix thoufand, and the other, the age and reign of evil, at the expiration of another fix thoufand.

" Their firft authors had meant by thefe recitals, the annual revolution of the great celeftial orb (a revolution compofed of twelve months or figns each divided into a thoufand parts), and the two fyftematic periods of winter and fummer, each confifting equally of fix thoufand. But thefe equivocal expref-fions having been erroneoufly explained, and having received an abfolute and moral, in-ftead of their aftrological and phyfical fenfe, the refult was, that the annual was taken for a fecular world, the thoufand periods for a thoufand years ; and judging, from the ap-pearance of things, that the prefent was the age of misfortune, they inferred that it would terminate at the expiration of the fix thoufand pretended years (90).

" Now, according to the Jewifh compu-tation, fix thoufand years had already nearly elapfed fince the fuppofed creation of the world (91). This coincidence produced confiderable

confiderable fermentation in the minds of the people. Nothing was thought of but the approaching termination. The Hierophants were interrogated, and their facred books examined. The great Mediator and final Judge was expected, and his advent defired, that an end may be put to fo many calamities. This was fo much the fubject of converfation, that fome one was faid to have feen him, and a rumour of this kind was all that was wanting to eftablifh a general certainty. The popular report became a demonftrated fact; the imaginary being was realized; and all the circumftances of mythological tradition being in fome manner connected with this phantom, the refult was an authentic and regular hiftory, which from henceforth it was blafphemy to doubt.

" In this mythological hiftory the following traditions were recorded : " That, " *in the beginning, a man and a woman had,* " *by their fall, brought fin and evil into the* " *world.*" (Examine plate II.)

" By this was denoted the aftronomical fact of the celeftial Virgin, and the herdfman

U   (Bootes)

(Bootes) who, fetting heliacally at the au-
tumnal equinox, refigned the heavens to the
wintry conftellations, and feemed, in fink-
ing below the horizon, to introduce into
the world the genius of evil, Ahrimanes,
reprefented by the conftellation of the Serpent (92.)

" *That the woman had decoyed and feduced*
" *the man* (93)."

" And in reality, the Virgin fetting firft,
appears to draw the Herdfinan (Bootes)
after her.

" *That the woman had tempted him, by*
" *offering him fruit pleafant to the fight and*
" *good for food, which gave the knowledge of*
" *good and evil.*"

" Manifeftly alluding to the Virgin, who
is depicted holding a bunch of fruit in her
hand, which fhe appears to extend towards
the Herdfman : in like manner the branch,
emblem of autumn, placed in the picture of
Mithra (94) on the front of winter and fummer, feems to open the door, and to give the
knowledge, the key, of good and evil.

" *That this couple had been driven from the*
" *celeftial garden, and that a cherub with a*
" *flaming*

" flaming fword had been placed at the door to " guard it."

" And when the Virgin and the Herdf-man fink below the Weftern horizon, Perfeus rifes on the oppofite fide (95), and fword in hand, this Genius may be faid to drive them from the fummer hea-ven, the garden and reign of fruits and flowers.

" That from this virgin would be born, " would fpring up a fhoot, a child, that fhould " crufh the ferpent's head, and deliver the " world from fin."

" By this was denoted the Sun, which, at the period of the fummer folftice, at the precife moment that the Perfian Magi drew the horofcope of the new year, found itfelf in the bofom of the Virgin, and which, on this account, was reprefented in their aftro-logical pictures in the form of an infant fuckled by a chafte virgin (96), and after-wards became, at the vernal equinox the Ram or Lamb, conqueror of the conftella-tion of the Serpent, which difappeared from the heavens.

" That in his infancy, this reftorer of the

" divine

" *divine or celeftial nature, would lead a mean,*
" *humble, obfcure and indigent life.*"

" By which was meant, that the winter fun was humbled, depreffed below the horizon, and that this firft period of his four ages, or the feafons, was a period of obfcurity and indigence, of fafting and privation.

" *That being put to death by the wicked, he*
" *would glorioufly rife again, afcend from hell*
" *into heaven, where he would reign for*
" *ever.*"

" By thefe expreffions was defcribed the life of the fame Sun, who, terminating his career at the winter folftice, when Typhon and the rebellious angels exercifed their fway, feemed to be put to death by them; but fhortly after revived and rofe again (97) in the firmament, where he ftill remains.

" Thefe traditions went ftill farther, fpecifying his aftrological and myfterious names, maintaining that he was called fometimes *Chris* or Confervator (98); and hence the Hindoo God, *Chris-en*, or *Chriftna*; and the Chriftian *Chris-tos*, the fon of Mary. That at other times he was called *Yes*, by the union

union of three letters, which, according to their numerical value, form the number 608, one of the folar periods (99). And behold, O Europeans, the name which, with a Latin termination has become your *Yts-us* or Jefus; the ancient and cabaliftical name given to young Bacchus, the clandeftine fon of the virgin Minerva, who in the whole hiftory of his life, and even in his death, calls to mind the hiftory of the God of the Chriftians; that is, the ftar of day, of which they are both of them emblems."

At thefe words a violent murmur arofe on the part of the Chriftian groupes; but the Mahometans, the Lamas and the Hindoos having called them to order, the orator thus concluded his difcourfe.

"You are not to be told," faid he, "in what manner the reft of this fyftem was formed in the chaos and anarchy of the three firft centuries; how a multiplicity of opinions divided the people, all of which were embraced with equal zeal and retained with equal obftinacy, becaufe alike founded on ancient tradition, they were alike facred. You know how, at the end of three centu-

U 3   ries,

turies, government having efpoufed one of
thefe fects, made it the orthodox religion ;
that is to fay, the predominant religion, to
the exclufion of the reft, which, on account
of their inferiority, were denominated here-
fics ; how, and by what means of violence
and feduction this religion was propagated
and gained ftrength, and afterwards became
divided and weakened ; how, fix centuries
after the innovation of Chriftianity, another
fyftem was formed out of its materials and
thofe of the Jews, and a political and theological empire was created by Mahomet at
the expence of that of Mofes and the vicars
of Jefus.

" Now, if you take a retrofpect of the
whole hiftory of the fpirit of religion, you
will find, that in its origin it had no other
author than the fenfations and wants of
man : that the idea of God had no other
type, no other model, than that of phyfical
powers, material exiftences, operating good
or evil, by impreffions of pleafure or pain on
fenfible beings. You will find that in the
formation of every fyftem, this fpirit of religion purfued the fame track, and was uniform

form in its proceedings; that in all, the
dogma never failed to reprefent, under the
name God, the operations of nature, and the
paffions and prejudices of men ; that in all,
morality had for its fole end, defire of happinefs and averfion to pain ; but that the
people and the majority of legiflators, ignorant of the true road that led thereto, invented falfe, and therefore contrary ideas
of virtue and vice, of good and evil ; that
is, of what renders man happy or miferable.
You will find, that in all, the means and
caufes of propagation and eftablifhment exhibited the fame fcenes, the fame paffions,
and the fame events, continual difputes about
words, falfe pretexts for inordinate zeal, for
revolutions, for wars, lighted up by the ambition of chiefs, by the chicanery of promulgators, by the credulity of profelytes, by
the ignorance of the vulgar, and by the
grafping cupidity and the intolerant pride of
all. In fhort, you will find that the whole
hiftory of the fpirit of religion, is merely that
of the fallibility and uncertainty of the human mind, which, placed in a world that it
does not comprehend, is yet defirous of folv-

ing

ing the enigma; and which, the aftonifhed fpectator of this myfterious and vifible prodigy, invents caufes, fuppofes ends, builds fyftems; then, finding one defective, abandons it for another not lefs vicious; hates the error that it has renounced, is ignorant of the new one that it adopts; rejects the truth of which it is in purfuit, invents chimeras of heterogeneous and contradictory beings, and, ever dreaming of wifdom and happinefs, lofes itfelf in a labyrinth of torments and illufions,"

CHAP.

C H A P. XXIII.

END OF ALL RELIGIONS THE SAME.

THUS ſpoke the orator, in the name of thoſe who had made the origin and genea-logy of religious ideas their peculiar ſtudy.

The theologians of the different ſyſtems now expreſſed their opinions of this diſcourſe. " It is an impious repreſentation," ſaid ſome, " which aims at nothing leſs than the ſub-" verſion of all belief, the introducing in-" ſubordination into the minds of men, and " annihilating our power and miniſtry."—" It is a romance," ſaid others, " a tiſſue of " conjectures, fabricated with art, but deſti-" tute of foundation."—The moderate and prudent ſaid, " Suppoſing all this to be true, " where is the uſe of revealing theſe myſte-" ries? Our opinions are doubtleſs pervaded " with errors, but thoſe errors are a neceſ-" ſary curb on the multitude. The world " has gone on thus for two thouſand years; " why ſhould we now alter its courſe?"

8   The

The murmur of difapprobation, which never fails to arife againft every kind of innovation, already began to increafe, when a numerous groupe of plebeians and untaught men of every country and nation, without prophets, without doctors, without religious worfhip, advancing in the fand, attracted the attention of the whole affembly; and one of them, addreffing himfelf to the legiflators, fpoke as follows:

" Mediators and umpires of nations! The ftrange recitals that have been made during the whole of the prefent debate, we never till this day heard of; and our underftanding, aftonifhed and bewildered at fuch a multitude of doctrines, fome of them learned, others abfurd, and all unintelligible, remains in doubt and uncertainty. One reflection however has ftruck us : in reviewing fo many prodigious facts, fo many contradictory affertions, we could not avoid afking ourfelves, Of what importance to us are all thefe difcuffions ? Where is the neceffity of our knowing what happened five or fix thoufand years ago, in countries of which we are ignorant, among men who will ever be be unknown to us? True or falfe, of what importance is it to us to know whether the world has exifted fix thoufand years or twenty thoufand; whether it was made of fomething or of nothing; of itfelf, or by an artificer, equally in his turn requiring an author? What! uncertain as we are of what is paffing around us, fhall we pretend to afcertain what is tranfacting in the fun, the moon, and imaginary fpaces? Having forgotten our own infancy, fhall we pretend to know the infancy of the world? Who can atteft what he has never feen? Who can certify the truth of what no one comprehends?

" Befide, what will it avail as to our exiftence, whether we believe or reject thefe chimeras? Hitherto neither our fathers nor ourfelves have had any idea of them, and yet we do not perceive that on that account we have experienced more or lefs fun, more or lefs fubfiftence, more or lefs good or evil.

" If the knowledge of thefe things be neceffary, how is it that we have lived as happily without it as thofe whom it has fo much difquieted? If it be fuperfluous, why fhould we now take upon ourfelves the burthen?"

then ?" — Then addreffing·himfelf to the
doctors and theologians : " How can it be
required of us, poor and ignorant as we are,
whofe every moment is fcarcely adequate to
the cares of our fubfiftence and the labours
of which you reap the profit ; how can it
be required of us to be verfed in the numerous hiftories you have related, to read the
variety of books which you have quoted,
and to learn the different languages in
which they are written ? If our lives were
protracted to a thoufand years, fcarcely
would it be fufficient for this purpofe."

" It is not neceffary," faid the doctors,
" that you fhould acquire all this fcience :
we poffefs it in your ftead."

" Meanwhile," replied thefe children of
fimplicity, " with all your fcience, do you
agree among yourfelves ? What then is its
utility ? Befides, how can you anfwer for
us ? If the faith of one man may be the
fubftitute of the faith of many, what need
was there that you fhould believe ? Your
fathers might believe for you ; and that
would have been the more reafonable, fince
they were the eye-witneffes upon whofe
credit you depend. Laftly, what is this
circumftance

circumftance which you call belief if it has no practical tendency? And what practical tendency can you difcover in this queftion, whether the world be eternal or no?"

" To believe wrong refpecting it would be offenfive to God," faid the doctors.

" How do you know that?" cried the children of fimplicity?

" From our fcriptures," replied the doc-tors.

" We do not underftand them," rejoined the fimple men.

" We underftand them for you," faid the doctors.

" There lies the difficulty," refumed the fimple men. " By what right have you ap-pointed yourfelves mediators between God and us?"

" By the command of God," faid the doctors.

" Give us the proof of that command," faid the fimple men.

" It is in our fcriptures," faid the doctors.

" We do not underftand them," anfwered the fimple men; nor can we underftand how a juft God can place you over our heads. Why does our common Father re-
quire

quire us to believe the fame propofitions with a lefs degree of evidence? He has fpoken to you; be it fo; he is infallible, he cannot deceive you. But we are fpoken to by you; and who will affure us that you are not deceived, or that you are incapable of deceiving? If we are miftaken, how can it confift with the juftice of God, to condemn us for the negleft of a rule with which we were never acquainted?"

" He has given you the law of nature," faid the doctors.

" What is the law of nature?" faid the fimple men. " If this law be fufficient, why does he give us another? If it be infufficient, why did he give us that?"

" The judgments of God," replied the doctors, " are myfterious; his juftice is not reftrained by the rules of human juftice."

" If juftice with him and with us," faid the fimple men, " mean a different thing, what criterion can we have to judge of his juftice? And once more, to what purpofe all thefe laws? What end does he propofe by them?"

" To render you more happy," replied a doctor, " by rendering you better and more virtuous.

virtuous. God has manifefted himfelf by
fo many oracles and prodigies to teach mankind the proper ufe of his benefits, and to
diffuade them from injuring each other."

" If that be the cafe," faid the fimple
men, " the ftudies and reafonings you told us
of are unneceffary : we want nothing but
to have it clearly made out to us, which is
the religion that beft fulfils the end that all
propofe to themfelves."

Inftantly, every groupe boafting of the
fuperior excellence of its morality, there arofe
among the partifans of the different fyftems
of worfhip, a new difpute more violent than
any preceding one. " Ours," faid the Mahometans, " is the pureft morality, which
teaches every virtue ufeful to men and ac-
ceptable to God. We profefs juftice, difin-
tereftednefs, refignation, charity, almfgiving,
and devotion. We torment not the foul
with fuperftitious fears ; we live free from
alarm, and we die without remorfe."

" And have you the prefumption," replied
the Chriftian priefts, " to talk of morality ;
you whofe chief has practifed licentioufnefs,
and preached doctrines that are a fcandal
to all purity, and the leading principle of
whofe

whofe religion is homicide and war. For
the truth of this we appeal to experience.
For twelve centuries paft your fanaticifm
has never ceafed to fpread defolation and
carnage through the nations of the earth;
and that Afia, once fo flourifhing, now
languifhes in infignificance and barbarifm,
is afcribable to your doctrine; to that doctrine, the friend of ignorance, the enemy
of all inftruction, which, on the one hand,
confecrating the moft abfolute defpotifm
in him who commands, and on the other,
impofing the moft blind and paffive obedience on thofe who are governed, has be-
numbed all the faculties of man, and plunged nations in a ftate of brutality.

" How different is the cafe with our fublime
and celeftial morality ! It is fhe that drew
the earth from its primitive barbarity, from
the abfurd and cruel fuperftitions of idolatry,
from human facrifices (100), and the orgies
of Pagan myftery: it is fhe that has purified
the manners of men, profcribed inceft and
adultery, polifhed favage nations, abolifhed
flavery, introduced new and unknown virtues
to the world, univerfal charity, the equality

of

of mankind in the eyes of God, forgivenefs and forgetfulnefs of injuries, extinction of the paffions, contempt of worldly greatnefs, and, in fhort, taught the neceffity of a life perfectly holy and fpiritual."

" We admire," faid the Mahometans, " the eafe with which you can reconcile that evangelical charity and meeknefs of which you fo much boaft, with the injuries and outrages that you are continually exercifing towards your neighbour. When you crimi-- nate with fo little ceremony the morals of the great character revered by us, we have a fair opportunity of retorting upon you in the conduct of him whom you adore: but we dif- dain fuch advantages, and, confining ourfelves to the real object of the queftion, we main- tain, that your gofpel morality is by no means characterifed by the perfection which you afcribe to it. It is not true, that it has in- troduced into the world new and unknown virtues : for example, the equality of man- kind in the eyes of God, and the fraternity and benevolence which are the confequence of this equality, were tenets formerly pro- feffed by the fect of Hermetics and Sama-

X   neans

neans (101), from whom you have your
defcent. As to forgivenefs of injuries, it
had been taught by the Pagans themfelves;
but in the latitude you give to it, it ceafes to
be a virtue, and becomes an immorality and
a crime. Your boafted precept, *to him that
ftrikes thee on thy right cheek turn the other
alfo*, is not only contrary to the feelings of
man, but a flagrant violation of every principle of juftice; it emboldens the wicked by
impunity, degrades the virtuous by the fervility to which it fubjects them; delivers up
the world to diforder and tyranny, and dif-
folves the bands of fociety: fuch is the true
fpirit of your doctrine. The precepts and
parables of your gofpel alfo never reprefent
God other than as a defpot, acting by no
rule of equity; than as a partial father,
treating a debauched and prodigal fon with
greater favour than his obedient and virtuous
children; than as a capricious mafter, giving
the fame wages to him who has wrought but
one hour, as to thofe who have borne the
burthen and heat of the day, and preferring
the laft comers to the firft. In fhort, your
morality throughout is unfriendly to human
                              intercourfe,

intercourfe, a code of mifanthropy, calculated
to give men a difguft for life and fociety, and
attach them to folitude and celibacy.

" With refpect to the manner in which
you have practifed your boafted doctrine, we
in our turn appeal to the teftimony of fact,
and afk : Was it your evangelical meeknefs
and forbearance which excited thofe endlefs
wars among your fectaries, thofe atrocious
perfecutions of what you called heretics,
thofe crufades againft the Arians, the Manicheans and the Proteftants; not to mention
thofe which you have committed againft us,
nor the facrilegious affociations ftill fubfifting
among you, formed of men who have fworn
to perpetuate them * ? Was it the charity
of your gofpel that led you to exterminate
whole nations in America, and to deftroy the
empires of Mexico and Peru; that makes
you ftill defolate Africa, the inhabitants of
which you fell like cattle, notwithftanding
the abolition of flavery that you pretend your
religion has effected; that makes you ravage

---

* The Oath taken by the Knights of the Order of
Malta, is to kill, or make the Mahometans prifoners, for
the glory of God.

India

India whofe domains you ufurp; in fhort, is it charity that has prompted you for three centuries paft to difturb the peaceable inhabitants of three continents, the moft prudent of whom, thofe of Japan and China, have been conftrained to banifh you from their country, that they might efcape your chains and recover their domeftic tranquillity?"

Here the Bramins, the Rabbins, the Bonzes, the Chamans, the priefts of the Molucca Iflands and of the coaft of Guinea, overwhelming the Chriftian doctors with reproaches, cried: "Yes, thefe men are robbers and hypocrites, preaching fimplicity to enveigle confidence; humility, the more eafy to enflave; poverty, in order to appropriate all riches to themfelves; they promife another world the better to invade this; and, while they preach toleration and charity, they commit to the flames, in the name of God, thofe who do not worfhip him exactly as they do."

"Lying priefts," retorted the miffionaries, "it is you who abufe the credulity of ignorant nations, that you may bend them to your yoke: your miniftry is the art of impof-

§   ture

ture, and deception : you have made religion a fyftem of avarice and cupidity : you feign to have correfpondence with fpirits, and the oracles they iffue are your own wills; you pretend to read the ftars, and your defires only are what deftiny decrees : you make idols fpeak, and the Gods are the mere inftruments of your paffions : you have invented facrifices and libations for the fake of the profit you would thus derive from the milk of the flocks, and the flefh and fat of victims; and under the cloak of piety you devour the offerings made to Gods who cannot eat, and the fubftance of the people, obtained by induftry and toil."

"And you," replied the Bramins, the Bonzes, and the Chamans, " fell to the credulous furvivor vain prayers for the fouls of his dead relatives. With your indulgences and abfolutions you have arrogated to yourfelves the power and functions of God himfelf : and making a traffic of his grace, you have put heaven up to auction, and have founded, by your fyftem of expiation, a tariff of crimes that has perverted the confciences of men (102)."

X 3   " Add

"Add to this," faid the Imans, "that with thefe men has originated the moft infidious of all wickednefs, the abfurd and impious obligation of recounting to them the moft impenetrable fecrets of actions, of thoughts, of *velléités*, (confeffion); by means of which their infolent curiofity has carried its inquifition even to the facred fanctuary of the nuptial bed (103), and the inviolable afylum of the heart."

By thus reproaching each other, the chiefs of the different worfhips revealed all the crimes of their miniftry, all the hidden views of their profeffion, and it appeared that the fpirit, the fyftem of conduct, the actions and manners of priefts were, among all nations, uniformly the fame: that, every where they had formed fecret affociations, corporations of individuals, enemies to the reft of the fociety (104):— that they had attributed to themfelves certain prerogatives and immunities, in order to be exempt from the burthens which fell upon the other claffes:—that they fhared neither the toil of the labourer, nor the perils of the foldier, nor the viciffitudes of the merchant:—that they led a life of celibacy,

to

to avoid domeſtic inconveniences and cares :
—that, under the garb of poverty, they found
the ſecret of becoming rich, and of procuring
every enjoyment:—that under the name of
mendicants, they collected impoſts more conſiderable than thoſe paid to princes:—that
under the appellation of gifts and offerings,
they obtained a certain revenue unaccompa-
nied with trouble or expence :—that upon
the pretext of ſecluſion and devotion, they
lived in indolence and licentiouſneſs : —
that they had made alms a virtue, that they
might ſubſiſt in comfort upon the labour of
other men:—that they had invented the ceremonies of worſhip to attract the reverence
of the people, calling themſelves the mediators and interpreters of the Gods, with the
ſole view of aſſuming all his power ; and that
for this purpoſe, according to the knowledge
or ignorance of thoſe upon whom they had
to work, they made themſelves, by turns,
aſtrologers, caſters of planets, augurers, magicians (106), necromancers, quacks, courtiers, confeſſors of princes, always aiming at
influence for their own excluſive advantage:
—that ſometimes they had exalted the pre-

rogative

rogative of kings, and held their perfons to be
facred, to obtain their favour or participate in
their power:—that at others they had decried this doctrine and preached the murder
of tyrants (referving it to themfelves to fpecify the tyranny), in order to be revenged of
the flights and difobedience they had experienced from them:—that at all times they
had called by the name of impiety what proved injurious to their intereft; had oppofed
public inftruction, that they might monopo-
lize fcience; and, in fhort, had univerfally
found the fecret of living in tranquillity
amidft the anarchy they occafioned; fecure,
under the defpotifm they fanctioned; in indolence, amidft the induftry they recommend-
ed; and in abundance, in the very bofom of
fcarcity; and all this, by carrying on the fingular commerce of felling words and geftures
to the credulous, who paid for them as for
commodities of the greateft value (107).

Then the people, feized with fury, were
upon the point of tearing to pieces the men
who had deceived them; but the legiflators,
arrefting this fally of violence, and addreffing
the chiefs and doctors, faid: "And is it thus,
O in-

O inftitutors of the people, that you have milled and abufed them ?"

And the terrified priefts replied: " O legif-lators, we are men, and the people are fo fuperftitious ! their weaknefs excited us to take advantage of it *."

And the kings faid : " O legiflators, the people are fo fervile and fo ignorant ! they have proftrated themfelves before the yoke which we fcarcely had the boldnefs to fhow to them †."

Then the legiflators, turning towards the people, faid to them: " Remember what you have juft heard; it contains two important truths. Yes, it is yourfelves that caufe the evils of which you complain ; it is you that encourage tyrants by a bafe flattery of their power, by an abfurd admiration of their pre-tended beneficence, by converting obedience into fervility, and liberty into licentioufnefs, and receiving every impofition with credulity.

---

* Confider in this view the Brabanters.

† The inhabitants of Vienna, for example, who har-neffed themfelves like cattle, and drew the chariot of Leopold.

Can

Can you think of punifhing upon them the errors of your own ignorance and felfifh-nefs ?"

And the people, fmitten with confufion, remained in a melancholy filence.

C H A P. XXIV.

SOLUTION OF THE PROBLEM OF CON-
TRADICTIONS.

THE legiflators then refumed their addrefs. " O nations!" faid they, " we have heard the difcuffion of your opinions; and the difcord that divides you has fuggefted to us various reflections, which we beg leave to propofe to you as queftions which it is neceffary you fhould folve.

" Confidering, in the firft place, the nu-merous and contradictory creeds you have adopted, we would afk on what motives your perfuafion is founded ? Is it from deliberate choice that you have enlifted under the banners of one prophet rather than under thofe of another ? Before you adopted this doctrine in preference to that, did you firft compare, did you maturely ex-amine them ? Or has not your belief been rather the chance refult of birth, and of the empire of education and habit ? Are you not

not born Chriftians on the banks of the
Tiber, Mahometans on thofe of the Euphrates, Idolaters on the fhores of India, in
the fame manner as you are born fair in
cold and temperate regions, and of a fable
complexion under the African fun! And if
your opinions are the effect of your pofition
on the globe, of parentage, of imitation, are
fuch fortuitous circumftances to be regarded as grounds of conviction and arguments
of truth?

" In the fecond place, when we reflect
on the profcriptive fpirit and the arbitrary
intolerance of your mutual claims, we are
terrified at the confequences that flow from
your principles. Nations! who reciprocally
doom each other to the thunder-bolts of
celeftial wrath, fuppofe the univerfal Being,
whom you revere, were at this moment to
defcend from heaven among this crowd of
people, and, clothed in all his power, were
to fit upon this throne to judge you: fuppofe
him to fay—" Mortals! I confent to adopt
" your own principles of juftice into my ad-
" miniftration. Of all the different reli-
" gions you profefs, a fingle religion fhall
" now

" now be preferred to the reft; all the others,
" this vaft multitude of ftandards, of nations,
" of prophets, fhall be condemned to ever-
" lafting deftruction. Nor is this enough:
" among the different fects of the chofen re-
" ligion one only fhall experience my favour,
" and the reft be condemned. I will go
" farther than this: of this fingle fect of
" this one religion, I will reject all the in-
" dividuals whofe conduct has not corre-
" fponded to their fpeculative precepts. O
" man! few indeed will then be the number
" of the elect you affign me! Penurious
" hereafter will be the ftream of beneficence
" which will fucceed to my unbounded
" mercy? Rare and folitary will be the ca-
" talogue of admirers that you henceforth
" deftine to my greatnefs and my glory."

And the legiflators arifing faid: " It is
enough; you have pronounced your will.
Ye nations, behold the urn in which your
names fhall be placed; one fingle name fhall
be drawn from the multitude; approach and
conclude this terrible lottery."—But the people, feized with terror, cried: " No, no; we
are brethren and equals, we cannot confent

to

to condemn each other."—Then the legiflators having refumed their feats, continued:
" O men! who difpute upon fo many fubjects, lend an attentive ear to a problem we
fubmit to you, and decide it in the exercife
of your own judgments."—The people accordingly lent the ftricteft attention; and the
legiflators lifting one hand towards heaven,
and pointing to the fun, faid: " O nations,
is the form of this fun which enlightens you
triangular or fquare?"—And they replied
with one voice, " It is neither, it is round."

Then taking the golden balance that was
upon the altar, " This metal," afked the
legiflators, " which you handle every day, is
a mafs of it heavier than another mafs of
equal dimenfions of brafs?"—" Yes," the
people again unanimoufly replied; " gold is
heavier than brafs."

The legiflators then took the fword. " Is
this iron lefs hard than lead?"—" No," faid
the nations.

" Is fugar fweet and gall bitter?—" Yes."

" Do you love pleafure, and hate pain?"—
" Yes."

" Refpecting thefe objects and a multiplicity

plicity of others of a fimilar nature, you have then but one opinion. Now tell us, is there an abyfs in the centre of the earth, and are there inhabitants in the moon?"

At this queftion a general noife was heard, and every nation gave a different anfwer. Some replied in the affirmative, others in the negative; fome faid it was probable, others that it was an idle and ridiculous queftion, and others that it was a fubjeft worthy of enquiry; in fhort there prevailed among them a total difagreement.

After a fhort interval, the legiflators having reftored filence : " Nations," faid they, " how is this to be accounted for ? We propofed to you certain queftions, and you were all of one opinion without diftinction of race or feft : fair or black, difciples of Mahomet or of Mofes, worfhippers of Bedou or of Jefus, you all gave the fame anfwer. We now propofe another queftion, and you all differ ! whence this unanimity in one cafe, and this difcordance in the other."

And the groupe of fimple and untaught men replied : " The reafon is obvious. Refpecting the firft queftions, we fee and feel the

the objects; we fpeak of them from fenfation : refpecting the fecond, they are above
the reach of our fenfes, and we have no
guide but conjecture."

"You have folved the problem," faid the
legiflators; "and the following truth is thus
by your own confeffion eftablifhed : Whenever objects are prefent and can be judged of
by your fenfes, you invariably agree in opinion ; and your differ in fentiment only when
they are abfent and out of your reach.

"From this truth flows another equally
clear and deferving of notice. Since you
agree refpecting what you with certainty
know, it follows, that when you difagree, it
is becaufe you do not know, do not underftand, are not fure of the object in queftion :
or in other words, that you difpute, quarrel
and fight among yourfelves, for what is uncertain, for that of which you doubt. But
is this wife ; is this the part of rational and
intelligent beings ?

"And is it not evident, that it is not truth
for which you contend; that it is not her
caufe you are jealous of maintaining, but the
caufe of your own paffions and prejudices ;
that

that it is not the object as it really exifts that
you wifh to verify, but the object as it appears to you; that it is not the evidence of
the thing that you are anxious fhould prevail, but your perfonal opinion, your mode
of feeing and judging? There is a power
that you want to exercife, an intereft that
you want to maintain, a prerogative that you
want to affume; in fhort, the whole is a
ftruggle of vanity. And as every individual,
when he compares himfelf with every other,
finds himfelf to be his equal and fellow, he
refifts by a fimilar feeling of right; and from
this right, which you all deny to each other,
and from the inherent confcioufnefs of your
equality, fpring your difputes, your combats
and your intolerance.

"Now, the only way of reftoring unanimity is by returning to nature, and taking
the order of things which fhe has eftablifhed for your director and guide; and this farther truth will then appear from your uniformity of fentiment:

"That real objects have in themfelves an
identical, conftant, and invariable mode of
exiftence, and that in your organs exifts a

Y   fimilar

fimilar mode of being affected and imprefied by them.

"But at the fame time, inafmuch as thefe organs are liable to the direction of your will, you may receive different impreflions, and find yourfelves under different relations towards the fame objects; fo that you are with refpect to them, as it were a fort of mirror, capable of reflecting them fuch as they are, and capable of disfiguring and mifreprefenting them.

"As often as you perceive the objects, fuch as they are, your feelings are in accord with the objects, and you agree in opinion; and it is this accord that conftitutes truth.

"On the contrary, as often as you differ in opinion, your diffentions prove that you do not fee the objects fuch as they are, but vary them.

"Whence it appears, that the caufe of your diffentions is not in the objects themfelves, but in your minds, in the manner in which you perceive and judge.

"If therefore we would arrive at uniformity of opinion, we muft previoufly eftablifh certainty, and verify the refemblance

blance which our ideas have to their models. Now this cannot be obtained, except
fo far as the objects of our enquiry can
be referred to the teftimony and fubjected
to the examination of our fenfes. Whatever cannot be brought to this trial is beyond the limits of our underftanding; we
have neither rule to try it by, nor meafure
by which to inftitute a comparifon, nor
fource of demonftration and knowledge concerning it.

" Whence it is obvious, that, in order to
live in peace and harmony, we muft confent
not to pronounce upon fuch objects, nor
annex to them importance; we muft draw
a line of demarcation between fuch as can be
verified and fuch as cannot, and feparate by
an inviolable barrier, the world of fantaftic
beings from the world of realities : that is to
fay, all civil effect muft be taken away from
theological and religious opinions.

" This, O nations, is the end that a great
people, freed from their fetters and prejudices, have propofed to themfelves; this is the
work in which, by their command, and under their immediate aufpices, we were en-

gaged,

gaged, when your kings and your priefts came to interrupt our labours. . . . Kings and priefts, you may yet for a while fufpend the folemn publication of the laws of nature; but it is no longer in your power to annihilate or to fubvert them."

A loud cry was then heard from every quarter of the general affembly of nations; and the whole of the people, unanimoufly teftifying their adherence to the fentiments of the legiflators, encouraged them to refume their facred and fublime undertaking. "Inveftigate," faid they, " the laws which nature, for our direction, has implanted in our breafts, and form from thence an authentic and immutable code. Nor let this code be calculated for one family, or one nation only, but for the whole without exception. Be the legiflators of the human race, as ye are the interpreters of their common nature. Shew us the line that feparates the world of chimeras, from that of realities; and teach us, after fo many religions of error and delufion, the religion of evidence and truth."

Upon this, the legiflators refuming their enquiry into the phyfical and conftituent attributes

attributes of man, and the motives and affections which govern him in his individual and focial capacity, unfolded in the following terms the laws on which Nature herfelf has founded his felicity.

END OF THE FIRST PART.

N O T E S.

$\mathbf{P}$ AGE 1. (*) *Eleventh year of Abd-ul Hâmid.* That is, 1784 of the Chriſtian æra, and 1198 of the Hegira. The emigration of the Tartars took place in March, imme‑ diately on the manifeſto of the empreſs declaring the Crimea to be incorporated with Ruſſia. ... *A Muſſul‑ man prince of the name of Gengis Khan.* It was Châhin Guerai. Gengis Khan was borne and ſerved by the kings whom he conquered : Châhin, on the contrary, after ſelling his country for a penſion of eighty thouſand roubles, accepted the commiſſion of captain of guards to Cathe‑ rine II. He afterwards returned home, and, according to cuſtom was ſtrangled by the Turks.

Page 7. (*a*). *The precious thread of Serica.* That is the ſilk originally derived from the mountainous country where the *great wall* terminates, and which appears to have been the cradle of the Chineſe empire. ... The *tiſſues of Caſ‑ ſimere.* The ſhawls which Ezekiel ſeems to have deſcribed under the appellation of Choud-choud. ... *The gold of Ophir.* This country, which was one of the twelve Arab

cantons,

cantons, and which has fo much and fo unfuccefsfully been fought for by the antiquaries, has left however fome trace of itfelf in Ofor, in the province of Oman, upon the Perfian Gulph, neighbouring on one fide to the Sabeans, who are celebrated by Strabo for their plenty of gold, and on the other to Aula or Hevila where the pearl fifhery was carried on. See the 27th chapter of Ezekiel, ✷ which gives a very curious and extenfive picture of the commerce of Afia at that period.

Page 8. (b). *This Syria contained a hundred flourifhing cities.* According to Jofephus and Strabo, there were in Syria twelve millions of fouls; and the traces that remain of culture and habitation confirm the calculation.

Page 12. (c). *A blind fatality.* This is the univerfal and rooted prejudice of the Eaft. " It was written," is there the anfwer to every thing. Hence refult an unconcern and apathy, the moft powerful impediments to inftruction and civilization.

Page 28. (d). *The too famous peninfula of India.* Of what real good has been the commerce of India to the mafs of the people ? On the contrary, how great the evil occafioned by the fuperftition of this country having been added to the general fuperftition ?

Page 29. (e). *Ancient kingdom of Ethiopia.* In the next volume of the Encyclopedia will appear a memoir refpecting the chronology of the twelve ages anterior to the paffing of Xerxes into Greece, in which I conceive myfelf to have proved, that Upper Egypt formerly compofed a diftinct kingdom, known to the Hebrews by the name of *Kous,* and to which the appellation of Ethiopia was fpecially given. This kingdom preferved its independence to the time of Pfammeticus, at which period, being

united

united to the Lower Egypt, it loft its name of Ethiopia, which thenceforth was beftowed upon the nations of Nubia, and upon the different hordes of Blacks, including Thebes, their metropolis.

Page *id.* (*f*). *Thebes with its hundred palaces.* The idea of a city with a hundred gates, in the common acceptation of the word, is fo abfurd, that I am aftonifhed the equivoque has not before been felt.

It has ever been the cuftom of the Eaft to call palaces and houfes of the great by the name of gates, becaufe the principal luxury of thefe buildings confifts in the fingular gate leading from the ftreet into the court, at the fartheft extremity of which the palace is fituated. It is under the veftibule of this gate that converfation is held with paffengers, and a fort of audience and hofpitality given. All this was doubtlefs known to Homer; but poets make no commentaries, and readers love the marvellous.

This city of Thebes, now Lougfor, reduced to the condition of a miferable village, has left aftonifhing monuments of its magnificence. Particulars of this may be feen in the plates of Norden, in Pocock, and in the recent travels of Bruce. Thefe monuments give credibility to all that Homer has related of its fplendour, and led us to infer of its political power and external commerce.

Its geographical pofition was favourable to this twofold object. For, on one fide, the valley of the Nile, fingularly fertile, muft have early occafioned a numerous population; and, on the other, the Red Sea giving communication with Arabia and India, and the Nile with Abyffinia and the Mediterranean, Thebes was thus naturally allied to the richeft countries on the globe; an

alliance

alliance that procured it an activity fo much the greater,
as Lower Egypt, at firft a fwamp, was nearly, if not totally, uninhabited. But when at length this country had
been drained by the canals and dikes which Sefoftris
conftructed, population was introduced there, and wars
arofe which proved fatal to the power of Thebes. Commerce then took another route, and defcended to the
point of the Red Sea, to the canals of Sefoftris (See
Strabo) and wealth and activity were transformed to
Memphis. This is manifeftly what Diodorus means,
when he tells us (Lib. I. fect. 2.) that as foon as Memphis was eftablifhed and made a wholefome and delicious
abode, kings abandoned Thebes to fix themfelves there.
Thus Thebes continued to decline, and Memphis to
flourifh till the time of Alexander, who, building Alexandria on the border of the fea, caufed Memphis to fall
in its turn; fo that profperity and power feem to have
defcended hiftorically ftep by ftep along the Nile: whence
it refults, both phyfically and hiftorically, that the exiftence of Thebes was prior to that of the other cities. The
teftimony of writers is very pofitive in this refpect. " The
" Thebans," fays Diodorus, " confider themfelves as the
" moft ancient people of the earth, and affert, that with
" them originated philofophy and the fcience of the
" ftars. Their fituation, it is true, is infinitely favourable
" to aftronomical obfervation, and they have a more accu-
" rate divifion of time into months and year than other
" nations, &c."

What Diodorus fays of the Thebans, every author and
himfelf elfewhere, repeat of the Ethiopians, which tends
more firmly to eftablifh the identity of place of which I
have fpoken. " The Ethiopians conceive themfelves (fays

" he,

" he, Lib. III.) to be of greater antiquity than any other
" nation : and it is probable that, born under the fun's path,
" its warmth may have ripened them earlier than other
" men. They fuppofe themfelves alfo to be the inventors
" of divine worfhip, of feftivals, of folemn affemblies,
" of facrifices, and every other religious practice. They
" affirm that the Egyptians are one of their colonies, and
" that the Delta, which was formerly fea, became land
" by the conglomeration of the earth of the higher
" country, which was wafhed down by the Nile. They
" have, like the Egyptians, two fpecies of letters, hiero-
" glyphics and the alphabet; but among the Egyptians
" the firft was known only to the priefts, and by them
" tranfmitted from father to fon, whereas both fpecies are
" common among the Ethiopians."

" The Ethiopians," fays Lucian, page 985, " were the
" firft who invented the fcience of the ftars, and gave
" names to the planets, not at random and without mean-
" ing, but defcriptive of the qualities which they con-
" ceived them to poffefs; and it was from them that
" this art paffed, ftill in an imperfect ftate, to the Egyp-
" tians."

It would be eafy to multiply citations upon this fubject;
from all which it follows, that we have the ftrongeft
reafon to believe that the country neighbouring to the
tropic, was the cradle of the fciences, and of confequence
that the firft learned nation was a nation of Blacks, for
it is incontrovertible, that by the term Ethiopians, the
ancients meant to reprefent a people of black complexion,
thick lips, and woolly hair. I am therefore inclined to
believe, that the inhabitants of Lower Egypt were originally a foreign colony imported from Syria and Arabia, a
medley

medley of different tribes of Savages, originally fhepherds
and fifhermen, who by degrees formed themfelves into a
nation, and who, by nature and defcent, were enemies of
the Thebans, by whom they were no doubt defpifed and
treated as barbarians.

I have fuggefted the fame ideas in my Travels into
Syria, founded upon the black complexion of the Sphinx.
I have fince afcertained, that the antique images of
Thebais have the fame characteriftic; and Mr. Bruce
has offered a multitude of analogous facts : but this
traveller, of whom I heard fome mention at Cairo, has
fo interwoven thefe facts with certain fyftematic opinions,
that we fhould have recourfe to his narratives with
caution.

It is fingular that Africa, fituated fo near us, fhould be
the country on earth which is the leaft known. The
Englifh are at this moment making attempts, the fuccefs
of which ought to excite our emulation.

Page 30. (g). *Here were the ports of the Idumeans,*
Ailah (Eloth), and Atfiom-Gaber (Hefion-Geber).
The name of the firft of thefe towns ftill fubfifts in its
ruins, at the point of the gulph of the Red Sea, and in
the route which the pilgrims take to Mecca. Hefion
has at prefent no trace, any more than Qolzoum and
Faran : it was, however, the harbour for the fleets of
Solomon. The veffels of this prince, conducted by the
Tyrians, failed along the coaft of Arabia to Ophir in the
Perfian Gulph, thus opening a communication with the
merchants of India and Ceylon. That this navigation
was entirely of Tyrian invention, appears both from the
pilots and fhipbuilders employed by the Jews, and the
names that were given to the trading iflands. viz. Tyrus

and

and Aradus, now Barhain. The voyage was performed in two diffent modes, either in canoes of ofier and rufhes, covered on the outfide with fkins done over with pitch : thefe veffels were unable to quit the Red Sea, or fo much as to leave the fhore. The fecond mode of carrying on the trade was by means of veffels with decks of the fize of our long boats, which were able to pafs the ftrait and to weather the dangers of the ocean : but for this purpofe it was neceffary to bring the wood from Mount Lebanus and Cilicia, where it is very fine and in great abundance. This wood was firft conveyed in floats from Tarfus to Phenicia, for which reafon the veffels were called fhips of Tarfus: from whence it has been ridiculoufly inferred, that they went round the promontary of Africa as far as Tortofa in Spain. From Phenicia it was tranfported on the backs of camels to the Red Sea, which practice ftill continues, becaufe the fhores of this fea are abfolutely unprovided with wood even for fuel. Thefe veffels fpent a complete year in their voyage, that is, failed one year, fojourned another, and did not return till the third. This tedioufnefs was owing, firft to their cruizing from port to port, as they do at prefent; fecondly, to their being detained by the Monfoon currents; and thirdly, becaufe, according to the calculations of Pliny and Strabo, it was the ordinary practice among the ancients to fpend three years in a voyage of twelve hundred leagues. Such a commerce muft have been very expenfive, particularly as they were obliged to carry with them their provifions and even frefh water. For this reafon Solomon made himfelf mafter of Palmyra, which was at that time inhabited, and was already the magazine and high road of merchants by the way of the Euphrates.

This

This conqueſt brought Solomon much nearer to the
country of gold and pearls. This alternative of a route
either by the Red Sea or by the river Euphrates was to
the ancients, what in later times has been the alternative
in a voyage to the Indies, either by croſſing the Iſthmus
of Suez or doubling the Cape of Good Hope. It appears
that till the time of Moſes this trade was carried on acroſs
the deſert of Syria and Theais; that afterwards it fell
into the hands of the Phenicians, who fixed its ſite upon
the Red ſea, and that it was mutual jealouſy that induced
the kings of Nineveh and Babylon to undertake the deſtruction of Tyre and Jeruſalem. I inſiſt the more upon
theſe facts, becauſe I have never ſeen any thing reaſonable
upon the ſubject.

Page 31. (*h*). *Babylon, the ruins of which are trodden under foot of men.* It appears that Babylon occupied on the
Eaſtern Bank of the Euphrates a ſpace of ground ſix
leagues in length. Throughout this ſpace bricks are found,
by means of which daily additions are made to the town
of Hellé. Upon many of theſe are characters written with
a nail ſimilar to thoſe of Perſepolis. I am indebted for
theſe facts to M. de Beauchamp, grand vicar of Babylon,
a traveller equally diſtinguiſhed for his knowledge of aſtronomy and his veracity.

Page 59. (*i*). *Thoſe wells of Tyre.* See reſpecting theſe
monuments, my Travels into Syria, vol. ii. p. 214.

Theſe artificial banks of the Euphrates. From the town
or village of Samaouät the courſe of the Euphrates is
accompanied with a double bank, which deſcends as far
as its junction with the Tygris, and from thence to the
ſea, being a length of about a hundred leagues French
meaſure. The height of theſe artificial banks is not uni-

form,

form, but increafes as you advance from the fea; it may
be eftimated at from twelve to fifteen feet. But for them,
the inundation of the river would bury the country
around, which is flat, to an extent of twenty or twenty-
five leagues; and even, notwithftanding thefe banks, there
has been in modern times an overflow which has covered
the whole triangle formed by the junction of this river
to the Tigris, being a fpace of country of 130 fquare
leagues. By the ftagnation of thefe waters an epidemical
difeafe of the moft fatal nature was occafioned. It follows
from hence, 1. That all the flat country bordering upon
thefe rivers was originally a marfh; 2. That this marfh
could not have been inhabited previoufly to the conftruc-
tion of the banks in queftion; 3. That thefe banks could
not have been the work but of a population prior as to
date: and the elevation of Babylon therefore muft have
been pofterior to that of Nineveh, as I think I have chro-
nologically demonftrated in the memoir above cited. See
Encyclopedie, vol. xiii. of Antiquities.

Page *id. (k)*. *Thofe conduits of Medea.* The modern
Aderbidjàn, which was a part of Medea, the mountains
of Kourdeftan, and thofe of Diarbekr, abound with
fubterranean canals, by means of which the ancient inhabitants conveyed water to their parched foil in order to
fertilize it. It was regarded as a meritorious act, and a
religious duty prefcribed by Zoroafter, who, inftead of
preaching celibacy, mortifications, and other pretended
virtues of the Monkifh fort, repeats continually in the
paffages that are preferved refpecting him in the Sad-der
and the Zend-avefta, " That the action moft pleafing to
" God is to plough and cultivate the earth, to water it
" with running ftreams, to multiply vegetation and living
" beings,

" beings, to have numerous flocks, young and fruitful
" virgins, a multitude of children, &c. &c."

Page 62. *(l)*. *This inequality, the result of accident, was
taken for the law of nature.* Almoſt all the ancient philoſophers and politicians have laid it down as a principle,
that men are born unequal, that nature has created ſome
to be free, and others to be ſlaves. Expreſſions of this
kind are to be found in Ariſtotle, and even in Plato,
called the divine, doubtleſs in the ſame ſenſe as the mythological reveries which he promulgated. With all the
people of antiquity, the Gauls, the Romans, the Athe-
nians, the right of the ſtrongeſt was the right of nations; and from the ſame principle are derived all the
political diſorders and public national crimes that at preſent exiſt.

Page *id. (m)*. *Paternal tyranny laid the foundation of
political deſpotiſm.* Upon this ſingle expreſſion it would
be eaſy to write a long and important chapter. We
might prove in it, beyond contradiction, that all the
abuſes of national governments have ſprung from thoſe
of domeſtic government, from that government called
patriarchal, which ſuperficial minds have extolled without
having analyzed it. Numberleſs facts demonſtrate, that
with every infant people, in every ſavage and barbarous
ſtate, the father, the chief of the family, is a deſpot, and a
cruel and inſolent deſpot. The wife is his ſlave, the
children his ſervants. This king ſleeps or ſmokes his
pipe, while his wife and daughters perform all the
drudgery of the houſe, and even that of tillage and cultivation, as far as occupations of this nature are practiſed
in ſuch ſocieties; and no ſooner have the boys acquired
ſtrength, than they are allowed to beat the females and.
make

make them ferve and wait upon them as they do upon
their fathers. Similar to this is the ftate of our own uncivilized peafants. In proportion as civilization fpreads,
the manners become milder, and the condition of the
women improves, till, by a contrary excefs, they arrive
at dominion, and then a nation becomes effeminate and
corrupt. It is remarkable, that parental authority is great
according as the government is defpotic. China, India,
and Turkey are ftriking examples of this. One would
fuppofe that tyrants gave themfelves accomplices, and
interefted fubaltern defpots to maintain their authority.
In oppofition to this the Romans will be cited; but it remains to be proved that the Romans were men truly
free; and their quick paffage from their republican defpotifm to their abject fervility under the emperors, gives
room at leaft for confiderable doubts as to that freedom.

Page 67. (*n*). *Always tending to concenter the power in
a fingle hand.* It is remarkable, that this has in all inftances been the conftant progrefs of focieties : beginning
with a ftate of anarchy or democracy, that is, with a great
divifion of power, they have paffed to ariftocracy, and from
ariftocracy to monarchy. Does it not hence follow, that
thofe who conftitute ftates under the democratic form,
deftine them to undergo all the intervening troubles between that and monarchy; and that the fupreme adminiftration by a fingle chief is the moft natural government, as well as that beft calculated for peace ?

Page 69. (*o*). *And kings followed the dictates of every
depraved tafte.* It is equally worthy of remark, that the
conduct and manners of princes and kings of every country and every age, are found to be precifely the fame at

Z   fimilar

fimilar periods, whether of the formation or diffolution of empires. Hiftory every where prefents the fame pictures of luxury and folly; of parks, gardens, lakes, rocks, palaces, furniture, excefs of the table, wine, women, concluding with brutality.

The abfurd rock in the garden of Verfailles has alone coft three millions. I have fometimes calculated what might have been done with the expence of the three pyramids of Gizah, and I have found that it would eafily have conftructed, from the Red Sea to Alexandria, a canal 150 feet wide and 30 deep, completely covered in with cut ftones and a parapet, together with a fortified and commercial town, confifting of 400 houfes furnifhed with cifterns. What difference in point of utility between fuch a canal and thefe pyramids?

Page 79. (p). *By their led horfes, &c.* A Tartar horfe-man has always two horfes, of which he leads one in hand. . . . The *Kalpak* is a bonnet made of the fkin of a fheep or other animal. The part of the head covered by this bonnet is fhaved, with the exception of a tuft about the fize of a crown-piece, and which is fuffered to grow to the length of feven or eight inches, precifely where our priefts place their tonfure. It is by this tuft of hair, worn by the majority of Muffulmans, that the angel of the tomb is to take the elect and carry them into Para-dife.

Page 80. (q). *Infidels are in poffeffion of a confecrated land.* It is not in the power of the fultan to cede to a foreign power a province inhabited by TRUE BELIEVERS. The people, inftigated by the lawyers, would not fail to revolt. This is one reafon which has led thofe who know the

§   Turks,

'Turks, to regard as chimerical the ceding of Candia, Cyprus, and Egypt, projected by certain European potentates.

Page 86. (*r*). *Pronouncing myfterioufly the word Aûm.* This word is in the religion of the Hindoos a facred emblem of the Divinity. It is only to be pronounced in fecret, without being heard by any one. It is formed of three letters, of which the firft, *a*, fignifies the principle of all, the creator, Brama; the fecond, *u*, the confervator, Vichenou; and the laft, *m*, the deftroyer, who puts an end to all, Chiven. It is pronounced like the monofyllable ôm, and expreffes the unity of thofe three Gods. The idea is precifely that of the Alpha and Omega mentioned in the New Teftament.

Page *id.* (*s*). *Whether he ought to begin the ceremony at the elbow, &c.* This is one of the grand points of fchifm between the partizans of Omar and thofe of Ali. Suppofe two Mahometans to meet on a journey, and to accoft each other with brotherly affection: the hour of prayer arrives; one begins his ablution at his fingers, the other at the elbow, and inftantly they are mortal enemies. O fublime importance of religious opinions! O profound philofophy of the authors of them!

Page 99. (*t*). *The horde of Oguzians.* Before the Turks took the name of their chief Othman I. they bore that of Oguzians; and it was under this appellation that they were driven out of Tartary by Gengis, and came from the borders of Gihoun to fettle themfelves in Anatolia.

Page 100. (*u*). *A general anarchy take place, as happened in the empire of the Sophis.* In Perfia, after the death of Thamas-Koulikan, each province had its chief, and for

forty

forty years thefe chiefs were in a conftant ftate of war.
In this view the Turks do not fay without reafon: " Ten
" years of a tyrant are lefs deftructive than a fingle night
" of anarchy."

Page 107. (x). *From people to people barbarous wars were
prevalent.* Read the hiftory of the wars of Rome and
Carthage, of Sparta and Meffina, of Athens and Syracufe,
of the Hebrews and the Phenicians : yet thefe are the nations of which antiquity boafts as being moft polifhed !

Page 114. (y). *The decifion of their difputes.* What is
a people ? An individual of the fociety at large. What
a war ? A duel between two individual people. In what
manner ought a fociety to act when two of its members
fight ? Interfere and reconcile, or reprefs them. In the
days of the Abbe de Saint-Pierre this was treated as a
dream, but happily for the human race it begins to be
realized.

Page 119. (z). *The Chinefe fubjected to an infolent defpotifm.* The emperor of China calls himfelf the fon of
heaven, that is, of God; for in the opinion of the Chinefe,
the material heaven, the arbiter of fatality, is the Deity
himfelf. " The emperor only fhows himfelf once in ten
" months, left the people, accuftomed to fee him, might
" lofe their refpect; for he holds it as a maxim, that
" power can only be fupported by force, that the people
" have no idea of juftice, and are not to be governed but
" by coercion." *Narrative of two Mahometan Travellers*
in 851 and 877, tranflated by the Abbe Renaudot in
1718.

Notwithftanding what is afferted by the miffionaries,
this fituation has undergone no change. The bamboo
ftill reigns in China, and the fon of heaven baftinades,

for

for the moſt trivial fault, the Mandarin, who, in his turn, baſtinades the people. The Jeſuits may tell us that this is the beſt governed country in the world, and its inhabitants the happieſt of men : but a ſingle letter from Amyot has convinced me, that China is a truly Turkiſh government, and the account of Sonnerat confirms it. See Vol. ii. of *Voyage aux Indes*, in 4to.

The irremediable vice of their language. As long as the Chineſe ſhall in writing make uſe of their preſent characters, they can be expected to make no progreſs in civilization. The neceſſary introductory ſtep muſt be the giving them an alphabet like our own, or the ſubſtituting in the room of their language that of the Tartars : the improvement made in the latter by M. de Lengles, is calculated to introduce this change. See the *Mantchou alphabet*, the production of a mind truly learned in the formation of language.

Page 119. (1.) *In the North I ſee nothing but ſerfs reduced to the level of cattle.* When this was written the revolution in Poland had not taken place. I beg leave to apologiſe to the virtuous nobles and the enlightened prince by whom it was effected.

Page 128. (2.) *And govern yourſelves.* This dialogue between the people and the indolent claſſes, is applicable to every ſociety ; it contains the ſeeds of all the political vices and diſorders that prevail, and which may tnus be defined ; men who do nothing, and who devour the ſubſtance of others ; and men who arrogate to themſelves particular rights and excluſive privileges of wealth and indolence. Compare the Mamlouks of Egypt, the nobility of Europe, the Nairs of India, the Emirs of Arabia, the Patricians of Rome, the Chriſtian clergy, the Imans,

the

the Bramins, the Bonzes, the Lamas, &c. &c. and you
will find in all the same characteristic feature,—" Men
" living in idlenefs at the expence of thofe who labour."

Page 138. (3). *Equality and liberty conflitute the phyfical
bafis.* In the declaration of rights there is an inverfion of
ideas in the firft article, liberty being placed before equality from which it in reality fprings. This defect is not
to be wondered at; the fcience of the rights of man is
a new fcience; it was invented yefterday by the Ameri-
cans, to day the French are perfecting it, but there yet
remains a great deal to be done. In the ideas that conflitute it there is a genealogical order which, from its
bafis, phyfical equality, to the minuteft and moft remote
branches of government, ought to proceed in an uninterrupted feries of inferences. This will be demonftrated
in the fecond part of this work.

Page 147. (4.) *A vaft hat of the leaves of the palm-tree.*
This fpecies of the palm-tree is called *Latanier.* Its leaf,
fimilar to a fan-mount, grows upon a ftalk iffuing directly
from the earth. A fpecimen may be feen in the botanic
garden.

Page 148. (5.) *The contemplation of one fpecies thus infinitely varied.* A hall of coftumes in one of the galleries
of the Louvre, would in every point of view be an interefting eftablifhment: it would furnifh an admirable
treat to the curiofity of a great number of men, excellent
models to the artift, and ufeful fubjects of meditation to
the phyfician, the philofopher, and the legiflator. Picture
to yourfelf a collection of the various faces and figures of
every country and nation, exhibiting accurately colour,
features and form: what a field for inveftigation and enquiry as to the influence of climate, manners, aliment,
&c.!

&c. ! It might truly be ftyled the fcience of man ! Buffon
has attempted a chapter of this nature, but it only ferves
to exhibit more ftrikingly our actual ignorance. Such a
collection it is faid is begun at Peterfburg, but it is faid at
the fame time, to be as imperfect as the vocabulary of
the 300 languages. The enterprize would be worthy of
the French nation.

Page 157. (6). *Thus are there fects to the number of feventy-two.* The Muffulmans enumerate in common feventy-two fects; but I read, while I refided among them,
a work which gave an account of more than eighty, all
equally wife and important.

Page *id.* (7). *Has never ceafed for twelve hundred years.*
Read the hiftory of Iflamifm by its own writers, and you
will be convinced that one of the principal caufes of the
wars which have defolated Afia and Africa fince the days
of Mahomet, has been the apoftolical fanaticifm of its
doctrine. Cæfar has been fuppofed to have deftroyed
three millions of men : it would be interefting to make a
fimilar calculation refpecting every founder of a religious
fyftem.

Page 161. (8). *The Neftorians, the Eutycheans, and a
hundred others.* Confult upon this fubject *Dictionnaire
des Herefies par l'Abbe Pluquet,* in two volumes, 8vo ; a
work admirably calculated to infpire the mind with philofophy, in the fenfe that the Lacedemonians taught
their children temperance, by fhewing to them the drunken
Heliotes.

Page 163. (9). *Difciples of Zoroafter.* They are the
Parfes, better known by the opprobrious name of Gaures
or Guebres, another word for infidels. They are in Afia

what the Jews are in Europe. The name of their pope
or high prieſt is Mobed.

Page 164. (10). *Their Deſcurs*; that is to ſay, their
prieſts. See, reſpecting the rites of this religion, *Henry
Lord, Hyde*, and the *Zendaveſta*. Their coſtuma is a robe
with a belt of four knots, and a veil over the mouth for
fear of polluting the fire with their breath.

Page *id.* (11). *The reſurrection of the body, or the ſoul,
or both.* The Zoroaſtrians are divided between two
opinions, one party believing that both ſoul and body will
riſe, the other, that it will be the ſoul only. The
Chriſtians and Mahometans have embraced the moſt ſolid
of the two.

Page 165. (12). *They wear a net over their mouths, &c.*
According to the ſyſtem of the Metempſychoſis, a ſoul, to
undergo purification, paſſes into the body of ſome inſect
or animal. It is of importance not to diſturb this penance,
as the work muſt in that caſe begin afreſh. . . . *Paria.*
This is the name of a caſt or tribe reputed unclean, becauſe they eat of what has enjoyed life.

Page *id.* (13). *Brhma.—reduced to ſerve as a pedeſtal to
the Lingam.* See *Sonnerat, Voyage aux Indes.* Vol. I.

Page 166. (14). *Hideous forms of a boar, a lion, &c.*
Theſe are the incarnations of Vichenou, or metamorphoſes
of the ſun. He is to come at the end of the world, that
is, at the expiration of the great period, in the form of a
horſe, like the four horſes of the apocalypſe.

Page *id.* (15). *In their devotion, &c.* When a ſectary
of Chiven hears the name of Vichenou pronounced, he
ſtops his ears, flies, and purifies himſelf.

Page 167. (16). *The Chineſe worſhip him under the name
ơf*

of Fôt. The original name of this God is *Baits*, which in Hebrew fignifies an egg. The Arabs pronounce in *Baidb*, giving to the *db* an emphatic found which makes it approach to *dz.* Kempfer, an accurate traveller, writes it *Budjo*, which muſt be pronounced *Boudſo*, whence is derived the name of Budfoiſt and of Bonze, applied to the prieſts. Clement of Alexandria, in his Stromata, writes it *Bedou*, as it is pronounced alfo by the Chingulais; and Saint Jerome, *Bouddi* and *Boutta.* At Thibet they call it *Budd :* and hence the name of the country called *Boud-tan* and *Ti-budd:* it was in this province that this fyſtem of religion was firſt inculcated in Upper Afia; *La* is a corruption of *Allah*, the name of God in the Syriac language, from which many of the Eaſtern dialects appear to be derived. The Chinefe having neither *b* nor *d*, have fupplied their place by *f* and *t*, and have therefore faid *Fout.*

Page 168. (17). *That the foul can exiſt independently of the fenfes.* See in Kempfer the doctrine of the Sintoiſts, which is a mixture of that of Epicurus and of the Stoics.

Page *id.* (18). *Talipat fcreen.* It is a leaf of the *Latanier* fpecies of the palm tree. Hence the Bonzes of Siam take the appellation of *Talapoin.* The ufe of this fcreen is an exclufive privilege.

Page 169. ('9). *Conjunction of the ſtars.* The fectaries of Confucius are no lefs addicted to aſtrology than the Bonzes. It is indeed the malady of every eaſtern nation.

Page *id.* (20). *The Grand Lama. The Delai-La-Ma,* or immenfe high prieſts of *La*, is the fame perfon whom we find mentioned in our old books of travels, by the

name

name of Prefter John, from a corruption of the Perfian word *Dschan,* which fignifies the world, to which has been prefixed the French word preftre or prêtre, prieft. Thus the *prieft world* and the *God world* are in the Perfian idiom the fame.

Page *id.* (21). *The excrements of their pontiff.* In a recent expedition, the Englifh have found certain idols of the Lamas filled in the infide with facred paftils from the clofe-ftool of the high-prieft. Mr. Haftings, and Colonel Pollier who is now at Laufanne, are living witneffes of this fact, and undoubtedly worthy of credit. It will be very extraordinary to obferve, that this difgufting ceremony is connected with a profound philofophical fyftem, to wit, that of the metempfychofis, admitted by the Lamas. When the Tartars fwallow thefe facred relics, which they are accuftomed to do, they imitate the laws of the univerfe, the parts of which are inceffantly abforbed and pafs into the fubftance of each other. It is upon the model of the ferpent who devours his tail, and this ferpent is Budd and the world.

Page 170. (22). *The inhabitant of Juida, &c.* It frequently happens, that the fwine devour the very fpecies of ferpents which the negroes adore, which is a fource of great defolation in the country. Prefident de Broffes has given us in his hiftory of the *Fetiche,* a curious collection of abfurdities of this nature. . . . *The Teleutean dreffes, &c.* The Teleuteans, a Tartar nation, paint God as wearing a vefture of all colours, particularly red and green; and as thefe conftitute the uniform of the Ruffian dragoons, they compare him to this defcription of foldiers. The Egyptians alfo drefs the God World in a

garment

garment of every colour. *Eusebius Præp. Evang. p.* 115.
l. 3. The Teleuteans call God *Bou*, which is only an alteration of Boudd, the God Egg and World.

Page *id.* (23). *The Kamchadale represents God under
the figure of an ill-natured and arbitrary old man.* Consult upon this subject a work entitled, *Description des Peuples soumis à la Russe*, and it will be found that the picture
is not overcharged.

Page 179. (24.) *His son-in-law Ali, or his vicars Omar
and Aboubekre.* These are the two grand parties into
which the Mussulmans are divided. The Turks have
embraced the second, the Persians the first.

Page 182. (25). *To make war upon infidels.* Whatever
the advocates for the philosophy and civilization of the
Turks may affirm, to make war upon infidels is confidered
by them as an obligatory precept and an act of religion.
See *Reland de Relig. Moham.*

Page 190. (26). *Your system rests entirely on mystical interpretations.* When we read the fathers of the church,
and see upon what arguments they have built the edifice
of religion, we are inexpressibly astonished with their
credulity, or their knavery; but allegory was the rage of
that period: the Pagans employed it to explain the actions
of their Gods, and the Christians acted in the same spirit
when they employed it after their fashion.

Page 195. (27). *It was not till four hundred years after.*
See the Chronology of the Twelve Ages, in which I conceive myself to have clearly proved that Moses lived about
1400 years before Jesus Christ, and Zoroaster about a
thousand.

Page 196. (28). *In the corrected publication of their sacred
books.* In the first periods of the Christian church, not
only

only the moſt learned of thoſe who have ſince been denominated heretics, but many of the orthodox, conceived
Moſes to have written neither the law nor the Penta-
teuch, but that the work was a compilation made by the
elders of the people and the Seventy, who, after the death
of Moſes, collected his ſcattered ordinances, and mixed
with them things that were extraneous; ſimilar to what
happened as to the Koran of Mahomet. See *Les Clemen-
tines*, Homel. 2. ſect. 51. and Homel. 3. ſect. 42.

Modern critics, more enlightened or more attentive
than the ancients, have found in Geneſis in particular,
marks of its having been compoſed on the return from
the captivity; but the principal proofs have eſcaped them.
Theſe I mean to exhibit in an analyſis of the book of
Geneſis, in which I ſhall demonſtrate that the tenth
chapter, among others, which treats of the pretended
generations of the Man called Noah, is a real geographical picture of the world, as it was known to the Hebrews
at the epoch of the captivity, which was bounded by
Greece or Hellas at the Weſt, mount Caucaſus at the
North, Perſia at the Eaſt, and Arabia and Upper Egypt
at the South. All the pretended perſonages from Adam
to Abraham or his father Terah, are mythological beings,
ſtars, conſtellations, countries. Adam is Bootes; Noah
is Oſyris, Xiſuthrus Janus, Saturn; that is to ſay Capricorn, or the celeſtial Genius that opened the year. The
Alexandrian Chronicle ſays expreſsly, page 85, that
Nimrod was ſuppoſed by the Perſians to be their firſt
king, as having invented the art of hunting, and that he
was tranſlated into heaven, where he appears under the
name of Orion.

Page 197. (29). *Creation of the world in ſix gahans*, or
periods,

periods, or into fix *gahan-bars*, that is, fix periods of time. Thefe periods are what Zoroafter calls the *thoufands of God* or of *light*, meaning the fix fummer months. In the firſt, ſay the Perſians, God created (arranged in order) the heavens; in the fecond the waters; in the third the earth; in the fourth trees; in the fifth animals; and in the fixth man: correfponding with the account in Genefis. For particulars fee *Hyde*, *ch*. 9. and *Henry Lord*, *ch*. 2. *On the religion of the ancient Perfians*. It is remarkable, that the fame tradition is found in the facred books of the Etrurians, which relate, " that the " Fabricator of all things had comprifed the duration of " his work in a period of twelve thoufand years, which " period was diſtributed to the twelve houfes of the fun." In the firſt thoufand, God made heaven and earth; in the fecond, the firmament; in the third, the fea and the waters; in the fourth, the fun, moon, and ſtars; in the fifth, the foul of animals, birds, and reptiles; in the fixth, man. See *Suidas*, at the word *Tyrrhena*; which ſhows firſt, the identity of their theological and aſtrological opinions; and fecondly, the identity, or rather confufion of ideas, between abfolute and fyſtematical creation, that is, the periods aſſigned for renewing the face of nature, which were at firſt the period of the year, and afterwards periods of 60, of 600, of 25,000, of 36,000, and of 432,000 years.

Page 198. (30). *Auricular confeſſion*, &c. The modern Parfes and the ancient Mithriacs, who are the fame fect, obferve all the Chriſtian facraments, even the laying on of hands in confirmation. " The prieſt of Mithra," fays Tertullian (de Præfcriptione, c. 40.) " promifes ab-
" folution from fin on confeffion and baptifm; and, if I
" rightly

" rightly remember, Mithra marks the foldiers in the fore-
" head (with the chrifm, called in Egyptian *Kouphi*) ; he
" celebrates the facrifice of bread, which is the refurrec-
" tion, and prefents the crown to his followers, menacing
" them at the fame time with the fword; &c."

In thefe mysteries they tried the courage of the initiated
with a thoufand terrors, prefenting fire to his face, a
fword to his breast, &c.; they alfo offered him a crown
which he refufed, faying, God is my crown : and this
crown is to be feen in the celeftial fphere by the fide of
Bootes. The perfonages in thefe mysteries were distin-
guifhed by the names of the animal conftellations. The
ceremony of mafs is nothing more than an imitation of
thefe mysteries and thofe of Eleufis. The benediction *the*
Lord be with you, is a literal tranflation of the formular
of admiffion *chen-k. am, p-ak.* See *Beaufob. Hist. Du*
Manicheifme, vol. ii.

Page 199. (31). *The Vedes, the Chaftres, and the Pourans.*
Thefe are the facred volumes of the Hindoos ; they are
fometimes written *Vedams, Pouranams, Chaftrans,* becaufe the Hindoos, like the Perfians, are accuftomed to
give a nafal found to the terminations of their words;
which we reprefent by the affixes *en* and *an,* and the
Portuguefe by the affixes *em* and *am.* Many of thefe
books have been tranflated, thanks to the liberal fpirit of
Mr. Haftings, who has founded at Calcutta a literary
fociety and a printing prefs. At the fame time, however, that we exprefs our gratitude to this fociety, we
muft be permitted to complain of its exclufive fpirit, the
number of copies printed of each book being fuch as it is
impoffible to purchafe them even in England; they are
wholly in the hands of the East India proprietors.
Scarcely

Scarcely even is the Afiatic Mifcellany known in Europe,
and a man muft be very learned in oriental antiquity before he fo much as hears of the Jones's, the Wilkins's
and the Halhed's, &c. As to the facred books of the
Hindoos, all that are yet in our hands are the Bhagvat
Geeta, the Ezour-Vedam, the Bagavadam, and certain
fragments of the Chaftres printed at the end of the
Bhagvat Geeta. Thefe books are in Indoftan what the
Old and New Teftament are in Chriftendom, the Koran
in Turkey, the Sad-der and the Zendavefta among the
Parfes, &c. When I have taken an extenfive furvey of
their contents, I have fometimes afked myfelf, what
would be the lofs to the human race if a new Omar condemned them to the flames; and unable to difcover any
mifchief that would enfue, I call the imaginary cheft that
contains them, the box of Pandora.

Page 201. (32). *Brama, Bichen or Vichenou, Chib or
Chiven.* Thefe names are differently pronounced according to the different dialects: thus they fay *Birmah,
Bremma, Breuma. Bichen* has been turned into *Vichen*
by the eafy exchange of a *B* for a *V*, and into *Vichenou*
by means of a grammatical affix. In the fame manner
Chib, which is fynonymous with Satan, and fignifies adverfary, is frequently written *Chib-a* and *Chiv-en*; he is
called alfo *Rouder* and *Routr-en*, that is, the deftroyer.

Page *id.* (33). *In the fhape of a tortoife.* This is the
conftellation *tefludo,* or the *lyre,* which was at firft a
tortoife, on account of its flow motion round the Pole;
then a lyre, becaufe it is the fhell of this reptile on which
the ftrings of the lyre are mounted. See an excellent
memoir of *M. Dupuis, fur l'Origine des Conftellations,
in 4to.*

Page 204. (34). *That you have borrowed the ancient
Paganifm*

Paganifm of the Weftern world. All the ancient opinions of the Egyptian and Grecian theologians are to be found in India, and they appear to have been introduced, by means of the commerce of Arabia and the vicinity of Perfia, time immemorial.

Page 205. (35). *Breathed upon the face of the waters.* This cofmogony of the Lamas, the Bonzes, and even the Bramins, as Henry Lord afferts, is literally that of the ancient Egyptians. "The Egyptians," fays Porphyry, "call "*Kneph*, intelligence, or efficient caufe of the univerfe. "They relate that this God vomitted an egg, from which "was produced another God named *Phtha* or Vulcan, "(igneous principle, or the fun,) and they add, that this "egg is the world." *Eufeb. Præp. Evang.* p. 115.

"They reprefent," fays the fame author in another place, "the God *Kneph*, or efficient caufe, under the form "of a man in deep blue (the colour of the fky), having "in his hand a fceptre, a belt round his body, and a fmall "bonnet royal of light feathers on his head, to denote "how very fubtile and fugacious the idea of that being "is." Upon which I fhall obferve, that *Kneph* in Hebrew fignifies a wing, a feather, and that this colour of fky-blue is to be found in the majority of the Indian Gods, and is, under the name of Narayan, one of their moft diftinguifhing epithets.

Page 208. (36). *That the Lamas were a degenerate fect of the Neftorians.* This is afferted by our miffionaries, and among others by Georgi in his unfinifhed work of the Thibetan alphabet: but if it can be proved that the Manicheans were but plagiarifts, and the ignorant echo of a doctrine that exifted fifteen hundred years before them, what becomes of the declarations of Georgi? See upon this fubject *Beaufob. Hift. du Manicheifme.*

But

But the Lama *demonftrated, &c.* The eaftern writers in general agree in placing the birth of *Bedou* 1027 years before Jefus Chrift, which makes him the cotemporary of Zoroafter, with whom, in my opinion, they confound him. It is certain that his doctrine notorioufly exifted at that epoch: it is found entire in that of Orpheus, Pythagoras, and the Indian gymnofophifts. But the gymnofophifts are cited at the time of Alexander as an ancient fect already divided into Brachmans and Sama- neans. See *Bardefanes en Saint Jerome, Epitre à Joviem.* Pythagoras lived in the ninth century before Jefus Chrift; See *Chronology of the Twelve Ages*; and Orpheus is of ftill greater antiquity. If, as is the cafe, the doctrine of Pythagoras and that of Orpheus are of Egyptian origin, that of Bedou goes back to the common fource; and in reality the Egyptian priefts recite that Hermes, as he was dying, faid: " I have hitherto lived an exile from my " country, to which I now return. Weep not for me, " I afcend to the celeftial abode, where each of you will " follow in his turn: there God is: this life is only " death." *Chalcidius in Thimæum.* Such was the profef- fion of faith of the Samaneans, the fectaries of Orpheus, and the Pythagoreans. Farther, Hermes is no other than Bedou himfelf; for among the Indians, Chinefe, Lamas, &c. the planet Mercury, and the correfponding day of the week (Wednefday) bear the name of Bedou: and this accounts for his being placed in the rank of mythological beings, and difcovers the illufion of his pretended exiftence as a man, fince it is evident that Mercury was not a human being, but the Genius or Decan, who, placed at the fummer folftice, opened the

A a   Egyptian

Egyptian year: hence his attributes taken from the
conftellation Syrius, and his name of Anubis, as well as
that of Efculapius, having the figure of a man and the
head of a dog: hence his ferpent, which is the Hydra,
emblem of the ' Nile (Hydor, humidity); and from this
ferpent he feems to have derived his name of Hermes, as
Remes (with a *fchin*), in the oriental languages, fignifies
ferpent. Now Bedou and Hermes being the fame
names, it is manifeft of what antiquity is the fyftem
afcribed to the former. As to the name of Samanean, it
is preeifely that of Chaman preferved in Tartary, China,
and India. The interpretation given to it is, *man of the
woods*, a *hermit mortifying the flefh*, fuch being the characteriftic of this fect; but its literal meaning is *celeftial*
(Samâoui), and explains the fyftem of thofe who are
called by it. This fyftem is the fame as that of the
fectaries of Orpheus, of the Eflenians, of the ancient
Anchorets of Perfia and the whole Eaftern country. See
Porphyry, de Abftin. Animal. Thefe celeftial and penitent
men, carried in India their infanity to fuch an extreme, as
to wifh not to touch the earth, and they accordingly
lived in cages fufpended to trees, where the people,
whofe admiration was not lefs abfurd, brought them
provifions. During the night there were frequent rob-
beries, rapes and murders, and it was at length difcovered that they were committed by thofe men, who,
defcending from their cages, thus indemnified themfelves
for their reftraint during the day. The Bramins, their
rivals, embraced the opportunity of exterminating them;
and from that time their name in India has been fynonymous with hypocrite. See *Hift. de la Chine*, in 5 vols.
4to.

4to. at the note page 50; *Hiſt. de Huns*, 2 vols.; and Preface to the *Ezour-Vedam*.

Page 209. (37). *Demonſtrate his exiſtence, &c.* There are abſolutely no other monuments of the exiſtence of Jeſus Chriſt as a human being, than a paſſage in Joſephus (*Antiq. Jud. lib.* 18. *c.* 3.), a ſingle phraſe in Tacitus, (*Annal. lib.* 15. *c.* 44.), and the Goſpels. But the paſſage in Joſephus is unanimouſly acknowledged to be apocryphal, and to have been interpolated towards the cloſe of the third century, (*See Trad. de Joſephe, par M. Gillet*); and that of Tacitus is ſo vague, and ſo evidently taken from the depoſition of the Chriſtians before the tribunals, that it may be ranked in the claſs of evangelical records. It remains to enquire of what authority are theſe records. "All the world knows," ſays Fauſtus, who, though a Manichean, was one of the moſt learned men of the third century, "All the world knows, that the Goſpels "were neither written by Jeſus Chriſt, nor his apoſtles, "but by certain unknown perſons, who, rightly judging "that they ſhould not obtain belief reſpecting things "which they had not ſeen, placed at the head of their "recitals the names of contemporary apoſtles." See *Beauſob.* vol. i. and *Hiſt. des Apologiſtes de la Relig. Chret. par Burigni*, a ſagacious writer, who has demonſtrated the abſolute uncertainty of theſe foundations of the Chriſtian religion; ſo that the exiſtence of Jeſus is no better proved than that of Oſiris and Hercules, or that of Fôt or Bedou, with whom, ſays M. de Guignes, the Chineſe continually confound him, for they never call Jeſus by any other name than Fôt. *Hiſt. de Huns.*

Page *id.* (38.) *Your Goſpels are taken from the books of the Mithriacs.* That is to ſay, from the pious romances

formed out of the facred legends of the Myfteries of
Mithra, Ceres, Ifis, &c.; from whence are equally derived the books of the Hindoos and the Bonzes. Our
miffionaries have long remarked a ftriking refemblance
between thofe books and the Gofpels. M. Wilkins exprefsly mentions it in a note in the Bhagvat-Geeta. All
agree that Krifna, Fôt, and Jefus, have the fame characteriftic features; but religious prejudice has ftood in the
way of drawing from this circumftance the proper and
natural inference. To time and reafon muft it be left to
. difplay the truth.

Page 210. (39). *The interior and fecret doctrine.* The
Budfoifts have two doctrines, the one public and often-
fible, the other interior and fecret, precifely like the
Egyptian priefts. It may be afked, why this diftinction?
It is, that as the public doctrine recommends offerings,
expiations, endowments, &c. the priefts find their profit in teaching it to the people; whereas the other, teaching the vanity of worldly things, and attended with
no lucre, it is thought proper to make it known only to
adepts. Can the teachers and followers of this religion,
be better claffed than under the heads of knavery and
credulity?

Page 212. (40). *That happinefs and misfortune, &c.*
Thefe are the expreffions of La Loubere, in his defcription of the kingdom of Siam and the theology of the
Bonzes. Their dogmas, compared with thofe of the
ancient philofophers of Greece and Italy, give a complete reprefentation of the whole fyftem of the Stoics and
Epicureans, mixed with aftrological fuperftitions, and fome
traits of Pythagorifm.

Page 224. (41). *The original barbarous ftate of mankind.*

It

It is the unanimous teſtimony of hiſtory, and even of legends, that the firſt human beings were every where ſavages, and that it was to civilize them, and teach them *to make bread*, that the Gods manifeſted themſelves.

Page *id.* (42). *Man receives no ideas but through the medium of his ſenſes.* The rock on which all the ancients have ſplit, and which has occaſioned all their errors, has been their ſuppoſing the idea of God to be innate and coeternal with the ſoul; and hence all the reveries developed in Plato and Jamblicus. See the *Timæus*, the *Phedon*, and *De Myſt. Ægyptiorum*, ſect. 1. c. 3.

Page 231. (43). *Record of all the monuments of antiquity.* It clearly reſults, ſays Plutarch, from the verſes of Orpheus and the ſacred books of the Egyptians and Phrygians, that the ancient theology, not only of the Greeks, but of all nations, was nothing more than a ſyſtem of phyſics, a picture of the operations of nature, wrapped up in myſterious allegories and enigmatical ſymbols, in a manner that the ignorant multitude attended rather to their apparent than to their hidden meaning, and even in what they underſtood of the latter, ſuppoſed there to be ſomething more deep than what they perceived. *Fragment of a work of Plutarch now loſt, quoted by Euſebius, Præpar. Evang. lib. 3. ch. 1. p.* 83.

The majority of philoſophers, ſays Porphyry, and among others Chæremon (who lived in Egypt in the firſt age of Chriſtianity), imagine there never to have been any other world than the one we ſee, and acknowledge no other Gods of all thoſe recognized by the Egyptians, than ſuch as are commonly called planets, ſigns of the Zodiac, and conſtellations; whoſe aſpects,

A a 3   that

that is, rifing and fetting, are fuppofed to influence the
fortunes of men; to which they add, their divifions of the
figns into decans and difpenfers of time, whom they ftyle
lords of the afcendant, whofe names, virtues in the re-
lieving diftempers, rifing, fetting, and prefages of future
events, are the fubjects of almanacks; (for be it obferved,
that the Egyptian priefts had almanacks the exact counterpart of Matthew Lanfberg's) for when the priefts
affirmed that the fun was the architect of the univerfe,
Chæremon prefently concludes that all their narratives
refpecting Ifis and Ofiris, together with their other facred
fables, referred in part to the planets, the phafes of
the moon, and the revolution of the fun, and in part to
the ftars of the daily and nightly hemifpheres and the
river Nile; in a word, in all cafes to phyfical and natural
exiftences, and never to fuch as might be immaterial and
incorporeal. . . . All thefe philofophers believe, that the
acts of our will, and the motion of our bodies, depend
upon thofe of the ftars to which they are fubjected, and
they refer every thing to the laws of phyfical neceffity,
which they call deftiny or *Fatum*, fuppofing a chain of
caufes and effects which binds, by I know not what connection, all beings together, from the meaneft atom to
the fupreme power and primary influence of the Gods;
fo that, whether in their temples or in their idols, the
only fubject of worfhip is the power of deftiny. *Por-
phyr. Epift. ad Junebonem.*

Page 232. (44). *The practice of agriculture required the
obfervation and knowledge of the heavens.* It continues to be
repeated every day, on the indirect authority of the book
of Genefis, that aftronomy was the invention of the children of Noah. It has been gravely faid, that, while

wandering

wandering fhepherds in the plains of Shinar, they employed their leifure in compofing a planetary fyftem : as
if fhepherds had occafion to know more than the Polar
ftar, and if neceffity was not the fole motive of every invention ! If the ancient fhepherds were fo ftudious and
fagacious, how does it happen that the modern ones are
fo ftupid, ignorant, and inattentive ? And it is a fact, that
the Arabs of the defert know not fo many as fix conftellations, and underftand not a word of aftronomy.

Page 233. (45). *Genii, Gods, authors of good and evil.*
It appears that by the words genius, the ancients denoted
a quality, a generative power ; for the following words,
which are all of one family, convey this meaning : *gene-
rary, genos, genefis, genus, gens.*

The Sabeans, ancient and modern, fays Maimonides,
acknowledge a principal God, the maker and inhabitant
of heaven ; but on account of his great diftance they conceive him to be inacceffible ; and in imitation of the
conduct of people towards their kings, they employ as
mediators with him, the planets and their angels, whom
they call princes and potentates, and whom they fuppofe
to refide in thofe luminous bodies as in palaces or taber-
nacles, &c. *More-Nebuchim, pars 3. c. 29.*

Page 234. (46). *And even a fex derived from the gender
of its appellation.* According as the gender of the object
was in the language of the nation mafculine or feminine,
the Divinity who bore its name was male or female.
Thus the Cappadocians called the moon God, and the
fun Goddefs ; a circumftance which gives to the fame
beings a perpetual variety in ancient mythology.

Page 235. (47). *Morality was a judicious practice of all
that is conducive to the prefervation of exiftence.* We may

add,

add, fays Plutarch, that thefe Egyptian prieſts always regarded the prefervation of health as a point of firſt importance, and as indifpenfably neceſſary to the practice of
piety and the fervice of the Gods. See his account of
Iſis and Oſiris, towards the end.

Page *id.* (48). *That its principles* (thofe of aſtronomy),
can be traced back to a period of 17,000 *years*. The hiſtori-
cal orator follows here the opinion of Mr. Dupuis, who, in
his learned memoir concerning the origin of the conſtellations, has aſſigned many plaufible reafons to prove that
Libra was formerly the fign of the vernal, and *Aries* of the
nocturnal equinox; that is, that fince the origin of the
actual aſtronomical fyſtem, the proceſſion of the equinoxes has carried forward by feven figns the primitive
order of the Zodiac. Now eſtimating the proceſſion at
about feventy years and a half to a degree, that is 2,115
years to each fign; and obferving that *Aries* was in
its fifteenth degree, 1,447 years before Chriſt, it follows, that the firſt degree of *Libra* could not have coincided with the vernal equinox more lately than 15,194
years before Chriſt, to which if you add 1790 years fince
Chriſt, it appears that 16,984 have elapfed fince the
· origin of the Zodiac. The vernal equinox coincided with
the firſt degree of *Aries* 2,504 years before Chriſt, and
with the firſt degree of *Taurus* 4,619 years before Chriſt.
Now it is to be obferved, that the worſhip of the Bull is
the principal article in the theological creed of the Egyptians, Perfians, Japanefe, &c.; from whence it clearly
follows, that fome general revolution took place among
thofe nations at that time. The chronology of five or
fix thoufand years in Genefis is little agreeable to this
hypothefis; but as the book of Genefis cannot claim to
be

be confidered as a hiftory farther back than Abraham, we are at liberty to make what arrangements we pleafe in the eternity that preceded.

Page *id.* (49). *When reafon finds there a zone of heaven equally free from the rains of the equator and the fogs of the North.* Mr. Bailli, in placing the firft aftronomers at Selingenfkoy, near the lake Baikal, paid no attention to this twofold circumftance: it equally argues againft their being placed at Axoum on account of the rains, and the *Zimb fly* of which Mr. Bruce fpeaks.

Page 238. (50). *Men gave to the ftars, &c.* " The " ancients," fays Maimonides, " directing all their at- " tention to agriculture, gave names to the ftars derived " from their occupation during the year." *More Neb. pars* 3.

Page 240. (51). *They call by the name of ferpents the figured traces of the orbits.* The ancients had verbs from the fubftantives *crab, goat, tortoife,* as the French have at prefent the verbs *ferpenter, coquetier.* The hiftory of all languages is nearly the fame.

Page 243. (52). *If they had not feen in them talifmans partaking of the nature of the ftars.* The ancient aftrolo- gers, fays the moft learned of the Jews (Maimonides), having facredly affigned to each planet a colour, an ani- mal, a tree, a metal, a fruit, a plant, formed from them all a figure or reprefentation of the ftar, taking care to felect for the purpofe a proper moment, a fortunate day, fuch as the conjunction of the ftar, or fome other favour- able afpect, They conceived, that by their magic cere- monies they could introduce into thofe figures or idols the influences of the fuperior beings after which they were modelled. Thefe were the idols that the Chaldean- Sabeans

Sabeans adored; and in the performance of their worfhip they were obliged to be dreffed in the proper colour.... The aftrologers, by their practices, thus introduced idolatry, defirous of being regarded as the
difpenfers of the favours of heaven; and as agriculture
was the fole employment of the ancients, they fucceeded
in perfuading them, that the rain and other bleffings of
the feafons were at their difpofal. Thus the whole art
of agriculture was exercifed by rules of aftrology, and the
priefts made talifmans or charms which were to drive
away locufts, flies, &c. See *Maimonides, More, Nebuchim,
pars* 3. *c.* 29.

The priefts of Egypt, Perfia, India, &c. pretended to
bind the Gods to their idols, and to make them come
from heaven at their pleafure. They threatened the fun
and moon, if they were difobedient, to reveal the fecret
myfteries, to fhake the fkies, &c. &c. *Eufeb. Præcep.
Evang. p.* 198, *and Iamblicus de Myfteriis Ægypt.*

Page *id.* (53). *The fun was fuppofed to affume their forms*
(the forms of the twelve animals). Thefe are the very
words of Iamblicus de Symbolis Ægyptiorum, c. 2. fect. 7.
The fun was the grand Proteus, the univerfal meta-
morphift.

Page 245. (54). *Your tonfure is the difk of the fun.* The
Arabs, fays Herodotus, fhave their heads in a circle and
about the temples, in imitation of Bacchus (that is the
fun,) who fhaves himfelf, they fay, in this manner. Jere-
miah fpeaks alfo of this cuftom. The tuft of hair which
the Mahometans preferve, is taken alfo from the fun,
who was painted by the Egyptians at the winter folftice,
as having but a fingle hair on his head.... *Your ftole its
Zodiac.* The robes of the goddefs of Syria and of Diana

of

of Ephefus, from whence are borrowed the drefs of
prieſts, have the twelve animals of the Zodiac painted on
them.....*Rofaries* are found upon all the Indian idols,
conſtructed more than four thoufand years ago; and
their ufe in the Eaſt has been univerfal for time immemorial.....The *crofier* is precifely the ſtaff of Bootes
or Ofiris (See Plate II.) All the Lamas wear the *mitre*
or cap in the ſhape of a cone, which was an emblem of
the fun.

Page 247. (55.) *Having faid that a planet entered into a
fign, their conjunction was denominated a marriage,* &c.
Thefe are the very words of Plutarch in his account of
Ifis and Ofiris. The Hebrews fay, in fpeaking of the generations of the Patriarchs, *et ingreffus eſt in eam.* From
this continual equivoque of ancient language, proceeds
every miſtake.

Page 248. (56). *The combination of thefe figures had alfo
a meaning.* The reader will doubtlefs fee, with pleafure,
fome examples of ancient hieroglyphics.

" The Egyptians (fays Hor-appolo) reprefent eternity
by the figure of the fun and moon. They defignate the
world by a blue ferpent with yellow fcales (ſtars, it is the
Chinefe Dragon). If they were defirous of expreffing the
year, they drew a picture of Ifis, who is alfo in their
language called *Sothis*, or dog-ſtar, one of the firſt conſtellations, by the rifing of which the year commences:
its infcription at Sais was, *It is I that rife in the conſtella-
tion of the Dog.*

" They alfo reprefent the year by a palm-tree, and the
month by one of its branches; becaufe it is the nature of
this tree to produce a branch every month. They farther
reprefent it by the fourth part of an acre of land." (The
whole

whole acre divided into four denotes the biffextile period
of four years. The abbreviation of this figure of a field
in four divifions, is manifeftly the letter *há* or *hét*, the
feventh in the Samaritan alphabet; and in general all
the letters of the alphabet are merely aftronomical hieroglyphics: and it is for this reafon that the mode of
writing is from right to left, like the march of the ftars).
—" They denote a prophet by the image of a dog, becaufe the dog-ftar (*Anoubis*) by its rifing gives notice of
the inundation. *Noubi* in Hebrew fignifies prophet.—
They reprefent inundation by a lion, becaufe it takes
place under that fign: and hence, fays Plutarch, the
cuftom of placing at the gates of temples figures of lions
with water iffuing from their mouths.—They exprefs the
idea of God and Deftiny by a ftar. They alfo reprefent
God, fays Porphyry, by a black ftone, becaufe his nature
is dark and obfcure. All white things exprefs the celeftial
and luminous Gods: all circular ones the world, the
moon, the fun, the deftinies: all femicircular ones, as bows
and crefcents, are alfo defcriptive of the moon. Fire and
the Gods of Olympus, they reprefent by pyramids and
obelifks: (the name of the fun *Baal* is found in this
latter word): the fun, by a cone (the mitre of Ofiris):
the earth, by a cylinder (which revolves): the generative
power of the air, by the *phalus*, and that of the earth, by
a triangle, emblem of the female organ. *Eufeb. Praecep.
Evang. p.* 98.

" Clay (fays Iamblicus de Symbolis, fect. 7. c. 2.) denotes matter, the generative and nutrimental power, every
thing which receives the warmth and fermentation of life.

" A man fitting upon the *Lotos* or *Nenuphar*, reprefents
the moving fpirit (the fun), which, in like manner as
the

the plant lives in the water without any communication with clay, exifts equally diftinᴄ̄t from matter, fwimming in empty fpace, refting on itfelf: it is round alfo in all its parts like the leaves, the flowers and the fruit of the Lotos. (Brama has the eyes of the Lotos, fays Chafter Neadirfen, to denote his intelligence: his eye fwims over every thing, like the flowers of the Lotos on the waters). A man at the helm of a fhip, adds Iamblicus, is defcriptive of the fun which governs all. And Porphyry tells us, that the fun is alfo reprefented by a man in a fhip refting upon an amphibious crocodile (emblem of air and water).

" At Elephantine they worfhipped the figure of a man in a fitting pofture, painted blue, having the head of a ram, and the horns of a goat which encompaffed a difk: all which reprefented the fun and moon's conjunᴄ̄tion at the fign of the ram; the blue colour denoting the power of the moon at the period of junᴄ̄tion, to raife water into clouds. *Eufeb. Præcep. Evang. p.* 116.

" The hawk is an emblem of the fun and of light, on account of his rapid flight, and his foaring into the higheft regions of the air where light abounds.

" A fifh is the emblem of averfion, and the *Hippopota-mus* of violence, becaufe it is faid to kill its father and ra-vifh its mother. Hence, fays Plutarch, the emblematical infcription of the temple of Sais, where we fee painted on the veftibule, 1. A child. 2. An old man. 3. A hawk. 4. A fifh. 5. A hippopotamus; which fignify, 1. Entrance (into life). 2. Departure. 3. God. 4. Hatred. 5. In-juftice. (See *Ifis & Ofiris*).

" The Egyptians, adds he, reprefent the world by a Scarabeus, becaufe this infeᴄ̄t pufhes, in a direᴄ̄tion con-trary

trary to that in which it proceeds, a ball containing its eggs, juſt as the heaven of the fixed ſtars cauſes the revo-lution of the ſun (the yolk of an egg) in an oppoſite di-rection to its own.

" They repreſent the world alſo by the number *five*, being that of the elements, which, ſays Diodorus, are earth, water, air, fire, and ether or *ſpiritus*. The Indians have the ſame number of elements, and according to Macrobius's Myſtics they are the ſupreme God, or *pri-mum mobile*, the intelligence, or *mens*, born of him, the ſoul of the world which proceeds from him, the celeſtial ſpheres and all things terreſtrial. Hence, adds Plu-tarch, the analogy between the Greek *pente*, five, and *pan*, all.

" The aſs," ſays he again, " is the emblem of Typhon, becauſe like that animal he is of a reddiſh colour. Now Typhon ſignifies whatever is of a mircy or clayey nature; (and in Hebrew I find the three words, *clay*, *red*, and *aſs*, to be formed from the ſame root, *hamr*. Iamblicus has farther told us, that clay was the emblem of matter; and he elſewhere adds, that all evil and corruption proceeded from matter: which, compared with the phraſe of Ma-crobius, *all is periſhable*, liable to change in the celeſtial ſphere, gives us the theory, firſt phyſical, then moral, of the ſyſtem of good and evil of the ancients."

Page 252. (57). *The ſenſeleſs cauſe of ſuperſtition.* Theſe are properly the words of Plutarch, who relates, that thoſe various worſhips were given by a king of Egypt to the different towns to diſunite and enſlave them (and theſe kings had been taken from the caſt of prieſts). See *Iſis & Oſiris.*

Page 255. (58). *In the projection of the celestial sphere.*
The ancient priests had three kind of spheres, which it
may be ufeful to make known to the reader.

" We read in Eufebius," fays Porphyry, " that Zoroafter was the firft who, having fixed upon a cavern
pleafantly fituated in the mountains adjacent to Perfia,
formed the idea of confecrating it to Mithra (the fun)
creator and father of all things: that is to fay, having
made in this cavern feveral geometrical divifions, reprefenting the feafons and the elements, he imitated on a
fmall fcale the order and difpofition of the univerfe by
Mithra. After Zoroafter, it became a cuftom to confe-
crate caverns for the celebration of myfteries: fo that in
like manner as temples were dedicated to the Gods,
rural altars to heroes and terreftrial deities, &c. fubterraneous abodes to infernal deities, fo caverns and grottoes
were confecrated to the world, to the univerfe, and to the
nymphs: and from hence Pythagoras and Plato borrowed
the idea of calling the earth a cavern, a cave, *de Antro
Nympharum.*"

Such was the firft projection of the fphere in relief:
though the Perfians give the honour of the invention to
Zoroafter, it is doubtlefs due to the Egyptians: for
we may fuppofe, from this projection being the moft
fimple, that it was the moft ancient; the caverns of
Thebes, full of fimilar pictures, tend to ftrengthen this
opinion.

The following was the fecond projection, " The prophets or hierophants," fays Bifhop Synnefius, " who had
been initiated in the myfteries, do not permit the common workmen to form idols or images of the Gods; but
they defcend themfelves into the facred caves, where
they

they have concealed coffers containing certain fpheres, upon which they conftruct thofe images fecretly and without the knowledge of the people, who defpife fimple and natural things, and wifh for prodigies and fables." (*Syn. in Calvit.*) That is, the ancient priefts had armillary fpheres like ours; and this paflage, which fo well agrees with that of Chæremon, gives us the key to all their theological aftrology.

Laftly, they had *flat models* of the nature of Plate II. with this difference, that they were of a very complicated nature, having every fictitious divifion of decan and fubdecan, with the hieroglyphic figns of their influence. Kircher has given us a copy of one of them in his Egyptian Œdipus, and Gybelin a figured fragment in his book of the calendar (under the name of the Egyptian Zodiac). The ancient Egyptians, fays the aftrologer Julius Firmicus (*Aftron. lib.* ii. and *lib.* iv. *c.* 16), divide each fign of the Zodiac into three fections; and each fection was under the direction of an imaginary being, whom they called *Decan*, or *chief of ten*; fo that there were three Decans a month, and thirty-three a year. Now thefe Decans, who were alfo called Gods (*Thoi*), regulate the deftinies of mankind—and they were placed particularly in certain ftars. They afterwards imagined in every *ten* three other Gods, whom they called *arbiters*; fo that there were nine for every month, and thefe were farther divided into an infinite number of powers. (The Perfians and Indians made their fpheres on fimilar plans; and if a picture thereof were to be drawn from the defcription given by Scaliger at the end of Manilius, we fhould find in it a complete explanation of their hieroglyphics, for every article forms one).

Page

Page *id.* (59) *The adverfe Genii.* It was for this reafon the Perfians always wrote the name of Ahrimanes inverted thus: ·sǝuɐɯ!ɹɥ∀

Page 256. (60). *Typhon, that is to fay deluge.* Typhon, pronounced Touphon by the Greeks, is precifely the *touphan* of the Arabs, which fignifies deluge; and thefe deluges in mythology are nothing more than winter and the rains, or the overflowing of the Nile; as their pretended fires which are to deftroy the world, are fimply the fummer feafon.   And it is for this reafon that Ariftotle (*De Meteor. lib.* I. *c.* xiv.), fays, that the winter of the great cyclic year is a deluge; and its fummer a conflagration.   " The Egyptians, fays Porphyry, " employ every year a talifman in remembrance of the world : at the fummer folftice they mark their houfes, flocks and trees with red, fuppofing that on that day the whole world had been fet on fire.   It was alfo at the fame period that they celebrated the pyrric or fire dance." (And this illuftrates the origin of purifications by fire and by water : for having denominated the tropic of Cancer the gate of heaven, and of genial heat or celeftial fire, and that of Capricorn the gate of deluge or of water, it was imagined that the fpirits or fouls who paffed through thefe gates in their way to and from heaven, were *roafted* or *bathed :* hence the baptifm of Mithra, und the paffage through flames, obferved throughout the Eaft long before Mofes).

Page *id.* (61). *In Perfia in a fubfequent period.* That is, when the ram became the equinoxial fign, or rather when the alteration of the fkies fhewed that it was no longer the Bull.   See Note 48.

Page 257. (62). *Whence are derived all religious acts of a gay nature.* All the ancient feftivals refpecting the return and exaltation of the fun were of this defcription: hence the *hilaria* of the Roman calendar at the period of the paffage (Pafcha) of the vernal equinox. The dances were imitations of the march of the planets. Thofe of the Dervifes ftill reprefent it to this day.

Page 258. (63). *All religious acts of the fombre kind.* " Sacrifices of blood," fays Porphyry, " were only offered to Demons and evil Genii to avert their wrath... Demons are fond of blood, humidity, ftench." *Apud. Eufeb. Præp. Ev. p.* 173.

" The Egyptians," fays Plutarch, "only offer bloody victims to Typhon. They facrifice to him a red ox, and the animal immolated is held in execration, and loaded with all the fins of the people." (The goat of Mofes). See *Ifis and Ofiris.*

Divifion of terreftrial beings into pure and impure, facred and abominable. Strabo fays, fpeaking of Mofes and the Jews, " Circumcifion and the prohibition of certain kinds of meat fprung from fuperftition."—And I obferve, refpecting the ceremony of circumcifion, that its object was to take from the fymbol of Ofiris (*Phallus*) the pretended obftacle to fecundity; an obftacle which bore the feal of Typhon, " whofe nature," fays Plutarch, " is made up of all that *hinders, oppofes, caufes obftruction.*"

Page 260. (64). *Elyfian-fields. Aliz,* in the Phenician or Hebrew language fignifies dancing and joyous.

Page 262. (65). *The Milky way.* See *Macrob. Som. Scip.* c. 12; and Note (78).

Page

Page 265. (66). *The bodies of its inhabitants caſt no
ſhade.* There is on this ſubjeƈt a paſſage in Plutarch, ſo
intereſting and explanatory of the whole of this ſyſtem,
that we ſhall cite it entire. Having obſerved that the
theory of good and evil had at all times occupied the attention of philoſophers and theologians, he adds : " Many
ſuppoſe there to be two Gods of oppoſite inclinations, one
delighting in good the other in evil; the firſt of theſe is
called particularly by the name of God, the ſecond by that
of Genius or Demon. Zoroaſter has denominated them
Oromaze and Ahrimanes, and has ſaid that, of whatever
falls under the cognizance of our ſenſes, light is the beſt
repreſentation of the one, and darkneſs and ignorance of
the other. He adds, that Mithra is an intermediate being, and it is for this reaſon the Perſians call Mithra the
mediator or *intermediator.* Each of theſe Gods has diſtinƈt
plants and animals conſecrated to him; for example, dogs,
birds and hedge-hogs belong to the good Genius, and all
aquatic animals to the evil one.

" The Perſians alſo ſay, that Oromaze was born or
formed out of the pureſt light; Ahrimanes, on the contrary,
out of the thickeſt darkneſs: that Oromaze made ſix Gods
as good as himſelf, and Ahrimanes oppoſed to them ſix
wicked ones: that Oromaze afterwards multiplied himſelf
threefold (Hermes triſmegiſtus), and removed to a diſtance
as remote from the ſun as the ſun is remote from the earth;
that he there formed ſtars, and, among others, *Syrius,*
which he placed in the heavens as a guard and centinel.
He made alſo twenty-four other Gods, which he incloſed
in an egg; but Ahrimanes created an equal number on his
part, who broke the egg, and from that moment good and
evil were mixed (in the univerſe). But Ahrimanes is

one

one day to be conquered, and the earth to be made *equal* and *fmooth*, that all men may live happy.

Theopompus adds, from the books of the Magi, that one of thefe Gods reigns in turn every three thoufand years, during which the other is kept in fubjection ; that they afterwards contend with equal weapons during a fimilar portion of time, but that in the end the evil Genius will fall (never to rife again). Then men will become happy, and their bodies caft no fhade. The God who mediates all thefe things reclines at prefent in repofe, waiting till he fhall be pleafed to execute them." See *Ifis and Ofiris.*

There is an apparent allegory through the whole of this paffage. The egg is the fixed fphere, the world ; the fix Gods of Oromaze are the fix figns of fummer, thofe of Ahrimanes the fix figns of winter.. The forty-eight other Gods are the forty-eight conftellations of the ancient fphere, divided equally between Ahrimanes and Oromaze. The office of *Syrius*, as guard and centinel, tells us that the origin of thefe ideas was Egyptian : finally, the expreffion that the earth is to become *equal* and *fmooth*, and that the bodies of happy beings are to caft no fhade, proves that the equator was confidered as their true paradife.

Page 265. (67). *The cave of Mithra.* See Note (58). In the caves which priefts every where conftructed, they celebrated myfteries which confifted (fays Origen againft Celfus) in imitating the motion of the ftars, the planets, and the heavens. The initiated took the name of conftellations and affumed the figures of animals. One was a lion, another a raven, and a third a ram. Hence the ufe of mafks in the firft reprefentation of the drama. See *Ant. Devoilé*, vol. ii. p. 244. "In the myfteries of Ceres the chief in the proceffion called himfelf the creator ; the bearer

of

of the torch was denominated the fun: the perfon near-
eft to the altar, the moon; the herald or deacon, Mercury.
In Egypt there was a feftival in which the men and women reprefented the year, the age, the feafons, the different
parts of the day, and they walked in proceffion after Bacchus. *Athen. lib.* v. *c.* 7. In the cave of Mithra was a
ladder with feven fteps, reprefenting the feven fpheres of
the planets, by means of which fouls afcended and defcended. This is precifely the ladder in Jacob's vifion,
which fhows that at that epocha the whole fyftem was
formed. There is in the French king's library a fuperb
volume of pictures of the Indian Gods, in which the ladder is reprefented with the fouls of men mounting it."

Page 267. (68). *Exact calculation.* Confult the ancient
aftronomy of M. Bailly, and you will find our affertions
refpecting the knowledge of the priefts amply proved.

Page 269. (69). *A reciprocal connection.* Thefe are the
very words of Jamblicus. *De Myft. Ægypt.*

Page *id.* (70.) *Or rather electrical fluid.* The more I
confider what the ancients underftood by *ether,* and
fpirit, and what the Indians call *akache,* the ftronger do
I find the analogy between it and electrical fluid. A
luminous fluid, principle of warmth and motion, per-
vading the univerfe, forming the matter of the ftars,
having fmall round particles, which infinuate themfelves
into bodies, and fill them by dilating itfelf, be their extent what it will, what can more ftrongly refemble elec-
tricity?

Page *id.* (71.) *Was fuppofed to have the fun for its heart.*
Natural philofophers, fays Macrobius, call the fun the
heart of the world. *Som. Scip. c.* 20. The Egyptians,
fays Plutarch, call the Eaft the *face,* the North the *right-*

B b 3   *fide,*

fide, and the South the *left-fide* of the world, becaufe there
the heart is placed. They continually compare the univerfe to a man; and hence the celebrated *microcofm* of
the Alchymifts. We obferve by the by, that the Alchymifts, Cabalifts, Free-mafons, Magnetifers, Martinifts,
and every other fuch fort of vifionaries, are but the miftaken difciples of this ancient fchool: we fay miftaken,
becaufe, in fpite of their pretenfions, the thread of the
occult fcience is broken.

Page *id.* (72). *That the world was eternal.* See the
Pythagorean *Ocellus Lucanus*.

Page 270. (73). *The Orphic egg.* This comparifon of
the fun with the yolk of an egg refers, 1. To its round
and yellow figure; 2. To its central fituation; 3. To
the germ or principle of life contained in the yolk. May
not the oval form of the egg allude to the elipfis of the
orbs? I am inclined to this opinion. The word Orphic
offers a farther obfervation. Macrobius fays (*Som. Scip.*
c. 14. and *c.* 20), that the fun is the brain of the univerfe,
and that it is from analogy that the fkull of a human
being is round, like the planet, the feat of intelligence.
Now the word Orph (with *ain*) fignifies in Hebrew
the brain and its feat (*cervix*): Orpheus, then, is the fame
as Bedou, or Baits; and the Bonzes are thofe very
Orphics which Plutarch reprefents as quacks, who ate
no meat, vended talifmans, and little ftones, and deceived individuals, and even governments themfelves.
See a learned Memoir of *Freret fur les Orphiques, Acad.*
des Infcrip. vol. 23. *in* 4to.

Page *id.* (74). *Wearing on his head a fphere of gold.*
See *Porphyry in Eufebius, Præp. Evang. lib.* 3. *p.* 115.

Page 271. (75). *Alluding to the wind.* The Northern

or

or *Elefian* wind, which commences regularly at the folftice, with the inundation.

Page 272. (76). *You-piter.* This is the true pronunciation of the Jupiter of the Latins. . . . *Exiftence itfelf.* This is the fignification of the word *You.* See Note (84).

Page 273. (77). *Producing the great egg.* See Note (35).

Page *id.* (78). *The immortality of the foul, which at firft was eternity.* In the fyftem of the firft fpiritualifts, the foul was not created with, or at the fame time as the body, in order to be inferted in it: its exiftence was fuppofed to be anterior and from all eternity. Such, in a few words, is the doctrine of Macrobius on this head. *Som. Scip. paffim.*

" There exifts a luminous, igneous, fubtle fluid, which, under the name of ether and fpiritus, fills the univerfe. It is the effential principle and agent of motion and life, it is the Deity. When an earthly body is to be animated, a fmall round particle of this fluid gravitates through the milky way towards the lunar fphere, where, when it arrives, it unites with a groffer air, and becomes fit to affociate with matter: it then enters and entirely fills the body, animates it, fuffers, grows, increafes, and diminifhes with it; laftly, when the body dies, and its grofs elements diffolve, this incorruptible particle takes its leave of it, and returns to the grand ocean of ether, if not retained by its union with the lunar air: it is this air or gas, which, retaining the fhape of the body, becomes a phantom or ghoft, the perfect reprefentation of the deceafed. The Greeks called this phantom the image or idol of the foul; the Pythagoreans, its chariot, its frame; and the Rabbinical fchool, its veffel, or boat. When a man had conducted himfelf well in this world, his

B b 4   whole

whole foul, that is, its chariot and ether, afcended to the
moon, where a feparation took place: the chariot lived in
the lunar Elyfium, and the ether returned to the fixed
fphere, that is, to God: for the fixed heaven, fays Macrobius, was by many called by the name of God (c. 14.)
If a man had not lived virtuoufly, the foul remained on
earth to undergo purification, and was to wander to and
fro, like the ghofts of Homer, to whom this doctrine
muft have been known, fince he wrote after the time of
Pherecydes and Pythagoras, who were is promulgators
in Greece. Heredotus, upon this occafion, fays, that the
whole romance of the foul and its tranfmigrations was
invented by the Egyptians, and propagated in Greece by
men, who pretended to be its authors. I know their
names, adds he, but fhall not mention them (*lib.* 2.).
Cicero, however has pofitively informed us, that it was
Pherecydes, mafter of Pythagoras. *Tufcul. lib.* 1. *fect.* 16.
Now admitting that this fyftem was at that period a
novelty, it accounts for Solomon's treating it as a fable,
who lived 130 years before Pherecydes. " Who know-
eth," fays he, " the fpirit of a man that it goeth upwards? I faid in my heart concerning the eftate of the
fons of men, that God might manifeft them, and that
they might fee that they themfelves are beafts. For that
which befalleth the fons of men, befalleth beafts; even
one thing befalieth them; as the one dieth, fo dieth the
other; yea they have all one breath, fo that a man hath
no pre-eminence above a beaft: for all is vanity." Eccles.
c. iii. v. 18.

And fuch had been the opinion of Mofes, as a tranf-
lator of Herodotus (M. Archer of the Academy of Infcriptions), juftly obferves in note 389 of the fecond book,

where

where he fays alfo, that the immortality of the foul was not introduced among the Hebrews till their intercourfe with the Affyrians. In other refpects, the whole Pythagorean fyftem, properly analyfed, appears to be merely a fyftem of phyfics badly underftood.

Page 275. (79). *The world is a machine*; *it has therefore an artificer.* All the arguments of the fpiritualifts are founded on this. See *Macrobius*, at the end of the fecond book, and *Plato*, with the comments of *Marcilius Ficinus*.

Page 276. (80). *The demi-ourgos, the logos, and the fpirit.* Thefe are the real types of the Chriftian Trinity. See Note (99).

Page 277. (81). *Its very names.* In our laft analyfis we found all the names of the Deity to be derived from fome material object in which it was fuppofed to refide. We have given a confiderable number of inftances; let us add one more relative to our word *God*. This is known to be the *Deus* of the Latins, and the *Theos* of the Greeks. Now by the confeffion of Plato (*in Cratylo*), of Macrobius (*Saturn, lib.* 1. *c.* 24), and of Plutarch (*Ifis & Ofiris*), its root is *thein*, which fignifies to wander, like *planeïn*, that is to fay, it is fynonimous with planets; becaufe, all our authors, both the ancient Greeks and barbarians particularly worfhipped the planets. I know that fuch enquiries into etymologies have been much decried : but if, as is the cafe, words are the reprefentative figns of ideas, the genealogy of the one becomes that of the other, and a good etymological dictionary would be the moft perfect hiftory of the human underftanding. It would only be neceffary in this enquiry to obferve certain precautions, which have

hitherto

hitherto been neglected, and particularly to make an exact comparifon of the value of the letters of the different alphabets. But, to continue our fubject, we fhall add, that in the Phenician language, the word *thab* (with *ain*) fignifies alfo to wander, and appears to be the derivation of *theïn*. If we fuppofe *Deus* to be derived from the Greek *Zeus*, a proper name of *You-piter*, having *zaw*, I live, for its root, its fenfe will be precifely that of *you*, and will mean *foul* of the world, *igneous* principle. See Note (84). *Div-us*, which only fignifies Genius, God of the fecond order, appears to me to come from the oriental word *div* fubftituted for *dib*, wolf and chacal, one of the emblems of the fun. At Thebes, fays Macrobius, the fun was painted under the form of a wolf or chacal, for there are no wolves in Egypt. The reafon of this emblem, doubtlefs, is that the chacal, like the cock, announces by its cries the fun's rifing; and this reafon is confirmed by the analogy of the words *lykos*, wolf, and *lyké*, light of the morning, whence comes *lux*.

Dius, which is to be underftood alfo of the fun, muft be derived from *dib*, a hawk. " The Egyptians," fays Porphyry (*Eufeb. Præcep. Evang. p.* 92.) " reprefent the fun under the emblem of a hawk, becaufe this bird foars to the higheft regions of air where light abounds." And in reality we continually fee at Cairo large flights of thefe birds, hovering in the air, from whence they defcend not but to ftun us with their fhrieks, which are like the monofyllable *dib :* and here, as in the preceding example, we find an analogy between the word *dies*, day, light, and *Dius*, God, Sun.

Page 278. (82). *The progrefs of fcience and difcovery.* One of the proofs that all thefe fyftems were invented in

Egypt,

Egypt, is, that this is the only country where we fee a complete body of doctrine formed from the remoteft antiquity.

Clemens Alexandrinus has tranfmitted to us (*Stromat. lib.* 6.), a curious detail of the 42 volumes which were borne in the proceffion of Ifis. " The prieft," fays he, " or chanter, carries one of the fymbolic inftruments of " mufic, and two of the books of Mercury; one contain-" ing hymns of the Gods, the other the lift of kings. " Next to him the *horofcope* (the regulator of time), " carries a palm and a dial, fymbols of aftrology; he " muft know by heart the four books of Mercury which " treat of aftrology : the firft on the order of the planets; " the fecond on the rifings of the fun and moon, and " the two laft on the rifing and afpect of the ftars. " Then comes the facred author, with feathers on his " head (like *Kneph*) and a book in his hand, together " with ink, and a reed to write with (as is ftill the " practice among the Arabs). He muft be verfed in " hieroglyphics, muft underftand the defcription of the " univerfe, the courfe of the fun, moon, ftars, and " planets, be acquainted with the divifion of Egypt into " 36 *nomes*, with the courfe of the Nile, with inftru-" ments, meafures, facred ornaments, and facred places. " Next comes the ftole bearer, who carries the cubit of " juftice, or meafure of the Nile, and a cup for the liba-" tions ; he bears alfo in the proceffion ten volumes on " the fubject of facrifices, hymns, prayers, offerings, " ceremonies, feftivals. Laftly arrives the prophet, bear-" ing in his bofom a pitcher, fo as to be expofed to view; " he is followed by perfons carrying bread (as at the " marriage of Cana). This prophet, as prefident of the

" myfteries,

" myſteries, learns ten other ſacred volumes, which treat
" of the laws, the Gods, and the diſcipline of the prieſts.
" Now there are in all forty-two volumes, thirty-ſix of
" which are ſtudied and got by heart by theſe perſonages,
" and the remaining ſix are ſet apart to be conſulted by
" the *paſtophores* : they treat of medicine, the conſtruction
" of the human body (anatomy), diſeaſes, remedies, in-
" ſtruments, &c. &c."

We leave the reader to deduce all the conſequences
of ſuch an Encyclopedia. It is aſcribed to Mercury; but
Jamblicus tells us that each book, compoſed by prieſts, was
dedicated to that God, who, on account of his title of
Genius or *decan* opening the zodiac, preſided over every
enterpriſe. He is the *Janus* of the Romans, and the *Guia-
neſa* of the Indians, and it is remarkable that *Yanus* and
Guianes are homonymous. In ſhort, it appears that theſe
books are the ſource of all that has been tranſmitted to us
by the Greeks and Latins in every ſcience, even in alchy-
my, necromancy, &c. What is moſt to be regretted in
their loſs, is that part which related to the principles of
medicine and diet, in which the Egyptians appear to have
made a conſiderable progreſs, and to have delivered many
uſeful obſervations.

Page 279. (83). *The reigning religion in Lower Egypt.*
" At a certain period," ſays Plutarch (*de Iſide*) " all the
Egyptians have their animal Gods painted. The Thebans are the only people who do not employ painters, becauſe they worſhip a God whoſe form comes not under
the ſenſes, and cannot be repreſented. And this is the
God whom Moſes, educated at Heliopolis, adopted; but
the idea was not of his invention.

Page 280. (84). *And Yehouh.* Such is the true pronunciation

nunciation of the Jehovah of the moderns, who violate in this refpect every rule of criticifm; fince it is evident that the ancients, particularly the Eaftern Syrians and Phenicians, were acquainted neither with the *Jé* nor the *V*, which are of Tartar origin. The fubfifting ufage of the Arabs, which we have re-eftablifhed here, is confirmed by Diodorus, who calls the God of Mofes *Iaw*, (*lib.* 1.), and *Iaw* and *Iahouh* are manifeftly the fame word: the identity continues in that of *Iou-piter*; but in order to render it more complete, we fhall demonftrate the fignification to be the fame.

In Hebrew, that is to fay, in one of the dialects of the common language of Lower Afia, *Yahouh* is the participle of the verb *hih*, to exift, to be, and fignifies exifting; in other words, the principle of life, the mover or even motion (the univerfal foul of beings). Now what is Jupiter? Let us hear the Greeks and Latins explain their theology. "The Egyptians," fays Diodorus, after Manatho, prieft of Memphis, " in giving names to the five elements, called *fpirit*, or ether, *Youpiter*, on account of the true meaning of that word: for *fpirit* is the fource of life, author of the vital principle in animals; and for this reafon they confidered him as the father, the generator of beings." For the fame reafon Homer fays, father, and king of men and gods (*Diod. lib.* 1. *fect.* 1.)

" Theologians," fays Macrobius, " confider You-piter as the foul of the world." Hence the words of Virgil: " Mufes let us begin with You-piter; the world is full of You-piter" (*Somn. Scip. ch.* 17.) And in the Saturnalia he fays, " Jupiter is the fun himfelf." It was this alfo which made Virgil fay: " The Spirit nourifhes the " life (of beings), and the foul diffufed through the vaft " members

" members (of the univerfe), agitates the whole mafs,
" and forms but one immenfe body."

"Ioupiter," fays the ancient verfes of the Orphic
fect, which originated in Egypt; verfes collected by
Onomacritus in the days of Pififtratus, " Ioupiter, repre-
" fented with the thunder in his hand, is the beginning,
" origin, end, and middle of all things: a fingle and
" univerfal power, he governs every thing; heaven,
" earth, fire, water, the elements, day, and night.
" Thefe are what conftitute his immenfe body: his eyes
" are the fun and moon: he is fpace and eternity; in
" fine," adds Porphyry, " Jupiter is the world, the uni-
" verfe, that which conftitutes the effence and life of all
" beings. Now," continues the fame author, " as phi-
" lofophers differed in opinion refpecting the nature and
" conftituent parts of this God, and as they could invent
" no figure that fhould reprefent all his attributes, they
" painted him in the form of man. . . . He is in a fitting
" pofture, in allufion to his 'immutable effence; the
" upper part of his body is uncovered, becaufe it is in
" the upper regions of the univerfe, (the ftars) that he
" moft confpicuoufly difplays himfelf. He is covered
" from the waift downwards, becaufe refpecting ter-
" reftrial things he is more fecret and concealed. He
" holds a fceptre in his left hand, becaufe on the left
" fide is the heart, and the heart is the feat of the under-
" ftanding, which (in human beings) regulates every
" action." *Eufeb. Præper. Evang. p.* 100.

The following paffage of the geographer and philofopher Strabo, removes every doubt as to the identity of
the ideas of Mofes and thofe of the heathen theologians,

" Mofes,

" Mofes, who was one of the Egyptian priefts, taught his followers, that it was an egregious error to reprefent the Deity under the form of animals, as the Egyptians did, or in the fhape of man, as was the practice of the Greeks and Africans. That alone is the Deity, faid he, which conftitutes heaven, earth, and every living thing; that which we call the *world*, the *fum of all things*, *nature*; and no reafonable perfon will think of reprefenting fuch a being by the image of any one of the objects around us. It is for this reafon, that, rejecting every fpecies of images or idols, Mofes wifhed the Deity to be worfhipped without emblems, and according to his proper nature; and he accordingly ordered a temple worthy of him to be erected, &c." *Geograph. lib.* 16. *p.* 1104, edition of 1707.

The theology of Mofes has, then, differed in no refpect from that of his followers, that is to fay, from that of the Stoics and Epicureans, who confider the Deity as the foul of the world. This philofophy appears to have taken birth, or to have been difleminated when Abraham came into Egypt (200 years before Mofes), fince he quitted his fyftem of idols for that of the God *Yahouh*; fo that we may place its promulgation about the feventeenth or eighteenth century before Chrift; which correfponds with what we have faid, Note (78).

As to the hiftory of Mofes, Diodorus, properly reprefents it when he fays, *lib.* 34 & 40, " That the Jews " were driven out of Egypt at a time of dearth, when the " country was full of foreigners, and that Mofes, a man " of extraordinary prudence and courage, feized this " opportunity of eftablifhing his religion in the moun- " tains of Judea." It will feem paradoxical to affert, that the 600,000 armed men whom he conducted thither

ought

ought to be reduced to 6,000; but I can confirm the affertion by fo many proofs drawn from the books themfelves, that it will be neceffary to correct an error which appears to have arifen from the miftake of the tranfcribers.

Page 280. (85). *Ei, exiftence.* This was the monofyllable written on the gate of the temple of Delphos. Plutarch has made it the fubject of a differtation.

Page 281. (86). *The name of Ofiris preferved in his fong.* Thefe are the literal expreffions of the book of Deuteronomy, ch. 32. " The works of *Tfour* are perfect." Now *Tfour* has been tranflated by the word creator; its proper fignification is to give *forms*, and this is one of the definitions of Ofiris in Plutarch.

Page 284. (87). *Of the Archangel Michael.* " The " names of the angels and of the months, fuch as Gabriel, " Michael, Yar, Nifan, &c. came from Babylon with " the Jews;" fays exprefsly the Talmud of Jerufalem. See *Peaufcb. Hift. du Manich.* Vol. II. p. 624, where he proves that the faints of the Almanac are an imitation of the 365 angels of the Perfians; and Jamblicus in his Egyptian Myfteries, *fcct.* 2. *c.* 3. fpeaks of angels, archangels, feraphim, &c. like a true Chriftian.

Page 285. (88). *Theology of Zoroafter.* " The whole phi- " lofophy of the gymnofophifts," fays Diogenes Lacrtius on the authority of an ancient writer, " is derived from " that of the Magi, and many affert that of the Jews to " have the fame origin." *Lib.* 1. *c.* 9. Magafthenes, an hiftorian of repute in the days of Seleucus Nicanor, and who wrote particularly upon India, fpeaking of the philofopy of the ancients refpecting natural things, puts the Brachmans and the Jews precifely on the fame footing,

Page

Page 287. (89). *To reftore the golden age upon earth.*
This is the reafon of the application of the many Pagan
oracles to Jefus, and particularly the fourth eclogue of
Virgil, and the Sybilline verfes fo celebrated among the
ancients.

Page 288. (90). *At the expiration of the fix thoufand
pretended years.* We have already feen, note 29, this tradition current among the Tufcans; it was diffeminated
through moft nations, and fhows us what we ought to
think of all the pretended creations and terminations of
the world, which are merely the beginnings and endings
of aftronomical periods invented by aftrologers. That of
the year or folar revolution, being the moft fimple and perceptible, ferved as a model to the reft, and its comparifon
gave rife to the moft whimfical ideas. Of this defcription
is the idea of the four ages of the world among the Indians. Originally thefe four ages were merely the four
feafons; and as each feafon was under the fuppofed influence of a planet, it bore the name of the metal appro-
priated to that planet: thus fpring was the age of the
fun, or of gold; fummer the age of the moon, or of filver;
antumn the age of Venus, or of brafs; and winter the
age of Mars, or of iron. Afterwards when aftronomers
invented the great year of 25 and 36 thoufand common
years, which had for its object the bringing back all the
ftars to one point of departure and a general conjunction,
the ambiguity of the terms introduced a fimilar ambiguity of ideas; and the myriads of celeftial-figns and
periods of duration which were thus meafured, were eafily
converted into fo many revolutions of the fun. Thus the
different periods of creation which have been fo great a
fource of difficulty and mifapprehenfion to curious en-

C e   quirers,

quirers, were in reality nothing more than hypothetical
calculations of aftronomical periods In the fame manner
the creation of the world has been attributed to different
feafons of the year, juft as thefe different feafons have
ferved for the fictitious period of thefe conjunctions ; and
of confequence has been adopted by different nations for
the commencement of an ordinary year. Among the
Egyptians this period fell upon the fummer folftice, which
was the commencement of their year; and the departure
of the fpheres, according to their conjectures, fell, in like
manner, upon the period when the fun enters Cancer.
Among the Perfians the year commenced at firft in the
fpring, or when the fun enters Aries; and from thence
the firft Chriftians were led to fuppofe that God created
the world in the fpring : this opinion is alfo favoured by
the book of Genefis; and it is farther remarkable, that
the world is not there faid to be created by the God of
Mofes (*Iahouh*), but by the *Elohim* or gods in the plural,
that is, by the *angels* or *genii*, for fo the word conftantly
means in the Hebrew books. If we farther obferve that
the root of the word *Elohim* fignifies ftrong or powerful,
and that the Egyptians called their *decans* ftrong and powerful leaders, attributing to them the creation of the world,
we fhall prefently perceive that the book of Genefis af-
firms neither more nor lefs than that the world was created
by the *decans*, by thofe very genii whom, according to
Sanchoniathon, Mercury excited againft Saturn, and who
were called *Elohim*. It may be farther afked, why the
plural fubftantive *Elohim* is made to agree with the fingular verb *bara* (the Elohim creates). The reafon is, that
after the Babylonifh captivity the unity of the Supreme
Being was the prevailing opinion of the Jews; it was
therefore

therefore thought proper to introduce a pious folecifm
in language, which it is evident had no exiftence before
Mofes : thus in the names of the children of Jacob many
of them are compounded of a plural verb, to which Elo‐
him is the nominative cafe underftood, as *Raouben* (Reü‐
ben), *they have looked upon me*, and *Samaoniti* (Simeon),
they have granted me my prayer, to wit, the Elohim. The
reafon of this etymology is to be found in the religious
creeds of the wives of Jacob, whofe gods were the *tara‐
phim* of Laban, that is, the angels of the Perfians, and the
Egyptian decans.

Page *id.* (91). *Six thoufand years had already nearly
elapfed fince the fuppofed creation of the world.* According
to the computation of the Seventy, the period elapfed con‐
fifted of about 5,600 years, and this computation was
principally followed. It is well known how much, in the
firft ages of the church, this opinion of the end of the
world agitated the minds of men. In the fequel, the ge‐
neral councils, encouraged by finding that the general con‐
flagration did not come, pronounced the expectation that
prevailed heretical, and its believers were called Millena‐
rians ; a circumftance curious enough, fince it is evi‐
dent from the hiftory of the Gofpels that Jefus Chrift
was a Millenarian, and of confequence a heretic.

Page 290. (92). *Conftellation of the ferpent.* " The
" Perfians," fays Chardin, " call the conftellation of the
" ferpent *Ophiucus*, ferpent of Eve: and this ferpent *Ophi‐
" ucus* or *Ophioneus* plays a fimilar part in the theology of
" the Phenicians," for Pherecydes, their difciple, and the
mafter of Pythagoras, faid " that *Ophioneus ferpentinus* had
" been chief of the rebels againft Jupiter." See Marf.

Ficin.

Ficin. Apol. Socrat. p. m. 797. col. 2. I ſhall add that *ephah* (with aïn) ſignifies in Hebrew ſerpent.

Page *id.* (93). *Seduced the man.* In a phyſical ſenſe to ſeduce, *ſeducere*, means only to attract, to draw after us.

Page *id.* (94). *Picture of Mithra.* See this picture in Hyde, page 111, edition of 1760.

Page 291. (95). *Perſeus riſes on the oppoſite ſide.* Rather the head of Meduſa; that head of a woman once ſo beautiful, which Perſeus cut off, and which he holds in his hand, is only that of the virgin, whoſe head ſinks below the horizon at the very moment that Perſeus riſes; and the ſerpents which ſurround it are Ophiucus and the Polar Dragon, who then occupy the zenith. This ſhews us in what manner the ancients compoſed all their figures and fables. They took ſuch conſtellations as they found at the ſame time on the circle of the horizon, and collecting the different parts, they formed groupes which ſerved them as an almanac in hieroglyphic characters. Such is the ſecret of all their picture⁼, and the ſolution of all their mythological monſters. The Virgin is alſo Andromeda, delivered by Perſeus from the whale that *purſues* her *(pro-ſequitur.)*

Page *id.* (96). *By a chaſte virgin.* Such was the picture of the Perſian ſphere, cited by Aben Ezra in the *Cœlum Poeticum* of Blacu, p. 71. " The picture of the firſt " decan of the Virgin," ſays that writer, " repreſents a " beautiful virgin with flowing hair, ſitting in a chair, " with two ears of corn in her hand, and ſuckling an infant, " called Jeſus by ſome nations, and Chriſt in Greek."

In the library of the king of France is a manuſcript in Arabic, marked 1165, in which is a picture of the twelve
ſigns;

figns; and that of the Virgin reprefents a young woman with an infant by her fide : the whole fcene indeed of the birth of Jcfus is to be found in the adjacent part of the heavens. The ftable is the conftellation of the charioteer and the goat, formerly Capricorn; a conftellation called *præfepe Jovis Heniochi*, *ftable* of *Iou*; and the word *Iou* is found in the name Iou-feph (Jofeph). At no great dif-tance is the afs of Typhon (the great fhe-bear), and the ox or bull, the ancient attendants of the manger. Peter the porter, is Janus with his keys and bald forehead: the twelve apoftles are the genii of the twelve months, &c. This Virgin has acted very different parts in the various fyftems of mythology: fhe has been the Ifis of the Egyptians, who faid of her in one of their infcriptions cited by Julian, *the fruit I have brought forth is the fun.* The majority of traits drawn by Plutarch apply to her, in the fame manner as thofe of Ofiris apply to Bootes : alfo the feven principal ftars of the fhe-bear, called David's chariot, were called the chariot of Ofiris (See *Kirker)*; and the crown that is fituated behind, formed of ivy, was called *Chen-Ofiris*, the tree of Ofiris. The Virgin has likewife been Ceres, whofe myfteries were the fame with thofe of Ifis and Mithra; fhe has been the Diana of the Ephefians ; the great goddefs of Syria, Cybele, drawn by lions; Minerva, the mother of Bacchus ; Aftræa, a chafte vir-gin taken up into heaven at the end of the golden age ; Thems, at whofe feet is the balance that was put in her hands ; the Sybil of Virgil, who defcends into hell, or finks below the hemifphere with a branch in her hand, &c.

Page 292. (97). *Rofe again in the firmament. Refurgere,* to rife a fecond time, cannot fignify to return to life, but

C c 3   in

in a metaphorical fenfe; but we fee continually miftakes of this kind refult from the ambiguous meaning of the words made ufe of in ancient tradition.

Page *id.* (98). *Chris, or confervator.* The Greeks ufed to exprefs by X, or Spanifh iota, the afpirated *hâ* of the Orientals, who faid *hâris.* In Hebrew *heres* fignifies the fun, but in Arabic the meaning of the radical word is, to guard, to preferve, and of *hâris,* guardian, preferver. It is the proper epithet of Vichenou, which demonftrates at once the identity of the Indian and Chriftian Trinities, and their common origin. It is manifeftly but one fyftem, which, divided into two branches, one extending to the eaft, and the other to the weft, affumed two different forms: its principal trunk is the Pythagorean fyftem of the foul of the world, or *Iou-piter.* The epithet *piter,* or father, having been applied to the demi-ourgos of Plato, gave rife to an ambiguity which caufed an enquiry to be made refpecting the fon of this father. In the opinion of the philofophers the fon was underftanding, *Nous* and *Logos,* from which the *Latins* made their *Verbum.* And thus we clearly perceive the origin of the *eternal father* and of the *Verbum* his fon, proceeding from him *(Mens ex Deo nata,* fays Macrobius): the *anima* or *fpiritus mundi* was the Holy Ghoft; and it is for this reafon that Manes, Bafilides, Valentinius, and other pretended heretics of the firft ages, who traced things to their fource, faid, that God the Father was the fupreme inacceffible light (that of the heaven, the *primum mobile,* or the *aplanes)*; the Son the fecondary light refident in the fun, and the Holy Ghoft the atmofphere of the earth (See *Beaufob.* Vol. II. p. 586): hence, among the Syrians, the reprefentation of the Holy Ghoft by a dove, the bird of Venus Urania, that is, of

the

the air. The Syrians (fays *Nigidius de Germanico*) affert
that a dove fat for a certain number of days on the egg of
a fifh, and that from this incubation Venus was born :
Sextus Empiricus alfo obferves (*Inft. Pyrrh. lib.* 3. *c.* 23.)
that the Syrians abftain from eating doves ; which inti-
mates to us a period commencing in the fign *Pifces*, in the
winter folftice. We may farther obferve, that if *Chris*
comes from *Harifch* by a *chin*, it will fignify *artificer*, an
epithet belonging to the fun. Thefe variations, which
muft have embarraffed the ancients, prove it to be the real
type of Jefus, as had been already remarked in the time of
Tertullian. " Many," fays this writer, " fuppofe with
" greater probability that the fun is our God, and they re-
" fer us to the religion of the Perfians." *Apologet. c.* 16.

Page 293. (99). *One of the folar periods.* See a curious
ode to the Sun, by Martianus Capella, tranflated by Ge-
belin.

Page 304. (100). *Human facrifices.* Read the cold
declaration of Eufebius (*Præp. Evang. lib.* 1. *p.* 11.)
who pretends that, fince the coming of Chrift, there have
neither been wars, nor tyrants, nor cannibals, nor fodo-
mites, nor perfons committing inceft, nor favages devour-
ing their parents, &c. When we read thefe fathers of
the church, we are aftonifhed at their infincerity or in-
fatuation.

Page 306. (101). *Sect of Samaneans.* The equality of
mankind in a ftate of nature, and in the eyes of God, was
one of the principal tenets of the Samaneans, and they
appear to be the only ancients that entertained this opinion.

Page 309. (102.) *Perverted the confciences of men.* As
long as it fhall be poffible to obtain purification from

crimes, and exemption from punifhment by means of
money or other frivolous practices; as long as kings and
great men fhall fuppofe that building temples or infti-
tuting foundations, will abfolve them from the guilt of
oppreffion and homicide; as long as individuals fhall imagine that they may rob and cheat, provided they obferve
faft during Lent, go to confeffion, and receive extreme
unction, it is impoffible there fhould exift in fociety any
morality or virtue; and it is from a deep conviction of
truth, that a modern philofopher has called the doctrine
of expiations *la vérole des fociétés.*

Page 310. (103). *Has carried its inquifition even to the
facred fanctuary of the nuptial bed.* The Muffulmans, who
fuppofe women to have no fouls, are fhocked at the idea
of confeffion, and fay; How can an honeft man think of
liftening to the recital of the actions or the fecret thoughts
of a woman? May we not alfo afk, on the other hand,
how can an honeft woman confent to reveal them?

Page id. (104). *That every where they had formed fecret
affociations, enemies to the reft of the fociety.* That we may
underftand the general feelings of priefts refpecting the
reft of mankind, whom they always call by the name of
the people, let us hear one of the doctors of the church.
" The people," fays Bifhop Synnefius, *in Calvit. page* 315,
" are defirous of being deceived, we cannot act otherwife
" refpecting them. The cafe was fimilar with the ancient
" priefts of Egypt, and for this reafon they fhut them-
" felves up in their temples, and there compofed their
" myfteries out of the reach of the eye of the people."
And forgetting what he has juft before faid, he adds—
" For had the people been in the fecret, they might have
" been offended at the deception played upon them. In
                                                      " the

" the mean time how is it poffible to conduct onefelf
" otherwife with the people fo long as they are the
" people ? For my own part, to myfelf I fhall always be
" a philofopher, but in dealing with the mafs of man-
" kind I fhall be a prieft."

" A little jargon," fays Gregory Nazianzen to St.
Jerome *(Hieron. ad Nep.)* " is all that is neceffary to
" impofe on the people. The lefs they comprehend, the
" more they admire. Our forefathers and doctors of
" the church have often faid, not what they thought,
" but what circumftances and neceffity dictated to
" them."

" We endeavour," fays Sanchoniathon, " to excite ad-
" miration by means of the marvellous." *(Præp. Evang.
lib.* 3.)

Such was the conduct of all the priefts of antiquity, and
is ftill that of the Bramins and Lamas, who are the exact
counterpart of the Egyptian priefts. Such was the practice of the Jefuits, who marched with hafty ftrides in the
fame career. It is ufelefs to point out the whole depravity
of fuch a doctrine. In general every affociation which has
myftery for its bafis, or an oath of fecrecy, is a league of
robbers againft fociety, a league divided in its very bofom
into knaves and dupes, or in other words agents and inftruments. It is thus we ought to judge of thofe modern
clubs, which, under the name of Illuminatifts, Martinifts,
Caglioftronifts, Free-mafons and Mefmerites, infeft Europe. Thefe focieties ape the follies and deceptions of the
ancient Cabalifts, Magicians, Orphics, &c. who, fays
Plutarch, led into errors of confiderable magnitude not
only individuals, but kings and nations.

Page 311. (106). *They made themfelves in turns aftrologers,*

logers, cafters of planets, magicians, &c. What is a magician, in the fenfe in which the people underftand the word ? a man who by words and geftures pretends to act on fupernatural beings, and compel them to defcend at his call and obey his orders. Such was the conduct of the ancient priefts, and fuch is ftill that of all priefts in idolatrous nations, for which reafon we have given them the denomination of magicians.

And when a Chriftian prieft pretends to make God defcend from heaven, to fix him to a morfel of leaven, and to render, by means of this talifman, fouls pure and in a ftate of grace, what is all this but a trick of magic ? And where is the difference between a Chaman of Tartary who invokes the genii, or an Indian Bramin, who makes his Vichenou defcend in a veffel of water to drive away evil fpirits ? Yes, the identity of the fpirit of priefts in every age and country is fully eftablifhed ! Every where it is the affumption of an exclufive privilege, the pretended faculty of moving at will the powers of nature ; and this affumption is fo direct a violation of the right of equality, that whenever the people fhall regain their importance, they will for ever abolifh this facrilegious kind of nobility, which has been the type and parent ftock of the other fpecies of nobility.

Page 312. (107). *Who paid for them as for commodities of the greateft value.* A curious work would be the comparative hiftory of the *agnufes* of the pope and the *paftils* of the grand Lama. It would be worth while to extend this idea to religious ceremonies in general, and to confront, column by column, the analogous or contrafting points of faith and fuperftitious practices in all nations. There is one more fpecies of fuperftition which it would

be

be equally falutary to cure, blind veneration for the great; and for this purpose it would be alone fufficient to write a minute detail of the private life of kings and princes. No work could be fo philofophical as this; and accordingly we have feen what a general outcry was excited among kings and the panders of kings, when the Anecdotes of the Court of Berlin firft appeared. What would be the alarm were the public put in poffeffion of the fequel of this work? Were the people fairly acquainted with all the crimes and all the abfurdities of this fpecies of idol, they would no longer be expofed to covet their fpecious pleafures, of which the plaufible and hollow appearance difturbs their peace, and hinders them from enjoying the much more folid happinefs of their own condition.

I N D E X.

INDEX.

I N D E X.

INDEX.